PELICAN BOOKS

MYSTICISM

F. C. Happold was born at Lancaster in 1893 and educated at Rydal and Peterhouse, Cambridge. He served in the First World War and was awarded a D.S.O. while still a second-lieutenant. After the war he started his career as a schoolmaster at the Perse School, Cambridge, where the foundations of his reputation as an educational pioneer were laid. In 1928 he became Headmaster of Bishop Wordsworth's School, Salisbury, from which post he retired in 1960. In the midst of a very active life as a schoolmaster he wrote a considerable number of books and articles on education, history, social studies, religion, and philosophy. These included *The Approach to History*, *Towards a New Aristocracy*, *The Adventure of Man*, and *Adventure in Search of a Creed*. He also published a nativity play, *The Finding of the King*. In 1937, in recognition of his educational work, he was made an Hon. Ll.D. of the University of Melbourne. After his retirement he wrote three Pelican Originals, *Mysticism, a Study and an Anthology*, *Prayer and Meditation* and *Religious Faith and Twentieth-Century Man*; as well as *The Journey Inwards*. He died in 1971.

Mysticism

A STUDY AND AN ANTHOLOGY

F. C. Happold

PENGUIN BOOKS

Penguin Books Ltd, Harmondsworth, Middlesex, England
Penguin Books Inc., 7110 Ambassador Road, Baltimore, Maryland 21207, U.S.A.
Penguin Books Australia Ltd, Ringwood, Victoria, Australia

—

First published 1963
Reprinted (with additions) 1964, 1967
Revised edition 1970
Reprinted 1971, 1973

—

Copyright © the Estate of F. C. Happold, 1963, 1964, 1970

—

Made and printed in Great Britain
by Cox & Wyman Ltd, London, Reading and Fakenham
Set in Monotype Garamond

Contents

THE ANTHOLOGY

Acknowledgements

SEVERAL have helped me considerably in the making of this book and I should like to thank them most sincerely here. First, I should like to thank Mr A. S. B. Glover, to whom it fell to read the first draft of my Study for Penguin Books, and who also, out of the goodness of his heart, read the revised book, including the Anthology, before it finally went to the printer. I owe much to his sound criticism and wide learning. I am also particularly grateful for the great interest taken in the book at all its stages by Mr Geoffrey Watkins, publisher and bookseller. He not only advised me on sources of information but also lent me books which I should not otherwise have been able to get. He also read and criticized my Study. Not content with that, so great was his interest that he declined to accept the normal publisher's fees for allowing me to use passages from the *Works* of Meister Eckhart, from Evelyn Underhill's edition of *The Cloud of Unknowing*, and from Wilmhurst's *Contemplations*, all published by his firm, as well as from *The Hymn of the Robe of Glory*, for which he held the copyright. I would also like to thank the Shrine of Wisdom for its interest, which was expressed by its allowing me to print the whole of its edition of *The Mystical Theology* of Dionysius the Areopagite without charge. I also owe a debt of gratitude to Professor A. J. Arberry, who not only helped me in the section in the Anthology on Sufism, but also allowed me to draw freely on his beautiful translations of the Sufi poet-mystics. And not least, I would thank my old friend Dr A. L. Peck for translating for me the passages I needed from St Bernard's *Sermons on the Song of Songs*.

I would also gratefully acknowledge the numerous permissions given me by publishers to print passages, often very long ones, from books of which they hold the copyright. I have shown publishers, authors, editors, and translators at the appropriate places, in the Anthology usually in the introductions to the several sections, the most convenient place for readers who might wish to refer to the works. In section 13 on Sufism, however, this could not conveniently be done. The names of translators are printed immediately below the prose or verse passages for the translation for which they were responsible. May I make formal acknowledgement to the holders of copyrights here: to the Cambridge University Press for two translations by R. A. Nicholson in sub-sections 1 and 2; to the Royal Asiatic Society for translations by E. H. Whinfield in sub-sections 2 and 5 and by R. B. Macdonald and W. H. T. Gairdner in sub-section 6; to John Murray for the translation by Margaret Smith in sub-section 5; to Luzac and Co. for the translation by E. J. Gibb in sub-section 2; to Professor Arberry himself for his own translations of poems by Iraqi, Iqbal, and Rumi in sub-sections 1, 3, and 4; the passage

from *Waiting on God* by Simone Weil on p. 141 and the passage from
The Vision of God by Nicholas Cusa on p. 335, are reprinted by permission
of G. P. Putnam's Sons (copyright 1951 by G .P. Putnam's Sons) and E. P.
Dutton and Co. Inc. respectively, as well as the English publishers mentioned in the text.

In addition to the above may I add formal acknowledgement to Mrs
Yeats and to the Macmillan Company of New York for the use of W. B.
Yeats's translation of *The Ten Principal Upanishads*, to the Tweedsmuir
Trustees for the use of a passage from John Buchan's *Memory Hold-the-door*,
and to Miss Vera Brittain for the use of a passage from *Testament of Friend-
ship*.

1963   F. C. HAPPOLD

The necessity of a new printing has given me the opportunity to include
in the anthology a section on Pierre Teilhard de Chardin.

In the new section the extracts from *The Wind and the Rain* are printed
by permission of the Seabury Press Inc., as well as the publishers mentioned in the text.

1964   F.C.H.

In this third edition I have left the Study in its original form, except that I
have rewritten the opening paragraphs of Chapter 9 and have revised
Chapter 17, 'The Mystical Element in Buddhism'. The numbering of
pages is the same as in previous editions.

In order to make it as complete as possible, three new sections have been
added to the Anthology, on the mystical philosophy of ancient China,
on Buddhist mysticism and on the mysticism of the Eastern Orthodox
Church.

I wish to acknowledge my immense debt to Mr Christmas Humphreys,
Q.C., to Brother George Every, S.S.M., and to Mr Geoffrey Watkins,
without whose advice and expert assistance I would not have been able to
do this work.

I also wish to acknowledge my debt to the following publishers who
have so generously allowed me to quote from books which they have
published, John Murray, J. M. Dent & Sons (and also to E. P. Dutton
& Co. Inc.), James Clarke & Co., and John M. Watkins, as well as to
my fellow Penguin Books author, Edward Conze.

1969   F.C.H.

THE STUDY

1. The Nature and Scope of this Book

THE first conception of this book was one of an anthology only. It was to be made up of passages from the writings of a few of the great mystics, of sufficient length to give the reader a more complete picture of their teachings than he could obtain from the short quotations from them to be found in most anthologies.

That first idea has developed into the present book. The book, as it is now presented to the reader, falls into two parts, first a Study of mysticism, then an anthology of the same type but of much wider scope than that originally conceived. Each part can be read as a separate book without reference to the other. On the other hand, the two parts supplement each other. The Study is an introduction to the Anthology, designed to help the reader, particularly if he has no previous acquaintance with mysticism, to understand the Anthology. The Anthology, while standing in its own right, is also designed to be a documentation of the Study through which the teachings of the mystics may be studied at first hand.

Of the nature and scope of the Anthology more is written in the introduction to it; nothing need be said here. On the Study a few observations may be useful in order that its character may be clearly appreciated.

In writing it, the easiest course would have been to assume the 'truth' of mysticism and then to try to describe what mysticism is and how it has expressed itself; in short, to be content with a summary of what had already been said, and said better than I could hope to say it. Though the easiest course, I felt that it was not the right one. The case for the validity of mystical experience is not a self-evident one. I was convinced, therefore, that the right way was to start, not by assuming from the first the validity of mystical experience, but rather on a note of scepticism. While one may rightly speak of the 'truth of mysticism' – that is, of the world-view of the mystic, arising out of his particular experience and his pondering on it – one may equally rightly speak of the 'truth of science', that is, the world-view of the scientist, arising out of his particular experience and his pondering on it. For a great many these two world-views seem to conflict; both cannot, it is felt, be 'true'. So before passing on to the main part of the Study I have tried to make out a case for regarding the validity of mystical experience and the world-view – the picture of the 'real', which stems from it – as a possible, and not unreasonable, hypothesis.

Secondly, since it was with the writings of the Christian mystics I was most familiar, it would have been easier for me to limit both Study and Anthology to Christian mysticism. Indeed, my Study has been criticized by one who has read it in manuscript as having too pronounced a Christian bias. If that is so, I make no apology. If one sincerely believes anything, it is not possible to be coldly objective. Nor is it necessary to be so, provided any bias is frankly acknowledged. While I am reluctant to apply to Christianity such concepts as 'final' and 'truer than', since neither can be logically demonstrated as valid (they partake of the truth of faith rather than of the truth of reason), I do, for reasons which will become apparent to the reader, recognize in Christianity a quality of 'uniqueness', something which I do not find in any of the other higher religions.

Any worth-while study of mysticism must, however, of its nature, be a study of comparative religion, for mysticism is a manifestation of something which is at the root of all religion and all the higher religions have their mystical expressions. I have not, therefore, confined myself, either in the Study or in the Anthology, to the expressions of mysticism within Christianity.

A common method used in the comparative study of religions is to compare them as one might compare the constitutions of Great Britain and France, concentrating particularly on the differences between them. Sometimes the underlying assumption is that the religion of the writer is in some way 'better' or 'truer' than those with which it is compared.

What, when one studies the mystical expressions of different religions, stands out most vividly, however, is not so much the differences as the basic similarities of vision. This is a phenomenon calling for explanation if any truly objective assessment of the significance of mystical experience is to be made.

I would maintain that the more fertile course is not to start with mystical expression in one particular religion, or with one particular type of mysticism, regarding it as a norm and comparing other expressions and types with it, but rather to take as the starting point the assumption of the fact of God. Assuming as the initial hypothesis that God, whatever He may be, simply *is*, and that in some way He reveals Himself to men, the task is then to examine quite objectively, avoiding at first all value-judgements, how this revelation or self-giving has manifested itself. Only then ought one to try to make a judgement.

Finally, it is essential that anyone writing about mysticism should define his terms as exactly as possible if he is not to be misunderstood. Some, particularly among Catholic writers, would restrict the term 'mystic' to those who have risen to the spiritual heights of what medieval writers called 'contemplation'. I have given, for reasons I have tried to make clear, the terms 'mystic', 'mysticism', 'mystical experience', 'mystical consciousness', no such restricted meaning. The theme of my Study is one of a particular form of consciousness, out of which arise types of experience, akin to, but not to be confused or equated with, those labelled 'religious', and which results in a special sort of 'spirituality', giving that word a wide connotation, and a predisposition to interrogate and interpret the universe in a particular way. Further, I have regarded it as a tenable hypothesis that this 'mystical consciousness' is, of its nature, in some way a development and extension of rational consciousness, resulting in an enlargement and refining of perception, and consequently having a noetic quality, so that through it knowledge of the 'real' is gained which could not be gained through rational consciousness.

Enough has been said to make the nature and scope of the book clear to the reader. Let us consider, as a start, what, in general terms, mysticism is.

2. The Perennial Philosophy

WHAT is mysticism? The word 'mystic' has its origin in the Greek mysteries. A mystic was one who had been initiated into these mysteries, through which he had gained an esoteric knowledge of divine things and been 'reborn into eternity'. His object was to break through the world of history and time into that of eternity and timelessness. The method was through initiation ceremonies of the sort so vividly described by the late Latin writer, Apuleius, in *The Golden Ass*. Through the mysteries the initiated entered into something holy and numinous, a secret wisdom about which it was unlawful for him to speak. The word 'mystery' (*mysterion*) comes from the Greek verb *muo*, to shut or close the lips or eyes.

Though we shall, in this study of mysticism, be intimately concerned with what may rightly be described as 'a break through the world of time and history into one of eternity and timelessness', we shall not be concerned with mysticism as it was originally conceived. In the course of time the word came to have an extended, indeed a different meaning. In that syncretism of Greek and Oriental philosophy which occurred in the centuries immediately preceding the birth of Christ, known as Neoplatonism, it came to mean a particular sort of approach to the whole problem of reality, in which the intellectual, and more especially the intuitive, faculties came into play. As a result of the fusion of Christian and Neoplatonist ideas in the early centuries of the Christian era, a system of so-called mystical theology came into existence, which was one of the main foundations of Christian mysticism.*

To speak more generally, mysticism has its fount in what is the raw material of all religion and is also the inspiration of much of philosophy, poetry, art, and music, a consciousness of a *beyond*, of something which, though it is interwoven with it,

* See *The Mystical Theology* of Dionysius the Areopagite in the Anthology, Section 11.

is not of the external world of material phenomena, of an *unseen* over and above the seen. In the developed mystic this consciousness is present in an intense and highly specialized form.

The mystical element enters into the commoner forms of religious experience when religious feeling surpasses its rational content, that is, when the hidden, non-rational, unconscious elements predominate and determine the emotional life and the intellectual attitude. In the true mystic there is an extension of normal consciousness, a release of latent powers and a widening of vision, so that aspects of truth unplumbed by the rational intellect are revealed to him. Both in feeling and thought he apprehends an immanence of the temporal in the eternal and the eternal in the temporal. In the religious mystic there is a direct experience of the Presence of God. Though he may not be able to describe it in words, though he may not be able logically to demonstrate its validity, to the mystic his experience is fully and absolutely valid and is surrounded with complete certainty. He has been 'there', he has 'seen', he 'knows'. With St Paul, in the poem by F. W. H. Myers, he can say:

> Whoso has felt the spirit of the Highest
> Cannot confound nor doubt Him nor deny.
> Yea with one voice, O world, though thou deniest,
> Stand thou on that side, for on this am I.

'Though he may not be able to describe it in words, though he may not be able logically to demonstrate its validity. . .' Let us be quite frank. To a man of the twentieth century, the heir of centuries of thought-techniques which had their roots in Greek logic – conditioned, consciously or unconsciously, by the scientific approach of our time – that may seem alien and incomprehensible. How, he may object, can anything be accepted which not only cannot be rationally proved but which also cannot even be described in words? It is a challenge that anyone setting out to write a study of mysticism must try to meet.

If the reader's initial approach is one of scepticism, I am quite content. I would, however, even at this early stage ask him to put to himself these questions: What is the nature of Reality, that which ultimately *is*? How much is our picture of it, what we know, or think we know, dependent on what we are able to see of it with our very limited range of perception? May it not be at least a possibility that, if our range of perception were enlarged, we should see it quite differently?

Not only have mystics been found in all ages, in all parts of the world and in all religious systems, but also mysticism has manifested itself in similar or identical forms wherever the mystical consciousness has been present. Because of this it has sometimes been called the Perennial Philosophy. Out of their experience and their reflection on it have come the following assertions:

1. This phenomenal world of matter and individual consciousness is only a partial reality and is the manifestation of a Divine Ground in which all partial realities have their being.

2. It is of the nature of man that not only can he have knowledge of this Divine Ground by inference, but also he can realize it by direct intuition, superior to discursive reason, in which the knower is in some way united with the known.

3. The nature of man is not a single but a dual one. He has not one but two selves, the phenomenal *ego*, of which he is chiefly conscious and which he tends to regard as his true self, and a non-phenomenal, eternal self, an inner man, the spirit, the spark of divinity within him, which is his true self. It is possible for a man, if he so desires and is prepared to make the necessary effort, to identify himself with his true self and so with the Divine Ground, which is of the same or like nature.

4. It is the chief end of man's earthly existence to discover and identify himself with his true self. By so doing, he will come to an intuitive knowledge of the Divine Ground and so apprehend Truth as it really is, and not as to our limited human perceptions it appears to be. Not only that, he will enter into a state of being which has been given different names, eternal life, salvation, enlightenment, etc.

Further, the Perennial Philosophy rests on two fundamental convictions:

1. Though it may be to a great extent atrophied and exist only potentially in most men, men possess an organ or faculty which is capable of discerning spiritual truth, and, in its own spheres, this faculty is as much to be relied on as are other organs of sensation in theirs.

2. In order to be able to discern spiritual truth men must in their essential nature be spiritual; in order to know That which they call God, they must be, in some way, partakers of the divine nature; potentially at least there must be some kinship between God and the human soul. Man is not a creature set over against God. He participates in the divine life; he is, in a real sense, 'united' with God in his essential nature, for, as the Flemish contemplative, the Blessed John Ruysbroeck, put it:

This union is within us of our naked nature and were this nature to be separated from God it would fall into nothingness.

This is the faith of the mystic. It springs out of his particular experience and his reflection on that experience. It implies a particular view of the nature of the universe and of man, and it seems to conflict with other conceptions of the nature of the universe and of man which are also the result of experience and reflection on it.

There is a poem by the late Latin poet and philosopher, Boethius, which, translated, opens as follows:

> This discord in the pact of things,
> This endless war 'twixt truth and truth,
> That singly held, yet give the lie
> To him who seeks to hold them both. . . .*

In the world, constituted as it is, men are faced not with one single truth but with several 'truths', not with one but with several pictures of reality. They are thus conscious of a 'discord in the pact of things', whereby to hold to one 'truth' seems to be to deny another. One part of their experience draws them to one, another to another. It has been the eternal quest of mankind to find the one ultimate Truth, that final synthesis in which all partial truths are resolved. It may be that the mystic has glimpsed this synthesis.

* Helen Waddell: *Mediaeval Latin Lyrics* (Penguin Classics).

3. The Astronomer's Universe

WHAT feelings were aroused in the minds of those who listened on their radios to the Reith Lectures given by Professor A. C. B. Lovell, under the title *The Individual and the Universe*? What were their emotional and intellectual reactions to the terrifying picture of the sidereal universe which he painted, so calmly and so objectively?

Gone is that picture, held for the greater part of man's history, of a universe with our earth as its centre, round which the heaven with its fixed stars rotated. Gone, too, that of a universe of fixed stars, with our solar system as its centre. Gone, too, that held by astronomers within the lifetime of some living today in which the sun was regarded as the centre of a stellar system of millions of stars, distributed throughout an extent of space which would take twenty thousand light years to traverse.

Now we are bidden by modern astronomers to envisage a universe so vast that the human mind faints in its attempt to grasp its immensity. The light-waves which now reach us from the Andromeda nebula, we are told, have travelled through space for two million light years; those from the cluster of galaxies in Hydra two thousand million light years. Not only this earth of ours, but also the solar system of which it is part, have, in the light of modern astronomical knowledge, faded into complete insignificance. The whole of our solar system is only a minute part of the Milky Way, a galaxy of some ten million stars, across which it would take a hundred thousand light years to travel. The Milky Way is, moreover, only one of a literally countless number of galaxies, separated from each other by immeasurably vast stretches of inter-galactic space, each one made up of thousands of millions of stars.

This is the astronomical picture of the universe. Against this awe-inspiring background what significance has this earth, this minute and unimportant speck in the immensities of space? What significance can be given to human history, this so brief story of civilizations which have risen and flourished, quickly to become dim memories and to be forgotten? Is it more than

> . . . a tale
> Told by an idiot, full of sound and fury,
> Signifying nothing?

If that be true of the whole of human history, what of each individual man, with his hopes and fears, his ardent dreams and noble strivings? Place each little life, place all the lives that ever were, or will be, against the astronomer's immensities of space and time. They are as nothing, individually and in totality, as transient and meaningless as a mayfly on a summer stream.

Must we now, if we are honest, acknowledge, regretfully perhaps, that man's dreams about his noble stature and destiny have been, after all, only the result of insufficient knowledge? That his immortal longings and his belief that behind everything there was a Supreme Being, with whom it was possible to have communion, have been only illusion? If there indeed be a Creator and Sustainer of this huge universe – and some astronomers doubt whether the concept of creation can any longer be held – can He have any interest in, or communion with, an insignificant dweller on a minute speck in the immensities of time and space? How can such a Creator-God, if indeed such exists, be 'Our Father'? If these doubts are justified, mysticism may have some psychological interest as a study of a particular aberration of the human mind. The high claims of the mystics are, however, demonstrably false. Their so-called 'knowledge' is founded on delusion. They can tell us nothing which will enable us to find the truth of the universe.

Before making that assumption, let us examine what this picture of the universe as given by the astronomer means. In order to do that let us first consider the nature of our knowledge of anything.

4. The Problem of Knowledge

WHEN we come to examine the problem of knowledge, we find that we must take into account three elements.

There is, first, what may be called the 'Ultimately Real', the Thing-as-it-is-in-itself. This may prove to be unknowable in its completeness. We may have to confess that we cannot hope to reach more than an approximation. Secondly, there is what we know, or, perhaps better, think we know, about it. And finally the question, how we know about it.

Now, it is axiomatic that we only perceive that which, with our particular organs of perception, we are capable of perceiving. The range of our normal perceptions is limited; thus we only perceive a fraction of what is actually *there*, and it is easy to be deceived. Further, the vision of each of us is selective; either consciously or unconsciously we select from our experiences, and different people interpret their selective experience in different ways, which are determined by their particular dispositions, and are dependent on such factors as heredity and environment, and their mental capacity. Finally, each of us is conscious of two worlds, an *outer* world of material phenomena and sense perception and an *inner* world of thoughts, emotions, and feelings. Within our experience we are conscious of what we name 'matter' and 'spirit'. But when we ask what 'matter' and 'spirit' are in their essential nature, or how they are interconnected, we have ultimately to confess that we do not know.

The starting-point in any exploration of the nature of what ultimately *is* cannot but be the fact of self-consciousness. Though I may know nothing else for certain, there is one thing I feel that I do know, that *I* exist, that *I* am *I*. Everything else may be illusion; but of that I am convinced.

But what is this *self*, this *ego*, this *I* of which I am conscious? St Augustine called the self an abyss. The more one ponders what it is, the more mysterious it becomes. Some have denied the existence of any continuing individual self at all, since all that can, on examination, be found to exist is a constantly changing series of material and psychological states. The *I* that I was a little while ago is not the same *I* that I am now. How then can I be said to exist as a continuous individual entity, or better, what is that *I*, if such there be, which continues to exist amid the slow changes of the organism, the flux of sensations, the dissipation of ideas, and the fading of memories?

This is not the place to attempt to give an answer. Some of the answers which men have given will emerge in the course of this Study. It is, however, clearly unsound to start with such an apparently obvious statement as '*I* exist', or '*I* am *I*'. It will be more cautious to say, with the Buddhist metaphysician, only 'There is an existent', and leave it at that for the moment.

Nevertheless, the fact remains that in the here and now I am conscious of an entity, whatever it may be, which I call myself, and it is with this fact of self-consciousness that willy-nilly one has got to start.

Through consciousness I have experience of two worlds, a world outside, and a world within, myself. I am impelled to explore and to try to understand these two worlds. By means of their reason, men, unlike the rest of creation, are in a position to interrogate and interpret their experiences, whether they come from outside through sense perception or from within themselves. Without experience, however, mankind would not be able to reason; there would be nothing to reason about. Experience is, therefore, the primary thing.

Now, in our acts of reflection on experience, we have, unless we are mere bundles of conditioned reflexes, a wide measure of freedom. First of all, we are free to decide which experiences we shall regard as primary and what authority we shall give to each. There is no logical compulsion to start with the experience of the external world, gained through sense perception, the reality of which is assumed, and then to examine and assess other aspects of experience in the light of this assumption. Instead of beginning with an assumption of the reality of the phenomenal world, and the possibility of knowing it through sense perception and conceptual reasoning, it is equally tenable to take as the starting-point man's inner experience (which includes the consciousness of the God-image in the soul) as the primary and most significant experience of the human race, and to interpret all other experience, including experience of the material world, in the light of it.

The validity of the choice which is made cannot, however, be rationally proved. It is inevitably based on faith. It cannot be too strongly realized that, in order to know at all, we are all forced to make what I will call *a primary act of intellectual faith*. Though other elements may enter, this act of faith is essentially an act of the intellect, a rational decision, a choice made, consciously or unconsciously, by the mind between several possibilities.

The necessity of this primary act of intellectual faith has been frankly recognized by some of the most profound thinkers throughout the ages. In the fifth century A.D., St Augustine of Hippo wrote:

Understanding is the reward of faith. Therefore do not seek to understand in order that you may believe, but make the act of faith in order that you may understand; for unless you make an act of faith you will not understand.

A thousand years later Nicholas of Cusa wrote in the same strain:

In every science certain things must be accepted as first principles if the subject matter is to be understood; and these first postulates rest only upon faith.

And it was a present-day astronomer, Sir Edward Appleton, who said:

So I want to make the assumption which the astronomer – and indeed any scientist – makes about the universe he investigates. It is this: that the same physical causes give rise to the same physical results anywhere in the universe, and at any time, past, present, and future. The fuller examination of this basic assumption, and much else besides, belongs to philosophy. The scientist, for his part, makes the assumption I have mentioned as an act of faith; and he feels confirmed in that faith by his increasing ability to build up a consistent and satisfying picture of the universe and its behaviour.

Therefore to know, to understand, to interpret the universe we rely on reflection on experience. But on what experience? Simply on our own individual experience? The experience of any particular individual is too limited to give more than a very partial picture. To arrive at the fullest knowledge and the deepest understanding it is necessary to take into account not our own personal experience only, not merely the experience of our own Western culture, but the total experience of the human race, past and present; not only the experience of the scientist, but also of the poet and the mystic; not only the experience of the world outside, but also of the world within us, the inner as well as the outer experiences of the race.

Not only are we free to select what within our experience we are prepared to regard as primary, we are also equally free to select the apparatus we use for its examination and interpretation. Here, again, the choice will of necessity be based on an act of faith.

The way we tend to think is the result of our mental heritage and environment. The mental heritage of Western European culture has its foundations in Classical Greece, where a capacity for logical reasoning was first developed and brought to a high state of perfection. Perhaps the finest achievements of Western European civilization have been in the domain of science. Since analysis and logic have proved themselves to be such efficient tools in the advance of scientific knowledge, there has been a tendency among the heirs of Western European culture more and more to regard them as the only valid tools of knowledge. They are, however, not the only tools of knowledge.

Our medieval ancestors acknowledged two valid ways of knowledge. The first was through *ratio*, i.e. discursive reason; the second through *intellectus*. The word '*intellectus*' is not easy to define exactly. It carried something of the meaning of intuition or creative insight or imagination, in the sense Blake used that word. *Intellectus* they considered a higher faculty of the mind than *ratio*; one capable of bringing men to a more profound knowledge than could be gained through discursive reason.

The status of intuition, creative insight, imagination, call it what you will, is an acknowledged one. It is recognized not only by the mystic, the poet, and many philosophers, but also by the scientist. It was one of the most eminent of quantum physicists, Max Planck, who wrote in his autobiography:

When the pioneer in science sends forth the groping fingers of his thoughts, he must have a vivid, intuitive imagination, for new ideas are not generated by deduction, but by an artistically creative imagination.

The greatest discoveries in every field of knowledge have had their origin in the intuitions of men of genius. Through intuition they see, sometimes in a flash, things not seen by other men. Through it they perceive relations between apparently isolated phenomena which others have missed. Through it they attain knowledge, which could have been attained in no other way.

How the insights gained through intuition come about it, is difficult to say. In the process of logical analysis and deduction the mind works from point to point; definite mental effort is involved; the stages of thought can be analysed. The insights of intuition, however, often have the appearance of something given, a sort of revelation coming from a something outside oneself. The mind, often in a state of passivity, makes a sudden leap. What has been before obscure becomes clear. Disconnected fragments fall into place, are integrated, and take on a pattern.

In his book, *The Faith of the Physicist*, Dr H. H. Huntley writes:

The physicist is driven by his own experience to conclude that his personality has depths and resources beyond the analysing conscious mind, wherein lie powers of synthesis, appreciation, and understanding, a latent skill and wisdom superior to that to which his consciousness is routinely accustomed. This suggests that the framework of physics, filled in with a host of facts, has been fabricated in mental regions where analysis is secondary to synthesis. Thus, both the inner experience of the individual scientist and the confessions of genius concerning the mental mechanism of discovery indicate that, no less than poetry and music, this framework of generalizations, principles, and laws which constitute science has been built up in mental levels below the levels of consciousness.

Let us carry the matter a little further. In his Inaugural Lecture at the University of Oxford in 1956, *Making, Knowing, and Judging*, Professor W. H. Auden distinguished between what he called Primary and Secondary Imagination. The Primary Imagination, according to Professor Auden, has contact with the sacred, in the widest possible sense of the word. This contact arouses a sense of awe, to which there is an impulse to respond. The response is, however, passive and there is no differentiation. What is met with at this level of awareness is simply that which is; it has no form. The function of the Secondary Imagination is to give form to this undifferentiated awareness, to allow it, as it were, to become incarnate. It is an active faculty; it differentiates, interprets, assesses, and transforms into words concepts and images.

Thus, at the Primary level of awareness, while the knowledge is of something which is real, what is known, since it is without form, cannot be grasped rationally, neither can it be communicated at the level of ordinary experience. It must pass through some sieve in order to be given intelligible form in words and concepts, or in music, colour, or shape. Let us, extending somewhat the usual connotation of the term, call this transforming medium of awareness *mind*.

Minds are conditioned by such factors as heredity, history, and environment, and, further, are of varying quality. So the clear but undifferentiated and formless vision, seen at the Primary level of awareness, as it passes through the medium of mind, is distorted and coloured. The result is, therefore, that we find different schools of thought, different theological and philosophical systems, different value-judgements, and different art forms. What may be the same vision seen at the level of Primary awareness may be given a variety of forms as it is interpreted by differently conditioned minds.

The eighteenth-century philosopher, Immanuel Kant,

maintained that, constituted as we are, we only know the world outside ourselves as a mental construction; things as they really are are unknown to us; we live in a world of appearances. The thing as it appears and is known to us Kant called the *phenomenon*, that which is unknown, perhaps unknowable, the *noumenon*. Further, he argued that through self-consciousness, nothing can be known about a noumenal world or a noumenal self, that is, a self as it really is in its essential nature, but only about a phenomenal world and a phenomenal self which is as much a part of the phenomenal world as anything else within our experience. Though he qualified his main thesis by allowing that through moral experience direct contact with a noumenal world was established, Kant's main argument was that the world we know is not the world as it really is, but only a mental construction of it.

Kant is not the only philosopher who has argued that we cannot know things as they really are, that the world we think we know so well is a construction of our minds. For Bertrand Russell, the fundamental stuff of the physical universe is something he calls *sense data*. These sense data, impinging on our sense organs, give rise to the impressions of shape, sound, colour, etc., which make up our world. Our world is, therefore, a *logical construction* from these sense data. What sense data are in themselves is unknowable; they cannot be examined or analysed; it is only possible to postulate their existence at all by their effects in our experience.

The deeper we delve, the more it becomes evident that the universe may not be what it seems to be. What we know is the particular picture of it possible within the range of human perception and capable of being interpreted by human reason.

5. The Nature of Scientific Truth

How does what has been written above affect our approach to the interpretation of the religious instinct in man, his conviction that his destiny is not solely bound up with the material universe, that he is not solely a creature of the phenomenal world? How, in particular, does it affect our assessment of the claims of the mystics? Before we attempt an answer, it will be useful to consider what a modern scientist regards as the nature of scientific truth and reality.

Unlike the materialists of the eighteenth and nineteenth centuries, twentieth-century scientists no longer regard their domain as all-inclusive, embracing everything in heaven and earth. They recognize that it is confined within relatively narrow limits. The results of recent specialist scientific activities have compelled them to conclude that it is necessary to consider orders of reality which are not amenable to the techniques and vocabulary of science. In the minds of some, at least, a doubt has arisen whether the natural world is, in its deeper recesses, rational, i.e. understandable beyond a certain point by the human mind as it is at present circumscribed. Physical realities, they have found, can no longer be adequately represented in terms of pictures and models of macroscopic phenomena. Matter has ceased to be the solid 'stuff' of the nineteenth-century scientist. It has dissolved into energy, something which is not known of itself but only by its effects. It is even accepted that the observer is, in some way, a part of that which he observes. Thus, in part at least, the source of scientific knowledge is within the scientist himself.

In physics the old conception of three-dimensional space passing simultaneously, moment by moment, through time, has been abandoned as no longer an adequate conception in the light of events as the physicist now perceives them. Time has become a mystery, having within it an ingredient of space. The scientist now envisages the universe in terms of a multi-dimensional space–time continuum, a continuum being defined as a series of component parts passing into one another. He does not consider it inconceivable, indeed it seems to fit in with his experience, both as a man and a scientist, that in those regions of personality which lie outside the orbit of normal consciousness the categories of time and space may be inappropriate and that man in his wholeness dwells in a realm which comprehends infinity. The world of his normal experience may be illusion, not in the sense that it does not exist, or is necessarily mere appearance, but in that what he perceives is only a section of a greater whole and, wholly or in part, the mental construction of a limited group of perceptions.

The astronomer's universe is thus a *mental* structure of austere beauty, which gives a coherent and satisfying account of its pattern and behaviour. It represents his particular reaction to that group of sense experiences which, as an astronomer, falls within his specialized field. His language is the language of mathematics, a complex of formulae and equations which express the *effects* on his instruments of whatever it is makes up the cosmos. He is, however, unable to say what matter and space and time are *in themselves*. Space and time may be only forms of perception; matter may have no objective existence. But, even if that is so, the mathematical equations whereby the physical universe is described will be the same as they would be if the opposite were true.

The expansion of human thought and the greater range and precision of the astronomer's instruments have resulted in the replacement of one *image* of the universe by another. The new image does not in itself destroy the dignity of man. Indeed, the fact that the mind of man can so explore and comprehend this vast sidereal world enhances his dignity. Nor does it annihilate God, or the possibility that there are spheres of existence other than the material and levels of consciousness and perception different from those of most human beings. It does, however, raise acute theological, metaphysical, and epistemological issues. It compels us to consider afresh our ideas of the nature of the universe, of man, and of God, to search for new and more adequate *images*. Perhaps in this task a study of mysticism may not be irrelevant or without value.

Before, however, we pass on to that study it will be useful to consider certain recent speculations in the field of the biological sciences.

6. The Evolution of Life: An Interpretation

THE evolution of life on this planet may be envisaged as a process of organic involution upon itself, as a movement from the extremely simple to the extremely complex. In this involution of complexity there has been a steady increase in interiorization, an enlargement of the psyche or consciousness. As they become more complex, structures become more vitalized and more conscious. It is tenable to assume the existence of a psyche, in an embryonic, undeveloped form, in every corpuscle, a *within* as well as a *without* even in the most elementary particles. As evolution proceeds the *within* becomes more and more the predominant factor.

Further, the evolutionary process has been one of groping, a progression by trial and error, particularly in the pre-reflexive zones, but there is also evident, at the same time, a hoarding and culminative improvement when favourable combinations are obtained. What, if anything, controls this groping and gives it direction most biologists are reluctant to say; they hesitate to assume the presence of some sort of purpose in the process. It is difficult, however, to avoid the conviction that there must be some *pattern of organization* inherent in the whole evolutionary process, a dynamic urge, whatever its origin, impelling structures to behave in certain ways and to develop in certain directions.

As seen within the time process, evolution takes the form of a series of unfoldings: from the building up of the universe, through the formation of the earth, to the appearance of life on this planet. Through countless ages the evolution of living forms has gone on, until the next stage, that of the emergence of Man, was reached, first the pre-hominids and finally *homo sapiens*.

With the appearance of the human line a new form of

biological existence emerges; there is, in effect, a new creation. This new creation is characterized by the emergence of the power of reflection. Father Pierre Teilhard de Chardin, in his *Phenomenon of Man*, coins the vivid word *hominisation* to describe this leap in the evolution of life. With the appearance of man, instinct is more and more supplemented by thought; there is a greater and greater interiorization; the *within* becomes more and more predominant. Invention more and more replaces chance as the controlling evolutionary directive. A new form of attraction and repulsion supplants that primitive type which operated at the levels of pre-life and the lower forms of life. Personal and social relations become ever more complex; and, very significantly, there arises a demand for unlimited survival, racial or personal, or both, the sort of demand which Tennyson expresses in *In Memoriam*:

> Thou wilt not leave him in the dust.
> Thou madest man, he knows not why.
> He thinks he was not made to die;
> And Thou hast made him, Thou art just.

The process of evolution may thus be envisaged as the adding of successive 'layers', or 'envelopes', to the globe. With the appearance of *homo sapiens*, to the *biosphere*, i.e. the envelope of life, is added the *noosphere*, the envelope of thought, another 'membrane to the majestic assembly of telluric layers'.

If this picture of the course of evolution be a true one, what line may evolution be expected to follow? May it not be the growth of an ever higher form of consciousness, spreading out ever wider and wider, until it embraces more and more of mankind, a greater and greater intensification of *noogenesis*, an expanding interiorization and spiritualization of man, which will result in an ability to see aspects of the universe as yet only faintly glimpsed? And, if that be so, may we not see in the mystics the forerunners of a type of consciousness, which will become more and more common as mankind ascends higher and higher up the ladder of evolution? It is not an irrational hypothesis.*

* Those of my readers who have read Father Pierre Teilhard de Chardin's

7. What we shall understand by the term Mysticism

WE are now ready to launch out on our study of mysticism. If the belief of the reader is that man is nothing more than a creature of the material world; that the only cognitive capacities available to him are sense perception, memory, and conceptual reason (and possibly introspection), by which he becomes aware of a material world, and possibly, of himself, but of nothing more – that so-called spiritual experience is merely the product of a physico-chemical process, acting according to predetermined patterns, the mere result of a particular conglomeration of atoms – then the claim of the mystics to know aspects of reality which are not apparent to normal consciousness will seem to him nonsense. If, on the other hand, he feels that there may possibly be

> ... More things in heaven and earth, Horatio,
> Than are dreamt of in your philosophy,

he may find the experiences and conclusions of the mystics of high relevance in the age-long effort of mankind to penetrate

---

The Phenomenon of Man (Collins) will have noted that what has been written above follows the thinking of Father de Chardin very closely. The English translation of his work appeared as I was working out the pattern of this study of mysticism and helped me to clarify certain speculations which were already taking shape in my mind, in part as a result of my reading of the work of other biologists, such as Dr Edmund Sinnott, whose *Biology of the Spirit* had impressed me very much. I think that Father de Chardin may, as a biologist and a palaeographer, have glimpsed one of those superb syntheses which have marked the development of human thought. The book must, of course, particularly its latter sections, at the moment be regarded as speculative, a possible, but as yet unproved, hypothesis. Nevertheless, his general picture of the shape of evolution, as a process of expanding interiorization, seems to ring true.

the ultimate secret of the universe, and of his own nature and destiny.

The word 'mysticism' is not a fully satisfactory one. Its origin was discussed and its character described in general terms at the beginning of our study. The word is, however, used with a number of different meanings and carries different connotations to different minds. To some it is simply a type of confused, irrational thinking. In the popular mind it is associated with spiritualism and clairvoyance, with hypnotism, and even with occultism and magic, with obscure psychological states and happenings, some of which are the result of neurasthenia and other morbid pathological conditions. To some it is bound up with visions and revelations. Others use it as a synonym for other-worldliness, or to describe a nebulous outlook upon the world or a religious attitude which does not care for dogma or the outward forms of religious observance. Some would limit its use to that rare state of consciousness which is found in the contemplative saints. It is, therefore, necessary in the interests of clarity that we should say as precisely as possible how the word will be used in this study or, more concretely, state what we are prepared to regard as falling within the range of mystical experience and of that type of consciousness which may, without misuse of the term, be termed mystical.

The use of the word in Christianity was largely due to the influence of Dionysius the Areopagite, often known as the Pseudo-Dionysius. Quite erroneously, he was thought to be a contemporary and disciple of St Paul, with the result that his *Mystical Theology* and other writings were regarded by medieval theologians as authoritative. The term used by medieval theologians was *theologia mystica*, by which they meant a particular type of insight and knowledge about God. The more common, and much more precise, word found in medieval times was *contemplatio* (contemplation). It was used to designate a rare and advanced form of spiritual experience, not found among ordinary, religious folk. To attain to a state of contemplation men and women withdrew from the world and followed a way of life entirely different from that led by those who remained in the world. The word 'mystical' did not become current until the later Middle Ages, and 'mysticism' is indeed quite a modern word.

It will be useful, therefore, at this stage to set out a number of definitions taken from medieval and modern sources.

Medieval theologians described what they termed 'mystical theology' as 'experimental wisdom', or as 'a stretching out of the soul into God through the urge of love', or as 'an experimental knowledge of God through unifying love'. These definitions all approach mysticism from the theological standpoint.

Others have approached it from the psychological angle, for instance Von Hartmann, who defines mysticism as 'the filling of the consciousness by a content (feeling, thought, desire) by an involuntary emergence of the same from the unconscious'. Du Prel wrote as follows:

The mystical phenomena of the soul-life are anticipations of the biological process. Soul is our spirit within the self-consciousness, spirit is the soul beyond the self-consciousness.

Goethe called mysticism 'the scholastic of the heart, the dialectic of the feelings'; others have used such phrases as 'intellectual intuition' and 'formless speculation'.

Again, some writers emphasize the noetic or intellectual quality of mystical experience, as, for instance, Lasson, when he writes:

The essence of mysticism is the assertion of an intuition which transcends the temporal categories of the understanding, relying on speculative reason. Rationalism cannot conduct us to the essence of things; we therefore need intellectual vision.

The Indian philosopher Radhakrishnan also emphasizes this noetic quality, when he calls mysticism 'integrated thought', in that it brings things together in a new pattern, i.e. integrates them, instead of, as in analytical thought, breaking them into parts. It thus relates them into a meaningful whole. It is a sort of creative insight, springing from a deep unconscious part of the psyche.

Evelyn Underhill, in *Practical Mysticism*, defines mysticism as the art of union with Reality, or God. She writes:

Mysticism is the art of union with Reality. The mystic is a person who has attained that union in a greater or lesser degree; or who aims at and believes in such attainment.

Professor A. Seth puts forward a similar point of view. He states:

It [mysticism] appears in connexion with the endeavour of the human mind to grasp the Divine essence or the ultimate reality of things and to enjoy the blessedness of actual communion with the highest.*

Thus our study is concerned with a form of experience and a type of consciousness, which can not only be approached from different angles but also be given different interpretations. We can put aside immediately all those false types of so-called mysticism such as spiritualism, occultism, and the like, which have been referred to above. We may also dismiss as inadequate and misleading such phrases as 'All religion is mystical'. Mystical experience may take more than one form. It is, however, a quite definite and recognizable form of experience. Nor need we concern ourselves with visions and states of ecstasy. Accounts of them are found in the writings of the contemplatives; they are, however, usually regarded with some suspicion and are in no way an essential element in mystical experience. Nor shall we regard all psychical experience as necessarily mystical. The characteristic of mystical experience is not determined by the *level of awareness* at which the experience takes place, but by the *quality* of the experience at that level.

We shall, however, regard as falling within the scope of our study a range of experience, which we shall maintain may rightly be called mystical, which extends far beyond that advanced and rare state which medieval writers called Contemplation. While few attain to that high state of mystical experience when it becomes a distinct form of consciousness,

* In Appendix A of his *Christian Mysticism* (Methuen) Dean Inge gives no less than twenty-six definitions of mysticism.

there is a wide range of spiritual and aesthetic experience which, I would maintain, is of the same character and proceeds from the same source. A man may be a mystic who is not, and never could be, a contemplative. There come to many the sudden moments of intuitive perception, elusive, fading quickly, but of deep significance, illuminations which they feel reveal to them new facets of reality. Perhaps only once or twice in a lifetime may come an experience more profound, of the sort which came to Warner Allen, and which he described in *The Timeless Moment*,* or to Blaise Pascal, which he recorded on the scrap of paper found sewn up in his doublet after his death:

> From about half past ten in the evening to
> about half an hour after midnight.
>   Fire.
> God of Abraham, God of Isaac, God of Jacob,
> Not the God of philosophers and scholars.
> Absolute Certainty: Beyond reason. Joy. Peace.
> Forgetfulness of the world and everything but God.
> The world has not known thee, but I have known thee.
>   Joy! joy! joy! tears of joy!

Such experiences, when they happen to a man, revolutionize his outlook, often change his life. He may carry on with his normal occupation as before. To his friends and acquaintances he may seem to be the same as he always was. But in himself he is changed. He feels that he has received a pure, direct vision of truth. Nothing can be the same again. These may not call themselves mystics, but in a lesser degree they have known something that the true contemplative knows in a more intense and continuous form. Their contact is with the same Reality as his.

We shall therefore accept a wide range of experience as falling within the province of our study, not limiting it to that rare type for which we shall use the medieval word, Contemplation. We shall regard mysticism as a particular and distinct sort of 'spirituality' and examine it from three points of view, as a type of experience, as a way of knowledge, and as a state of consciousness.

* Anthology, Section 1.

8. The Mysticism of Love and Union and the Mysticism of Knowledge and Understanding

FOR convenience one may divide mystical experience into two types, which may be called the *mysticism of love and union* and the *mysticism of knowledge and understanding*. They are in no way exclusive, indeed they are always, in some degree, combined. The distinction lies in the predominant urge.

In the first the urge is to escape from a sense of separation, from the loneliness of selfhood, towards a closer participation and reunion with Nature or God, which will bring peace and rest to the soul. This sort of urge is expressed in some words of St Augustine:

Thou hast made us for thyself, O God, and our hearts are restless till they rest in Thee.

There are two urges in life. One is towards selfhood, individualization, and separation; the other towards an escape from the loneliness of self into something bigger than self. Man is the most individualized of all created beings, and yet, at the same time, the one most capable, through thought and imagination, of participating in everything. These two urges are constantly at war within him. He clings to his selfhood and self-love; he is reluctant to give them up; and yet at the same time he has an inherent longing for reunion with something to which he feels he belonged and from which he feels himself to be separated.

This urge has its origin, if one accepts the only thesis on which a case for the validity of mysticism is based, in the fact that man is in some way a sharer in the divine life. He therefore longs to return to that from which he feels he has come, to be more closely and consciously linked with it. He feels himself to be a pilgrim of eternity, a creature in time but a citizen of a timeless world.

Since man is a sharer in the divine life, there is a mutual and reciprocal attraction. The mysticism of love and union can be described not only in terms of man's search for God but also in terms of God's search for man.

'I sought for God for thirty years,' writes the Moslem mystic Abū Yazid, 'I thought it was I who desired Him, but, no, it was He who desired me.'

And in the anonymous medieval poem, *Quia amore langueo*, God in the person of Christ speaks to the soul in these words:

> I am true love that false was never;
> My sister, man's soul, I loved her thus;
> Because I would in no wise dissever,
> I left my kingdom glorious;
> I provided for her a place full precious;
> She fled, I followed, I loved her so;
> That I suffered these pains most piteous
> *Quia amore langueo*.*

The mysticism of knowledge and understanding springs from the urge, inherent in man, to find the secret of the universe, to grasp it not in parts but in its wholeness. This aspect of mysticism appears in a number of the definitions given earlier in this book. Mysticism is defined as *experimental wisdom* and as *experimental knowledge of God*, i.e. a knowledge of God based on direct experience of Him; as intellectual intuition or formless speculation; as the endeavour of the human mind to grasp the Divine essence or the ultimate reality of things; as the assertion of an intuition which transcends the temporal categories of the understanding, relying on speculative reason; as integrated thought, bringing things together in a new pattern, integrating them instead of breaking them down into parts, as in analytical thought.

The philosopher also attempts to describe a complete reality over against special realities, to comprehend the universe as a whole and not in fragments. His method is, however, by way of deductive reasoning from first principles, which must be axiomatic. But if one tries to find the truth of things in this way it is easy to become bogged down and to end in

* The spelling has been modernized.

philosophical scepticism. Not only is it difficult to decide what
is axiomatic; even the apparent axioms can fail. For instance,
the statement 'A thing cannot at the same time be and not be'
seems obvious enough to common-sense perception. It is
doubtful, however, whether it is acceptable in the domain of
non-dualistic thought or in those ranges of experience where
the concepts of time and space do not seem to be applicable.

Philosophy can, moreover, easily become a game of conceptual counters. The mystic puts aside this game of conceptual counters. He relies not on deductive reason but on
intuitive unifying vision to pierce to the secret. As a result of
direct intuitive experience, he finds not only a coherent pattern,
which is not contrary to his reason, but also a certainty of a
sort which cannot be given by philosophy.

In the letter in which he presents his book, *De docta ignorantia*
(*Of Learned Ignorance*), to the Cardinal Julian, Nicholas of Cusa
writes:

Take now, Reverend Father, what for long I have by divers paths
of learning sought to attain. Attainment, however, was denied me
until I was returning by sea from Genoa, when, by what I believe was
a supreme gift of the Father of Lights from whom is every perfect
gift, I was led in the learning that is ignorance to grasp the incomprehensible; and this I was able to achieve not by way of comprehension but by transcending those perennial truths that can be
reached by reason.

The urge to know through mystical intuition is not the
same urge as that which is the impulse in the search for scientific and metaphysical knowledge. There is often a common
element, the desire to make sense of the universe, but for the
mystic another element enters, the desire for 'salvation'. The
sort of knowledge which comes through *intuitus mysticus*, unlike scientific and metaphysical knowledge, has a 'saving'
quality; it leads to 'eternal life'. 'This is eternal life,' said
Jesus, 'to know God and him whom He has sent.'

9. Nature-Mysticism, Soul-Mysticism, and God Mysticism

WE have in the previous pages considered mysticism as falling into two main types: of love and union, and of knowledge and understanding. Approached from a different angle, it is possible to consider it in its three aspects of nature-mysticism, soul-mysticism and God-mysticism. Again, the aspects are not necessarily mutually exclusive; they may and often do intermix.

With the exception of pure soul-mysticism, mystical experiences may take several analogous forms. They may be (1) *pan-en-henic*, i.e. the sense of the all in an undifferentiated non-dual One and this One in the all; or (2) *pan-en-theistic*, i.e. the sense that all is in God and God is in all; or (3) *pan-theistic*. In this latter either Deity or the 'divine' is felt as being 'contained' within creation, or that, to quote from the *Upanishads*, 'there is nothing in the world which is not God'.

Nature-mysticism is characterized by a sense of the immanence of the One or God or soul in Nature. In a very typical form it is expressed in Wordsworth's lines:

> A motion and a spirit, that impels
> All thinking things, all objects of all thought,
> And rolls through all things.

or in the lines:

> That Light whose smile kindles the Universe,
> That Beauty in which all things work and move

of Shelley. In Richard Jefferies* it is linked up with a sort of soul-mysticism. Francis Thompson rejects nature-mysticism as in itself inadequate:

* See Anthology, Section 30.

But not by that, by that, was eased my human smart,
In vain my tears were set on Heaven's grey cheek.
For ah! we know not what each other says,
These things and I; in sound *I* speak,
Their sound is but their stir, they speak by silences.
Nature, poor stepdame, cannot slake my drouth.

In pure soul-mysticism the idea of the existence of God is, in any expressible form, absent. The soul is in itself regarded as numinous and hidden. The uncreated soul or spirit strives to enter not into communion with Nature or with God but into a state of complete isolation from everything that is other than itself. The chief object of man is the quest of his own self and of right knowledge about it.

While not alien to the thought of some schools of Hindu and Buddhist mysticism, soul-mysticism is not easy for the Western mind to comprehend. What is meant, it may be asked, by the soul's striving to isolate itself from everything which is other than itself? What indeed is the object of trying to do so?

Soul-mysticism may, however, be combined with God-mysticism, as in the teaching of the Hindu Sankara* and the Christian Meister Eckhart. Both emphasize the numinous, hidden quality of the soul and its glory in its own eternal nature. In both is found the inherent idea of soul-mysticism, that of the absolute character of the soul when it is separated from all which is not soul, when it has realized its being in self-knowledge and is freed alike from the sense of I-ness and from the world. In both, however, there is also the idea of the soul's knowing and finding itself through union with the Godhead or with Brahman.

The basic idea always found in God-mysticism is that of the return of the spirit to its immortal and infinite Ground, which is God. It may take more than one form. In one type the uncreated spirit, the real self, is thought of as 'absorbed' into the essence of God. The individual personality and the whole objective world are felt to be entirely obliterated. This type is typical of most forms of Eastern mysticism. In another type,

* Sri Samkaracarya (eighth century A.D.); sometimes spelt Shankara or Samkara.

more characteristic of the West, the soul or spirit, created by God, is said to be 'deified' so that, as it were, it 'becomes' God, yet without losing its identity, by a process of 'union' and 'transformation' whereby it becomes a new creature.

At this stage it is only necessary to describe each of these aspects in general terms. Their character will become clearer as we proceed.

10. Characteristics of Mystical States

MYSTICAL states have certain marked characteristics:

1. First of all, a mystical state has the quality of *ineffability*, that is, it defies expression in terms which are fully intelligible to one who has not known some analogous experience. It thus resembles a state of feeling rather than a state of intellect. It is not possible to make a state of feeling clear to one who has not experienced it. For instance, neither toothache, nor the smell of a rose, nor the sensation of being in love, nor the pleasure which comes to one while listening to a great symphony, are amenable to adequate communicable description.

2. Nevertheless, while mystical states are akin to states of feeling, they are also states of knowledge. They have a *noetic* quality. They result in insight into depths of truth unplumbed by the discursive intellect, insights which carry with them a tremendous sense of authority. Things take on a new pattern and a new, often unsuspected, significance. Even though he may not be able to say, in the language of the intellect, what he knows, one who has undergone mystical experience is convinced with absolute certainty that he does know.

3. Mystical states can seldom be sustained for long; they rarely last for any length of time. They have thus the quality of *transiency*. There is invariably a speedy return to normality. The following of a particular way of life can, however, increase their frequency. At that stage of the Mystic Way known as the Illuminative Life, they can be very frequent and, it would

seem, controllable. In the words of St John of the Cross, 'the soul has it in its power to abandon itself, whenever it wills, to this sweet sleep of love'.

4. It is possible to prepare oneself for the reception of mystical experience. Indeed, in the writings of the mystics, much space is given to instructions on the following of the so-called 'Way of Purgation'. Nevertheless, when they occur, mystical states invariably carry with them a feeling of something given. They have the quality of *passivity*. The mystic feels as if his own will were in abeyance, as if he were grasped and held by a power not his own.

5. A common characteristic of many mystical states is the presence of a *consciousness of the Oneness of everything*. All creaturely existence is experienced as a unity, as All in One and One in All. In theistic mysticism God is felt to be in everything and everything to exist in God.

In ancient Chinese philosophy the creation of the phenomenal universe is envisaged as a coming out of *Tao*, the Primal Meaning and Undivided Unity behind everything, by the pulling asunder of polar opposites. Out of *Tao* sprang the principles of phenomenal reality, the two poles of *yang* (light) and *yin* (darkness), which are evident throughout the whole of the universe as it appears to us. We cannot conceive of light except as the opposite of darkness, of above except as the opposite of below, of before except as the opposite of after, of goodness except as the opposite of evil. Our perception is conditioned by the existence of these polar opposites. Yet though *yang* and *yin* have their origin in the Undivided Unity, they are only active in the realm of phenomena.

In this realm of polar opposites man is imprisoned. He is conscious, therefore, of a division in his soul. His deepest spiritual instinct is to break through the polar opposites and find again the Primal Meaning, so that he may once again be restored to the Undivided Unity which he has lost.

God is to be found, said Nicholas of Cusa, beyond 'the coincidence of contradictories'. There can, however, be no escape from duality through sense perception, for sense perception is conditioned by the presence of polar opposites, nor through discursive thought, which is bound by the same dualism. In mystical experience the dilemma of duality is resolved. For to the mystic is given that unifying vision of the One in the All and the All in the One.

There is little doubt that this sense of the Oneness of everything in the universe and outside it is at the heart of the most highly developed mystical consciousness. All feelings of duality and multiplicity are obliterated, including the duality between man and Deity. Though it may be expressed differently, this is equally true of Hindu and Sufi mystics, of Plotinus and of the great contemplatives of Christianity.

6. A further characteristic of mystical experience is the *sense of timelessness*. The nature of time has puzzled men ever since they started to think about it. Does it exist in its own right or is it only a particular sort of perception, bound up with the way we, as creatures of a phenomenal world, see things?

As the perception of the modern physicist has expanded, he has, as we have seen, been compelled to abandon the idea of three-dimensional space passing simultaneously, moment by moment, through time. Instead he finds himself impelled to think in terms of a four-dimensional universe, in which time is one of the dimensions. Considered as an abstraction the universe simply *is*. In itself it is timeless. It is simply a multiplicity of points which only begin to form stretches of time among themselves when the human mind provides a reference system.

Some of our experiences fall into a time-series in which there is always a past, a present, and a future. A moment ago the present moment was in the future; in another moment it will be in the past. In this series the relationship between events is constantly changing. There is another series, that of 'earlier than', 'later than', in which the relationship between events remains constant. The hour I got up this morning will always remain earlier than the time I shall go to bed tonight. Normal sense experience falls into these two series. There are, however, other experiences, and these are the most profound and significant, in which the relationships are not capable of being adequately described in terms of past, present, and future, or of earlier than, later than. These experiences have a timeless quality. They are not bounded by *clock* time.

Whatever time may be, and it is a mystery, the experiences of the mystics are not understandable unless one is prepared to accept that there may be an entirely different dimension from that of clock time or indeed of any other sort of time. For the mystic feels himself to be in a dimension where time is not, where 'all is always now'.

7. Bound up with the sense of oneness and the sense of timelessness there is another characteristic of mystical experience, the conviction that the familiar phenomenal *ego* is not the real I.

This conviction finds expression in one form in the Atman doctrine of Hinduism. The self, the *ego* of which we are normally conscious, it is asserted, is not the true self. It is conscious only by fits and starts; it is bound up with bodily organizations and mental happenings which are subject to change and decay; it is, therefore, only an ephemeral, phenomenal self.

In man there is another self, the true Self, which is not affected by ordinary happenings and which gives him a sense of identity through numerous bodily and mental transformations. It does not change in the slow changes of the organism, in the flux of sensations, in the dissipation of ideas, or in the fading of memories. This true Self Hinduism calls the *Atman*. The Atman is immortal, constant, and unchanging, and is not bound by space–time. It is not only an individual self, it also has a universal quality. It is 'that by which the universe is pervaded, which nothing pervades, which causes all things to shine, but which all things cannot make to shine'.* In its nature, moreover, this True or Greater Self is divine. 'The knowledge that Brahman and Atman are one and the same' wrote Sankara, 'is true knowledge.'†

It also finds expression in a somewhat different form, and with a somewhat different emphasis, in Christian mysticism under several names, the *spark*, the *centre*, or *apex of the soul*,

* Sankara: *The Crest-Jewel of Wisdom.*
† ibid.

and the *ground of the spirit*. Though the theological and meta-physical expression may be different, the insight and the experience on which it is based is clearly the same.

The spark of the soul is described by Ruysbroek in these words:

The third property [of the soul] we call the spark of the soul. It is the inward and natural tendency of the soul towards its source. And here we receive the Holy Spirit, the Charity of God. By this inward tendency we are like the Holy Spirit; but in the act of receiving we become one spirit and love with God.

Meister Eckhart uses more vigorous language:

For the power of the Holy Ghost seizes the very highest and purest, the spark of the soul, and carries it up in the flame of love. . . . The soul-spark is conveyed aloft into its source and is absorbed into God and is identified with God and is the spiritual light of God.

Whatever the spark is, a faculty or organ of the soul whereby the soul has communion with and knows God, and therefore created, or whether it is the very essence of the Being and Nature of God Himself, and therefore uncreated, Eckhart appears to be uncertain. He sometimes expresses one point of view, sometimes another. He always seems to be saying, however, that at the 'apex of the mind' there is a divine spark which is so closely akin to God that it is 'one' with, not merely 'united to' Him. In one place he writes:

There is in the soul something which is above the soul, Divine, simple, a pure nothing; rather nameless than named, unknown than known. . . . It is absolute and free from all names and all forms, just as God is free and absolute in Himself. It is higher than knowledge, higher than love, higher than grace. For in these there is still distinction. In this power God doth blossom and flourish with all his Godhead and the spirit flourisheth in God.

Tauler, one of Eckhart's followers, seems to assume that there are two grounds of the soul. One is uncreated and is the abyss of the Godhead. Yet it is 'in us'. The other is created. This, according to Tauler, is both the empirical self and the self as it is in its potentiality as sharing in the life of God.

It is the task of the psychologist to explore the workings of

the human psyche. It is therefore of interest to find in Dr
C. G. Jung's concept of the *self* an idea not dissimilar to that
of the *spark*.

To understand what Jung means by the self, it will be
necessary to say a little about his psychology. One of the most
important elements in it is his theory of the *archetypes of the
collective unconscious*. These archetypes are not innate inherited
images, but dispositions to form certain symbols and images.
They cannot be known of themselves nor can they be en-
countered directly, but only through their manifestations in
these symbols or images. Jung calls them 'the organs of the
prerational psyche' and explains that as our physical organs
are the result of a long process of bodily development, so the
archetypes are the outcome of the whole inner experience of
the human race. They are centres of energy, of immense power,
and the symbols through which they are manifested enshrine
the deepest spiritual wisdom of mankind.

By the *self* Jung does not mean what we normally mean by
the word. It has affinities with the self of Hindu religious
psychology. Jung defines the term as 'the archetypal image
that leads out of polarity to the union of both partial systems –
through a common mid point'. It therefore contains the idea
of something which leads to synthesis, wholeness, the coming
together of those polar-opposites present in the phenomenal
world. Since, according to Jung, the self itself is an archetype,
it cannot be directly known, but only through the symbols
which are the manifestations of its archetypal energy.

Jung sometimes calls the self the *whole*, sometimes the *peri-
phery*, at other times the *centre of the psyche*. It is, without doubt,
described in psychological terms, that faculty or organ of the
psyche which the mystics call the spark, apex, centre, or
ground of the soul. It is that in the personality through which
man has contact with the Divine. Indeed, Jung once wrote:

The soul must possess some possibility of contact with God, that is
something which corresponds to the divine essence; otherwise no
association could possibly have taken place. This corresponding
quality described in psychological terms is the archetype of the
divine image.

11. The Nature of Mystical Experience

IN *The Sparkling Stone* Ruysbroeck describes four ascending religious types, under the names of the hirelings, the faithful servants, the secret friends, and the hidden sons of God.

The *hirelings*, he says, are 'those who love themselves so inordinately that they will not serve God save for their own profit and because of their own reward'. These 'dwell in bondage and in their own selfhood; for they seek, and aim, at their own in all they do'.

The *faithful servants* are those who serve God in the outward and active life. They love and serve God in their own way and have, in some degree, subdued the dictates of self, but they have not yet learned to turn wholly inward. Consequently they are divided in heart, unstable in mind, and easily swayed by joy and grief in temporal things.

Though he [the faithful servant] may live according to the commandments of God, inwardly he abides in darkness. He lives more in the world of the senses than of the spirit.

The *secret friends* are those who have conquered self and entered on the inward life, which is for them 'an upward stirring exercise of love'. They have not as yet, however, become fully inward men. They possess their inwardness, in Ruysbroeck's term, as an *attribute*,

. . . for they have, as images and intermediaries, between themselves and God, their own being and their own activity. And though in their loving adherence they feel united with God, yet, in their union, they always feel a difference and otherness between God and themselves. For the simple passing into the Bare and Wayless they do not know and love; and therefore their highest inward life ever remains in Reason and Ways.

How great [continues Ruysbroeck] is the difference between the secret friend and the *hidden son*. For the friend makes only loving, living, and measured ascents towards God. But the son presses on to lose his own life upon the summits in that simplicity which knoweth not itself. [Only when] we and all our selfhood die in God do we become his hidden sons.

The highest state of the mystic life can only be reached when there has been a complete death of the selfhood, when all images and intermediaries have been abandoned, and when a man has entered that Dark Silence, that Nothingness, that Wayless Way, where the hidden sons of God lose and, at the same time, find themselves.

One may be a 'faithful servant' of God without being in any sense a mystic or having known any sort of mystical illumination; nor does an awakening of the transcendental sense necessarily result in mystical insight, still less in the birth of a contemplative. The state of dark contemplation, known by the 'hidden sons of God', is one which few are capable of attaining. True mysticism, however, begins in an awakening of the transcendental sense, that sense of something beyond material phenomena which lies at the root of all religious feeling. But it is only the beginning; there must be something more.

No one chooses to be a mystic of his own volition. He must undergo some sort of experience which is of sufficient intensity to lead to an expansion of normal consciousness and perception, so that there comes to him a new vision of reality which dominates his life and thought. He must experience some sort of 'conversion'.

The illumination may be gradual, almost imperceptible, or sudden and violent. If there is a sudden conversion, a swift, overwhelming experience, it is usually preceded by and is the result of a long period of restlessness, uncertainty, and mental stress. The classic example of sudden conversion and illumination, resulting in a complete change of outlook and life, is that of St Paul on the road to Damascus. Yet here, though the actual change was abrupt, there seems to have been a period of mental stress leading up to it. If not, what is the meaning of the words, 'Saul, Saul, why persecutest thou me? It is hard for thee to kick against the goad'?

There was a long, hard struggle in the mind of St Francis of Assisi between the life of the world and the call of the spirit, which lasted for several years, before the illumination in the little, ruinous church of San Damiano, when (in the words of Thomas of Celano):

... being led by the Spirit he went in to pray; and he fell down before the Crucifix in devout supplication, and having been smitten by unwonted visitations, found himself another man than he who had gone in.

St Paul and St Francis were true mystics, adepts in the spiritual life. In this Study we are, however, concerned with the whole range of mystical consciousness. I have, therefore, as a prologue to the Anthology, which forms the second section of the book, included descriptions of a number of experiences, clearly mystical in character, of men and women who are in no sense contemplatives. Each contains one or more of the characteristic marks of mystical states which have been described in earlier pages. Let us consider some of them.

Consider first the vivid, illuminating experience which came to Warner Allen between two notes of a symphony and which he describes in his book, *The Timeless Moment.** In it one finds not only that sense of the oneness of everything which has been noted as typical of a mystical state, but also the feeling of absorption without loss of identity, the feeling of ceasing to be oneself and yet at the same time discovering what one is convinced is one's true self. There is also the feeling of amazement, of intense joy and peace, and, at the same time, intense unworthiness, which is also typical.

Consider next the experience of the adolescent boy on the cricket field.

What had been merely an outside became an inside. The objective was somehow transformed into a completely subjective fact, which was experienced as 'mine', but on a level where the world had no meaning; for 'I' was no longer the familiar ego.*

Here is the typical reconciliation of the polar opposites of 'outside' and 'inside', of 'objective' and 'subjective', and the sense of the familiar phenomenal self being not the real self. Though at the time his background of experience prevented

* Anthology, Section 1.

him from understanding the meaning of what he had seen, its effect on him can be gauged by the fact that he was able to describe it so exactly and vividly many years later.

The experience of Winifred Holtby,* knowing, from what the doctors had told her, that the work she loved was at an end and that she had not long to live, is typical of one particular type of mystical experience, the vision of a Love which is inherent, though not obvious, in the texture of the universe, which once glimpsed brings peace, acceptance, joy, and faith, and enables a man or woman to say with confidence that 'there is nothing anywhere in the world or without that can make us afraid'.

The small girl in the orchard* can only use phrases such as 'I saw the heavens open' and 'so it's like this; now I know what Heaven is like, now I know what they mean in church'.

John Buchan, later Lord Tweedsmuir and Governor-General of Canada, in his autobiography, *Memory Hold-the-Door* tells of his own experience in these words:

Then and there came on me the hour of revelation. . . . Scents, sights, and sounds blended into a harmony so perfect that it transcended human expression, even human thought. It was like a glimpse of the peace of eternity.*

The hour of revelation! Mystical states are more than states of feeling, they are states of knowledge.

The experience which befell Dr R. M. Bucke at the age of thirty-five and which dominated all his later thinking is described as follows:

Directly afterwards there came upon me a sense of exultation, of immense joyousness, accompanied or immediately followed by an intellectual illumination quite impossible to describe.*

It was this experience which enabled him in his book, *Cosmic Consciousness* (Innes, Philadelphia, 1905), to write one of the clearest and most precise descriptions of that intellectual illumination, that new access of knowledge, which comes through

* All these passages are printed in Section 1 of the Anthology.

mystical intuition, a knowledge which reveals aspects of the universe not accessible to the intellect:

Like a flash there is presented to his consciousness a conception (a vision) of the meaning and drift of the universe. He does not come to believe merely; but he sees and knows that the cosmos, which to the self-conscious mind seems made up of dead matter, is in fact far otherwise – is in truth a living presence. He sees that the life which is in man is eternal ... that the foundation principle of the world is what we call love. ... Especially does he obtain such a conception of *the whole* – as makes the old attempts mentally to grasp the universe and its meaning petty and ridiculous.

None of these experiences are experiences of mystics in the restricted sense of the word, i.e. those who have ascended the Mount of Contemplation. Yet can one doubt that they are of the same character and spring from the same source as that described by St Augustine, one of the greatest of Western contemplatives, in the famous passage in his *Confessions*:

Thus with the flash of one trembling glance it [the soul] arrived at THAT WHICH IS. And then I saw Thy invisible things understood by the things that are made. But I could not fix my gaze thereon; and my infirmity being struck back, I was thrown again on my wonted habits, carrying along with me only a loving memory thereof, and a longing for what I had, as it were, perceived the odour of, but was not yet able to feed on.*

The difference between the mystic, in the wide sense, as the term is here used, and the contemplative is thus one of degree. The primary experience and the primary effect are the same. Those called to that high state of spirituality named Contemplation, by a greater concentration and a more thorough purgation, attain to a state of consciousness, in which that which for those not called to the following of this way is only occasional and spasmodic can become so frequent, so much a way of life, that, in the words of St John of the Cross already quoted, 'the soul has it in its power to abandon itself, *whenever it wills*, to this sweet sleep of love'.

* Anthology, Section 13.

12. The Mystic Way

THE Mystic Way is usually, particularly by Catholic theologians, divided into three stages: the Way of Purgation, the Way of Illumination, or the Illuminative Life (which is also called Proficiency and Contemplation), and the Way of Union, or the Unitive Life.

This classification should, however, be regarded as a rough diagram only, useful as a general guide, but not to be thought of as a description of clearly defined and recognizable stages, which have been universally followed by mystics. There is actually, a good deal of variety in the experience of different mystics and, moreover, as one reads the descriptions of their experiences, it is often difficult to decide what stage is being described or at what stage of the Mystic Way a particular contemplative is. The Mystic Way is more like a slope than a staircase, and it is sometimes a slippery slope, with constant slippings back. In her Seventh Revelation Dame Julian of Norwich tells how she passed from one stage to another time after time:

After this He shewed me a sovereign ghostly pleasance in my soul. . . . I was in all peace and rest. . . . This lasted but a while and I was turned and left to myself in heaviness and weariness of life. . . . And anon after this our blessed Lord gave me again comfort and rest in the soul. . . . And then the pain showed again to my feeling, and then the joy and the blessing, and now this one, and now that other, diverse times – I suppose about twenty times.

Though less precise, the divisions used by Ruysbroeck in *The Adornment of the Spiritual Marriage* are, in some ways, more satisfactory and realistic. He divides the Mystic Way into the three stages: the Active Life, a life which may be in a real sense illuminated, but is not yet that of the truly 'inward' man; the Interior Life, the full life of the 'inward man', which, in its advanced stages, seems to be one of definite union, or something so close to it as to be hardly distinguishable from it; and the Superessential or God-seeing Life, the life of complete and permanent attainment.

The Indian philosopher Radhakrishnan uses a somewhat different scheme to describe this path to perfection:

The way of growth lies through a gradual increase in impersonality by an ever deeper and more intense unifying of the self with a greater than itself. In this process prayer, worship, meditation, philosophy, art, and literature all play their part, since all help in purifying the inner being and disposing it more and more for contact with the divine.*

The three stages of the way of perfection he calls Purification, Concentration, and Identification.

In his allegory *The Conference of the Birds*† the Sufi mystic Farid al-din 'Attar pictures the journey of the mystic from the start of his pilgrimage to his final attainment as one through seven valleys. First comes the Valley of the Quest, the stripping away of all encumbrances, so that the heavenly light may enter. It corresponds to the Way of Purgation. Next comes the Valley of Love, the beginning of the true mystic life, the first stage of Illumination. In the next valley, that of Knowledge and Enlightenment, the mystic enters into the state of Contemplation proper; the soul partakes of the divine, the contemplative glimpses the mystery of Being; God is seen in all things. In the fourth valley, the Valley of Detachment, the soul becomes utterly absorbed in the Divine Love. In the fifth, that of Unity, the contemplation of the naked Godhead, stripped of all images, is reached. The vision is as yet transient, and in the Valley of Bewilderment it seems to have disappeared. The light is too bright; the soul is dazzled and blinded. But it is now ready to enter the Valley of Annihilation, where the self is completely merged in God.

* Radhakrishnan: *Eastern Religions and Western Thought* (O.U.P.).
† Anthology, Section 16.

13. The Purgation of the Self

WHATEVER the scheme of classification, whatever the labels used for the different stages, the first step in the Mystic Way is the purgation of the self.

The Way of Purgation has two main objectives: first of all complete detachment from and renunciation of the things of sense, and the death of the egocentric life, so that the divine life may be born in the soul and union with the Godhead attained; and secondly, a continuous cleansing of the perceptions and a scouring of the windows of the soul, so that the light of a new reality may stream in and completely illuminate and transform it.

One can hardly read a page of the writings of the great contemplatives without finding a constant reiteration of the necessity of renunciation, detachment, and self-mortification, if any progress towards illumination and union is to be made.

'A man should stand and be so free of himself, that is from selfhood, I-hood, me, mine and the like,' writes the author of *Theologia Germanica*, 'that in all things he should no more regard himself and his own than if he did not exist.'

'The only provisions for the journey in the Path of Truth,' says the Hoopoe in 'Attar's allegory, 'are total renunciation and self-annihilation. Consume to ashes whatsoever thou hast . . . I can think of no better fortune for a valiant man than this, that he loses himself from himself.'*

It is, however, to the famous chapter in *The Ascent of Mount Carmel*† by St John of the Cross that we may turn to find the summons to renunciation and detachment in one of its most vigorous and vivid forms.

St John of the Cross says that for the soul to attain to a state of perfection it must pass through two *nights*. The first night (or purgation) is of the senses, the second, of the spiritual

---

* 'Attar: *Conference of the Birds*, trans. R. P. Masani.
† Anthology, Section 27.

part of the soul. In Chapter 13 of *The Ascent of Mount Carmel*
he describes 'the manner and way which the soul must follow
in order to enter this night of sense'. He bids those who would
attain complete detachment to renounce all the pleasures of
the senses, to prefer not that which is easiest, but that which
is most difficult, not that which is most restful but that which
is most wearisome, not that which is loftiest and most precious
but that which is lowest and most despised, not the best of
temporal things but the worst. He sums up his teaching in a
series of epigrams:

> In order to arrive at having pleasure in everything,
> Desire to have pleasure in nothing.
> In order to arrive at possessing everything,
> Desire to possess nothing.
> In order to arrive at being everything,
> Desire to be nothing.
> In order to arrive at knowing everything,
> Desire to know nothing.

for

> When the mind dwells upon anything,
> Thou art ceasing to cast thyself upon the All.
> For, in order to pass from the all to the All
> Thou hast to deny thyself wholly in all.

He who would tread the Mystic Way is bidden not only
painfully to learn to annihilate the selfhood but also to turn
his attention more and more from the multiplicity of the
phenomenal world, with its classifying and image-making, its
logical reasoning and discursive thinking, so as to attain that
'simple seeing' of which the mystics speak; for not until the
eye has become single can the whole body be filled with light.

If we desire to find the truth of things, the *truth-in-essence*,
where shall we look for it? The mysticism of every religion
speaks with a common voice. 'The Kingdom of Heaven is
within you.' 'Hold fast to thy centre and all things shall be
thine.' 'Take your seat within the heart of the thousand-
petalled lotus.' Robert Browning echoes the same truth:

> Truth is within ourselves; it takes no rise
> From outward things, whate'er you may believe.

There is an inmost centre in us all,
Where truth abides in fulness; and around
Wall upon wall, the gross flesh hems it in,
This perfect, clear perception – which is truth.

A baffling and perverting carnal mesh
Binds it, and makes all error: and to *know*
Rather consists in opening out a way
Whence the imprisoned splendour may escape,
Than in effecting entry for a light
Supposed to be without.

Reality is one single whole; but within the one reality there are different levels of significance. Man participates in all these interrelated levels. There are, however, as it were, screens separating each region of significance from the rest. What is seen at the normal level of awareness is the result of a particular combination of image-making faculties, revealing a picture, true and real within its own limitations, but, compared with the complete whole, only an appearance, what in Eastern philosophies is termed *maya*. By turning inward, away from the flux of phenomena, towards the centre of the soul, by putting aside all concepts and images, spiritual as well as bodily, in a state of stillness and passivity, it is possible to penetrate through these separating screens, and to see deeper into that which more completely *is*; perhaps, in the end, to ascend to the contemplation of God Himself.

St John of the Cross speaks, as we have seen, of a passage through two kinds of 'night'.* The first he calls the dark night of the senses, the second, which is more difficult to understand, the dark night of the spirit. In the first night there is, he says, still some light, for understanding and reason still operate; but in the second all is darkness; both the understanding and the senses are in abeyance; all that remains is the ardent longing of pure faith.

The anonymous medieval author of *The Cloud of Unknowing* uses the image of a 'cloud', in which all the normal tools of perception, knowledge, and understanding are discarded.

* Anthology, Section 27.

For [he says] of all other creatures and their works, yea, and of the works of God's self, may a man through grace have fullhead of knowing, and well he can think of them: but of God Himself can no man think.*

To see God and be united to Him a man must enter into darkness, for

... the higher part of contemplation, as it may be had here, hangeth all wholly in this darkness and in this cloud of unknowing; with a loving stirring and a blind beholding of the naked being of God Himself only.

Nicholas of Cusa, the fifteenth-century cardinal and states-man, mathematician and mystic, speaks of a *docta ignorantia*, that is, an 'instructed' or 'learned' ignorance, a form of awareness which is not that of the intellect, but which alone can lead men to deeper truth.

Normal perception is, as we have seen, conditioned by the existence in the phenomenal world of polar opposites. God is to be found beyond the realm of these polar opposites, for, he writes:

The place wherein Thou art found unveiled is girt round with the coincidence of contradictories, and this is the wall of Paradise wherein Thou dost abide. The door whereof is guarded by the most proud spirit of Reason, and, unless he be vanquished, the way in will not lie open. [Therefore] I observe how needful it is for me to enter into the darkness, and to admit the coincidence of opposites, beyond all the grasp of reason, and there to seek the truth where impossibility meeteth me.†

Thus [he goes on] while I am borne to loftiest heights, I behold Thee as infinity. By reason of this, Thou mayest not be attained, comprehended, or named, or multiplied, or beheld. He that ap-proacheth Thee must needs ascend above every limit and end and finite thing. But how shall he attain unto Thee who art the End towards whom he striveth, if he must ascend above the end? He who ascendeth above the end, doth he not enter into what is unde-fined and confused, and thus, in regard to the intellect, into

* Anthology, Section 22.
† Anthology, Section 25.

ignorance and obscurity, which pertain to intellectual confusion? It behoveth, then, the intellect to become ignorant and to abide in darkness if it would fain see Thee. But what, O my God, is this intellectual ignorance? Is it not an instructed ignorance?*

14. Man's Knowledge of God

To those familiar only with the popular and more elementary forms of religious thought and expression, much of this may sound alien and strange. What is the meaning of all this talk about 'darkness' and 'unknowing' and 'ignorance'? It will be desirable at this point, therefore, to consider what the more profound religious thinkers have thought about God and the possibility of man's having knowledge of Him.

A great deal of our knowledge is merely *about* things. Yet, within our normal experience, there is another sort of knowledge. When we say we *know* someone we love, we are describing a different sort of knowledge than when we say that we know that it is ten miles to X or that if we mix certain chemicals together we shall blow ourselves up. This other kind of knowledge is based on something which can only be called 'union'. The more subject and object, the observer and that which is observed, merge into each other, that is, are 'united' with each other, the more profound and illuminating the knowledge becomes; and the less it becomes capable of description.

The knowledge we may have of God is knowledge of this sort; but it goes beyond it; for God can only be fully known by *becoming* God, by taking Him into the inmost self as the fulfilment of that self, and by the self's being taken fully into the divine life and being transformed therein. The idea of man *becoming* or being *made* God may be alien to popular religious conceptions of the nature of God and man, wherein man is thought of as standing over against God. It constantly appears,

*Anthology, Section 25.

however, in the writings of the mystics, and it was one of the greatest champions of Catholic orthodoxy, St Athanasius, who wrote:

God was made man in order that man might be made God.

At the heart of religious experience there is a paradox. Men of spiritual insight are, in the depths of their souls, conscious of a Presence, which they call God, and this Presence is more real to them than anything else that they know. They are not, however, able to describe It as other things can be described nor do they know It as they know other things. They are compelled to say that, in terms of the human intellect, God, since He cannot be comprehended by the rational faculty, is unknown and unknowable. That, however, is only half the picture. Though unknown and unknowable by the intellect, by what Dionysius the Areopagite calls the *higher faculty*, it is possible for a man to be united 'to Him Who is wholly unknowable; thus by knowing nothing he knows That Which is beyond his knowledge'.* The unknowable and unknown God is 'closer than breathing, nearer than hands and feet'. He is 'more inward to us than we are to ourselves'.

In the history of man's attempt to penetrate the mystery of the Being of God two ways have been followed, two modes of speaking used, the way of negation, the *via negativa*, and the way of affirmation. These two ways are not in opposition, they are what the scientists would call complementary, each true in its own setting, each supplementing the other.

The *via negativa* is known to all the higher religions. When the authors of the Upanishads write:

Who says that Spirit is not known, knows; who claims that he knows, knows nothing,†

and:

He is not knowable by perception, turned inwards or outwards, or by both combined. He is neither that which is known, nor that

* Anthology, Section 11.
† Anthology, Section 2.

which is not known, nor is he the sum of all that might be known. He cannot be seen, grasped, bargained with. He is undefinable, unthinkable, indescribable,*

they are echoed by the contemplative saints of Christianity; among others, by St Bernard:

What is God? I can think of no better answer than, He who is.

by Meister Eckhart:

Why dost thou prate of God? Whatever thou sayest of Him is untrue.

and by St Augustine:

There is in the mind no knowledge of God except the knowledge that it does not know Him.

But He, of whom the mind can have no knowledge, can be known in the deep centre of the soul; He, who is neither perceptible to the senses nor conceivable by the intellect, is sensible to the heart.

In his commentary on *The Secret of the Golden Flower*, a Chinese Book of Life, Jung wrote:

Every statement about the transcendental ought to be avoided because it is a laughable presumption on the part of the human mind, unconscious of its limitations.

Nevertheless, though the negation may be truer than the affirmation, it is possible and legitimate to make affirmations about the nature of the Divine Being. One must, however, be conscious of their limitations and realize that they can never be more than symbols, images, approximations, always inadequate, always, in a sense, untrue. When we speak of God as Goodness, Beauty, Truth, or Love, we are not guilty of a 'laughable presumption', provided we realize that what we are actually doing is translating into inadequate word-concepts something which springs from inner experience of Him. One has only to study the experiences of the mystics to feel that these affirmations have real meaning. Not only that, but

* Anthology, Section 2.

these affirmations spring from an innate natural reason. There is something in men which compels them instinctively to rebel against an irrational universe and which will not allow them to conceive of a Divine Being except as One who is the sum total, and much more, of everything they, in their highest moments, feel to be most beautiful and good and true.

In the second part of his Eddington Memorial Lecture, *Time and Universe for the Scientific Conscience*, the astronomer Dr Martin Johnson spoke of the 'incomparable perceptiveness of Jesus' in His use of the word Father as a symbol revealing the nature of God. We cannot turn our flashes of spiritual insight, our moments of worship, he declares, into any rational account of God, for the notion of God is beyond our grasp. The word Father, however, is a symbol which is not misleading, one which, to quote Dr Johnson's own words, 'made God accessible to the learned and unlearned, the former unable and the latter unwanting to penetrate beyond the symbol'.

The Blessed John Ruysbroeck, the *doctor ecstaticus*, stands very high among the exponents of speculative Christian mysticism. While his vision of God is framed in the language of the great dogmas of the Christian Faith, particularly the mysterious dogma of the Blessed Trinity, he interprets these dogmas in such a way that one feels that, had he lived in the twentieth instead of the fourteenth century, he would not have regarded such concepts as Energy, Pattern, Structure, Process, Organism, and Complementarity as alien to his thought.

In his attempt to describe the Being of God, Ruysbroeck, following Eckhart, distinguishes between 'the Godhead' and 'God'. The Godhead is One, Eternal Rest, the Primal Unity, the Nameless Being, and as such cannot be comprehended by man. There is, however, a fruitive outpouring of God, and this outpouring is manifested in differentiation. As human beings we can be aware of God, not as He is in Himself, but in this differentiation. Let Ruysbroeck speak for himself.

In *The Book of the Twelve Béguines* he writes that there is

. . . a distinction and a differentiation *according to our reason* between God and the Godhead, between action and rest. The fruitful nature of the Persons of whom is the Trinity in Unity and the Unity in

Trinity ever worketh in living differentiation. But the Simple Being of God, *according to the nature thereof*, is an Eternal Rest of God and of all created things.

Again, in the *Seven Degrees of Love*, he says that in the eternal Now

we can speak no more of Father, Son, and Holy Spirit or of any creature, but only of one Being, which is the very substance of the Divine Persons. There we all are before our creation. . . . There the Godhead is, in simple essence, without activity; Eternal Rest, Unconditioned Dark, the Nameless Being, the Superessence of all created things.

Here, in these two passages, expressed in the language of Catholic theology, is the essence of that perennial mystical philosophy which is found in all the higher theistic religions:

1. That the Godhead is absolute Stillness and Rest, free of all activity and inaccessible to human thought, yet alive through and through, a tremendous Energy, pouring Itself out into the created world and drawing that world back into Itself.
2. That there is a complete unity in everything; all is in God and God is in all.
3. That man's real self is divine.

All are present; for in Ruysbroeck's thought, set out in these passages, the Simple Being of God is not only an Eternal Rest of God Himself, but also of all created things; the Godhead is not only Eternal Rest, Unconditioned Dark, the Nameless Being, but also the Superessence of all created things.

Man is, thus, not a creature set over against God; he is united with His triune life, and 'this union is within us by our naked nature and were this nature to be separated from God it would fall into pure nothingness'. The union of God and man, though the impress of the Eternal Image of God on man is received passively – it has to be realized as an actuality by man himself – is not something which may or may not happen; it exists eternally and was a fact before man was created in time.

A similar conviction is expressed by Meister Eckhart in these words:

The knower and the known are one. Simple people imagine they should see God, as if He stood there and they here. God and I, we are one in knowledge.

And even more paradoxically:

The eye with which I see God is the same as that with which he sees me.

And in one of his most superb passages Ruysbroeck thus sums up his teaching:

Through the Eternal Birth all creatures have come forth in eternity before they were created in time. So God has seen and known them in Himself, according to distinction, in living ideas, and in an otherness from Himself, but not as something other in all ways, for all that is in God is God.

This eternal going out and this eternal life, which we have and are in God eternally, without ourselves, is the cause of our created being in time. And our created being abides in the Eternal Essence, and is one with it in its essential existence.*

In an even more paradoxical form Ruysbroeck is echoed by 'Attar in the allegory *The Conference of the Birds* already referred to. At the end of their long pilgrimage the thirty bedraggled birds enter the Presence of the Simurg.

> And in the centre of the Glory there
> Beheld the Figure of *themselves* as 'twere
> Transfigured – looking to *themselves* beheld
> The Figure on the Throne en-miracled†

And, in the last canto of the *Paradiso* Dante, gazing on the vision of Ultimate Reality, saw amid the circles of blazing light the image of a man:

> Eternal light, that in Thyself alone
> Dwelling, alone dost know Thyself, and smile
> On Thy self-love, so knowing and so known!
> The sphering thus begot, perceptible

* Anthology, Section 19.
† Anthology, Section 16.

In Thee like mirrored light, now to my view –
When I had looked on it a little while –
Seemed in itself, and in its own self-hue,
Limned with our image.*

15. The State of Contemplation

To describe the experience of the mystical awakening and
illumination of the self is not unduly difficult. While it is an
experience not known to all, it is known to many. The descriptions of it given in the first section of the Anthology, and
commended on pages 53–5, will doubtless strike chords in
the minds of some at least of my readers. Nor is it too hard
to convey some idea of what is meant by the Way of Purgation; for this is a path which, to a lesser or greater degree,
many are called, in one way or another, to follow. When,
however, one tries to describe the higher states of the mystical
life, the task becomes more difficult.

First of all, we are now dealing with states of consciousness
and types of experience which are rare. Some of us have had
an experience which we might describe as 'an intellectual illumination quite impossible to describe', or as 'an hour of
revelation', or as a vision of a sustaining Love inherent in the
very texture of the universe. But the 'Dark Silence', the 'Wayless Way', the 'Nakedness' and 'Nothingness', if they strike
any answering chords at all, strike only faint and elusive ones.
They are descriptions of states which are outside normal
experience.

Further, our language has evolved primarily as an instrument for describing experience through the five senses. It
does not lend itself easily to descriptions of rare spiritual and
psychological states, which, though they may be states of
knowledge, are also states of feeling. Like the poet and the

* Anthology, Section 17. Cary translates the last lines:
      'For I therein, methought, in its own hue
      Beheld our image painted.'

musician, the mystic has to find a language of his own; it is to a great extent a language of symbols, and it is of the nature of symbolism that it conceals as well as reveals.

Nor are the mystics themselves always very helpful. Though the descriptions they have left are many and detailed, though immense pains have been taken to convey, as exactly as possible, what has been felt and seen and known, there is great variety in description and terminology. The basic similarities are striking, but the pure, undifferentiated vision has inevitably been distorted as it has passed through the prisms of individual temperament and predisposition. Even the traditional labels are used by the same writer in different ways at different times. The exact and painstaking St Teresa uses a different classification in each of her three works, the *Life*, *The Way of Perfection*, and *The Interior Castle*.

I trust, therefore, that I may be forgiven if there is a certain lack of precision in what follows, and if, in order to make myself as clear as possible, I may sometimes repeat myself.

In the study of Contemplation we are considering a movement of consciousness towards a higher level, as the result of the emergence and cultivation of powers which in most men and women remain latent. As found in the true contemplative it is an extreme form of the withdrawal of attention from the sensible world and a total dedication of action and mind towards a particular interior object. It is essentially a creative activity, similar to the highest activity of poet, painter, and musician. All great creative artists, whether their medium be words or paint or sound, must be in a real sense illuminated, and in some is clearly seen that remaking of consciousness which is found in the religious contemplative. Some, for instance William Blake, seem, without doubt, to have lived the Illuminative Life. Contemplation is thus a developed form of that inward turning towards the deep centre of the soul to which we have referred earlier, for it is only here that God is to be found.

To mount to God is to enter into one's self. For he who inwardly entereth and intimately penetrateth into himself gets above and beyond himself and truly mounts up to God.

And it is also a losing of that individual self we think we are.

How can you take your soul to Him if you carry with you your soul [i.e. consciousness of self].*

The word, 'contemplation', may be used in two senses; first, in a technical sense, as a term to describe a state of mystical consciousness, and secondly to describe a way of knowing.

One view of the world is that it is an intelligible presentation which is spread out before us for our detached and dispassionate examination; its nature can be grasped by thought, analysis, and classification alone. This view has been held by most philosophers and scientists.

Another view is that the world is not like that at all, that it is a 'mystery', the secret of which can only be partially grasped by thought, analysis, and classification. To penetrate its deepest secrets one must not stand aside from it but try, as it were, to feel it, to become part of it. One must be content, intently and humbly, to 'contemplate' it, to gaze at it as one might gaze at a picture, not in order to analyse the technique of its brushwork or colour arrangement, but to penetrate its meaning and significance. This intent, loving gazing in order to know and understand is what is meant when we say that contemplation is a tool of knowledge.

The contemplative attitude of mind is seen in its most highly developed form in one who has entered the *state* of Contemplation.

In the *state* of Contemplation there is found a self-forgetting attention, a humble receptiveness, a still and steady gazing, an intense concentration, so that emotion, will, and thought are all fused and then lost in something which is none of them, but which embraces them all. Gradually, by a deeper and deeper process of self-merging, a communion is established between the seer and what is seen, between him who feels and that which he feels.

Normal perception, as we have seen, is conditioned by those spatial and temporal polarities which operate in the phenomenal world. Much of our thinking and speaking, which is

* 'Attar: *The Conference of the Birds*.

chiefly concerned with the world of phenomena, reflects the existence of these polarities; it is dualistic; it is founded on the principle of opposites. Unity is opposed to multiplicity; the subject cannot be the object, *this* cannot be *that*.

More and more, as Contemplation proceeds, these polar opposites of normal thought and perception fade away. As Nicholas of Cusa said:

The place wherein Thou dost abide is girt round with the coincidence of contradictories. . . . 'Tis beyond the coincidence of contradictories Thou mayest be seen and nowhere this side thereof.

The concepts of personal and impersonal, transcendence and immanence, beginning and ending, unity and multiplicity cease to have meaning. The experience of the dark abyss of the Godhead and of the intimate personal union of love are seen as one. To lose one's self is to find it; the divine Dark is filled through and with a glowing light. Perception, thought, expression cease to be dualistic and become non-dualistic. That sense of Oneness and Timelessness, which we have seen as characteristic of mystical states, is found in a highly developed form. The all is seen as the One and the One as the all; time and timelessness intersect. Unless this idea of non-duality can be grasped the whole range of mystical experience is incomprehensible.

Not only that, but also this sense of passing out of dualism into non-dualism explains in great measure the symbols and expressions, sometimes startling, which many mystics use and the theological and metaphysical statements of such religions as Hinduism.

The great difference between the formal theologies of Hinduism on the one hand and Judaism, Christianity, and Islam on the other, is that the thought of the former is non-dualistic, of the latter dualistic. The fundamental Hindu assertion, *Thou art That*, i.e. that the true self of man is 'identical' with Brahman, springs from the realization of this 'identity' in the mystical consciousness of Hinduism, the most mystical of all the higher religions. To Jew, Christian, and Moslem a gulf is felt to exist between God and man, Creator and creature, which can never be crossed. To assert that 'Thou' art 'That' sounds blasphemous. Consequently, since, whatever it may mean, this sense of a sort of identification, in which the personal self is absorbed in the Divine, is at the heart of the most highly developed form of mystical consciousness, there has always been a state of tension between the contemplatives and the ecclesiastical authorities of Christianity and Islam.

For instance, Meister Eckhart, who was never afraid of the startling phrase when it seemed best to express what he wanted to say, stated, 'The eye with which I see God is the same as that with which he sees me', and he found himself in trouble with the official Church. The Mohammedan saint, Al-Hallaj, was crucified because he was accused of saying, though he never actually did so in the sense his accusers maintained, 'I am the Truth', and so identifying himself with God. As he was about to be executed, he is reported to have uttered this prayer:

And these thy servants who are gathered to slay me, in zeal for Thy religion and in desire to win Thy favour, forgive them, O Lord, and have mercy upon them; for verily if Thou hadst revealed to them that which Thou hast revealed to me, they would not have done what they have done; and if Thou hadst hidden from me that which Thou hast hidden from them, I should not have suffered this tribulation.

Perhaps it will help the reader to understand better if a word is said here about what is called the *mystic copula*. When one makes a statement such as 'This boy is John', one is using the copula 'is' to express identity as identity is understood logically. When, however, Sankara says that the Atman is Brahman or Al-Hallaj said 'I am the Truth', neither are making logical statements. In both the copula has a significance which it does not contain in logic. Both are mystical not logical statements of identity. Mysticism has its logic, but it is, to use Rudolf Otto's word, a 'wonder' logic.

This is one of the most important and difficult issues in the whole range of mystical experience and its interpretation. It will be discussed more fully when we come to consider the Unitive Life.

16. The Degrees of Prayer

To enter into that advanced state of Contemplation which St John of the Cross calls *dim or dark Contemplation*, education and training are necessary. Much of the writings of the contemplatives is given over to detailed descriptions of this education of the contemplative. We have already described some of its general characteristics and objectives. It is now necessary to write in greater detail.

The steps of the ladder whereby the would-be contemplative ascends to the state of advanced Contemplation are generally known among Christian mystics as the 'degrees of prayer', or, as it is sometimes called, orison. Mystical prayer is nothing to do with the words and petitions of what is commonly called prayer. It is not articulate; it has no form. It is, in the words of a medieval English mystic, 'naught else but a yearning of soul', wherein the soul is united to God in its ground without the intervention of imagination or reason or of anything but a simple attention of the mind and a humble, self-forgetting action of the will.

There is much variation in the ways the degrees of prayer are described, and it is easy to become confused. For the sake of simplicity we shall divide them into the stages of Recollection, Quiet, and Contemplation proper.

Recollection has been described by Father Thomas Merton in these words:

Recollection makes me present to myself by bringing together two aspects, or activities, of my being as if they were two lenses of a telescope. One lens is the basic semblance of my spiritual being, the inward soul, the deep will, the spiritual intelligence. The other is my outward soul, the will engaged in the activities of life. . . . When the active soul knows only itself, then it is absent from its true self. It does not know its own inward spirit. It never acts according to the need and measure of its own true personality, which exists where my spirit is wedded with the silent presence of the Lord's Spirit and

where my deep will responds to his gravitation towards the secrecy
of the Godhead.*

Recollection usually begins with acts of meditation on some
object or idea, in which imagination and thought play a predominant part. It develops through various states into the
Prayer of Inward Silence and Simplicity. Here imagination and
thought begin to fade out. This, in turn, merges into the true
Prayer of Quiet. As the Prayer of Quiet becomes deeper, the
stage of true *Contemplation* is reached and, as this grows in
intensity, the heights (or ought one to say the depths?) of *Dark
Contemplation* or the *Prayer of Passive Union*, which Ruysbroeck
and others describe so vividly, are attained. Throughout the
progress the attitude of the self becomes more and more one
of pure receptivity and loving trust. Thought, imagination,
and individual activity more and more cease. The self is fully
sunk in That which is both One and All.

In her autobiography St Teresa compares these degrees of
mystical prayer with four ways of watering a garden. At first
the water has to be drawn up by hand as from a deep well; a
great deal of human effort is called for. Then things become
easier. The senses have been stilled and it is as if the well had
been fitted with a windlass; more water can be got by less
effort. Later still, when all voluntary activities of the mind have
ceased, it is as if a little river ran through the garden. In the
last and highest degree it is as if God Himself watered the
garden with His rain.†

Recollection is a form of spiritual gymnastics, a deliberate
concentration of the self in an effort to penetrate to its centre.
The faculties of the mind are still wide awake: the self is fully
aware of its own individual personality. Though conscious of
it, it still feels its separateness from the divine Reality. It has
not yet reached the stage of the Prayer of Inward Silence and
Simplicity, still less those higher degrees of prayer, which are
technically known as 'infused orison'.

* *No Man is an Island* (Hollis and Carter).
† See Anthology, Section 26, for St Teresa's description of the degrees
of prayer as contained in her *Life*.

The self [writes Evelyn Underhill] is as yet unacquainted with the strange plane of silence which so soon becomes familiar to those who attempt even the lowest activities of the contemplative life; where the self is released from succession, the voices of the world are never heard and the great adventures of the spirit take place.*

The Master, in one of the *Dialogues* of the seventeenth-century German mystic, Jacob Boehme, gives these instructions to the Disciple:

Cease from thine own activity, fix thine eye upon one point. . . . Gather in all thy thoughts and by faith press into the Centre. . . . Be silent before the Lord, sitting alone with Him in thy inmost and most hidden cell, thy inward being centrally united in itself, and attending His will in the patience of hope.

The soul's progress from Recollection to the Prayer of Quiet need not be described in detail. It is sufficient to say that a deep, slow brooding and pondering, a deliberate effort of attention and concentration, an equally deliberate effort to bring the mind to a complete state of stillness result, at length, in the consciousness reaching a plane characterized by an immense increase in receptivity, an almost complete suspension of the reflective powers and the surface-consciousness, and a strange and indescribable silence. The self is content to rest in a new level of vivid awareness, marked by a deep peace and living stillness. The strain and effort which have been so evident and often painful in Recollection have disappeared. There is still a consciousness of selfhood, but the very meaning of I, Me, Mine, has been somehow transformed.

In *The Way of Perfection* St Teresa thus describes the Prayer of Quiet:

This is a supernatural thing, which we cannot obtain by any effort on our part. The soul rests in peace . . . all [her] powers are at rest. The soul understands, with an understanding quite different from that given by the external senses, that she is now quite close to God and that, if she drew just a little nearer, she would become one thing with Him by union. She does not see Him with eyes of the body or the soul. . . . The soul understands He is here, though not so clearly. She does not know herself how she understands; she sees only that she is in the Kingdom. . . .

* *Mysticism* (Methuen).

It is like the suspension of all internal and external powers. The external man . . . does not wish to make the slightest movement but rests, like one who has almost reached the end of his journey, that he may resume his journey with redoubled strength. . . . The soul is so happy to find herself near the fountain that she is satisfied even without drinking. She seems to have no more to desire. The faculties are at peace and do not wish to move. . . . However, the faculties are not so lost that they cannot think of Him whom they are near. Two of them are free. The will alone is held captive. . . . The understanding desires to know but one thing, and the memory to remember only one. They both see that only one thing is necessary, and everything else disturbs it. . . . I think, therefore, that since the soul is so completely happy in this prayer of quiet, the will must be united, during most of the time, with Him who alone can satisfy it.*

St Teresa's description of the Prayer of Quiet reads like a passage from a manual of psychology. Meister Eckhart's treatment is somewhat different. The passages I quote are taken from two of his Christmas Day sermons,† in which he speaks of the Divine Birth as taking place, not only in Bethlehem, but also in the human soul.

What does it behove a man to do to deserve and procure this birth to come to pass in him: is it better for him to do his part towards it, to imagine and think about God, or should he keep still in peace and quiet so that God can speak and act in him while he merely waits on God's operation? . . . The best and utmost of attainment in this life is to remain still and let God act and speak in thee. When the powers have all been withdrawn from their bodily forms and functions, then is this Word spoken. Thus he says: 'In the midst of the silence the secret word was spoken to me.' The more completely thou art able to in-draw thy faculties and to forget those things and their images which thou has taken in, the more, that is to say, thou forgettest the creature, the nearer thou art to this and the more susceptible thou art to it.

Here the soul is scattered abroad among her powers and dissipated in the act of each: the power of seeing is in the eye, the power

* St Teresa: *The Way of Perfection*, trans. Alice Alexander (The Mercier Press, Cork).

† Included in the *Works* of Meister Eckhart, vol. I, trans. by C. de B. Evans (Watkins); part of the first of these sermons is quoted in Anthology.

of hearing in the ear, the power of tasting in the tongue, and her powers are accordingly enfeebled in their interior work, scattered forces being imperfect. It follows that for her interior work to be effective, she must call in all her powers, recollecting them out of external things to one interior act.

To achieve the interior act one must assemble all one's powers as it were into one corner of one's soul, where, secreted from images and forms, one is able to work. In this silence, this quiet, the Word is heard. There is no better method of approaching this Word than in silence, in quiet: we hear it and know it aright in unknowing. To one who knows naught it is clearly revealed.

17. The Mystical Element in Buddhism

IN our study of mystical consciousness, while Christianity, Hinduism, and Islam have all come into our purview, so far Buddhism has not been mentioned. Has it anything to say which will be of value to us?

Buddhism has been called the most mystical and the least mystical of the higher religions, the most spiritual religion and not a religion at all. How is it possible for there to be such conflicting points of view?

One reason is that it is impossible to give a precise, unequivocal and unified statement of Buddhist teaching. There are so many schools of Buddhism, all, it is true, stemming from the original Theravada School and all accepting the basic teaching of that school, but all in various ways different, seeing the original inspiration in different lights. While Theravada Buddhism, the Old Wisdom School, is primarily ethical and non-mystical, Mahayana Buddhism, the New Wisdom School, with its numerous divisions, has a different complexion. It is more speculative, more cosmic and more mystical.

Further, the main concern of the Buddha himself was to find a reason and a remedy for the suffering and wretchedness involved in the corruptibility of all things born. All abstract metaphysical and theological speculations he regarded as sterile, on the ground that no satisfactory and demonstrable answers were possible and that it was not necessary to enter into them in order that his main purpose might be achieved. On many of the issues with which religion and philosophy have concerned themselves he maintained a 'noble silence', or, when questioned, answered in paradoxes.

What are the basic principles of Buddhism? They are summed up in the doctrines of the Three Signs of Being, of the Four Noble Truths, and in the Noble Eightfold Path (the Middle Way), a way of life which leads to the realization of *Nirvana*.

The three Signs of Being, or life on this earth, are impermanence, suffering, and *anatta* (no soul). The doctrine of *anatta* is difficult to interpret. It has been defined as follows. If what we call a man is examined, all that is found are the so-called *Five Aggregates,* matter, sensations, perceptions, mental formations, and consciousness; and these are all seen to be in a perpetual state of flux. How then can one speak of any sort of 'soul' or 'self', in the sense of an enduring entity which can be thought of as passing over from one state or embodiment to another? There is no *I* which is a doer of anything; 'it is the senses which move among their objects'; 'the deeds are, but there is no doer thereof'; of nothing in a man can it be said that it *is*. There are, however, other interpretations.

The first of the Four Noble Truths is *Dukkha*, i.e. the impermanence and unsubstantiality of life, its suffering, sorrows, and joys, its imperfections and unsatisfactoriness. This, by analysis, one must try to understand. The second is the *Origin of Dukkha*. This, according to the Buddha, is the existence of 'desire', which is the source of all passions, suffering, and defilement. The third is the *Cessation of Dukkha,* which is found in the realization of *Nirvana*. The fourth is the *Noble Eightfold Path,* which, if followed to the end, leads to the realization of *Nirvana*. All are called upon to follow this Path as far as they can.

Buddhist doctrine is founded on an acute, objective analysis of the world and man. It leads to a way of life, redolent with tolerance, compassion, and love for all creatures. Its goal is the realization of *Nirvana*. Its teaching is very subtle and full of paradoxes; consequently it is not easy to understand. The way to the cessation of *Dukkha* and the realization of *Nirvana* is through the Noble Eightfold Path, with its eight categories or divisions of Right Understanding, Right Thought, Right Speech, Right Action, Right Livelihood, Right Effort, Right Mindfulness, and Right Concentration.

Can there be said to be any idea of a God in Buddhism? It is difficult to say. What, in any case, does one mean by the word, God? What does the doctrine of *anatta* imply? Does it refer to the phenomenal ego only? What is meant by *Nirvana*? To answer these questions at all adequately one would have to write at far greater length than is possible in this Study. We may, however, find the key we need in a passage in the *Parinirvana Sutra*, which brings out the basic Mahayana teaching on *Self*, as contrasted with *the self*, on *Nirvana* and on the cosmic application of *anatta*.

It is only when all outward appearances are gone that there is left that one principle of life which exists independently of all external phenomena. It is the fire which burns in the eternal light, when the fuel is expended and the flame is extinguished; for that fire is neither in the flame not in the fuel, nor yet inside either of the two, but above, beneath, and everywhere.*

Let us expand. Absolute Reality is inconceivable by man in his present state. The finite mind can never 'know' the Infinite. It must accept an absolute and a relative Truth. This life (called *Be-ness*) is the highest that man can conceive of the Absolute. Be-ness is manifest in time–space phenomena. Consequently, everything within the domain of *Samsara* (the world of becoming, life on this earth) partakes of the essential nature of Be-ness. This is called by the obscure name of *Suchness*. Suchness, however, is conceived as an ultimate spiritual essence, beyond the opposites which condition human perception. Psychologically, it equates with *Alayavijnana*, 'repository-consciousness', which seems to be the same as Jung's collective unconscious; religiously it equates with the

* Quoted in Christmas Humphreys: *Buddhism* (Penguin Books).

Dharmakaya, the body of the *Dharma*, the principle of cosmic unity seen as the object of religious consciousness, akin to the *Tao* of Chinese religio-philosophy.

In the Buddhist scriptures one comes across such phrases as, 'Have Self as a lamp, Self as a refuge, and no other refuge'; 'Through Self one should urge on the self, one should restrain the self by Self – for Self is the lord of the self'. What is this 'Self' and how does it differ from 'the self'? 'Self' is the universal principle of life, the That which some call God, over and above 'the self', the phenomenal ego. It is the common denominator of all forms of life. It is not the property of any man; yet it is 'my-Self'.

What is not Self, that is not mine, that I am not, that is not my Self.

Self alone is eternal. All except Self is impermanent. It is the object of a man to slay the fires of attachment, hatred, and illusion so that Self may be freed from the bondage of self. Since one can say nothing of the contents of the Self, the relation between Self and the self cannot be intellectually known: it can only be realized intuitively.

In the deepest religious experience, whether it be Christian, Buddhist, Hindu, or Mohammedan, when all ideas, thoughts, sensations, and volitions which make up the self are exhausted, there is found to remain only a Void, the One of Plotinus, the Godhead of Eckart and Ruysbroeck, the Brahman of Hinduism. The Void is not only Emptiness. In mystical experience it is found to be a Plenum-Void. The Emptiness and the Fullness are one.

How shall we interpret Nirvana, the Cessation of *Dukkha*, the end of the Path? Nirvana simply *is*. It cannot be conceived; it can only be experienced. It is the extinction of the not-Self in the completion of the Self. It is not annihilation but the goal of perfection, through the destruction of all that is individual in us. It is a death, a 'being finished', in the sense of both an ending and a perfecting. It is neither a place, nor an effect, nor in time, nor 'attainable'; but it can be 'seen'. The aim of the Path is to remove the screens which obscure the vision of Nirvana. Further, Samsara, the 'Wheel of Becoming', is a mode of Nirvana. Consequently, Nirvana need not be sought beyond this life; like the 'kingdom of heaven', it is here and now.

This is clearly the language of mysticism. Nirvana is a purely mystical conception; it cannot be conceived or expressed; it can only be realized by what can only be called mystical intuition.

Buddhist mysticism is not typical God-mysticism. Whether Buddhism is theistic or non-theistic cannot be answered by a categorical 'Yes' or 'No'. There is in it no 'personal' God, a Being with whom man can have communion. What one finds is something which seems to be akin to the naked Godhead of Eckhart or the undifferentiated abstract Brahman of Hinduism. Further, from one point of view at least, the Buddhist Self is similar to the 'noble soul' of Eckhart, which is itself the undifferentiated unity from which the multiplicity of ideas, thoughts, etc. has been excluded and is indistinguishable from the undifferentiated unity of the Godhead.

The idea of a personal 'Saviour', if not of a personal 'God', is, however, found in the Bodhisattva ideal of Mahayana Buddhism. The Bodhisattva is one who, having become completely enlightened, and having attained Nirvana, and so freed at last from the melancholy wheel of birth and death, renounces his blessedness in order that he may remain to help suffering humanity. In his divine compassion he says, 'for others' sake this great reward I yield.' He accomplishes the Great Renunciation and becomes a Saviour of the World.

If one desires a label for Buddhist mysticism, it might be called 'metaphysical mysticism' (or 'mystical metaphysics') or 'analytical soul-mysticism'. One particular interest for the student of mysticism lies in the fact that it springs out of a religio-philosophy which was in its beginnings so strictly analytical and scientific. The statements on the Three Signs of Being and Conditioned Genesis might have been set out by a modern materialist; the resultant philosophy and way of life are, however, very different from his.

The eighth division of the Path is called Right Concentration. It leads those able to follow it through four stages. In the first lust, hatred, worry, restlessness, and sceptical doubts are conquered and feelings of joy and happiness cultivated. In the second, intellectual activities are suppressed and tranquillity and 'one-pointedness' of mind attained; the sensation of joy, however, still remains. In the third stage the feeling of joy, which is an active sensation, disappears and the state is simply one of happy calm. In the fourth all sensations whatsoever, even of happiness and unhappiness, of joy and sorrow, fade away and all that remains is pure, bare equanimity and awareness.

There are obvious dissimilarities, but surely here one can hear echoes of St Teresa's Degrees of Prayer and of the descriptions of the Mystic Way found in the writings of St John of the Cross.

In the *Book of the Golden Precepts,** a Tibetan manual intended for the use of Lanoos (disciples), what is clearly a Mystic Way in its final stages is described as a journey through seven gates, each narrower than the preceding one, each opened by a golden key. Before the first gate can even be approached, a hard path has had to be followed, so that the disciple has already learnt to obey the moral law and to live in the eternal, to feel himself abiding in all things and all things in the Self, to be in full accord with all lives and to love all men.

The key of the first gate is the attainment of utter charity; of the second of complete harmony and balance in word and act; and of the third a patience which nothing earthly can disturb. Before the fourth gate can be unlocked a state must be reached in which there is complete indifference to pleasure, in which all illusion has been conquered and in which truth only is seen. To open the fifth gate is needed the spiritual power to attain to supreme Truth. The sixth gate leads to eternal rest and contemplation; while he who can use the seventh key becomes a God and is created a Bodhisattva.

It was not until this book was already in production that

* Translated by H.P.B. under the title, *The Voice of the Silence*, Theosophy Company (India).

Anne Gage's moving and brilliant account of her spiritual Odyssey, *The One Work, a Journey towards the Self*,* came into my hands. In it she records two conversations, one with a Buddhist monk in Bangkok, the other with a saintly Hindu at Arunachala, the Hill of Light, in India. I cannot end this chapter better than by quoting a part of the first of these conversations. Anne Gage has put the question, 'How can one say what has value in this present world?' The monk replies:

'Only one thing has value: Enlightenment.'
'Does Enlightenment mean Nirvana?'
'Yes.'
'But doesn't that mean annihilation and the death of the soul?'
'Not of the soul, but of ignorance and separation.'
'But I have read that the Buddha did not believe in any permanent entity or essence like the Real Self: that Nirvana is an experience of bliss followed by utter dissolution; that he denied the existence of both God and the soul.'
'That is the interpretation given to Buddhism by men who have understood neither the teaching nor themselves.'
'Why did he say that everything was unreal?'
'Can you say of what passes through you, of your fleeting emotions and thoughts, of the circumstances that come to you, this is I; this is permanent; this is real?'
'No, I suppose not.'
'Do you know what is permanent and real?'
'No, unless God is, but I don't know that God exists. Did the Buddha believe in God?'
'He didn't speak of God, which is different. If a man realizes God and is among other men who do not, it is useless to speak about Him for they would not understand. It is better to indicate how they can come to know Him themselves. Man must discover God and his true Self or Ego by following the Path of Enlightenment.'

Later in the conversation the monk defines Enlightenment in these words: 'Then Samsara which is life as you know it now becomes Nirvana or life as it really is.'

---

* Published by Vincent Stuart, 1961.

The fundamental teaching of Buddhism could hardly be more clearly and concisely expressed.

18. The Higher Stages of Contemplation

As we pass on to the consideration of true Contemplation, since we are dealing with rare states of consciousness for the description of which no precise and adequate language is available, our task increases in difficulty. Its main characteristics may be summed up as follows.

The contemplative has now ascended above the multiplicity and divisions of his general consciousness and has been raised above himself. His consciousness of I-hood and of the world has disappeared. Thought, love, and will have become a unity, and feeling and perception have been fused.

Further, Contemplation has a profound noetic quality. Though what is known can only be communicated in evocative symbols which, on the face of them, look like attempts to tell what the contemplative has felt, it brings new knowledge and insight. This knowledge is acquired not by way of observation, but by way of participation. The subject does not stand over against the object; the two merge and unite. The knower and the known are one. The contemplative participates in Divinity. He has the consciousness of being that which he knows and knowing that which he is.

Of the act of pure contemplation, the experience of the poets, indeed of any who have had moments of intuition and illumination, can give us hints. Here, however, in pure Contemplation, is something more complete and more profound, a complete act of perception involving the whole man, sometimes of very brief duration, taking place in 'a flash', in 'an instant', and yet continuing in a joyous radiance, its noetic and transforming qualities perpetually expanding.

All this is what our earlier considerations of mystical experience and consciousness would lead us to expect. Nor will it surprise us that there is found in Contemplation in a very vivid form that sense of the 'coincidence of contradictories' to which we have already referred. The vision is a twofold one. It partakes of 'darkness' and 'light', of 'deprivation' and 'acquisition', of 'emptiness' of everything and of a fuller realization and possession of everything, of the Dark Abyss of the Godhead and an intimate personal communion of the soul with the Heavenly Bridegroom, of the utter transcendence and otherness of God and of His complete immanence in the depths of the self.

Not only that, but side by side with an existential perception of the Presence and Being of God, a joyous apprehension of the Absolute, there is found a new vision of the phenomenal world, which lights it up and makes it appear quite different, as if there had been an abnormal sharpening of the senses. Sometimes the one, sometimes the other vision may predominate. In the greatest of the mystics both are exquisitely blended. The more complete the simplification, the deeper the cleansing of perception, the more everything is seen *sub specie aeternitatis*. Every visible and invisible creature appears as a revelation of God.

The transcendental experience of the numinous is analysed by Rudolf Otto in *The Idea of the Holy*. To describe its content he uses the phrase '*mysterium tremendum et fascinans*'. The word *mysterium* implies the idea of something wholly other than man; *tremendum* the ideas of awefulness, overpoweringness, and urgency; *fascinans* the idea of something which draws one in spite of one's self.

This experience of the utter transcendence of the Divine Being is evident in the well-known description of that vision of God which started Isaiah on his prophetic career:

In the year that King Uzziah died, I saw the Lord sitting upon a throne, high and lifted up, and his train filled the temple. Above him stood the seraphim: each one had six wings; with twain he covered his face, and with twain he covered his feet, and with twain he did fly. And one cried unto another: Holy, holy, holy is the Lord of hosts. The fullness of the whole earth is his glory!

The effect of this vision on Isaiah is typical. He cries out:

Woe is me, for I am undone! Because I am a man of unclean lips, and I dwell in the midst of a people of unclean lips: For mine eyes have seen the King, the Lord of hosts.

The transcendental vision is given what is perhaps its most perfect, literary expression in the last canto of Dante's *Paradiso* in which, in the triple circles of dazzling light, the poet saw in intellectual illumination the Love 'that moves the sun and the other stars'.

Dominating the vision of Transcendence is the recipient's feeling of his own littleness, his complete unworthiness, his utter ignorance of Something which so much surpasses his infinitesimally small selfhood. He is filled with awe and self-abasement, his sole desire is to lose himself within this *mysterium tremendum et fascinans*. How can It be known? To name It is presumption. It can only be spoken of in negatives. It is, *not this, not that*. It is the fathomless abyss, the Desert of the Godhead, the Wilderness 'where no one is at home'.

Yet in the negation there is a vast affirmation. The Dark Silence is filled with light and heavenly music, in the Nothingness everything is contained. It is 'a lightsome dark and a rich naught'. The austere, still Wilderness, where no one is at home, is the long-sought-for home; and, hidden in the dazzling obscurity of the secret Silence, is the garden of lilies where the soul is united with the Beloved.

> All things I then forgot,
> My cheek on Him who for my coming came.
> All ceased, and I was not,
> Leaving my cares and shame
> Among the lilies, and forgetting them.*

We have reached the highest stage of Contemplation, called dim or dark Contemplation. In order that we may see what it is, let some of those who have entered it speak.

The great wastes to be found in this divine ground [wrote Tauler, the fourteenth-century friar-preacher of Strasbourg, one of the most

* St John of the Cross; trans. by Arthur Symons.

virile of the German mystics] have neither image nor form nor condition, for they are neither here nor there. They are like unto a
fathomless Abyss, bottomless and floating in itself. . . . A man who
deserves to enter will surely find God here, and himself simply in
God; for God never separates Himself from this ground. God will
be present with him and he will find and enjoy Eternity here. There
is no past nor present here, and no created light can reach unto or
shine into this divine ground; for here only is the dwelling-place of
God and His sanctuary. . . . This ground is so desert and bare that
no thought can ever enter there. . . . It is so close and yet so far off,
and so far beyond all things, that it has neither time nor place. It is
a simple and unchanging condition. A man who really and truly
enters, feels as though he had been here throughout eternity, and as
though he were one therewith.*

Here [writes Ruysbroeck] he meets God without intermediary. And
from out the Divine Unity, there shines into him a simple light; and
this light shows him Darkness and Nakedness and Nothingness. In
this Darkness he is enwrapped and falls into somewhat which is in
no wise, even as one who has lost his way. In the Nakedness, he
loses the perception and discernment of all things, and is transfigured and penetrated by a simple light. In the Nothingness, all his
activity fails him; for he is vanquished by the working of God's
abysmal love, and in a fruitive inclination of his spirit he vanquishes
God, and becomes one spirit with Him.†

This is the highest degree of Contemplation, the ascent of
the 'secret stair' of which St John of the Cross writes:

It is secret wisdom, and happens secretly and in darkness, so as to
be hidden from the world of the understanding and of other
faculties. . . .

It is secret not only in the darkness and afflictions of purgation,
when the wisdom of love purges the soul, and the soul is unable
to speak of it, but equally so afterwards in illumination, when this
wisdom is communicated to it most clearly. Even then it is still so
secret that the soul cannot speak of it and give it a name whereby it
may be called; for, apart from the fact that the soul has no desire to
speak of it, it can find no suitable way or manner or similitude by
which it may be able to describe such lofty understanding and such
delicate spiritual feeling. . . .

* Tauler: *The Inner Way*, quoted in Underhill: *Mysticism*.
† Anthology, Section 19.

This mystical knowledge has the property of hiding the soul within itself . . . so that it considers itself as having been placed in a most profound and vast retreat, to which no human creature can attain, such as an immense desert, which nowhere has any boundary, a desert the most delectable, pleasant and lovely for its scenery, vastness and solitude, wherein the more the soul has been raised up above all temporal creatures, the more deeply does it find itself hidden.*

Probably many of my readers will find all this puzzling, perhaps entirely incomprehensible. Yet these descriptions have a strange ring of truth in them. Though they describe a state of consciousness we can never hope to know, we somehow feel that, if we could attain to it, that is what it would be like. We subconsciously feel that what is described is something utterly real. Commenting on this state of consciousness, in his Introduction to Ruysbroeck's *Adornment of the Spiritual Marriage*, Maeterlinck wrote:

Here we stand suddenly at the confines of human thought, and far beyond the Polar circle of the mind. . . . Here we are concerned with the most exact of sciences: with the exploration of the harshest and most uninhabitable headlands of the divine 'know thyself': and the midnight sun reigns over that rolling sea where the psychology of man mingles with the psychology of God.

And there we must leave it.

19. The Contemplation of Immanence

THE Contemplation of Immanence is complementary to the Contemplation of Transcendence. In the latter God is apprehended as the 'naked Godhead', as the 'Nameless Being of whom naught can be said', as the heavenly Truth, 'hidden in the dazzling obscurity of the secret silence', as the 'higher than the highest'. In the former He is seen as very near and very dear, 'closer to us than our most inward part'. He is the ador-

* *Dark Night of the Soul*, Allison Peers's translation.

able, personal Comrade, the courteous and most dearworthy Lord, of Julian of Norwich or the Divine Lover of St John of the Cross.

Yet the two aspects of Contemplation are not distinct and separate. Consider this passage from Ruysbroeck's *Adornment of the Spiritual Marriage*:

When we have thus become seeing we can behold in joy the coming of the eternal Bridegroom. . . . And the coming of the Bridegroom is so swift that he is perpetually coming and dwelling within with unfathomable riches; and ever coming anew in His Person, without interception, with such new brightness that it seems as though He had never come before. For His coming consists beyond time, in an eternal Now, which is ever received with new longings and new joy. Behold, the delight and the joy which this Bridegroom brings with Him in his coming are boundless and without measure, for they are Himself.

Here is the Contemplation of Immanence, yet only a few lines later he continues:

Now this active meeting and this loving embrace are in their ground fruitive and wayless; for the abysmal Waylessness of God is so dark and so unconditioned that it swallows up in itself every Divine way and activity, and all the attributes of the Persons, within the rich compass of the essential Unity.

The experience of the Spiritual Marriage and of the naked Godhead merge in the same vision.

Consider again how, in one of his *Sermons on the Song of Songs*, St Bernard describes and tries to explain his own vision:

By what way then did He enter? Can it be that He did not enter at all, because He did not come from outside? for He is not one of the things that are without. Yet again, He did not come from within me, for He is good, and I know that *no good thing dwelleth in me*. I have gone up to the highest that I have, and behold, the Word was towering yet higher. My curiosity took me to the lowest depth to look for Him, nevertheless He was found still deeper. If I looked outside me, I found He was beyond my farthest; if I looked within He was more inward still.*

Or yet again, how, in his *Confessions*, St Augustine tells how
* Anthology, Section 14.

he found the Divine Light in the innermost recesses of his heart:

And I entered and beheld with the eye of my soul (such as it was), above the same eye of my soul, above my mind, the Light Unchangeable. Not this ordinary light, which all flesh may look upon, nor, as it were, greater of the same kind, as though the brightness of this should be manifold brighter, and with its greatness take up all space. Not such was this light, but other, yea, far from all these. Nor was it above my soul, as oil is above water, nor yet as heaven above earth; but above my soul, because It made me; and I below It, because I was made by It. He that knows the Truth, knows what that Light is; and he that knows It, knows eternity.*

The vision of the mystic not only contains an existential perception of the Presence and Being of God, a joyous apprehension of the Absolute, of the Reality upholding all things, but is also a new vision of the phenomenal world, so that it is seen differently from what it was before. This new vision of the phenomenal world is essentially one of Immanence, of the One, however the One may be conceived, present in and permeating the All.

There is an exquisite description of it in a novel, *The Winthrop Woman* by Anya Seton,† which, though in the guise of fiction, is so vivid in quality and so penetrating in its insight, that one cannot but feel that it is founded on first-hand experience. Here it is:

A ray of sunlight started down between the tree trunks. It touched the pool with liquid gold. The pool became transparent to its green depths and her self was plunged in those depths and yet upraised with joy upon the rushing wind. The light grew stronger and turned white. In this crystal whiteness there was ecstasy. Against the light she saw a wren fly by; the wren was made of rhythm, it flew with meaning, with a radiant meaning. There was the same meaning in the caterpillar as it inched along the rock, and the moss, and the little nuts which had rolled across the leaves.

And still the apperception grew, and the significance. The significance was bliss, it made a created whole of everything she

* Anthology, Section 13.
† Hodder & Stoughton.

watched and touched and heard – and the essence of this created whole was love. She felt love pouring from the light, it bathed her with music and with perfume; the love was far off at the source of the light, and yet it drenched her through. And the source and she were one.

The minutes passed. The light moved softly down, and faded from the pool. The ecstasy diminished, it quietened, but in its stead came a serenity and sureness she had never known.

Here all the chief characteristics of the *pan-en-henic* experience are present, the perception of the fusion of the One in the All, and the All in the One, of a hidden meaning and significance lying behind external phenomena, of the underlying love upholding and permeating everything, of the unity of the knower and known; and, through it all, a feeling of intense joy, sureness, and serenity.

One of the most vivid descriptions of this fresh vision of the phenomenal world is found in the *Journal* of George Fox, the founder of the Society of Friends. 'All things were new,' and 'all creation gave another smell unto me than before.'

It has been known by many of the poets, for instance by William Blake:

> To see a world in a grain of sand
> And heaven in a wild flower,
> Hold infinity in the palm of your hand
> And eternity in an hour.

by Tennyson:

> Flower in the crannied wall,
> I pluck you out of the crannies; –
> Hold you here, root and all, in my hand,
> Little flower – but if I could understand
> What you are, root and all, and all in all,
> I should know what God and man is.

by Shelley:

> That Light whose smile kindles the Universe,
> That Beauty in which all things work and move,
> That Benediction which the eclipsing Curse
> Of birth can quench not, that sustaining Love

Which through the web of being blindly wove
By man and beast and earth and air and sea,
Burns bright or dim, as each are mirrors of
The fire for which all thirst. . . .

by Browning:

God is seen God
In the star, in the stone, in the flesh, in the soul and the clod.

and by William Wordsworth:

. . . something far more deeply interfused,
Whose dwelling is the light of setting suns,
And the round ocean, and the living air,
And the blue sky, and in the mind of man:
A motion and a spirit, that impels
All thinking things, all objects of all thought,
And rolls through all things.

Francis Thompson knew it and gave it expression in *The Mistress of Vision*:

When to the new heart of thee
All things by immortal power
Near or far,
Hiddenly
To each other linked are,
That thou canst not stir a flower
Without troubling of a star. . . .

While John Masefield puts it into the mouth of the converted drunkard in *The Everlasting Mercy*:

The station brook to my new eyes
Was babbling out of Paradise,
The waters rushing from the rain
Were singing Christ is risen again.
I thought all earthly creatures knelt
For rapture of the joy I felt.
The narrow station wall's brick ledge
The wild hop withering in the hedge,
The lights in huntsman's upper story
Were parts of an eternal glory.

Thomas Traherne, the seventeenth-century poet and mystic, felt it intensely; it runs through the whole of his *Centuries of Meditations*:

All things abided eternally as they were in their proper places. Eternity was manifest in the light of the day, and something infinite behind everything appeared.*

In the poets the movement is usually one from the *without* to the *within*; in the contemplatives always from the *within* to the *without*. Of this movement from the within to the without, the seventeenth-century French contemplative, Malaval, wrote:

From the moment in which the soul receives the impression of Deity in infused vision she sees him everywhere.

While that master of dark Contemplation, Meister Eckhart, could write:

The nearest thing that one knows in God – for instance, if one could understand a flower as it has its being in God – this would be higher than the whole world.

In a well-known passage from the *Relevations of Divine Love* of Julian of Norwich there is a most subtle fusion:

Also in this He showed me a little thing, the quality of an hazel-nut in the palm of my hand; and it was round as a ball. I looked thereupon with the eye of my understanding, and thought: What may this be? And it was answered generally thus: It is all that is made. And I marvelled how it might last, for methought it might suddenly have fallen to naught for littleness. And I was answered in my understanding: It lasteth and ever shall last, for that God loveth it. And so All-Thing hath the Being by the love of God.

In this Little Thing, I saw three properties. The first is that God made it, the second that God loveth it, the third that God keepeth it. But what is to me verily the Maker, the Keeper, and the Lover – I cannot tell.†

* Anthology, Section 28.
† Anthology, Section 24.

20. The Unitive Life

THE Unitive Life, or, to use Ruysbroeck's perhaps better term, the Superessential Life, is nothing less than the final triumph of the spirit, the attainment of a complete and permanent synthesis and reconciliation between the *within* and the *without*.

When a man can be said to have passed through the state of Illumination to that of Union it is difficult to determine. Since we are dealing with a state of consciousness which is outside that of normal experience, all we have to help us are the descriptions of that state given by those who have attained it. As one reads these descriptions, however, one is often puzzled as to whether the writer is describing dim Contemplation or full Union. Even St John of the Cross, the most precise and analytical of all the writers on the mystical life, does not really make clear the difference between what he calls the Spiritual Betrothal and the Spiritual Marriage.*

We need not, however, try to be too precise. It is sufficient to say that, when a man follows the Mystic Way to its end, this is the state which is attained. The death of selfhood is complete, an utter transformation of personality has taken place, so that a new creature is born, a new and permanent change of consciousness has been brought about. The soul is fully united with That which beyond all appearances is; it is 'oned' with God. The dark nights which have characterized the long and arduous steps of the Mystic Way are over. The climber has reached the summit.

Delacroix, in his *Études sur le mysticisme*, gives this description:

The beginning of the mystic life introduces into the personal life of the subject a group of states which are distinguished by certain characteristics, and which form, so to speak, a special psychological system. At its term it has, as it were, suppressed the ordinary self, and by the development of this system has established a new per-

* See Anthology, Section 27.

sonality, with a new method of feeling and action. Its growth results in the transformation of personality: it abolishes the primitive consciousness of selfhood, and substitutes for it a wider consciousness; the total disappearance of the selfhood in the divine, the substitution of a Divine Self for the primitive self.*

When, however, we speak of a complete death of selfhood, of an utter transformation of the personality, of union with God, what precisely do we mean? What is selfhood? What is the nature of personality? From what has already been written the reader will have gathered that here is a problem which has puzzled many minds and to which more than one answer has been given. The word 'union' can be given different meanings. Do we mean by it some sort of *annihilation*, in which 'personality', whatever it may be, completely disappears, or *transformation*, in which the personality is changed into something which before it was not and yet, in some way, still remains itself? And when we add the words 'with God' we have to confess that in terms of the intellect God is unknowable and unknown.

The life of union of the soul with God is sometimes called the *Spiritual Marriage*. As in human marriage two 'persons' are 'oned' and 'become one flesh', so in the Spiritual Marriage are, metaphorically, God and the soul. A close, permanent, joyous communion of love and knowledge has been established. What were before two have, as it were, been merged into one. Here the imagery is not difficult to understand. It is personal imagery, drawn from human experience.

Union is, however, not uncommonly described as *deification*. This is a more difficult description. How can a human being be 'made God'? What does the word imply? Some mystics, especially in the East, have tended to speak of deification in terms of a complete *annihilation* of the self, as if the self were wholly absorbed into the divine so that no difference in essence existed any longer between the self and God. Others, intent on maintaining the essential 'otherness' of God and the creature have preferred to speak in terms of *transformation* or *transmutation* of the self.

* Quoted in Underhill: *Mysticism*.

If the issue were put to an enlightened Hindu he might reply somewhat as follows: 'What do you mean by self? The self which gives you a sense of being an individual personality is not your real self. It is a phenomenal, ephemeral self which you think of as "I" since you are deceived by *maya*. Your true self is the Atman, which is Universal Self, of which you are, as it were, a "part". Not only that, Atman is "identical", if I may use that word without being misunderstood, with Brahman, the undifferentiated Unity.

'Therefore, I would say that a man who has entered into the mystical state of which we are speaking has thrown off the illusion of his phenomenal ego; he has *realized*, that is the word I should use, his Greater Self. Since that always has been and always will be, one can apply neither the word, "annihilated" nor the word "transformed" to it. By this process of realization of his true nature a man "identifies" himself with, and so "becomes", Self, Brahman, Universal Spirit.

'Let me put it in this way. The task of one who treads the Mystic Way, indeed it is the task of everyone, is to extirpate in himself the illusory multiplicity of objects and acts. He must strive to retire within the Atman, the absolute Unity which he is. If you ask whether he will then know the Atman, I should answer, "Yes and no." He will not know it objectively, for that would mean the continuance of a subject–object relationship. He will have become the Atman, he will have become Brahman. Beyond that there is nothing.'

Islam is the most transcendent of all the higher religions; in no other is the complete 'otherness' of God so strongly emphasized. Yet out of it came one of the most beautiful and profound upsurges of mystical insight in the whole history of mysticism. In Sufism, as this manifestation is called, one finds a most subtle blending of the experience of God as the Divine Lover and of utter self-loss in Him. While the Hindu deity is an abstract deity, in Sufism He is the Beloved. The Beloved is, however, also the 'Truth', and the 'Truth' admits of no duality either in fact or idea; the union must be complete, the self must die absolutely.

There is a story which expresses this idea very vividly. The lover knocks at the door of the Beloved. 'Who is there?' asks the Beloved. 'It is I,' replies the lover. 'This house will not hold Me and thee,' comes the reply. The lover goes away and weeps and prays in solitude. After a long time he returns and knocks again. The Voice asks, 'Who is there?' 'It is Thou.' Immediately the door opens; lover and Beloved are face to face at last.

We find in Sufism a doctrine similar to that of Ruysbroeck's 'There we all are [i.e. in God] before our creation [i.e. in time]'. The Sufi mystic and poet, Jalalud-din Rumi, puts it, in his *Diwan*, thus:

Ere there was a garden and vine and grape in the world
Our soul was intoxicated with immortal wine.
In the Baghdad of Eternity we proudly were proclaiming, 'I am God.'

Since that was so, the heart is the mirror of Divinity.

'Your Self is a copy made in the image of God. Seek in yourself all that you desire to know.'

'O heart, we have searched from end to end; I saw in thee naught save the Beloved.'

We have approached very close to the Hindu, *Thou art That*. Man's own true self, which cannot be taken away from him, though his material self, and indeed the whole material creation, are no more, belongs to the Eternal Self, which is God, and from which it is temporarily estranged, but to which it is destined to return.

The return can, however, only be through self-loss. Until the selfhood, the ego, is utterly dead, the union can only be partial. In the highest state of the mystical life the death of selfhood is complete. The man has been 'deified', he has 'become' or 'been made' God. Therefore, when, animated by a passionate and selfless love, he looks to his centre, he sees only God. As St Paul wrote:

I live, yet not I, but Christ liveth in me.

T-D

mysticism

It is the intensity of the experience which explains the words which those who have climbed to the heights of the life of union use.

> In this course thou must persevere until He mingles Himself with thy soul, and thine own individual existence passes out of sight. Then, if thou regardest thyself, it is He whom thou art regarding; if thou speakest of thyself, it is He of whom thou art speaking. The relative has become the Absolute, and 'I am the Truth' is equivalent to 'He is the Truth'.*

So wrote the Persian mystic, Jami. He is echoed by the earliest Sufi poet of Persia, Baba Kuhi of Shiraz:

> I passed away into nothingness, I vanished,
> And lo, I am the All-Living – only God I saw.*

And by another Persian poet-mystic, 'Iraqi:

> I have no other in my cloak but God. . . .
> When thou transcendest, 'Glory be to God',
> Wipe off the dust of selfhood from thy soul!

While 'Attar, in the allegory *The Conference of the Birds*, makes the Voice from the blazing Throne speak thus to the thirty bedraggled birds who, through toil and pain, have at last reached the Presence:

> 'Come, you lost atoms, to your Centre draw,
> And *be* the Eternal Mirror that you saw;
> Rays that have wandered into darkness wide,
> Return, and back into your Sun subside.'*

It fell to the brilliant Abu Hamid al-Ghazali, the 'Proof of Islam', to reconcile the apparent heresy inherent in Sufi teaching with the orthodox theology of Islam. In an illuminating passage in his *Mishkat al-Anwar*, when he is writing of those who, 'on their return from their Ascent into the heaven of Reality, use such exaggerated expressions as, "I am the One Real" or, "Within this robe is nothing but Allah"', remarks, 'The words of Lovers passionate in their intoxication and ecstasy must be hidden away and not spoken of,' and goes on:

* Anthology, Section 16.

Now, when this state prevails, it is called in relation to him who experiences it, Extinction, nay, Extinction of Extinction, for the soul has become extinct to itself, extinct to its own extinction, for it becomes unconscious of itself and unconscious of its own unconsciousness, since were it conscious of its own unconsciousness, it would be conscious of itself. In relation to the man immersed in this state, the state is called, in the language of metaphor, 'Identity'; in the language of reality, 'Unification'.*

One and a half centuries earlier the ninth-century al-Junaid of Baghdad had interpreted the central Sufi doctrine of *fanā*, i.e. the 'dying to self', in this way. The mystic, in passing away from self, does not cease to exist, *in the true sense of existence*, as an individual. His individuality is perfected, transmuted, and eternalized through God and in God. He expresses this very succinctly in a verse of one of his poems:

> So in a manner we
> United are, and One;
> Yet otherwise disunion
> Is our estate eternally!†

Among the Christian mystics, though the language used sometimes seems to carry a different meaning, an essential 'otherness' between God and the creature is always maintained.

In *The Spiritual Canticle* St John of the Cross, for example, speaks of deification in these words:

Then the two natures are so united, what is divine so communicated to what is human, that, *without undergoing any essential change each seems to be God* – yet not perfectly so in this life, though still in a manner which can neither be described nor conceived.

The fourteenth-century German Dominican, the Blessed Henry Suso, expresses himself thus:

He forgets himself, he is no longer conscious of his selfhood; he *disappears and loses himself in God*, and becomes one spirit with Him, as a drop of water which is drowned in a great quantity of wine.

Yet a little later in the same passage he adds, '*His being remains, but in another form.*'

* Anthology, Section 16.
† Trans. by A. J. Arberry and quoted in his *Sufism* (Allen & Unwin).

At times, for instance in this passage on *The Spiritual Marriage*, Ruysbroeck seems to imply complete absorption:

For to comprehend and understand God above all similitudes, such as he is in Himself, *is to be God with God,* without intermediary, and without any otherness that can become . . . an intermediary.*

But he constantly qualifies this possible impression, for instance in *The Sparkling Stone*:

Though I have said before that we are one with God, and this is taught by Holy Writ, yet now I will say that *we must eternally remain other than God, and distinct from Him,* and this too is taught us by Holy Writ. *And we must understand and feel both within us,* if all is to be right with us.

When the author of the *Theologia Germanica* is asked who it is who becomes a partaker of the Divine Nature and is made a Godlike or deified man, he replies:

He who is *imbued with or illuminated* by the Eternal or Divine Light and *inflamed or consumed* by Eternal or Divine Love, he is a deified man and a partaker of the Divine Nature.

Little more can usefully be said. We are dealing with a rare state of consciousness which cannot be assessed from personal experience. We can only study the evidence of those who have known this state and try to interpret it. Let us leave it at that.

21. The Lesser Mystic Way: The Mysticism of Action

IN that lovely but comparatively little-known treatise on the mystic life, the *Four Degrees of Passionate Charity*, Richard of St Victor writes as follows:

In the first degree God enters into the soul and she turns inward into herself. In the second she ascends above herself and is lifted up to God. In the third the soul, lifted up to God, passes over altogether

* Anthology, Section 19.

into Him. *In the fourth the soul goes forth on God's behalf and descends below herself.* *

Here, in this fourth degree of Love, we have something new. There has been throughout the history of mysticism a tendency towards an extreme form of passivity and an entire withdrawal from the active life of the world. In the seventeenth century this extreme passivity took the form of Quietism and was condemned by the Church. The goal of the Mystic Way is not, however, to rest lazily in a mass of pleasant sensations. The true mystic is not like a cat basking in the sun, but like a mountaineer. At the end of his quest he finds not the enervating isle of the Lotus Eaters, but the sharp, pure air of the Mount of Transfiguration. The greatest contemplatives, transfigured on this holy mountain, have felt themselves called upon to 'descend below themselves', to take on the humility of Christ, who 'took upon Him the form of a servant', and, coming down to the plain, to become centres of creative energy and power in the world. In whatever field of active life they may engage, because they have become completely detached, because the selfhood has been entirely subdued in them, because they partake of the Divine life and are united with that Ultimate Reality we call God, the world can no longer touch them. Hidden in God, inflamed with the Divine Love, serene and confident, they possess a creative strength and power, which ordinary men, tossed hither and thither by the passions of the primitive self, do not possess.

Consider the career of St Augustine, thinking, writing, and administering his diocese of Hippo in a world which was collapsing about him, or of St Gregory and St Bernard, whose creative geniuses had so profound an influence on the temporal pattern of their respective ages, or of St Catherine of Genoa, said to have leapt, after her four years of intense purgation, into the experience of the Unitive Life, organizing and administering her hospitals, or of St Catherine of Siena, correspondent and adviser of popes, emperors, and kings. The list could go on and on.

To the mysticism of understanding and knowledge and of

* Anthology, Section 15.

union and love I would add the mysticism of action. It is not a separate type, but originates in the first two and is their expression in the temporal world. I would extend it beyond the high, creative, selfless manifestation of Divine love as it is seen in a St Bernard or a St Catherine of Genoa, which is its supreme manifestation. I would call it the Lesser Mystic Way – the word 'lesser' implies no value-judgement. It is a way of ordinary living, but one inspired and controlled by the particular sort of insight, however slight, which we have termed mystical. It is the outward expression of a particular view of the nature of the world.

When one considers carefully and objectively that collection of the sayings of Jesus, grouped together in the Sermon on the Mount, it becomes evident that what Jesus is implicitly saying is something like this: You did not make the world or determine its nature or the moral laws which govern it. If you are to live in it successfully, you must conform with these laws. If you frame your actions in accordance with them you will be like a man who builds his house on a firm foundation; for you will be living in accordance with the real pattern of the universe. The stars in their courses will fight for you; you cannot fail. If you do not, you will be like a man who builds on sand. Sooner or later, however beautiful and solid it may look, your house will collapse.

The Sermon on the Mount is neither impractical idealism nor a collection of unlivable moral precepts. It is a superb analysis of right action in the light of things as they really are and not as they appear to be. It is an expression of the mysticism of action.

Possibly about the same time the mysticism of action was given expression in the *Bhagavad Gita*,* the Song of God, one of the wisest and most beautiful of the religious writings of India.

The *Gita* opens with the story of the Indian prince, Arjuna, faced with a perplexing moral decision. He finds himself the leader of one of the opposing armies in a civil war. On the

* The date of the *Gita* is uncertain, but is now regarded as being some time between 200 B.C. and A.D. 100.

other side are many of his friends and relatives. Victory in the impending battle will give him a throne, but at what a price! In deep mental anguish he turns for advice to his charioteer, Krishna, the Indian incarnation of God. What, he asks, is his duty in the face of this painful dilemma? There is no space to set down Krishna's argument. His answer is, however, clear: 'As a prince and a warrior your duty is to fight.'

But Arjuna is still perplexed. How, he asks Krishna, can you at the same time tell me that knowledge of God is superior to all action and yet at the same time bid me to do these terrible deeds? There follows the famous discourse on the basis of right action.

There are two ways to God, says Krishna, the way of contemplation and the way of action; but action of a particular sort, which he sums up in these words:

The world is imprisoned in its own activity, except when actions are performed as worship of God. Therefore you must perform every action sacramentally and be free from all attachment to results.*

Here again is an expression of the mysticism of action.

If life is to be lived in the right and most effective way, and men are to realize their true potentialities, the nature of human action must be understood. In the light of the ungraspable immensities of space and time, revealed by the astronomers, in the light of the vastness of the history of life on this planet, human action is, of itself, as nothing, ephemeral, insignificant, and meaningless. It only takes on significance and meaning when it is seen in relation to something higher than itself, when it is performed not for itself alone but in the light of something beyond it. To act as if action were all-important in itself is to be imprisoned in one's own activity, to be shut up in a closed universe.

Devote yourself, therefore [says Krishna] to reaching union with God. To unite the heart with God and then to act, that is the secret of unattached work.

* For a more complete picture of the teaching of the *Gita* on action see Anthology, Section 4.

And Jesus, in the Sermon on the Mount, gives a similar precept:

Seek ye first the Kingdom of God and His righteousness and all these things shall be added unto you.

To tread the hard, stern way of Contemplation and to enter into the full Unitive Life is for the few. Though later there may be a return, a descent from the heights to the plain, it demands withdrawal from the world and an intense concentration on a particular objective. For far more their destiny is to lead a creative, active life. That too can be, in a real sense, a Mystic Way, different, but with its own hardness and sternness, its own high moments of illumination and its own spirituality. For such it is their road to blessedness and eternal life.

22. Mysticism and Dogma: The Insights of India, Palestine, and Greece

> Go, go, go, said the bird: human kind
> Cannot bear very much reality.

ONLY the great mountaineers of the Spirit can breathe the rare air of the summit. The, for most, unendurable and unattainable experience must be translated. Dogma is the translation of mystical experience and the insights which spring from it into symbols. Without an original mystical experience there would be no dogma, for there would be nothing to dogmatize on. The object of dogma is to transmit the essence of the original vision to those unable or unwilling to ascend the Mount of Revelation. It is usually the result of the meditation of a community on its inner experience. Its function is to conserve the experience, to enrich and explain it, and to guard it against what may be felt to be false or inadequate interpretations of it. When examined, credal statements are found to be varying combinations of theological, metaphysical, psychological, and symbolic elements; in the Christian creeds an all-important historical element is present.

In so far as any credal statement is framed and understood in terms of the intellect, it is of its nature inadequate and imperfect; the truth which springs from spiritual vision is only capable of partial expression in conceptual terms. Further, any particular credal statement is inevitably framed in the language and thought-patterns of the age in which it was formulated; and language and thought-patterns change with time.

Dogmatic statements have been understandably condemned, not only on the grounds that they are inadequate and, when wrongly understood, misleading, but also because they have, throughout history, been a source of division, hatred, and persecution. When, however, its character is rightly appreciated and its limitations fully recognized, dogma is a source of spiritual and mental illumination of exquisite beauty and immense value.

How ought dogma to be understood? In the interpretation of dogma all approaches are legitimate, for the object is, through the medium of dogma, to find truth. One may try to understand it metaphysically; in all dogma there is a metaphysical element, an explicit or implicit statement about the nature of the universe. On the other hand, one may accept Jung's contention that to understand metaphysically is impossible, that it is only possible to understand dogma psychologically. Or, with Berdyaev, one may regard it as the symbolic expression of mystical and eternal fact and decline to give the symbols a logical connotation or more than an implicit metaphysical sanction. What matters is the degree of spiritual understanding reached through it.

In primitive and elementary forms of religion God is regarded as an Object. Man stands over against this Object as observing Subject. So long as this attitude was maintained man's ideas of Deity were necessarily limited and circumscribed. It was only when this subject–object relationship could be put aside that the essential advance could be made, for, to quote from the Upanishads, 'the only proof of His existence is union with Him'. At the apex of the soul the knower and the known must in some way become one.

About the middle of the millennium before the birth of Christ there occurred a profound revolution in Indian religious thought and spiritual awareness. It was the result not primarily of philosophical reflection; it sprang rather out of an apparently widespread wave of mystical and psychological experience; it was the result of a deliberate turning inward. Out of it came a spiritual revelation of immense profundity and significance.

To state the beliefs of Hinduism exactly and in detail is impossible; there is no codified Hindu dogma, nothing, for instance, corresponding to the Christian Creeds. There are many schools of thought within it. One may concentrate one's attention on those two fundamental tenets, which implicitly contain all the rest. They have been referred to several times already, but may with advantage be summarized at this point.

The first may be summed up in some words from the Mundaka Upanishad:

My son! There is nothing in this world that is not God. He is action, purity; everlasting Spirit. Find Him in the cavern; gnaw the knot of ignorance.

Shining, yet hidden, Spirit lives in the cavern. Everything that sways, breathes, opens, closes, lives in Spirit; beyond learning, beyond everything, better than anything; living, unliving.

It is the undying blazing Spirit, that seed of all seeds, wherein lay hidden the world and all its creatures. It is life, speech, mind, reality, immortality.*

The second is expressed in two passages from the Chhandogya Upanishad:

In this body, in this town of Spirit, there is a little house shaped like a lotus and in that house there is a little space. . . . There is as much in that little space within the heart as there is in the whole world outside. Heaven, earth, fire, wind, sun, moon, lightning, stars; whatever is and whatever is not, everything is there. . . . What lies in that space does not decay when the body decays, nor does it fall when the body falls. That space is the home of Spirit. Every desire

* Anthology, Section 2.

is there. Self is there, beyond decay and death; sin and sorrow; hunger and thirst; His aim truth; His will truth.

and

My son! Though you do not find that Being in the world, He is there. That Being is the seed; all else but His expression. He is truth. He is Self. Shwetaketu! *You are That.**

Here are fundamental statements on the nature of God, the universe, and man of immense significance in the development of human thought. Something new has come into the world, a fresh vision of reality. What do they say?

The basic stuff of the universe is spirit; the Reality behind all phenomena is Spirit. There is nothing in the universe that is not God, everlasting Spirit. Everything lives in Spirit; it is the seed of all seeds; from it everything comes.

Man is the house of Spirit; in a sense he is Spirit, for 'You are That'. The self he thinks he knows is not his true self; it is an empirical, phenomenal self, conscious only in fits and starts, unstable, subject to change, decay, and death; it has no fixed identity. Within man dwells, however, a Greater Self, the Atman, which is immortal and unchanging, a divine light, the unsleeping seer, the true self. This Self is present in all, yet distinct from all. It is a Universal Self and at the same time a personal Self.

Hindu thought, unlike most Western thought, is, as we have already seen, non-dualistic. The object is not set over against the subject; the knower and the known are one; God is the One without a second; there is nothing in the world which is not God. Therefore it is possible for the Hindu to say not only, 'Perceive the Atman in thyself as "this I am",' but also, 'The knowledge that Brahman (God) and Atman (the divine Self in man) are one and the same is true knowledge.'

Man, however, lives in the illusion of multiplicity; he does not see the world and himself as they truly are; he is deceived by *maya*, a difficult term which is used with more than one meaning. In general, it is used to indicate the tendency to identify ourselves with our apparent selves and an apparent

* Anthology, Section 2.

universe, to be deceived by the appearance which conceals the reality. It does not mean that the empirical world and the selves in it are mere illusion or are not, in their way, real; it means that they are not seen as, in their essential nature, they really are.

It was a magnificent achievement in spiritual understanding. Hinduism has, however, been criticized by Albert Schweitzer, for instance, as a religion of life-negation and a denial of the significance of human life and human history. Though this has been denied and must not be pressed too far, it is, to a great extent, borne out by Indian history and the development of much of Hindu thought.

Man cannot contain within himself too much at one time. Every advance in human thought demands a concentration, the exclusion of something in favour of something else. The splendid Hindu vision of the spiritual nature of the universe and of man tended to result in an exaggerated otherworldliness, and too great an emphasis on the virtue of passivity as opposed to action. In Hindu religious thought the true object of man is to be annihilated in Spirit, to escape from the bonds of historical succession, from the endless cycle of birth and death. Human history, if not entirely meaningless, has only minor significance. The meaning of existence is not to be found in history; the goal of creation is outside history.

These are, of course, generalizations; in order to be scrupulously exact, one would have to add several qualifications. For instance, one would have to draw attention to that wise and penetrating discourse on the nature of right action contained in the *Bhagavad Gita*. Nevertheless, in the light of Indian history the judgement is not a biased one. Neither those great advances in science nor the zeal to create a just social order which have been characteristics of Western history took place, or could have taken place, in India. The urge was lacking.

The Indian vision, splendid as it was, was incomplete. It failed satisfactorily to reconcile 'spirit' and 'matter'. A further revelation was necessary in order that a deeper and more satisfying synthesis might be reached. Its setting was in the West.

The revolution in the religious thought in India, which has

been described, coincided approximately in time with the rise of the great Hebrew prophets and with the Classical Age of Greece.

Hebrew religion lacked the deep mystical and psychological insight of the Hindu revelation. While Hinduism had given little significance to history, the Hebrew religion was in essence a meditation on history. While Hinduism turned inward away from the phenomenal world, Hebraism turned outward towards it. God was the God of history, the Holy and utterly transcendent, you revealing Himself within the historical process, and so giving to it significance and meaning. The mystical element in Hebraism was slight, except, perhaps, in its later developments, when it came into contact with other religious systems. But out of its particular insight sprang the idea of a 'living' God, a God of righteousness and justice, whose service demanded from His servants moral rectitude and social justice.

He hath shown thee, O man, what is good; and what doth the Lord require of thee, but to do justly, and to love mercy, and to walk humbly with thy God.

Here again we are, for the sake of clarity and brevity, generalizing (there are other elements in the Hebrew religion which are not mentioned), but not unfairly or inexactly.

The Greeks were not, in general, a spiritually minded race. Their eyes were, for the most part, turned outward to the world of material phenomena. Their great contribution to the development of human thought was the conception of an orderly, rational universe, governed by law. This universe was, moreover, one which men could, by a divinely implanted reason, explore and hope to comprehend. The possession of reason was to the thinkers of Greece what distinguished man from the rest of creation and put him above it.

That is not to say that there were no mystical strains in the Greek transition from a primitive polytheistic naturalism to rational philosophy. There is, for instance, a marked mystical element in Plato, which later developed into that Neoplatonism, which, as we have seen, profoundly influenced

Christian mysticism. It was inevitable that there should be, for no rational philosophical system can alone satisfy the deep religious and psychological needs inherent in mankind.

23. Mysticism and Dogma: The Christian Revelation

AT the time of the birth of Christ, the Mediterranean world was, if not waiting for, at least ripe for a new revelation. That revelation came in Jesus Christ.

The contact of Jesus with his disciples was an experience of so compelling a character that it impelled them to declare with complete and utter conviction that the Man who had died on a cross on Calvary had risen and was alive again. He was the Son of God. Though He had returned to the eternal world, at Pentecost the Spirit had descended on them.

To their contemporaries it was an astounding and incredible statement, 'to the Jews a stumbling block, to the Greeks foolishness'. To call a man the divine Son of God was to the Jews blasphemy; it was in complete contradiction to that strict monotheism which was their particular pride. To the Greek philosophical mind it was equally alien, for one of its chief difficulties had been to explain how a transcendent, perfect God could create an imperfect world. How, the philosophers asked, could the imperfect come out of the perfect, the Many from the One? How then could God become incarnate?

It was, therefore, inevitable that, as Christianity spread throughout the Greco-Roman world, the question should be asked: If you assert that Jesus Christ was the Son of God, that he was divine, what exactly do you mean? For over four centuries the great debate on the Nature of Christ continued; it still goes on.

A fundamental metaphysical issue was involved. Any statement about the nature of Jesus Christ could not avoid being also a fundamental statement about the nature of God, the universe, and man. Though these early Christians were called upon to deal with a special case in which an inner experience was bound up with a particular group of historical events, they could not interpret that special case without making, at least implicitly, a general metaphysical statement about everything.

The experience of Christ, as described in the New Testament, was a dual experience. It was, first of all, the experience of the earthly Jesus, a man whom his disciples had known as man, who had died and, they believed, had risen again. It was also the experience of the divine indwelling of the Spirit of the risen Christ. These two experiences could not be separated. The man who died on a cross on a desolate hill was also the immanent Christ of whom St Paul spoke when he said, 'I live, yet not I, but Christ liveth in me.'

An inner experience of the immanence of God in man had been known in India and reflection on it had resulted in those two fundamental statements which are the glory of the Hindu faith. This inner experience was, however, unrelated to history. In consequence Hinduism failed to find and express – though, in the *Gita*, it moves towards it – a completely satisfactory synthesis between history and not-history, between time and timelessness, between matter and spirit. It fell to Christianity to try to find and express a richer synthesis.

It is no part of this book to describe in detail that long theological debate which resulted in the formulation of the great Creeds of Christendom.* Outwardly the story is not a pretty one. The debate was characterized by much hatred and conflict. On the face of it, it looks like a futile splitting of theological hairs. Yet out of it came what was in essence a new and significant statement on the nature of Reality. The insights of India, of Palestine, and of Greece were not superseded. They were fulfilled.

First one formula, then another, was suggested and rejected as erroneous, misleading, or inadequate. All in one way or another failed to express the Christian revelation in its fullness.

* It is well told in Wand: *The Four Great Heresies* (Mowbrays). For a reinterpretation in present-day concepts see Matthews: *The Problem of Christ in the Twentieth Century* (Oxford).

Some clearly could not stand. For instance, to say that, since there could be no relation between God and the material world, Jesus was not a human person but a phantom, as did the Docetists, could be rejected out of hand. Adoptionism, however, which said that Jesus was a good man on whom the Power of God had rested and who had been 'adopted' as God's Son, so that he was able to reveal the nature of God, in so far as it could be revealed at the human level, was eminently reasonable. Equally so was Apollinarianism. Apollinarius, starting with the thesis that a human being is a union of a physical body and rational soul, explained the relationship of the divine and human in Christ by arguing that in Him the Divine Logos* replaced the rational soul. This interpretation would have implied, however, that Jesus Christ was not truly a man as ordinary men are men.

Adoptionism and Apollinarianism, and this is also true of Arianism and most of the other so-called heresies, expressed only an *association* of the divine and human in Christ. What the most profound thinkers of the early Christian Church were intent on doing was to assert categorically, not a mere *association* of the divine and human, but a full and perfect *union* of the divine and the human in the one person of Jesus Christ; that He was at the same time completely, truly, and perfectly God and man.

The credal formula eventually accepted by the Church was that Jesus Christ was 'of one *substance* (or in Greek *ousia*) with the Father', i.e. that He had the same underlying reality as God; and that in Him the Divine Logos had been made flesh and become man; i.e. that He had taken upon Himself all that makes man man. Further, the two natures, the human and the divine, were recognized as being integrated, without any confusion, change, division, or separation, in the one *person* (i.e. *hypostasis*, i.e. the reality in a distinct instance) of Christ; in the words of the Declaration of Faith of Chalcedon, 'the distinction of the natures in no way being annulled by the union, but rather the characteristics of each nature being preserved and

* See the Prologue to the Fourth Gospel, Anthology, Section 7.

coming together to form one person and subsistence, not as parted or separated into two persons but one and the same'.

It was not very satisfactory. The concepts available were inadequate, the approach to the whole issue was faulty. It might have been better if the debate could have been conducted through psychological concepts; but no adequate ones were available. The attempt to give a theological and metaphysical interpretation to what was in its essence an inner experience resulted in the reality being obscured and treated objectively in an almost physical-chemical fashion. The divine and the human were regarded as if they were two kinds of material elements, which in some way were fused together without losing their separate identities as, for instance, when wine and water are mixed and yet remain two distinct elements in the mixture. Further, all that emerged was an assertion without explanation, a statement incapable of rational proof.

24. The Coinherence of Spirit and Matter

YET in spite of all that, the conception of the relationship of God and the phenomenal world, of spirit and matter, were reorientated and reordered. The map of thought was redrawn and extended. Though these early Christian theologians persisted in declaring that they were only stating 'the faith once given to the saints', they were, though the issue was presented to them in a highly specialized form, unknowingly groping after a solution of the perennial metaphysical problem of how that which we call God was related to the world, of how spirit and matter were connected. Anything which was said could not but be, implicitly, if not explicitly, a fundamental statement on the whole problem of the nature of God, the material universe and man.

In Hinduism there was richness of inner experience and profound meditation on the problem, but in the end the material world was seen only as the 'play' of God and the chief end of man was to escape from the melancholy wheel of birth and death. No Hindu thinker could have written that magnificent passage in St Paul's Epistle to the Romans about the whole creation waiting for deliverance from the bondage of corruption into the liberty of the glory of the sons of God. In Judaism, essential as were its insights as a prelude for the deeper insights which came out of it, there was a blind spot which resulted in the rejection by the Jews of the revelation when it came. The Greek philosophical mind proved itself incapable of reconciling the One and the Many.

What the Christian Church asserted was the complete *coinherence* – there is no better word – of matter and spirit, of the One and the All and the All and the One. Only by such an assertion could the experience of the earthly Jesus and the experience of the indwelling Christ be intellectually fused, only thus could the full immanence of God in the world, as it had been seen in the Jesus of history, be adequately explained.

In early Christian thought Christ did not stand alone. He was the second Adam, the first-born of many brothers, the Archetypal Man, man as he is in his essential being. In Christ, said St Athanasius, God was made man (*hominized*), that man might be made God (*deified*).

The mystical identification – one can use no other word – of Christ with the whole of mankind and with the whole of man's nature, flesh as well as spirit, is emphasized time and time again by early Christian thinkers.

We hold that to the whole of human nature the whole essence of the Godhead was united. . . . He in his fullness took upon himself me in my fullness, and united whole to whole that he might in his grace bestow salvation on the whole man. [St John of Damascus]

God so united himself to us and us to him, that the descent of God to the human level was at the same time the ascent of man to the divine level. [St Leo]

By dwelling in one the Word dwelt in all, so that the one being constituted the Son of God in power, the same dignity might pass to the whole human race. [St Cyril of Alexandria]

In the Saviour we are all risen, we have all been restored to life, we have all ascended into heaven. For a portion of the flesh and blood of each of us is in the man Christ. [St Maximus of Turin]*

The Christian Creeds are a complex of theological, metaphysical, psychological, and historical elements. Running through them are the great mythological archetypes of the Great Mother and the Divine Son who is slain and rises again. These great mythological archetypes are to be found in the religious insights of all ages and in all parts of the globe. They rise, according to Jung, out of the collective unconscious and express the most profound spiritual insights of the human race on its nature and destiny.

The story of Jesus Christ is not the first or only story of a dying God. 'Behind the figure of the dying demigod,' wrote Arnold Toynbee in his great *Study of History*,

there looms the greater figure of a very god who dies for different worlds under diverse names – for a Minoan World as Zagreus, for a Sumeric World as Tammuz, for a Hittite World as Attis, for a Scandinavian World as Balder, for a Syriac World as Adonis, for a Shī'ī World as Husayn, for a Christian World as Christ. Who is this God of many Epiphanies but only one Passion?

'Many Epiphanies but only one Passion'; but with, in the Passion of Christ, this essential difference. What had been before a myth became a fact of history. In Him, the Eternal Lamb of God, slain before the foundation of the world, died in time. In His Incarnation, Passion, and Resurrection what had been before an inner experience passed from dream to actuality. The reality glimpsed and expressed in ancient ritual and mythology was incarnate in the phenomenal world. The perennial dream of mankind became true.

In Jesus Christ, Archetypal Man, God and man were one, in Him spirit and matter coinhered. That was the mystical truth the Church believed, that is what it asserted. By that assertion of faith, for it could not be logically demonstrated, something of vast significance was added to man's ever-expanding picture of reality. Human thought passed into a new

* Quoted in Watts: *Myth and Ritual in Christianity* (Thames and Hudson).

dimension. The Christian Creed is the expression, inadequate and capable of different interpretations in the light of different world views, of a profound corporate mystical insight of knowledge and understanding. Since the timeless vision was bound up with time, it inevitably led to a new and fertile mysticism of action. It is not strange that it was the Christian West and not the East that saw the emergence of humanism and modern science. Both were the logical outcome of the Christian vision of the coinherence of matter and spirit.

Man burns to find the secret of the universe. But neither knowledge nor action alone can satisfy. To the mysticism of knowledge and understanding and the mysticism of action must be added the mysticism of union and love. Only thus may the deepest spiritual and psychological needs of men be met. In the Christian vision, because it was equally one of spirit and of matter, the need was met in a more satisfying form than ever before. The Eternal Christ, 'begotten of His Father before all worlds, God of God, Light of Light, very God of Very God', was also the human Teacher, flesh of our flesh, bone of our bone, who taught His disciples to say, 'Our Father which art in heaven', and thus gave to men the most intimate symbol of the personal union of God and man, the Mediator and the Saviour, who brought the unknowable God-head within the reach of frail humanity. In him heaven was brought down to earth and earth taken up to heaven.

Though the vision had, in order that it might become incarnate, to be expressed in the language of the intellect, it cannot be grasped intellectually.

He [Christ] is grasped only when movement ceases and faith takes its place. By this faith we are caught up into simplicity above all reason and intelligence to the third heaven of pure simple intellectuality. ... And this is no other than that very learned ignorance, by which the blessed Paul himself, raised higher and into a closer knowledge, perceived that the Christ with whom he was at one time acquainted, he never really knew.*

* Nicholas of Cusa: *Of Learned Ignorance*. See Anthology, Section 25.

25. The Validity of Mysticism

WE started our study with the dilemma created in the mind by the contemplation of the vast immensities of time and space revealed by modern astronomy. In the light of that picture of the universe what, if any, we asked, was the significance of man? What validity could now be accorded to those long-accepted beliefs in his nature and destiny which had their origin in world-views so very different from that of the present day?

The attempt to answer these questions led us to examine the nature of human knowledge and perception in general and of scientific knowledge in particular. As a result of that examination we found that neither the discoveries of modern astronomy, nor indeed any other discovery in the field of science, in themselves destroyed the dignity of man or proved that the old religious beliefs about his nature and destiny were illusions.

In our study of mystical experience and mystical consciousness we have examined a range of consciousness which extends beyond that of the rational consciousness, and a mode of perception wider than that of normal human beings. In the mystics we have seen a procession of men and women who have claimed to have broken into a 'spiritual' world and there found an answer to the perennial riddle which has fully satisfied them. What authority, however, can be accorded to their testimony?

For the mystic himself his vision is completely authoritative. For himself his position is invulnerable. Does it, however, carry any authority for one who has had no analogous experience, to whom any sort of mystical state is unknown? While it is not strictly true to say that the mystic is unable to describe what he has experienced, he cannot describe it in rational terms, nor can its validity be logically demonstrated as can, for instance, a proposition in mathematics or a scientific statement. What he says he knows cannot be 'proved'.

Certain things can, however, be said. Firstly, the result of a study of the whole range of mystical consciousness is inevitably to throw doubt in any unbiased mind on any claim of the non-mystical and rational consciousness, based on intellect and the senses alone, to be the only valid organ of perception. Unless it is dismissed as pure delusion, the experience of the mystics makes it impossible to accept the rational consciousness as the only form of consciousness. The possibility of orders of truth concealed from, or only half-revealed by, the rational consciousness, cannot be dismissed as an untenable hypothesis. Indeed, it can be argued that in the light of the totality of human experience it is the most likely one.

Secondly, the more one explores the writings of the mystics, the deeper one tries to delve into their meaning and significance, the more one finds a most impressive basic unanimity. To say that is not to make any claim for the 'oneness' of mystical experience; it is not possible to substantiate any such claim. The mystic's particular psychological make-up, his geographical, environmental, metaphysical, and theological background, the particular urge which has started him on his quest, all affect the character of his vision. It is not possible to assert that all mystics 'see' the same thing, that all have an identical experience. These factors, too, influence the descriptions different mystics have left of their experiences and the varying ways they have interpreted them. Their unanimity is found at a deeper level. At the level of what I have called the Primary Imagination, it is difficult to escape the conclusion that all have glimpsed in varying degrees and in varying forms the same Reality and found the same Truth.

If that be so, the age-long quest of mankind, the search for the ultimate Truth which lies hidden beyond all the partial truths, behind all the polar opposites which condition human perception, is not a vain one. We need not rest content with the partial truths revealed by astronomy, by physics, by biology, by history, each true in its own field, sometimes contradicting, or seeming to contradict, each other, none complete in itself, none giving the whole picture; nor yet with the truth of mathematics or the truth of language, primarily truths of expression, obeying rules which men themselves have made. Beyond all these, beyond the contradictories of each separate truth, lies concealed the supreme and final Truth, the ultimate synthesis which mankind has longed to find, but has never found. Whether through mystical intuition it is seen more clearly and fully must be left to the reader, on the evidence which has been presented to him, to reach his own conclusion. That will depend in the last resort on the primary act of intellectual faith he is prepared to make.

26. Conclusion:
The Mystic's Universe

OUR Study moves to its close. In it we have tried not only to understand the nature and scope of mystical experience and consciousness, but also to assess its significance. Throughout it we have been moving towards a possible interpretation of all experience and all consciousness.

Mysticism is like a great fugal pattern, each part interwoven with the other, sometimes one theme, sometimes another predominating, but together forming one whole. It is seen to have three interconnected aspects, which we have called the mysticism of knowledge and understanding, the mysticism of love and union, and the mysticism of action.* In it are found four interrelated visions; the vision of Oneness, the vision of Timelessness, the vision of a Self other than the empirical self, and the vision of a Love enfolding everything that exists.

If the witness not only of the great pioneers of the spirit, but also of those lesser ones who have tasted something of the same experience and caught something of the same vision, is accepted, it is surely here that a revealing synthesis is, if anywhere, most likely to be found.

Mystical states, however, since in their purity they are states

* They have affinities with jnana-yoga, bhakti-yoga, and karma-yoga of Hinduism.

of undifferentiated awareness at the level of the Primary Imagination, have no intellectual content. Since they happen in conditions of space–time, however, they have a quality whereby the imageless state of pure awareness can be translated into intellectual vision and becomes capable of expression. We have considered these translations of intellectual vision as they have been given expression in different religious systems and in different parts of the globe.

When we contemplate these interrelated and evolving insights, what picture of reality emerges? It is one of a universe which is a dynamic unfolding of Spirit. There is nothing in it which is not Spirit, 'the seed of all seeds'. By us this dynamic unfolding of Spirit is experienced and seen in the setting of space–time. We are involved in an evolutionary process which contains the elements of succession and expansion. The evolutionary process is, however, the unfolding of Spirit in a timeless Now. The higher consciousness advances in the process of evolution, the more it moves out of succession. To be fully conscious is to escape from time, from expansion, from separateness, from contradictories. Growth, movement, and change dissolve in permanence, stillness, and completeness.

Though the universe we perceive has the quality of *maya*, there is in it a mysterious coinherence between spirit and matter. Matter has, as it were, a reality in its own right. It is, as it were, an incarnation of spirit. But since man is contained in space–time phenomena, he does not easily perceive the real nature of the world or of himself. He imagines he is wholly bound up with his ephemeral, phenomenal self. He does not easily perceive that his true self is of that changeless Spirit, with which it is, of its nature, one.

Only in God, timeless Spirit, undifferentiated Energy, impersonal yet personal, far yet near, unknown and unknowable yet intimately known, hidden beyond the coincidence of opposites, the sustaining, all-pervading Love 'which moves the sun and the other stars', can the nature of the universe and of man be understood and then only in part, 'as in a glass darkly', and only, as Nicholas of Cusa knew, by 'transcending those perennial truths that can be reached by reason'.

There I might end; but the picture would not be complete. To know, to understand is not enough; the deep spirit of man craves for something more, for something which has been given many names, salvation, redemption, eternal life, the kingdom of heaven, union with God. A lonely being, contained in the brief span between birth and death, as a material entity he is only an insignificant bundle of atoms in a vast, frightening, impersonal universe, soon to return to dust and be known no more. Yet he feels that he is more than this. He is conscious of a 'spark' within him, of himself as an image, perhaps more than an image, of divinity, of an undivided Unity from which he is separated and to which he longs to return. He may forget for a time that he is a King's son, forget the Pearl he was sent down to Egypt to find, forget the Glorious Robe which once he wore in his Father's kingdom and be sunk in the sleep of spiritual oblivion.* But the divine light is there within him and cannot for ever be quenched.

Not only has mysticism its fount in what is the raw material of all religion, but also all the most profound insights of religious truth have their origin in the mystical experiences of those who have led the spiritual progress of the human race. Not only have they received a vision of a reality which is beyond that of space–time, they have also found a way from separation to union, a way of timeless life.

The Way springs out of the Vision; for without the Vision the Way would not be known. It is the Way of Union through reciprocal love, of like calling unto like, of the love of God stretching down to man and of the love of man stretching up to God. But it is not an easy way. It is the Royal Road of the Holy Cross, a way of utter self-loss, of the shedding of every vestige of self-love, of the abandonment of everything, even of one's own selfhood.

But the supreme loss is the supreme finding. Within the wild desert of the naked Godhead is found the divine Bridegroom to whom the soul, all cares and shame forgotten, is united in the garden of lilies, the dear Comrade, the heavenly Father

---

* The imagery is that of *The Hymn of the Robe of Glory*; see Anthology, Section 9.

with outstretched arms, who is also the Mother on whose breast the weary child may rest, the Redeemer and Mediator, a Love encompassing everything. Here mysticism becomes lyrical, warm, and glowing. Here it speaks to the most intimate longings of the human soul.

Is the vision of the mystic remote and irrelevant to us who, since we have not the spiritual gifts nor are prepared to pay the price, cannot hope to know the high experiences of the contemplatives or attain to their certain empirical knowledge? Not entirely. Much of our knowledge is inevitably based on the wisdom and experience of others. The picture of reality which they have seen and described is there for us to study and ponder over, to accept or reject. We cannot hope to have the profound experiences given to the contemplative saints, but mystical consciousness is much more common than a capacity to rise to the heights of Contemplation. To more than is supposed, since they seldom talk about it, there has come, even if only dimly, the experience of 'the intersection of the timeless moment'.

There are times when the awakened soul, craving for a revelation which will make sense of the riddle of the universe, of the apparent futility of life, and of its own inadequacy, may feel that there is no answer. Sick with longing, it can only cry, '*De profundis, Domine*'. But the desire is everything; for the prayer of desire is not seldom the prelude of the revelation. Suddenly 'the timeless moment' is there, the morning stars sing together, a sense of utter joy, utter certainty, and utter unworthiness mingle, and in awe and wonder it murmurs: 'I know'.

THE ANTHOLOGY

Introduction

WHAT is included in an anthology may be dictated solely by the personal preferences of its compiler; some of the best anthologies have been of this sort. On the other hand, it may be built up round some special topic, or to illustrate some literary or historical movement or some particular literary form. Whatever the intent of the compiler, it is desirable that he should make it clear to his readers. Every anthology throws itself open to criticism; every anthology thus calls for a preliminary apologia.

To decide what to include and what to omit has not been an easy task. What indeed is mysticism? As the reader of the Study will have realized, there are many differences of interpretation. The choice of material is vast; among Christian mystics alone, at least fifty, perhaps more, have claims to be included. Mystical experience and speculation, moreover, is not limited to one religion. Should I attempt to give as complete and balanced a picture as possible of mysticism as it has manifested itself in all religions, and even outside them? Or should I, in the interests of clarity and compactness, limit it to its expression on one religious system only, in an anthology intended for Western readers, to its expression in Christianity? Let me therefore say what I have tried to do.

In the first place, I have tried to make an anthology which would be both an anthology pure and simple, which could be read quite apart from the Study which precedes it, and also an extension and documentation of that study. Other factors which have operated in the choice of material have been:

1. The space at my disposal. The original plan of the book was one of a study of some 30,000 words and an anthology of 40,000 to 50,000 words. It has worked out longer than that and it has only been by a ruthless elimination of much that I would have liked to include that the anthology has been kept within bounds at all.

2. My desire to avoid compiling an anthology of mere snippets. It seemed to me to be better to omit some mystics and some schools of mysticism with strong claims to inclusion in order that the passages from the writings of those who were included should be of sufficient length to allow the reader to get a reasonably full and clear idea of their thought as a whole.

3. The availability of material and its suitability for inclusion in an anthology not intended primarily for scholars.

4. My own personal preferences and knowledge.

So, in the first place, and particularly in order that the Anthology might be more useful as a documentation of the Study, I have concentrated on illustrating various types of mystical consciousness and experience rather than attempted to include all those who had claims to inclusion. Thus, though the *Dialogues* of St Catherine of Siena and St Catherine of Genoa would have been well worthy of inclusion, I did not feel that either of these great contemplative saints had said anything which was not said as well or better by the German and Flemish mystics who are included. Again, though there were a number of great Catholic mystics in the centuries following that of St Teresa and St John of the Cross, for instance the Venerable Augustine Baker, St François de Sales, Madame Guyon, and Father Pierre Caussade, it seemed to me that nothing of real significance was added by them to what had been said earlier. I have therefore followed the passages from St John of the Cross with selections from the writings of Thomas Traherne, William Law, and Richard Jefferies, whose mysticism was of types not previously illustrated. In the second edition (1964) an additional section, illustrating yet another type, particularly relevant for our times, that of Father Pierre Teilhard de Chardin, *The Mysticism of the Divine Milieu*, was added.

Though Jacob Boehme is probably the greatest of the Protestant mystics, and the mystical insights of William Blake are of particular interest and significance, I decided to omit them on account of their obscurity. Most of the writings of Jacob Boehme and the Prophetic Books of William Blake are incomprehensible without an intimate knowledge of the symbols these writers used.

Since my Study was an attempt to survey mysticism in general and is not confined to its expression in one particular religion, the logical course would have been to aim at a greater balance than the Anthology actually has. If it is criticized as being too predominantly drawn from Christian sources, I must accept such criticism as valid. It is, however, not due solely to my own Christian bias.

When I prepared the Anthology of the original edition I was reasonably well acquainted with the Hindu *Upanishads* and the *Bhagavada Gita*, with the writings of Plato and Plotinus and with the Sufi mystics of Islam, and good translations were available. All were, therefore, included in the Anthology of the first edition. Though I knew Lossky's *Mystical Theology of the Eastern Church* and the Faber and Faber edition of *Writings from the Philokalia*, I had failed to appreciate the central place the doctrine of *theosis* (deification) played in the mystical theology of the Eastern Orthodox Church; nor had I made a sufficient study of the mantric Prayer of Jesus, the Prayer of the Heart, to realize its mystical significance. I therefore did not include examples of the expression of mystical consciousness in that branch of the Christian Church.

Further, my understanding of the richness of Buddhist spirituality and my acquaintance with the vast corpus of Buddhist scriptures were so limited that I did not feel myself capable of including a section on the manifestations of mystical consciousness in Buddhism. Nor did I feel that I sufficiently understood that difficult work, the *Tao Te Ching*, to be able to include a section on the essentially mystical conception of *Tao* in ancient Chinese metaphysics.

Now that a third edition of *Mysticism* is called for I have tried, however inadequately, to make this Anthology as catholic (in the widest sense of the word) as possible. I have therefore added sections on Chinese (Taoist) and Buddhist mysticism and on the mysticism of the Eastern Orthodox Church. I do not, however, feel yet capable of compiling satisfactorily a section on the rich vein of Jewish mysticism.*

Finally, some of the material included in the anthology is not easy reading, particularly for one who has no previous acquaintance with the literature and ideas of mysticism. Some readers may find it better to start by dipping in here and there, so as to discover what appeals to them, what, for the moment, they find alien and even incomprehensible, rather than to try to read from beginning to end. For example, Julian of Norwich, Thomas à Kempis, St Teresa, and Traherne are easy to understand, Plotinus and Eckhart may be at first difficult. Much, however, depends on the taste and mental and spiritual background of each reader.

* A good chapter on Jewish mysticism is included in Spencer's *Mysticism in World Religion* (Penguin Books and Allen and Unwin (Library edition)). There are some interesting examples in Gollancz's *Year of Grace*.

1. Prologue: The Timeless Moment

I HAVE argued in this Study of mysticism that mystical experience is not something confined to those who have risen to the heights of Contemplation, but that it can be present in a less developed form in quite ordinary men and women. An experience of the sort which may, without unjustifiably stretching the meaning of the word, be called mystical may happen to anyone, sometimes quite unexpectedly; but, when it occurs, it is clearly recognizable. It may happen only once in a lifetime; but, when it does happen, it brings an illumination and a certainty which can rarely, if ever, be reached by the rational consciousness and may change the whole tenure of a life.

As a Prologue, therefore, to this Anthology, which is made up, for the most part, of the writings of those who have progressed far along the Mystic Way, I have set out a number of descriptions – call them 'case histories' if you will – of mystical experiences which have happened to those who would make no claim to be called mystics in the fullest sense. They are of different types, happening to people of different ages, temperaments, and walks of life – two are the experiences of children – but all reveal one or more of the characteristics which, in the Study, we have listed as typical of mystical experience. A reading of them may, perhaps, convince the reader of the relevance of mysticism to himself.*

*

This experience and the one which follows happened to children, the first to a girl of nine, the second to a boy of fifteen. Both were recalled in later life.

Suddenly the Thing happened, and, as everybody knows, it cannot be described in words. The Bible phrase, 'I saw the heavens open', seems as good as any if not taken literally. I

---

* In *Watcher on the Hill* Dr Raynor Johnson sets out and examines thirty-six similar 'case histories'. See also his *The Imprisoned Splendour* (both Hodder and Stoughton).

T-E

remember saying to myself, in awe and rapture, 'So it's like this; now I know what Heaven is like, now I know what they mean in church'. The words of the 23rd Psalm came into my head and I began repeating them: He maketh me to lie down in green pastures; He leadeth me beside the still waters. Soon it faded and I was alone in the meadow with the baby and the brook and the sweet-smelling lime trees. But though it passed and only the earthly beauty remained, I was filled with great gladness. I had seen the 'far distances'.

From Margaret Isherwood, The Root of the Matter (*Gollancz*)

The thing happened one summer afternoon, on the school cricket field, while I was sitting on the grass, waiting my turn to bat. I was thinking about nothing in particular, merely enjoying the pleasures of midsummer idleness. Suddenly, and without warning, something invisible seemed to be drawn across the sky, transforming the world about me into a kind of tent of concentrated and enhanced significance. What had been merely an outside became an inside. The objective was somehow transformed into a completely subjective fact, which was experienced as 'mine', but on a level where the word had no meaning; for 'I' was no longer the familiar ego. Nothing more can be said about the experience, it brought no accession of knowledge about anything except, very obscurely, the knower and his way of knowing. After a few minutes there was a 'return to normalcy'. The event made a deep impression on me at the time; but, because it did not fit into any of the thought patterns – religious, philosophical, scientific – with which, as a boy of fifteen, I was familiar, it came to seem more and more anomalous, more and more irrelevant to 'real life', and was finally forgotten.

From the same source

*

Vera Brittain wrote Testament of Friendship *as a tribute to her friend, Winifred Holtby. At the age of thirty-three, while at the height of her power as a novelist, Winifred Holtby was told by a specialist that she might have not more than two years to live. Compelled by bodily weakness to give up her work, her whole being in rebellion, she was one day, feeling very tired and dispirited, walking up a hill and came to a trough outside a farmhouse. Its surface was frozen over and some lambs were gathered round it.*

She broke the ice for them with her stick, and as she did so heard a voice within her saying 'Having nothing, yet possessing all things'. It was so distinct that she looked round startled, but she was alone with the lambs on the top of the hill. Suddenly, in a flash, the grief, the bitterness, the sense of frustration disappeared; all desire to possess power and glory for herself vanished away, and never came back. . . . The moment of 'conversion' on the hill of Monks Risborough, she said with tears in her eyes, was the supreme spiritual experience of her life. She always associated it afterwards with the words of Bernard Bosanquet on Salvation:

'And now we are saved absolutely, we need not say from what, we are at home in the universe, and, in principle and in the main, feeble and timid creatures as we are, there is nothing within the world or without it that can make us afraid.'

From *Vera Brittain*, Testament of Friendship (*Macmillan*)

*

I had been ploughing all day in the black dust of the Lichtenburg roads, and had come very late to a place called the eye of Malmani – Malmani Oog – the spring of a river which presently loses itself in the Kalahari. We watered our horses and went supperless to bed. Next morning I bathed in one of the Malmani pools – and icy cold it was – and then basked in the early sunshine while breakfast was cooking. The water made a pleasant music, and near by was a covert of willows filled with singing birds. Then and there came on me the hour of revelation, when, though savagely hungry, I forgot about breakfast. Scents, sights, and sounds blended into a harmony so perfect that it transcended human expression, even human thought. It was like a glimpse of the peace of eternity.

From *John Buchan*, Memory Hold-the-Door (*Hodder and Stoughton*)

*

In his book, The Timeless Moment, *Warner Allen tells how at the*

*age of fifty he realized that he had gone through life without discovering
in it any pattern or rational purpose. He started to trace back the
events of his past life in the hope of finding in them some sort of significant pattern which might help him to find what he sought. He goes on
to tell, though without giving any details, how this quest for enlightenment led him through paths of 'unforeseen darkness and danger' – he
was obviously going through a period of what is called purgation – but
how 'within a year of clock-time' an answer came. This is how he
describes the coming of the answer:*

It flashed up lightning-wise during a performance of Beethoven's Seventh Symphony at the Queen's Hall, in the trium-
phant fast movement when 'the morning stars sang together
and all the sons of God shouted for joy'. The swiftly flowing
continuity of the music was not interrupted, so that what T. S.
Eliot calls 'the intersection of the timeless moment' must have
slipped in between two demi-semi-quavers.

What followed he tells in these words:

When, long afterwards, I analysed the happening in the
cold light of retrospect, it seemed to fall into three parts: first
the mysterious event itself, which occurred in the infinitesimal
fraction of a second; this I learnt afterwards from St Teresa to
call the Union with God; then Illumination, a *wordless* stream
of complex feelings in which the experience of Union combined
with the rhythmic emotion of the music like a sunbeam striking with iridescence the spray above a waterfall – a stream that
was continually swollen by tributaries of associated Experience; lastly Enlightenment, the recollection in tranquillity
of the whole complex of Experience as it were embalmed in
thought-forms and words.

*Of the stage of Illumination (similarities to Pascal's Memorial
will be noted) he writes:*

It was a time of mingled feeling and dawning thought. In the
coalescence of new and old Experience inchoate phrases were
beginning to shape themselves. A dim impression of the condition of the objective self might be given by a jumble of
incoherent sentences. 'Something has happened to me – I am

utterly amazed – can this be that? (*That* being the answer to
the riddle of life) – but it is too simple – I always knew it – it is
remembering an old forgotten secret – like coming home – I am
not "I", not the "I" I thought – there is no death – peace
passing understanding – yet how unworthy I – '

*The stage of Enlightenment is told in the form of a 'symbolic story
of a journey into the heart of the Self':*

Rapt in Beethoven's music, I closed my eyes and watched
a silver glow which shaped itself into a circle with a central
focus brighter than the rest. The circle became a tunnel of
light proceeding from some distant sun in the heart of the
Self. Swiftly and smoothly I was borne through the tunnel and
as I went the light turned from silver to gold. There was an
impression of drawing strength from a limitless sea of power
and a sense of deepening peace. The light grew brighter but
was never dazzling or alarming. I came to a point where time
and motion ceased. In my recollection it took the shape of a
flat-topped rock, surrounded by a summer sea, with a sandy
pool at its foot. The dream scene vanished and I am absorbed
in the Light of the Universe, in Reality glowing like fire with
the knowledge of itself, without ceasing to be one and myself,
merged like a drop of quicksilver in the Whole, yet still separate as a grain of sand in the desert. The peace that passes all
understanding and the pulsating energy of creation are one in
the centre in the midst of conditions where all opposites are
reconciled.

From *Warner Allen*, The Timeless Moment (*Faber and Faber*)

*

It happened in my room in Peterhouse on the evening of
1 February 1913, when I was an undergraduate at Cambridge.
If I say that Christ came to me I should be using conventional
words which would carry no precise meaning; for Christ
comes to men and women in different ways. When I tried to
record the experience at the time I used the imagery of the
vision of the Holy Grail; it seemed to me to be like that. There
was, however, no sensible vision. There was just the room,

with its shabby furniture and the fire burning in the grate and the red-shaded lamp on the table. But the room was filled by a Presence, which in a strange way was both about me and within me, like light or warmth. I was overwhelmingly possessed by Someone who was not myself, and yet I felt I was more myself than I had ever been before. I was filled with an intense happiness, and almost unbearable joy, such as I had never known before and have never known since. And over all was a deep sense of peace and security and certainty.

Some experiences of this sort, which I have found recorded, lasted a very short time. Mine lasted several hours. What time I went to bed I do not know, but when I awoke in the morning it was still there. During the day it faded. It was very wonderful and quite unforgettable.

Though I now recognize the experience as of the kind described by the mystics, at that time I knew nothing of mysticism. . . .

The other experience of which I must tell, happened a little later in the same room. I have always thought of it as a continuation and completion of that I have described; it 'felt' the same. This time, however, it seemed that a voice was speaking to me. It was not sensibly audible; it spoke within me. The words were strange: 'Those who sought the city found the wood: and those who sought the wood found the city.' Put into cold print they sound nonsensical. Yet I felt vividly that they meant something very important, that they were the key to a secret.*

I shall have more to say of this second experience; but first I would tell of two others. The first of these occurred in late 1916, during the Battle of the Somme. I crouched in the darkness in a front-line trench, which was nothing but a muddy ditch, stinking with unburied corpses, amid a tangle of shell-holes. At dawn my battalion was due to attack. I watched the slow movement of the luminous dial of my wrist-watch,

---

* Not until years later did the author realize that what he had grasped intuitively was Nicholas of Cusa's 'coincidence of contradictories (or opposites)'. See the passage from *The Vision of God* printed in the Anthology, page 305.

dreading the moment when I must get up and lead my men forward towards the German lines. And suddenly, with absolute certainty, I knew that I was utterly safe. It was not Rupert Brooke's:

> Safe though all safety's lost, safe where men fall;
> And if these poor limbs die, safest of all.

Still less was it the sort of fatalism not uncommon among fighting men in action. Rather it was a vivid sense of being completely safe physically. When the thunder of the barrage broke I went forward quite unafraid.

Baldly set down, the experience may not sound very important; it may be thought to have been merely the effect of a particularly heavy strain. It must be considered side by side with another experience which happened to me on the evening of 18 April 1936, the evening of the day before my son was born. My first child had been still-born and, as I lay in bed, I was very anxious about my wife and much disturbed in mind. And then a great peace came over me. I was conscious of a lovely, unexplainable pattern in the whole texture of things, a pattern of which everyone and everything was a part; and weaving the pattern was a Power; and that Power was what we faintly call Love. I realized that we are not lonely atoms in a cold, unfriendly, indifferent universe, but that each of us is linked up in a rhythm, of which we may be unconscious, and which we can never really know, but to which we can submit ourselves trustfully and unreservedly.

From F. C. Happold, Adventure in Search of a Creed (*Faber and Faber*)

*

It was the experience recorded below which led the Canadian psychologist, Dr R. M. Bucke, to investigate similar experiences in others and resulted in his writing Cosmic Consciousness: a Study in the Evolution of the Human Mind. *The description printed below is the version of it in the privately printed pamphlet which preceded the larger work.*

I had spent the evening in a great city, with two friends

reading and discussing poetry and philosophy. We parted at midnight. I had a long drive to my lodgings. My mind, deeply under the influence of the ideas, images, and emotions called up by the reading and talk, was calm and peaceful. I was in a state of quiet, even passive enjoyment, not actually thinking, but letting ideas, images, and emotions flow of themselves, as it were, through my mind. All at once, without warning of any kind, I found myself wrapped in a flame-coloured cloud. For an instant I thought of fire, an immense conflagration somewhere close by in that great city; the next instant I knew that that fire was in myself. Directly afterwards there came upon me a sense of exultation, of immense joyousness, accompanied or immediately followed by an intellectual illumination quite impossible to describe. Among other things, I did not merely come to believe, I saw that the universe is not composed of dead matter, but is, on the contrary, a living Presence; I became conscious in myself of eternal life. It was not a conviction that I would have eternal life, but a consciousness that I possessed eternal life then; I saw that all men are immortal; that the cosmic order is such that without any peradventure all things work together for the good of each and all; that the foundation principle of the world, of all the worlds, is what we call love, and that the happiness of each and all is in the long run certain. The vision lasted a few seconds and was gone; but the memory of it and the sense of the reality of it has remained during the quarter of a century which has since elapsed. I knew that what the vision showed was true. I had attained to a point of view from which I saw that it must be true. That view, that conviction, I may say that consciousness, has never, even during the periods of the deepest depression, been lost.

From William James, The Varieties of Religious Experience
(*Longmans, Green*)

*

The experience recorded below took place in a village church during the singing of the Te Deum. *It was of quite short duration. The* Te Deum *was still going on when it ended. The person who experienced it had had no psychical or mystical experience previously.*

While thus reflecting I caught sight, in the aisle at my side, of what resembled bluish smoke issuing from the chinks of the stone floor, as though from fire smouldering beneath. Looking more intently I saw it was not smoke, but something finer, more tenuous – a soft impalpable self-luminous haze of violet colour, unlike any physical vapour, and for which there was nothing to suggest a cause. Thinking I experienced some momentary optical defect or delusion, I turned my gaze farther along the aisle, but there too the same delicate haze was present. . . . I perceived the wonderful fact that it extended farther than the walls and roof of the building and was not confined by them. Through these I could now look and see the landscape beyond. . . . I saw all parts of my being simultaneously, not from my eyes only. . . . Yet for all this intensified perceptive power there was no loss of touch with my physical surroundings, no suspension of my faculties of sense. . . . I felt happiness and peace beyond words.

Upon that instant the luminous haze engulfing me and all around me became transformed into golden glory, into light untellable. . . . The golden light of which the violet haze seemed now to have been as the veil or outer fringe, welled forth from a central immense globe of brilliancy. . . . But the most wonderful thing was that these shafts and waves of light, that vast expanse of photosphere, and even the great central globe itself, were crowded to solidarity with the forms of living creatures . . . a single coherent organism filling all place and space, yet composed of an infinitude of individuated existences. . . . I saw, moreover, that those beings were present in teeming myriads in the church I stood in; that they were intermingled with and were passing unobstructedly through both myself and my fellow-worshippers. . . . The heavenly host drifted through the human congregation as wind passes through a grove of trees; beings of radiant beauty and clothed in shimmering raiment. . . .

But this vast spectacle of heaven and earth was succeeded by an even richer experience; one in which everything in time and space and form vanished from my consciousness and only the ineffable eternal things remained. . . . And as the point of a candle-flame leaps suddenly upward, when an object is held just above it, so the flame of my consciousness leapt to its utmost limit and passed into the region of the formless and uncreated to tell of which all words fail. . . . For a few moments of mortal time, which are no measure of the spirit's experience in the world immortal, all consciousness of my physical surroundings was withdrawn. . . .

Eventually, while thus rapt, the remembrance of the outer world from which my consciousness had been transported returned to me, like an old half-forgotten memory. The world and my recent surroundings were exhibited to me, but at a remote distance, as when one looks upon a scene through a reversed telescope. . . . Without shock or violence the consciousness which had been so highly exalted relapsed and sank to its normal limits and became adjusted to physical conditions; the spirit was returned to its fleshly sheath as a jewel is replaced in its casket after use and locked away. Once more I was standing in the church, perfectly well and unmoved.

From W. L. Wilmhurst, Contemplations (J. M. Watkins)

*

I remember the night, and almost the very spot on the hillside, where my soul opened out, as it were, into the Infinite, and there was a rushing together of the two worlds, the inner and the outer. It was deep calling unto deep – the deep that my own struggle had opened up within being answered by the unfathomable deep without, reaching beyond the stars. I stood alone with Him who had made me, and all the beauty of the world, and love, and sorrow, and even temptation. I did not seek Him, but felt the perfect union of my spirit with His. The ordinary sense of things around me faded. For the moment nothing but an ineffable joy and exaltation remained. It is impossible fully to describe the experience. It was like the effect of some great orchestra when all the separate notes have melted into one swelling harmony that leaves the listener conscious of nothing save that his soul is being wafted upwards, and almost bursting with its own emotion. The perfect stillness of the night was thrilled by a more solemn silence. The darkness held a presence that was all the more felt because it was not seen.

I could not any more have doubted that *He* was there than that
I was. Indeed, I felt myself to be, if possible, the less real of
the two.

My highest faith in God and truest idea of Him were then
born in me. I have stood upon the Mount of Vision since, and
felt the Eternal round about me. But never since has there come
quite the same stirring of the heart. Then, if ever, I believe,
I stood face to face with God, and was born anew of His spirit.

From William James, The Varieties of Religious Experience

*

I was in perfect health: we were on our sixth day of tramping
and in good training. We had come the day before from Sixt to
Trient by Buet. I felt neither fatigue, hunger, nor thirst, and
my state of mind was equally healthy. ... I can best describe
the condition in which I was by calling it a state of equilibrium.
When all at once I experienced a feeling of being raised above
myself, I felt the presence of God – I tell of the thing just as I
was conscious of it – as if his goodness and his power were
penetrating me altogether. The throb of emotion was so
violent that I could barely tell the boys to pass on and wait for
me. I then sat down on a stone, unable to stand any longer,
and my eyes overflowed with tears. ... Then, slowly, the
ecstasy left my heart; that is, I felt that God had withdrawn
the communion which he had granted, and I was able to walk
on, but very slowly, so strongly was I still possessed by the
interior emotion. ... The state of ecstasy might have lasted
four or five minutes, although it seemed at the time to last
much longer. ... I think I may add that in this ecstasy of mine
God had neither form, colour, odour, nor taste; moreover,
that the feeling of his presence was accompanied by no deter-
minate localization. It was rather as if my personality had been
transformed by the presence of a *spiritual spirit*. But the more
I seek words to express this intimate intercourse, the more I
feel the impossibility of describing the thing by any of the usual
images. At bottom the expression most apt to render what I
felt is this: God was present, though invisible; he fell under no
one of my senses, yet my consciousness perceived him.

From William James, The Varieties of Religious Experience

This experience happened to the Indian poet Rabindranath Tagore⁊ while he was standing watching the sun rise above the trees in a street in Calcutta. He told it to his friend C. F. Andrews, who records it in his collection of letters.

As I was watching it, suddenly, in a moment, a veil seemed to be lifted from my eyes. I found the world wrapt in an inexpressible glory with its waves of joy and beauty bursting and breaking on all sides. The thick cloud of sorrow that lay on my heart in many folds was pierced through and through by the light of the world, which was everywhere radiant. . . .

There was nothing and no one whom I did not love at that moment. . . . I stood on the veranda and watched the coolies as they tramped down the road. Their movements, their forms, their countenances seemed strangely wonderful to me, as if they were all moving like waves in the great ocean of the world. When one young man placed his hand upon the shoulder of another and passed laughingly by, it was a remarkable event to me. . . . I seemed to witness, in the wholeness of my vision, the movements of the body of all humanity, and to feel the beat of the music and the rhythm of a mystic dance.

From C. F. Andrews, Letters to a Friend (*Allen and Unwin*)

*

Perhaps Simone Weil merits a place in the main body of this anthology. She is, however, a particularly suitable choice to conclude this section. The spiritual autobiography of this talented girl, with her philosophical genius and rare powers of thought, who was born in Paris in 1909, is contained in the long letter (Letter IV in her book, Waiting on God*) which she wrote to her friend, the Dominican Father Perrin, before leaving France in 1942 and a little over a year before her death in England.*

It is a spiritual autobiography of peculiar interest for our times. In it she tells how, as an adolescent, though remaining within the Christian inspiration, she saw the problem of God as one insoluble for the human mind. So she decided to leave it alone, neither affirming nor denying anything. Prayer she avoided since she feared its power of suggestion; she desired above all to keep her intellectual integrity.

In 1938 she spent ten days, from Palm Sunday to Easter Tuesday, at Solesmes, following, in spite of the splitting headaches to which she was subject, all the liturgical services. There she met an English Catholic, who introduced her to the English metaphysical poets of the seventeenth century. Thus she came in contact with George Herbert's poem Love, *which she learnt by heart and used to recite to herself.*

It was during one of these recitations that, as I told you, Christ himself came down and took possession of me.

In my arguments about the insolubility of the problem of God I had never foreseen the possibility of that, of a real contact, person to person, here below, between a human being and God. I had vaguely heard tell of things of this kind, but I had never believed in them. In the *Fioretti* the accounts of apparitions rather put me off if anything, like the miracles in the Gospels. Moreover, in this sudden possession of me by Christ, neither my senses nor my imagination had any part; I only felt in the midst of my suffering the presence of a love, like that which one can read in the smile of a beloved face. . . . God in his mercy had prevented me from reading the mystics, so that it should be evident to me that I had not invented this absolutely unexpected contact.

Yet I still half refused, not my love but my intelligence. For it seemed to me certain, and I still think so today, that one cannot wrestle enough with God if one does it out of pure regard for truth. Christ likes us to prefer truth to him because, being Christ, he is truth. If one turns aside from him to go towards truth, one will not go far before falling into his arms.

To some an experience of this sort comes only once in a lifetime. With Simone Weil it was not isolated. She used to say the 'Our Father' in Greek every morning with absolute attention and often while she was working in the vineyard.

At times the very first words tear my thoughts from my body and transport it to a place outside space where there is neither perspective nor point of view. The infinity of the ordinary expanses of perception is replaced by an infinity to the second or sometimes the third degree. At the same time, filling every part of this infinity of infinity, there is a silence, a silence which is not an absence of sound but which is the object of a positive sensation, more positive than that of sound. Noises, if there are any, only reach me after crossing the silence.

Sometimes, also, during this recitation or at other moments, Christ is present with me in person, but his presence is infinitely more real, more moving, more clear than on the first occasion he took possession of me.

This is a description of mystical prayer at the stage of the Prayer of Quiet, or beyond. Simone Weil had become a true mystic. Those who read her story may say, perhaps, that she had become a saint. Yet, and this is her particular interest for our times, she refused to be baptized into the Church which she loved. In her letter to Father Perrin she gives her reasons. For her Plato was a mystic, Dionysius and Osiris in a certain sense Christ himself, the Bhagavad Gita *a revelation of God. Christianity, she felt, was catholic by right but not in fact, not a truly incarnated Christianity; too much was outside it.*

Having so intense and painful a sense of this urgency, I should betray the truth, that is to say the aspect of truth which I see, if I left the point, where I have been since my birth, at the intersection of Christianity and everything that is not Christian.

I have always remained at this exact point, on the threshold of the Church, without moving, quite still ἐν ὑπομένη (it is so much more beautiful a word than *patientia*); only now my heart has been transported, for ever, I hope, into the Blessed Sacrament exposed on the altar.

From Simone Weil, Waiting on God, *trans. by Emma Cranford*
(Routledge and Kegan Paul)

2. There is Nothing that is not Spirit

THE UPANISHADS

THE *Vedas, the oldest sacred literature of Hinduism, were composed from about 1500 to 1000 B.C. They consist for the most part of hymns in praise of personified elements, sacrificial prayers and hymns, and incantations against the powers of evil. They represent a comparatively primitive stage of religious development.*

Sometime before 500 B.C. a profound change took place in the religious consciousness of India, a great leap forward in spiritual insight occurred, analogous to those advances in the human mind which were happening at approximately the same time in Palestine and Greece. This change of religious outlook found its expression in the Upanishads.

If one seeks in the Upanishads for any consistent system of doctrine, one will not find it. What one finds is a series of gropings, some of the earlier ones crude, for answers to fundamental metaphysical questions: What is the nature of reality? What is the self of which man is conscious? What is God? Some of the Upanishads take the form of dialogues, in which various questions are posed and answers suggested. The quest on which these spiritual explorers were engaged is summed up in the beautiful prayer in the Brihadaranyaka-Upanishad:

> *Lead me from the unreal to the real;*
> *Lead me from darkness to light;*
> *Lead me from death to immortality.*

Out of this groping emerged something of immense significance, the most profound and revolutionary statement on the nature of reality which mankind had as yet made.

The basic teaching of the Upanishads has been discussed more than once in the course of our Study. In order, however, that the reader may the better understand the passages which follow, it may be useful to summarize it again here.

Everything has its origin and being in Spirit, 'the seed of all seeds'. Everything in the world is a manifestation of Spirit. There is nothing in the world which is not God, everlasting Spirit.

What then is man? Not the phenomenal, transient ego, the bundle of ever-changing memories, sensations, and physical transformations of which he is mainly conscious. His real self is the Atman, the Greater Self, unborn, changeless, and immortal, the Thou. As in the doctrine of Plotinus, the Atman is a Universal as well as a personal Self. Not only that, it is in its essence one with Everlasting Spirit, Brahman, God, the That, the Self which is behind, indeed is, every Self.

Most translations of the Upanishads into English are cumbrous and difficult to understand. The passages printed below are taken from The Ten Principal Upanishads, *beautifully and clearly put into English by Shree Purohit Swami and the Irish poet, W. B. Yeats.* From them the essential insights, which the Upanishads strive to express, will become clear. Where confusion may possibly arise in the reader's mind is in the use of the word, 'self', sometimes written with a small, sometimes with a capital letter. The word is used in four ways, in reference to the ephemeral, phenomenal self, always written with a small 's'; to the two aspects of Atman as a personal and as a universal impersonal Self, usually written with a capital, but occasionally, in the translation used, with a small 's', when it refers to the personal self; and to Brahman, Spirit, the undifferentiated Godhead. In some of the passages quoted the word refers to both Atman and Brahman at the same time.*

Let it be remembered that Hindu thought and expression is non-dualistic. It apprehends the reality of the Self without as identical with the Self within. Thou (Atman) is That (Brahman); everything is one Self. This approach is summed up in the last passage from the Brihadaranyaka-Upanishad quoted below.

I have felt it best to arrange the passages under the titles of the Upanishads in which they appear, so that the whole section reads like a series of variations on the same theme.

The Self is one. Unmoving, it moves faster than the mind. The

* Reprinted with the permission of The Macmillan Company (first published in 1937 by Faber and Faber Ltd).

senses lag, but Self runs ahead. Unmoving, it outruns pursuit. Out of Self comes the breath that is the life of all things.

Unmoving, it moves; is far away, yet near; within all, outside all.

The Self is everywhere, without a body, without a shape, whole, pure, wise, all knowing, far shining, self-depending, all transcending; in the eternal procession assigning to every period its proper duty.

From the Isha-Upanishad

Who says that Spirit is not known, knows; who claims that he knows, knows nothing. The ignorant think that Spirit lies within knowledge, the wise man knows It beyond knowledge. Spirit is known through revelation. The living man who finds Spirit, finds Truth.

From the Kena-Upanishad

The Self knows all, is not born, does not die, is not the effect of any cause; is eternal, self-existent, imperishable, ancient. How can the killing of the body kill Him?

He who thinks that He kills, he who thinks that He is killed, is ignorant. He does not kill nor is He killed.

The Self is lesser than the least, greater than the greatest. He lives in all hearts.

The individual self and the universal Self, living in the heart, like shade and light, though beyond enjoyment, enjoy the result of action. All say this, all who know Spirit.

He who calls intellect to manage the reins of his mind reaches the end of his journey, finds there all-pervading Spirit.

Above the senses are the objects of desire, above the objects of desire mind, above the mind intellect, above the intellect manifest nature.

Above manifest nature the unmanifest seed, above the unmanifest seed, God. God is the goal; beyond Him nothing.

God does not proclaim Himself, He is everybody's secret, but the intellect of the sage has found Him.

Eternal creation is a tree, with roots above, branches on the ground; pure eternal Spirit, living in all things and beyond whom none can go; that is Self.

From the Katha-Upanishad

My son! There is nothing in this world, that is not God. He is action, purity; everlasting Spirit. Find Him in the cavern; gnaw the knot of ignorance.

Shining, yet hidden, Spirit lives in the cavern. Everything that sways, breathes, opens, closes, lives in Spirit; beyond learning, beyond everything, better than anything; living, unliving.

It is the undying blazing Spirit, that seed of all seeds, wherein lay hidden the world and all its creatures. It is life, speech, mind, reality, immortality.

In a beautiful golden scabbard hides the stainless, indivisible, luminous Spirit.

Neither sun, moon, star, neither fire nor lightning, lights Him. When He shines, everything begins to shine. Everything in the world reflects His light.

Spirit is everywhere, upon the right, upon the left, above, below, behind, in front. What is the world but Spirit?

Two birds, bound one to another in friendship, have made their homes on the same tree. One stares about him, one pecks at the sweet fruit.

The personal self, weary of pecking here and there, sinks into dejection; but when he understands through meditation that the other – the impersonal Self – is indeed Spirit, dejection disappears.

He who has found Spirit, is Spirit.

From the Mundaka-Upanishad

There is nothing that is not Spirit. The personal self is the impersonal Spirit.

The Self is the lord of all; inhabitant of the hearts of all. He is the source of all; creator and dissolver of beings. There is nothing He does not know.

He is not knowable by perception, turned inward or outward, nor by both combined. He is neither that which is known, nor that which is not known, nor is He the sum of all that might be known. He cannot be seen, grasped, bargained with. He is undefinable, unthinkable, indescribable.

The only proof of His existence is union with Him. The world disappears in Him. He is the peaceful, the good, the one without a second.

From the Mandookya-Upanishad

'Put this salt into water, see me tomorrow morning,' said Uddālaka. Shwetaketu did as he was told.

Uddālaka said: 'Bring me the salt you put into water last night.'

Shwetaketu looked, but could not find it. The salt had dissolved.

Uddālaka asked his son how the top of the water tasted.

Shwetaketu said: 'It is salt.'

Uddālaka asked how the middle of the water tasted.

Shwetaketu said: 'It is salt.'

Uddālaka asked how the bottom of the water tasted.

Shwetaketu said: 'It is salt.'

Uddālaka said: 'Throw away the water; come to me.'

Shwetaketu did as he was told and said: 'The salt will always remain in the water.'

Uddālaka said: 'My son! Though you do not find that Being in the world, He is there.

'That Being is the seed; all else but His expression. He is truth. He is Self. Shwetaketu! You are That. . . .'

In this body, in this town of Spirit, there is a little house shaped like a lotus, and in that house there is a little space. One should know what is there.

What is there? Why is it so important?

There is as much in that little space within the heart as there is in the whole world outside. Heaven, earth, fire, wind, sun, moon, lightning, stars; whatever is and whatever is not, everything is there.

If everything is in man's body, every being, every desire,

what remains when old age comes, when decay begins, when the body falls?

What lies in that space does not decay when the body decays, nor does it fall when the body falls. That space is the home of Spirit. Every desire is there. Self is there, beyond decay and death; sin and sorrow; hunger and thirst; His aim truth; His will truth.

From the Chhandogya-Upanishad

This Self is nearer than all else; dearer than son, dearer than wealth, dearer than anything. If a man call anything dearer than Self, say that he will lose what is dear; of a certainty he will lose it; for Self is God. Therefore one should worship Self as Love. Who worships Self as Love, his love never shall perish.

It is said everything can be got through the knowledge of Spirit. What is that knowledge?

In the beginning there was Spirit. It knew itself as Spirit; from that knowledge everything sprang up. He who knows that he is Spirit, becomes Spirit, becomes everything.

For as long as there is duality, one sees the other, one smells the other, one hears the other, one speaks to the other, one thinks of the other, one knows the other; but when everything is one Self, who can see another, how can he see another; who can smell another, how can he smell another; who can hear another, how can he hear another; who can speak to another, how can he speak to another; who can think of another, how can he think of another; who can know another, how can he know another? Maitreyi! How can the knower be known?

From the Brihadaranyaka-Upanishad

3. The Tao Which Can Be Spoken Is Not The True Tao

THE TAO TE CHING

IN general the philosophy of Ancient China was essentially practical. Confucius (551–479 B.C.), its outstanding and most influential figure, taught a system of personal and social ethics which was not based on a belief in any sort of Transcendent Reality. In every culture, however, a mystical strain always appears. Its supreme expression in ancient Chinese thought is in the book known as Tao te Ching. *Both the date and authorship of the book are obscure. It is commonly attributed to Lao-Tzu, who lived some fifty years before Confucius. It is possible, however, that later elements were incorporated. For our purpose it does not matter very much.*

The Tao te Ching *is a 'poetical' work; one might call it mystical poetry, for its thought is definitely in the tradition of mysticism. It consists of a collection of often paradoxical aphorisms. To build up a short anthology out of these aphorisms is made difficult owing to the obscurity of the exact meaning of the original and the difficulty of translating it. To read through different translations of the* Tao te Ching *is sometimes to wonder whether one is reading a translation of the same work at all.*

The key concept is that of Tao. *Though Tao is sometimes translated the Way, in its transcendental aspect it is the Primal Meaning, the Undivided Unity, which lies behind all phenomena. The phenomenal world that we know is seen as a coming-out of Tao through the breaking up of the Undivided Unity of Tao into the polar opposites of yang and yin, light and darkness, which dominate and determine all human perception. Nothing can be realized except in relation to its opposite. One cannot realize light except in relation to dark, masculine except in relation to feminine (yang is the masculine, the light, yin the feminine, the dark, principle in the universe), before except in relation to after, good except in relation to evil etc. These polar opposites, however, exist only in the phenomenal world. They do not exist in Tao, the Undivided Unity, to which the spiritual man longs to return. This doctrine of the coincidence of opposites (contradictories) in an Ultimate Reality is stressed in the teaching of Nicholas of Cusa (see Section 25).*

The word, Tao, is sometimes quite accurately translated 'the Way'. In the Tao Te Ching the word has a double meaning. In addition to its transcendental aspect, Tao is a way of life bound up with a moral principle or 'virtue' inherent in the very nature of the cosmos. One who has realized Tao is impelled to lead a particular sort of life, the life of 'actionless activity':

> ††This is why the sage abides by actionless activity,
>   And puts into practice wordless teaching.
>   Since all things have been made, he does not
>   turn his back on them:
>   Since they have life, he does not own them:
>   Since they act, he does not entrust himself to them.
>   When he has achieved any success, he does not stay by it,
>   In this not staying by his success he is unique;
>   And this is why he is not deprived of it.

In the passages printed below I have used the translation by Lionel Giles in The Sayings of Lao Tzu (Wisdom of the East Series, published by John Murray), except for those passages marked **, which are taken from J. J. L. Duyvendak's edition of Tao Te Ching (also John Murray), and those marked ††, which are from E. R. Hughes' Chinese Philosophy in Classical Times (Everyman Library, Dent).

The Tao which can be expressed in words is not the eternal Tao; the name which can be uttered is not the eternal name. Without a name it is the Beginning of Heaven and Earth; with a name, it is the Mother of all things. Only one who is ever free of desire can apprehend its spiritual essence; he who is ever a slave to desire can see no more than its outer fringe. These two things, the spiritual and the material, though we call them by different names, in their origin are one and the same. This sameness is a mystery – the mystery of mysteries. It is the gate of all wonders.*

How unfathomable is Tao! It seems to be the ancestral progenitor of all things. How pure and clear is Tao! It would seem to be everlasting. I know not of whom it is the offspring.

Tao eludes the sense of sight, and is therefore called colourless. It eludes the sense of hearing and is therefore called soundless. It eludes the sense of touch and is therefore called incorporeal. These three qualities cannot be apprehended, and hence may be blended into a unity.

---

* This first chapter of the *Tao Te Ching* (or *King*) is the key to the whole book. In order to assist the reader to understand it, two other translations are printed below:

**The Way that may truly be regarded as the Way is other than a permanent Way.

The terms that may be regarded as terms are other than permanent terms.

The term Non-Being indicates the beginning of heaven and earth; the term Being indicates the mother of the ten thousand things.

For indeed it is through the constant alternations between Non-Being and Being that the wonder of the one, and the limitation of the other will be seen.

These two, having a common origin, are named with different terms.

What they have in common is called the Mystery, the Mystery of Mysteries, the Gate of all Wonders.

††If the Tao could be comprised in words, it would not be the unchangeable Tao:

(For) if a name may be named, it is not an unchangeable name.

When the Tao had no name, that was the starting point of heaven and earth.

Then when it had a name, this was the mother of creation.

Because this is so, to be constantly without desire is the way to have a vision of the mystery (of heaven and earth).

For constantly to have desire is the means by which their limitations are seen.

These two entities although they have different names emerge together;

And (emerging) together means 'in the very beginning'.

But the very beginning has also a beginning before it began – this door into all mystery!

Yet another translation of the first sentence is:

The Tao which can be spoken is not the true Tao.

From of old until now, its name has never passed away. It watches over the beginning of all things. How do I know this about the beginning of things? Through Tao.

Man takes his law from the Earth; the Earth takes its law from Heaven; Heaven takes its law from Tao; but the law of Tao is its own spontaneity.

As soon as Tao creates order, it becomes nameable.

All-pervading is the Great Tao. It can be at once on the right hand and on the left. All things depend on it for life, and it rejects them not. . . . It loves and nourishes all things. . . . All things return to it.

All things under Heaven are products of Being, but Being itself is the product of Not-Being.

Tao is a great square with no angles, a great vessel which takes long to complete, a great sound which cannot be heard, a great image with no form.

Tao lies hid and cannot be named, yet it has the power of transmitting and perfecting all things.

Tao produced Unity; Unity produced Duality; Duality produced Trinity; and Trinity produced all existing objects. These myriad objects leave darkness behind them and embrace the light, being harmonized by contact with the Vital Force.

††Everyone in the world recognizes beauty as beauty, and thus ugliness (is known).

Everyone recognizes the good as good, and thus what is not good (is known).

And indeed,
Being and Non-Being produce one another,
Hard and easy complete one another,
Long and short are relative to one another,
High and low are dependent on one another,
Tones and voice harmonize with one another,
First and last succeed one another.

** Though thirty spokes may be joined on one hub, the utility of the carriage lies in what is not there.

Though clay may be moulded into a vase, the utility of the vase lies in what is not there.

Though doors and windows may be cut to make a house, the utility of the house lies in what is not there.

Therefore, taking advantage of what is, we recognize the utility of what is not.

The Way of Heaven is like the drawing of a bow; it brings down what is high and raises what is low.

It is the Way of Heaven to take from those who have too much and to give it to those who have too little. But the way of man is not so. He takes away from those who have too little, to add to his own superabundance. What man is there that can take of his own superabundance and give it to mankind. Only he who possesses Tao.

4. The Mysticism of Loving Faith and Selfless Action

THE BHAGAVAD GITA

MAGNIFICENT *as were the insights enshrined in the Upanishads, something was lacking. Their mysticism was primarily a mysticism of knowledge and understanding; it lacked the element of love and, further, did not lead logically to a mysticism of action. The goal was deliverance from the melancholy wheel of death and birth; action was shunned as an inevitable source of bondage.*

Sometime between 100 B.C. and A.D. 200 – the date is uncertain – the poem, the Bhagavad Gita, *the 'Song of God', was composed, perhaps by one, perhaps by several individuals. It added what was absent in the Upanishads. It humanized God and redeemed action. It quickly took its place among the sacred books of India and its influence down the centuries has been profound.*

The doctrine of the Gita *is not consistent throughout. Its fundamental teaching is, however, clear. It is summed up in the following words of Krishna, the Indian incarnation of God, to Prince Arjuna:*

'The world is imprisoned in its own activity, except when actions are performed as worship of God. Therefore you must perform every action sacramentally, and be free of all attachment to results. . . .

'Mentally resign all your action to me. Regard me as your dearest loved one. Know me as your only refuge. Be united always in heart and consciousness to me. United with me, you shall overcome all difficulties by my grace. . . .

'The Lord lives in the heart of every creature. He turns them round and round on the wheel of his Maya. Take refuge utterly in him. By his grace you will find supreme peace, and the state which is beyond all change.'

Here, in addition to a mysticism of action, we have a mysticism of faith – the Indian word for it is 'bhakti', which has been translated 'loving faith' – and of action. The insights of the Upanishads are not superseded; they are extended.

The mysticism of the Upanishads and, even more so, the mysticism of Theravada Buddhism, lacked warmth and humanity. The heart can never rest content with the conclusions of the head; it demands love as well as wisdom. The possibility of love of God was absent and, particularly in Theravada Buddhism, the demands on ordinary folk were too great. What was missing was now added, and not in the Gita alone. For the Gita coincides approximately in time with the development of Mahayana Buddhism, with its Bodhisattva ideal. The Bodhisattva, who has attained a state of supreme wisdom and has won his blessedness, whose essential nature is a great loving heart and whose love embraces all sentient beings, is able, through loving faith in him, to act as a mediator between God and man and so assist ordinary men on their path to Nirvana.

Later we shall see, in the Christo-mysticism of St Paul, bhakti mysticism in its most profound manifestation.

The text used is that of The Bhagavad-Gita, Song of God, translated by Swami Prabhavananda and Christopher Isherwood (Phoenix House).

THE WAY OF SELFLESS ACTION

ARJUNA: But, Krishna, if you consider knowledge of Brahman superior to any sort of action, why are you telling me to do these terrible deeds?

Your statements seem to contradict each other. They confuse my mind. Tell me one definite way of reaching the highest good.

KRISHNA: I have already told you that, in this world, aspirants may find enlightenment by two different paths. For the contemplative is the path of knowledge; for the active is the path of selfless action.

Freedom from activity is never achieved by abstaining from action.

Nobody can become perfect by merely ceasing to act. In fact, nobody can ever rest from his activity* even

---

* Here 'activity' includes mental action, conscious and subconscious.

for a moment. All are helplessly forced to act, by the gunas.*

A man who renounces certain physical actions but still lets his mind dwell on the objects of his sensual desire, is deceiving himself. He can only be called a hypocrite. The truly admirable man controls his senses by the power of his will. All his actions are disinterested. All are directed along the path to union with Brahman.

Activity is better than inertia. Act, but with self-control. If you are lazy, you cannot even sustain your own body.

The world is imprisoned in its own activity, except when actions are performed as worship of God. Therefore you must perform every action sacramentally, and be free from all attachment to results.

> In the beginning
> The Lord of beings
> Created all men
> To each his duty.
> 'Do this,' he said
> 'And you shall prosper.
> Duty well done
> Fulfils desire.'

> *

> The ignorant work
> For the fruit of their action:
> The wise must work also
> Without desire
> Pointing man's feet
> To the path of his duty.

* The three forces of Prakriti, the power of Brahman as the basis of all mind and matter, called *sattwa*, *rajas*, and *tamas*. Psychologically *sattwa* manifests itself as tranquillity and purity, *rajas* as passion and aggressive action, *tamas* as stupidity and sloth. All are present in the psychological make-up of each individual and influence the way he acts, one or other predominating. None is, however, his true self.

Let the wise beware
Lest they bewilder
The minds of the ignorant
Hungry for action:
Let them show by example
How work is holy
When the heart of the worker
Is fixed on the Highest.

*

Seer and leader,
Provider and server:
Each has the duty
Ordained by his nature
Born of the gunas.

The seer's duty,
Ordained by his nature,
Is to be tranquil
In mind and in spirit,
Self-controlled,
Austere and stainless,
Upright, forbearing;
To follow wisdom,
To know the Atman,
Firm of faith
In the truth that is Brahman.

The leader's duty,
Ordained by his nature,
Is to be bold,
Unflinching and fearless,
Subtle of skill
And open-handed,
Great-hearted in battle,
A resolute ruler.

Others are born
To the tasks of providing:

These are the traders,
The cultivators,
The breeders of cattle.

To work for all men,
Such is the duty
Ordained for the servers:
This is their nature.

All mankind
Is born for perfection;
And each shall attain it
Will he but follow
His nature's duty.

THE WAY OF LOVING FAITH

Now you shall hear how a man may become perfect, if he devotes himself to the work which is natural to him. A man will reach perfection if he does his duty as an act of worship to the Lord, who is the source of the universe, prompting all action, everywhere present.

When a man has achieved non-attachment, self-mastery, and freedom from desire through renunciation, he reaches union with Brahman, who is beyond all action.

Mentally resign all your action to me. Regard me as your dearest loved one. Know me to be your only refuge. Be united always in heart and consciousness with me.

United with me, you shall overcome all difficulties by my grace. But if your heart is full of conceit, and you do not heed me, you are lost. If, in your vanity, you say: 'I will not fight,' your resolve is vain. Your own nature will drive you to the act. For you yourself have created the karma that binds you. You are helpless in its power. And you will do that very thing which your ignorance seeks to avoid.

The Lord lives in the heart of every creature. He turns them round and round upon the wheel of his Maya. Take refuge utterly in him. By his grace you will find supreme peace, and the state which is beyond all change.

5. Emptiness and Compassion

BUDDHIST MYSTICISM

TO compile an anthology which will give a clear idea of the mystical elements in a faith which has been called the most mystical and the least mystical of all the higher religions, the most spiritual religion and not a religion at all, is not an easy task. Further, there are so many schools of Buddhism and the corpus of Buddhist scriptures is a huge one.

Theravada Buddhism, the Little Vehicle, the Old Wisdom School, is not primarily mystical in any real sense; it is essentially a way of life, a code of ethics, of great beauty and depth. The Mahayana School of Buddhism, the Greater Vehicle, the New Wisdom School, took the teaching of the original Theravada school as its foundation, reinterpreted and extended it, and gave it a cosmic and often mystical flavour. It is in Mahayana Buddhism that one finds a mystical interpretation of the Buddhist Faith, expressed in various forms, but with an underlying unity.

One of the difficulties for the Westerner in his effort to understand Buddhism is the particular language in which so many Buddhist writings are couched. It is often a language of paradox and non-duality. One is called upon to penetrate through this paradoxical, non-dualistic language to get at the inner meaning. This will be evident in some of the examples of Buddhist writings which are given below. Those, however, who are familiar with the writings of such Christian mystics as Dionysius the Areopagite, Eckhart and Ruysbroeck (see Sections 11, 18 and 19) will find the key to understanding.

The language of Buddhist mysticism is not the language of logic, but that of a not uncommon type of mystical expression. Consider, for example, these verses of the Zen Buddhist, Hsuan-chiao:

> *You cannot take hold of it, nor can you get rid of it;*
> *While you can do neither, it goes on its own way;*
> *You remain silent and it speaks, you speak and it is silent;*
> *The great gate of charity is wide open with no obstruction*
> *whatever before it.*

While Buddhism does not recognize a 'God' of the sort found in the theologies of religions such as Christianity and Islam, at the heart of the deepest Buddhist insight and spirituality there is some non-personal Ultimate Reality, a Primal Meaning, an Undivided Unity. It is found in the concept of the Void, *which resembles the Godhead of Eckhart, and the* Dharmakaya, *which has affinities with the* Tao *of the Chinese mystical tradition and perhaps with the mystical interpretation of the* Torah *of Judaism. This 'Deity', this Buddhist God-image, can only be realized in that ultimate mystical experience in which all images, all mental processes, all forms, fade away in a bare, undifferentiated awareness.*

If one is called upon to give a label to the most significant type of Buddhist mysticism one might call it the mysticism of the Void *or of* Emptiness *or of* Non-duality. *One might call it a metaphysical mysticism; or mystical metaphysics.*

Perhaps the most important Buddhist scripture in which the doctrine of Emptiness is set out is the Mahayana Heart Sutra, *the quintessence of the vast* Prajna-Paramita *literature, which is concerned with 'the Wisdom which has gone beyond'. If, on his first reading of it the reader finds himself lost and bewildered, his puzzlement is understandable. It is strange reading. Its meaning may perhaps become clearer if one compares the thought and mode of expression of the* Heart Sutra *with those of Meister Eckhart.*

In different ways, at different times, Eckhart writes of what he calls 'the birth of Christ in the soul'. This birth is, for Eckhart, a profound inner mystical experience, 'a noble birth' which takes place in what, following other Christian mystics, he calls the core *or* essence, *or the* apex, *or the* summit *of the soul. Some Christian mystics have called it the* centre *or* spark *of the soul, or the* ground *of the spirit. It is, in Eckhart's words, 'the central silence, the pure peace and abode of the heavenly birth'. In order to bring about this 'noble birth' consciousness must be stripped of all its empirical contents, of all sensations, images and thought processes; it must become 'empty', a 'pure self' in which the ego has discarded all ideas of multiplicity and differentiation. This pure self is identical with the* Essence of Mind *which, in the scripture,* The Awakening of Faith, *is defined as an ultimate purity and unity, a wholeness which embraces everything, which is uncreated and eternal:*

'*If the mind could be kept free from discriminative thinking there would be no more arbitrary thoughts to give rise to appearances of form, existences and conditions.*'

Emptiness may be thought of as God, or a form of realization of God, in His negative aspect, the Godhead of Meister Eckhart, the Void (sunyata) of Buddhism. Eckhart and other mystics of his school call it a desert, *a* barren wilderness, *or a* waste; *sometimes Eckhart uses the phrase '*the barren Godhead*'.*

Yet this negative Godhead, this Void, has a positive aspect. In Christianity It manifests Itself in the Unity of the Holy Trinity, which is not a 'mode' or 'aspect' of Deity, but the outpouring of the un-knowable, ineffable, attributeless Godhead Itself. In Buddhism the 'emptiness' of the Void is experience as a Plenum-Void; *para-doxically the Emptiness is also a Fullness. In Its Darkness and Nothingness there glows not only the dazzling light of Ultimate Reality but also a new vision of the material world. At the heart of the mystical quest of Buddhism, as of every other supreme mystical quest, is the urge to realize this highest of all spiritual experiences.*

That, however, is not the whole picture. At the centre of Buddhist spirituality there is something else, which stems from the urge which impelled the Buddha to forsake the luxuries of his palace, even his beloved Yasôdhara, a vast compassion for suffering humanity. In Buddhist writings two words are used, metta *and* karuna. Metta *carries the meaning of loving kindness, benevolence, friendliness and affection. It is an attitude of mind to be cultivated so that it may influence disposition and action.* Karuna *is something different and higher. It is the supreme virtue, an inherent spiritual quality, similar to the* agapē [caritas, *love) of St Paul's great hymn to Love (I Corin-thians XIII). In Buddhism it finds its supreme expression in the Great Renunciation of the Bodhisattva, the vow to relinquish the blessedness which has been won, so long as any sentient being remains in sorrow and ignorance.*

Since any short anthology of the mystical element in Buddhism must of necessity be selective, in the passages I have chosen I have concen-trated on the elements of Emptiness, Non-duality and Compassion.

The translations of the Heart Sutra (No. 1) *and of the* Metta-Sutra [No. 8), *are those of Edward Conze, printed in his* Buddhist Scriptures (Penguin Books). *All the other passages are taken, with his permission, from Christmas Humphreys' anthology,* The Wisdom of Buddhism (*Michael Joseph*). *The books from which the passages were originally taken are as follows: No. 2, from* The Path of Light, *trans. by D. L. Barnett (John Murray); No. 3 from* Buddhist Texts through the Ages *by Edward Conze (Bruno Cassirer); Nos. 4 and 5 from* Manual of Zen Buddhism *by D. T. Suzuki (Eastern Buddhist Society); No. 6 from* The Dhammapada, *a New Version by J. A. (Buddhist Society, London); No. 7a from* The Sutra of Wei Lang (*Hui Neng*), *trans. by Wong Mou-Iam (Luzac); Nos. 7b and 10 from* The Voice of the Silence, *trans. by H. P. B. (Theosophical Publishing Coy.); No. 9 from* The Buddha's Philosophy *by G. F. Allen (Allen and Unwin).*

I. THE HEART SUTRA

(i) *The invocation.* Homage to the Perfection of Wisdom, the lovely, the holy!

(ii) *The prologue.* Avalokita, the holy Lord and Bodhisattva, was moving in the deep course of the wisdom which has gone beyond. He looked down from on high, he held but five heaps, and he saw that in their own-being they were empty.

(iii) *The dialectics of emptiness. First stage.* Here, O Sariputra, form is emptiness, and the very emptiness is form; emptiness does not differ from form, form does not differ from emptiness; whatever is form, that is emptiness, whatever is emptiness, that is form. The same is true of feelings, perceptions, impulses, and consciousness.

(iv) *The dialectics of emptiness. Second stage.* Here, O Sariputra, all dharmas are marked with emptiness; they are not produced or stopped, not defiled or immaculate, not deficient or complete.

(v) *The dialectics of emptiness. Third stage.* Therefore, O Sariputra, in emptiness there is no form, nor feeling, nor perception, nor impulse, nor consciousness; no eye, ear, nose, tongue, body, mind; no forms, sounds, smells, tastes, touchables or objects of mind; no sight-organ-element, and so forth, until we come to: no mind-consciousness-element; there is no ignorance, no extinction of ignorance, and so forth, until we come to: there is no decay and death, no extinction of decay and death; there is no suffering, no origination, no stopping, no path; there is no cognition, no attainment, and no non-attainment.

(iv) *The concrete embodiment and practical basis of emptiness.* Therefore, O Sariputra, it is because of his indifference to any kind of personal attainment that a Bodhisattva, through having relied on the perfection of wisdom, dwells without thought-coverings. In the absence of thought-coverings he has not been made to tremble, he has overcome what can upset, and in the end he attains to Nirvana.

(vii) *Full emptiness is the basis also of Buddhahood.* All those who appear as Buddhas in the three periods of time fully awake to the utmost, right and perfect enlightenment because they have relied on the perfection of wisdom.

(viii) *The teaching brought within reach of the comparatively un-enlightened.* Therefore one should know the Prajñaparamita as the great spell, the spell of great knowledge, the utmost spell, the unequalled spell,* allayer of all suffering, in truth – for what could go wrong? By the Prajñaparamita has this spell been delivered. It runs like this: Gone, Gone, Gone beyond, Gone altogether beyond, O what an awakening, All Hail!

This completes the Heart of Perfect Wisdom.

2. THE PERFECT KNOWLEDGE

We deem that there are two verities, the Veiled Truth and the Transcendent Reality. The Reality is beyond the range of the understanding; the understanding is called Veiled Truth ...

from The Path of Light

3. BEYOND THOUGHT

A thought is like the stream of a river, without any staying power; as soon as it is produced it breaks up and disappears. A thought is like the flame of a lamp, and it proceeds through causes and conditions. A thought is like lightning, it breaks up

* or mantra.

in a moment and does not stay on. Thought is like space, and it is defiled by adventitious defilements. Thought is like a bad friend, for it generates all kind of ill. Thought is like a fish-hook, which looks pleasant although it is not. Thought is like a blue-bottle-fly, because it looks for what is lovely in what is not. Thought is like an enemy, because it inflicts much agony. Thought, though one searches for it all around, cannot be found. What cannot be found, that cannot be apprehended. What cannot be apprehended, that cannot be past, future or present. What is not past, future or present, that is beyond the three dimensions of time. What is beyond the three dimensions of time, that neither is nor is not. . . .

4. ON TRUST IN THE HEART

The perfect way knows no difficulties
Except that it refuses to make preferences;
Only when freed from hate and love
It reveals itself fully and without disguise;
A tenth of an inch's difference,
And heaven and earth are set apart.
If you wish to see it before your own eyes
Have no fixed thoughts either for or against it.

To set up what you like against what you dislike –
That is the disease of the mind:
When the deep meaning (of the Way) is not understood
Peace of mind is disturbed to no purpose.

(The Way) is perfect like unto vast space,
With nothing wanting, nothing superfluous,
It is indeed due to making choice
That its Suchness is lost sight of.

Pursue not the outer entanglements,
Dwell not in the inner Void;
Be serene in the oneness of things,
And dualism vanishes by itself.

When you strive to gain quiescence by stopping motion,
The quiescence thus gained is ever in motion;
As long as you tarry in the dualism,
How can you realize oneness?

And when oneness is not thoroughly understood,
In two ways loss is sustained:
The denying of reality is the asserting of it,
And the asserting of emptiness is the denying of it.*

Wordiness and intellection –
The more with them, the further astray we go;
Away therefore with wordiness and intellection,
And there is no place where we cannot pass freely.

When we return to the root, we gain the meaning;
When we pursue external objects we lose the reason.
The moment we are lightened within,
We go beyond the voidness of a world confronting us.

Transformations going on in an empty world which
    confronts us
Appear real all because of ignorance:
Try not to seek after the true,
Only cease to cherish opinions.

Abide not with dualism,
Carefully avoid pursuing it;
As soon as you have right and wrong,
Confusion ensues, and Mind† is lost.

The two exist because of the One,
But hold not even to this One;

    * This verse means that when the absolute oneness of things is not
understood, both affirmation and negation tend to be one-sided views of
reality.
    † In the sense not of psychological mind, but of absolute mind or Mind.
The Chinese word could also be translated 'heart', 'soul' or 'spirit'.

When a mind is not disturbed,
The ten thousand things offer no offence.

No offence offered, and no ten thousand things;
No disturbance going, and no mind set up to work;
The subject is quieted when the object ceases,
The object ceases when the subject is quieted.

The object is an object for the subject,
The subject is a subject for the object;
Know that the relativity of the two
Rests ultimately on one emptiness.

In one emptiness the two are not distinguished,
And each contains in itself all the ten thousand things;
When no discrimination is made between this and that,
How can a one-sided and prejudiced view arise?

The Great Way is calm and large-hearted,
For it nothing is easy, nothing hard;
Small views are irresolute, the more in haste, the tardier
    they go.

Clinging is never kept within bounds,
It is sure to go the wrong way;
Quit it, and things follow their own courses,
While the essence neither departs not abides.

Obey the nature of things, and you are in concord with
The Way, calm and easy, and free from annoyance;
But when your thoughts are tied, you turn away from the
    truth,
They grow heavier and duller, and are not at all sound.

When they are not sound, the spirit is troubled;
What is the use of being partial and one-sided then?
If you want to walk the course of the One Vehicle,
Be not prejudiced against the six sense-objects.

When you are not prejudiced against the six sense-objects,
You are then one with the enlightenment.
The wise are non-active,
While the ignorant bind themselves up;
While in the Dharma itself there is no individuation,
They ignorantly attach themselves to particular objects.
It is their own mind that creates illusions;
Is this not the greatest of all self-contradictions?

The ignorant cherish the idea of rest and unrest,
The enlightened have no likes and dislikes;
All forms of dualism
Are contrived by the ignorant themselves.
They are like unto visions and flowers in the air;
Why should we trouble ourselves to take hold of them?
Gain and loss, right and wrong –
Away with them once for all!

If an eye never falls asleep,
All dreams will by themselves cease;
If the Mind retains its absoluteness,
The ten thousand things are of one Suchness.

When the deep mystery of one Suchness is fathomed,
All of a sudden we forget the external entanglements;
When the ten thousand things are viewed in their oneness,
We return to the origin and remain where we ever have
    been.

Forget the wherefore of things,
And we attain to a state beyond analogy;
Movement stopped and there is no movement,
Rest set in motion and there is no rest;
When dualism does no more obtain,
Oneness itself abides not.

The ultimate end of things where they cannot go any further,
Is not bound by rules and measures:

In the Mind harmonious (with the Way) we have the
    principle
Of identity, in which we find all strivings quieted;
Doubts and irresolutions are completely done away with,
And the right faith is straightened;
There is nothing left behind,
There is nothing retained;
All is void, lucid, and self-illuminating,
There is no exertion, no waste of energy –
This is where thinking never attains,
This is where the imagination fails to measure.

In the higher realms of true Suchness
There is neither 'self' nor 'other':
When direct identification is sought,
We can only say 'not two'.

In being 'not two', all is the same,
All that is is comprehended in it;
The wise in the ten quarters,
They all enter into this Absolute Reason.

This Absolute Reason is beyond quickening (time) and
    extending (space),
For it one instant is ten thousand years;
Whether we see it or not,
It is manifest everywhere in all the ten quarters.

Infinitely small things are as large as large things can be,
For here no external conditions obtain;
Infinitely large things are as small as small things can be,
For objective limits are here of no consideration.

What is the same as what is not,
What is not is the same as what is;
Where this state of things fails to obtain,
Indeed, no tarrying here.

One in All,
All in One –
If only this were realized,
No more worry about your not being perfect.

When Mind and each believing mind are not divided,
And undivided are each believing mind and Mind,
This is where words fail;
For it is not of the past, present, and future.*

5. HAKUN'S SONG OF MEDITATION

For such as, reflecting within themselves,
Testify to the truth of Self-nature,
To the truth that Self-nature is no-nature,
They have really gone beyond the ken of sophistry.
For them opens the gate of oneness of cause and effect,
And straight runs the path of non-duality and non-trinity.
Abiding with the not-particular which is in particulars,
Whether going or returning, they remain for ever unmoved;
Taking hold of the no-thought which lies in thoughts,
In every act of theirs they hear the voice of the truth.
How boundless the sky of Samhadi unfettered!
How transparent the perfect moon-light of the Fourfold
     Wisdom!
At that moment what do they lack?
As the Truth eternally calm reveals itself to them,

---

*Author's Note: This superb mystical poem, composed by the third
Patriarch of Zen, contains the quintessence of Mahayana mystical insight.
It is difficult to understand at the first reading, since it is full of paradox,
couched in the non-dualistic language of polarity, of what Nicholas of
Cusa calls 'contradictories', which can only be resolved at a higher level
of perception than the rational (see Section 25). Like T. S. Eliot's Four
Quartets, however, as one reads and rereads it, first one verse or line, then
another, becomes luminous and full of profound meaning.

Suchness (tathata) is the 'thusness', the 'be-ness', of everything, an
ultimate spiritual essence beyond the opposites which condition human
perception, akin to the 'Isness' of Meister Eckhart and the 'mystical' of
Wittgenstein: 'There is the inexpressible; it shows itself; it is the mystical.'

This very earth is the Lotus Land of Purity,
And this body is the body of the Buddha.

The concluding lines of a Zen meditation

6. THE TWIN VERSES

All that we are is the result of what we have thought: it is founded on our thoughts and made up of our thoughts. If a man speak or act with an evil thought, suffering follows him as a wheel follows the hoof of the beast that draws the cart.

All that we are is the result of what we have thought: it is founded on our thoughts and made up of our thoughts. If a man speak or act with a good thought, happiness follows him like a shadow that never leaves him.

Hatred does not cease by hatred; hatred ceases only by love. This is the eternal law.

Many do not realize that all must one day die. In those who know this fact all strife is stilled.

As the wind throws down a shaky tree, so temptation overthrows him who lives only for pleasure, who is immoderate, idle and weak.

As the wind does not throw down a mountain, so temptation does not overthrow him who lives without looking for pleasure, who is moderate, faithful and strong.

As rain breaks into an ill-thatched house, so craving breaks into an ill-trained mind.

As rain does not break into a well-thatched house, so craving does not break into a well-trained mind.

The man who talks much of the Teaching but does not practise it himself is like a cowman counting others' cattle: he has no part in the Brotherhood.

The man who can repeat but little of the Teaching, but lives it himself, who forsakes craving, hatred and delusion, possesses right knowledge and calmness, clings to nothing in this or any other world, he is a follower of the Blessed One.

From the Dhammapada

7. THE BUDDHA WHO DWELLS WITHIN

(a)

Within the domain of our mind there is a Tathagata of Enlightenment who sends forth a powerful light which illumines externally the six gates (of sensation) and purifies them. This light is strong enough to pierce through the six heavens of desire, and when it is turned inwardly to the Essence of Mind it eliminates at once the three poisonous elements, purges away our sins which might lead us to the hells, and enlightens us thoroughly within and without.

*

Within our mind there is a Buddha, and that Buddha within is the real Buddha. If Buddha is not to be sought within our mind, where shall we find the real Buddha? Doubt not that a Buddha is within your mind, apart from which nothing can exist.

From the Sutra of Wei Lang (Hui Neng)

(b)

Avert thy face from world deceptions; mistrust thy senses, they are false. But within the body, the shrine of thy sensations, seek in the impersonal for the 'Eternal Man', and having sought him out, look inward; thou art Buddha.

From the Tibetan Book of the Golden Precepts
(The Voice of the Silence)

8. THE METTA SUTRA

This is what should be done by the man who is wise, who seeks the good, and who knows the meaning of the place of peace.

Let him be strenuous, upright, and truly straight, without conceit of self, easily contented and joyous, free of cares; let him not be submerged by the things of the world; let him not take upon himself the burden of worldly goods; let his senses be controlled; let him be wise but not puffed up, and let him not desire great possessions even for his family. Let him do nothing that is mean or that the wise would reprove.

May all beings be happy and at their ease! May they be joyous and live in safety!

All beings, whether weak or strong – omitting none – in high, middle, or low realms of existence, small or great, visible or invisible, near or far away, born or to be born – may all beings be happy and at their ease!

Let none deceive another, or despise any being in any state! Let none by anger or ill-will wish harm to another!

Even as a mother watches over and protects her child, her only child, so with a boundless mind should one cherish all living beings, radiating friendliness over the entire world, above, below, and all around without limit. So let him cultivate a boundless good will towards the entire world, uncramped, free from ill-will or enmity.

Standing or walking, sitting or lying down, during all his waking hours, let him establish this mindfulness of good will, which men call the highest state!

Abandoning vain discussions, having a clear vision, free from sense appetites, he who is made perfect will never again know rebirth.

9. THE FOUR SUBLIME STATES
(Brahma Viharas)

Benevolence (Metta)

Here, with thoughts of benevolence, one pervades first one direction, then a second direction, then a third direction, then a fourth direction, then above, then below, then all around. Identifying oneself with all, one pervades the entire universe with thoughts of compassion, with heart grown great, wide, deep, boundless, purified of all ill-will.

Compassion (Karuna, Love)

Here, with thoughts of compassion, one pervades first one direction, then a second direction, then a third direction, then a fourth direction, then above, then below, then all around.

Identifying oneself with all, one pervades the entire universe with thoughts of compassion, with heart grown great, wide, deep, boundless, purified of all ill-will.

Joyous Sympathy (or Sympathetic Joy)

Here, with thoughts of joyous sympathy, one pervades first one direction, then a second direction, then a third direction, then a fourth direction, then above, then below, then all around. Identifying oneself with all, one pervades the entire universe with thoughts of joyous sympathy, with heart grown great, wide, deep, boundless, purified of all ill-will.

Equanimity (or Peace of Mind)

Here, with thoughts of equanimity, one pervades first one direction, then a second direction, then a third direction, then a fourth direction, then above, then below, then all around. Identifying oneself with all, one pervades the entire universe with thoughts of equanimity, with heart grown great, wide, deep, boundless, purified of all ill-will.

10. LIBERATION OR RENUNCIATION?
THE CHOICE OF THE BODHISATTVA

But stay, Disciple . . . Canst thou destroy divine COMPASSION? Compassion is no attribute. It is the Law of LAWS – eternal Harmony, Alaya's SELF; a shoreless universal essence, the light of everlasting right, and fitness of all things, the law of love eternal.

The more thou dost become at one with it, thy being melted in its BEING, the more thy Soul unites with that which IS, the more thou wilt become COMPASSION ABSOLUTE.

Such is the Arya Path, Path of the Buddhas of perfection.

*

Now bend thy head and listen well, O Bodhisattva – Compassion speaks and saith: 'Can there be bliss when all that lives must suffer? Shalt thou be saved and hear the whole world cry?'

Now thou hast heard that which was said.

Thou shalt attain the seventh step and cross the gate of final knowledge, but only to wed woe – if thou wouldst be Tathagata, follow upon thy predecessor's steps, remain unselfish till the endless end.

Thou art enlightened – chooose thy way.

From the Book of the Golden Precepts
(The Voice of the Silence)

6. The Father of Christian Mysticism

PLATO

PLATO lived when the great period of Classical Greece was drawing to its close. The city states, which had been the homes of the vigorous flowering of intellectual and artistic life which was the glory of the Classical period of Greek history, had failed to develop into the wider political groupings which the time demanded as a condition of survival. Instead, the fratricidal strife of the Peloponnesian War (431–404 B.C.) so weakened the Greek city states that they fell an easy prey to the Macedonian power, which had arisen in the North.

Plato was born in Athens in 437 B.C. Like St Augustine, he wrote in an age of transition, when old things were passing away and new things were being born.

Few, if any, thinkers have had a deeper and more permanent influence on European thought. Much of his writing was concerned with politics; he has sometimes been called the Father of the Modern State. Behind all his writings on political issues, however, lay a profound spiritual philosophy. It was his intense sense of the world of spirit which impelled him to strive to create on earth the sort of state in which the life of the spirit would be possible.

The fundamental issue with which Plato concerned himself was a dual one; what was the nature of the truly Real over against appearance, and what and how do we know about it.

What was Plato's basic theory? It has been called the Theory of Ideas, or better, Forms. Put briefly the theory is as follows: We know objects, for instance a table, through our senses; we can see and touch them. There are, however, many tables, all slightly different from each other. How do we recognize them as tables? It is because all tables possess certain common qualities, such as hardness, smoothness, and colour, which place them in the class of objects we recognize as tables. These qualities do not, according to Plato, constitute the real table. Take them all away and there still remains the Idea of the table, the 'ideal' table, to which all actual tables approximate. It is the same *with abstract things, such as beauty or justice. Behind all beautiful objects lies the Idea of Beauty, in virtue of which they are called beautiful. The Idea cannot be known through the senses, but only through the mind.*

Plato, however, went further. If the concrete table, which can be seen and touched, is not the real table, if the real, the completely perfect thing is the Idea or Form, then the real world is an eternal world of Ideas. To this world a man must try to ascend and the ascent from shadows and images to the Truth can only be made by the soul. The soul is, therefore, for Plato the most important and significant part of a man.

Here is not only a theory of knowledge, but also a profound spiritual philosophy. Plato may not be a mystic in the way St John of the Cross was a mystic; he was, however, the Father of Christian mysticism. The pure Platonism of Plato himself was the stem from which branched out that Neoplatonism, of which Plotinus is the greatest exponent, on which much of the later speculative mysticism of Christianity was founded.

In the three passages printed below I have tried to give some idea of Plato's spiritual philosophy. The first and last are from recent translations, published in the Penguin Classics, the second from Jowett's well-known translation.

ILLUSION AND REALITY

'I want you to go on to picture the enlightenment or ignorance of our human conditions somewhat as follows. Imagine an underground chamber, like a cave with an entrance open to the daylight and running a long way underground. In this chamber are men who have been prisoners there since they were children, their legs and necks being so fastened that they can only look straight ahead of them and cannot turn their heads. Behind them and above them a fire is burning, and between the fire and the prisoners runs a road, in front of which a curtain-wall has been built, like the screen at puppet shows between the operators and their audience, above which they show their puppets.'

'I see.'

'Imagine, further, that there are men carrying all sorts of gear

along behind the curtain-wall, including figures of men and
animals made of wood and stone and other materials, and that
some of these men, as is natural, are talking and some not.'

'An odd picture and an odd sort of prisoner.'

'They are drawn from life,' I replied. 'For, tell me, do you
think our prisoners could see anything of themselves or their
fellows except the shadows thrown by the fire on the wall of
the cave opposite them?'

'How could they see anything else if they were prevented
from moving their heads all their lives?'

'And would they see anything more of the objects carried
along the road?'

'Of course not.'

'Then if they were able to talk to each other, would they not
assume that the shadows they saw were real things?'

'Inevitably.'

'And if the wall of their prison opposite them reflected
sound, don't you think that they would suppose, whenever
one of the passers-by on the road spoke, that the voice belonged to the shadow passing before them?'

'They would be bound to think so.'

'And so they would believe that the shadows of the objects
we mentioned were in all respects real.'

'Yes, inevitably.'

'Then think what would naturally happen to them if they
were released from their bonds and cured of their delusions.
Suppose one of them were let loose, and suddenly compelled
to stand up and turn his head and look and walk towards the
fire; all these actions would be painful and he would be too
dazzled to see properly the objects of which he used to see the
shadows. So if he was told that what he used to see was mere
illusion and that he was now nearer reality and seeing more
correctly, because he was turned towards objects that were
more real, and if on top of that he were compelled to say what
each of the passing objects was when it was pointed out to him,
don't you think he would be at a loss, and think that what he
used to see was more real than the objects now being pointed
out to him?'

'Much more real.'

'And if he were made to look directly at the light of the fire, it would hurt his eyes and he would turn back and take refuge in the things which he could see, which he would think really far clearer than the things being shown him.'

'Yes.'

'And if,' I went on, 'he were forcibly dragged up the steep and rocky ascent and not let go till he had been dragged out into the sunlight, the process would be a painful one, to which he would much object, and when he emerged into the light his eyes would be so overwhelmed by the brightness of it that he wouldn't be able to see a single one of the things he was now told were real.'

'Certainly not at first,' he agreed.

'Because he would need to grow accustomed to the light before he could see things in the world outside the cave. First he would find it easiest to look at shadows, next at the reflections of men and other objects in water, and later on at the objects themselves. After that he would find it easier to observe the heavenly bodies and the sky at night than by day, and to look at the light of the moon and stars, rather than at the sun and its light.'

'Of course.'

'The thing he would be able to do last would be to look directly at the sun, and observe its nature without using reflections in water or any other medium, but just as it is.'

'That must come last.'

'Later on he would come to the conclusion that it is the sun that produces the changing seasons and years and controls everything in the visible world, and is in a sense responsible for everything that he and his fellow-prisoners used to see.'

'That is the conclusion which he would obviously reach.'

'And when he thought of his first home and what passed for wisdom there, and of his fellow-prisoners, don't you think he would congratulate himself on his good fortune and be sorry for them?'

'Very much so.'

'There was probably a certain amount of honour and glory

to be won among the prisoners, and prizes for keen-sighted-ness for anyone who could remember the order of sequence among the passing shadows and so be best able to predict their future appearances. Will our released prisoner hanker after these prizes or envy this power or honour? Won't he be more likely to feel, as Homer says, that he would far rather be "a serf in the house of some landless man", or indeed any-thing else in the world, than live and think as they do?'

'Yes,' he replied, 'he would prefer anything to a life like theirs.'

'Then what do you think would happen,' I asked, 'if he went back to sit in his old seat in the cave? Wouldn't his eyes be blinded by the darkness, because he had come in suddenly out of the daylight?'

'Certainly.'

'And if he had to discriminate between the shadows, in com-petition with the other prisoners, while he was still blinded and before his eyes got used to the darkness – a process that might take some time – wouldn't he be likely to make a fool of himself? And they would say that his visit to the upper world had ruined his sight, and that the ascent was not worth even attempting. And if anyone tried to release them and lead them up, they would kill him if they could lay hands on him.'

'They certainly would.'

'Now, my dear Glaucon,' I went on, 'this simile must be connected, throughout, with what preceded it. The visible realm corresponds to the prison, and the light of the fire in the prison to the power of the sun. And you won't go wrong if you connect an ascent into the upper world and the sight of the objects there with the upward progress of the mind into the intelligible realm – that's my guess, which is what you are anxious to hear. The truth of the matter is, after all, known only to God. But in my opinion, for what it is worth, the final thing to be perceived in the intelligible realm, and perceived only with difficulty, is the absolute form of Good; once seen, it is inferred to be responsible for everything right and good, producing in the visible realm light and the source of light, and being, in the intelligible realm itself, the controlling source of reality and intelligence. And anyone who is going to act rationally either in public or private must perceive it.'

From The Republic, *trans. by H. D. P. Lee (Penguin Books)*

THE NATURE AND DESTINY OF THE SOUL

Of the nature of the soul, though her true form be ever a theme of large and more than mortal discourse, let me speak briefly, and in a figure. And let the figure be composite – a pair of winged horses and a charioteer. Now the winged horses and the charioteers of the gods are all of them noble and of noble descent, but those of other races are mixed; the human charioteer drives his in a pair; and one of them is noble and of noble breed, and the other is ignoble and of ignoble breed; and the driving of them of necessity gives a great deal of trouble to him. I will endeavour to explain to you in what way the mortal differs from the immortal creature. The soul in her totality has the care of inanimate being everywhere, and traverses the whole heaven in divers forms appearing; – when perfect and fully winged she soars upward, and orders the whole world; whereas the imperfect soul, losing her wings and dropping in her flight, at last settles on the solid ground – there, finding a home, she receives an earthly frame which appears to be self-moved, but is really moved by her power; and this composition of soul and body is called a living and mortal creature. For immortals no such union can be reasonably believed to be; although fancy, not having seen nor surely known the nature of God, may imagine an immortal creature having both a body and also a soul which are united throughout all time. Let that, however, be as God wills, and be spoken of acceptably to him. And now let us ask the reason why the soul loses her wings!

The wing is the corporeal element which is most akin to the divine, and which by nature tends to soar aloft and carry that which gravitates downwards into the upper region, which is the habitation of the gods. The divine is beauty, wisdom, goodness, and the like; and by these the wing of the soul is nourished, and grows apace; but when fed upon evil and foulness and the opposite of good, wastes and falls away. . . .

Of the heaven which is above the heavens, what earthly poet ever did or ever will sing worthily? It is such as I will describe; for I must dare to speak the truth, when truth is my theme. There abides the very being with which true knowledge is concerned; the colourless, formless, intangible essence, visible only to mind, the pilot of the soul. The divine intelligence, being nurtured upon mind and pure knowledge, and the intelligence of every soul which is capable of receiving the food proper to it, rejoices at beholding reality, and once more gazing upon truth, is replenished and made glad, until the revolution of the world brings her round again to the same place. In the revolution she beholds justice, and temperance, and knowledge absolute, not in the form of generation or of relation, which men call existence, but knowledge absolute in existence absolute; and beholding the other true existences in like manner, and feasting upon them, she passes down into the interior of the heavens and returns home; and there the charioteer putting up his horses at the stall, gives them ambrosia to eat and nectar to drink. . . .

Every soul of man has in the way of nature beheld true being; this was the condition of her passing into the form of man. But all souls do not easily recall the things of the other world; they may have seen them for a short time only, or they may have been unfortunate in their earthly lot, and, having had their hearts turned to unrighteousness through some corrupting influence, they may have lost the memory of the holy things which once they saw. Few only retain an adequate remembrance of them; and they, when they behold here any image of that other world, are rapt in amazement; but they are ignorant of what this rapture means, because they do not clearly perceive. For there is no light of justice or temperance or any of the higher ideas which are precious to souls in the earthly copies of them: they are seen through a glass dimly; and there are few who, going to the images, behold in them the realities, and these only with difficulty. There was a time when with the rest of the happy band they saw beauty shining in brightness, – we philosophers following in the train of Zeus, others in company with other gods; and then we beheld the beatific vision and were initiated into a mystery which may be truly called most blessed, celebrated by us in our state of innocence, before we had any experience of evils to come, when we were admitted to the sight of apparitions innocent and simple and calm and happy, which we beheld shining in pure light, pure ourselves and not yet enshrined in that living tomb which we carry about, now that we are imprisoned in the body, like an oyster in his shell.

From the Phraedus, *trans. by Benjamin Jowett*

THE ASCENT TO ABSOLUTE BEAUTY

The Symposium, *or* Dinner Party, *deals with the nature of love. As his contribution to the discussion, Socrates, who was one of the guests, describes a conversation he had with Diotima, a prophetess of Mantinea.*

'So far, Socrates, I have dealt with love-mysteries into which even you could probably be initiated, but whether you could grasp the perfect revelation to which they lead the pilgrim if he does not stray from the right path, I do not know. However, you shall not fail for any lack of willingness on my part: I will tell you of it, and do you try to follow if you can.

'The man who would pursue the right way to this goal must begin, when he is young, by applying himself to the contemplation of physical beauty, and, if he is properly directed by his guide, he will first fall in love with one particular beautiful person and beget noble sentiments in partnership with him. Later he will observe that physical beauty in any person is closely akin to physical beauty in any other, and that, if he is to make beauty of outward form the object of his quest, it is great folly not to acknowledge that the beauty exhibited in all bodies is one and the same; when he has reached this conclusion he will become a lover of all physical beauty, and will relax the intensity of his passion for one particular person, because he will realize that such a passion is beneath him and of small account. The next stage is for him to reckon beauty of soul more valuable than beauty of body; the result will be that, when he encounters a virtuous soul in a body which has little of the bloom of beauty, he will be content to love and cherish it and to bring forth such notions as may serve to make young people better; in this way he will be compelled to contemplate beauty as it exists in activities and institutions, and to recognize that here too all beauty is akin, so that he will be led to consider physical beauty taken as a whole a poor thing in comparison. From morals he must be directed to the sciences and contemplate their beauty also, so that, having his eyes fixed upon beauty in the widest sense, he may no longer be the slave of a base and mean-spirited devotion to an individual example of beauty, whether the object of his love be a boy or a man or an activity, but, by gazing upon the vast ocean of beauty to which his attention is now turned, may bring forth in the abundance of his love of wisdom many beautiful and magnificent sentiments and ideas until at last, strengthened and increased in stature by this experience, he catches sight of one unique science whose object is the beauty of which I am about to speak. And here I must ask you to pay the closest possible attention.

'The man who has been guided thus far in the mysteries of love, and who has directed his thoughts towards examples of beauty in due and orderly succession, will suddenly have revealed to him as he approaches the end of his initiation a beauty whose nature is marvellous indeed, the final goal, Socrates, of all his previous efforts. This beauty is first of all eternal; it neither comes into being nor passes away, neither waxes nor wanes; next, it is not beautiful in part and ugly in part, nor beautiful at one time and ugly at another, nor beautiful in this relation and ugly in that, nor beautiful here and ugly there, as varying according to its beholders; nor again will this beauty appear to him like the beauty of a face or hands or anything else corporeal, or like the beauty of a thought or a science, or like beauty which has its seat in something other than itself, be it a living thing or the earth or the sky or anything else whatever; he will see it as absolute, existing alone with itself, unique, eternal, and all other beautiful things as partaking of it, yet in such a manner that, while they come into being and pass away, it neither undergoes any increase or diminution nor suffers any change.

'When a man, starting from this sensible world and making his way upward by a right use of his feeling of love for boys, begins to catch sight of that beauty, he is very near his goal. This is the right way of approaching or being initiated into the mysteries of love, to begin with examples of beauty in this world, and using them as steps to ascend continually with that absolute beauty as one's aim, from one instance of physical beauty to moral beauty, and from moral beauty to the beauty of knowledge, until from knowledge of various kinds one arrives at the supreme knowledge whose sole object is that absolute beauty, and knows at last what absolute beauty is.

'This above all others, my dear Socrates,' the woman from Mantinea continued, 'is the region where a man's life should be spent, in the contemplation of absolute beauty. Once you have seen that, you will not value it in terms of gold or rich clothing or of the beauty of boys and young men, the sight of whom at present throws you and many people like you into such an ecstasy that, provided that you could always enjoy the sight and company of your darlings, you would be content to go without food and drink, if that were possible, and to pass your whole time with them in the contemplation of their beauty. What may we suppose to be the felicity of the man who sees absolute beauty in its essence, pure and unalloyed, who, instead of a beauty tainted by human flesh and colour and a mass of perishable rubbish, is able to apprehend divine beauty where it exists apart and alone? Do you think that it will be a poor life that a man leads who has his gaze fixed in that direction, who contemplates absolute beauty with the appropriate faculty and is in constant union with it? Do you not see that in that region alone where he sees beauty with the faculty capable of seeing it, will he be able to bring forth not mere reflected images of goodness but true goodness, because he will be in contact not with a reflection but with the truth? And having brought forth and nurtured true goodness he will have the privilege of being beloved of God, and becoming, if ever a man can, immortal himself.'

From The Symposium, *trans. by* W. Hamilton *(Penguin Books)*

7. Christo-Mysticism

ST JOHN AND ST PAUL

WE need not concern ourselves here with such controversial issues as to whether or not all the epistles attributed to St Paul were actually written by him or whether the Fourth Gospel was actually the work of the Beloved Disciple. Our concern is with a particular manifestation of mystical consciousness and insight which we find in the Christian tradition. There is little doubt that its fount is the Fourth Gospel and the Pauline writings; both clearly speak the dialect of mysticism. That some have questioned the mystical character of the Fourth Gospel is probably due to their limiting the term, mysticism, to the state of Contemplation and to those manifestations of it which are Neoplatonist in origin. Clement of Alexandria, one of the early Fathers of the Church, called the Fourth Gospel the 'spiritual' Gospel, while Origen remarked that no one could fully understand it who had not, like St John, lain upon the breast of Jesus. Dean Inge, in his Christian Mysticism, calls it the charter of Christian mysticism.

Two points must, however, be made. First, the, Johannine and Pauline writings are not mystical treatises of the type of, for instance, those of Ruysbroeck and St John of the Cross, works composed for those desirous of following the contemplative life. St John's Gospel is a biography of Jesus of a particular sort, designed, as its author states, to demonstrate that Jesus was indeed the Christ. The Pauline letters are in the main essentially practical, dealing, for the most part, with the practical problems of the Churches to which they are addressed. Interwoven with these practical matters, however, sometimes arising from them, are superb passages of mystical illumination and insight. Secondly, the Johannine and Pauline tradition is not the only fount of Christian mysticism. Another stream flows into and intermingles with it. This stream originates in Neoplatonist in the Christian form given to it in the Mystical Theology of Dionysius the Areopagite.

In the writings of the Christian mystics sometimes one sometimes the other predominates.

The mysticism of St John and St Paul has been termed Christo-mysticism and contrasted with God-mysticism, as if the two were incompatible with each other. True they are not the same; mystical illumination takes more than one form. They do not, however, conflict. Christo-mysticism has similarities with the bhakti-mysticism of the Gita and is akin to the mysticism of the Bodhisattva ideal of Mahayana Buddhism. It is a mysticism of loving faith in a Mediator between the naked Godhead and weak, suffering humanity. The key doctrine of St Paul is that of the indwelling of the Spirit of the Risen Christ, and this indwelling Spirit is intimately bound up in his mind with Christ crucified, with the man who died on a cross in time. For St John and St Paul Jesus Christ is both the Life and the Life-giver, both the Revelation and the Revealer, both the Way and the Guide. In him are gathered into one things earthly and heavenly. In Christo-mysticism something significant is added to the pure God-mysticism of the Upanishads and the bhakti-mysticism of the Gita. Spirit and matter, the eternal and the temporal, coinhere and are at last seen no longer in opposition.

In the Christian mystics the two streams of Johannine–Pauline and Pseudo-Dionysian inspiration combine in different ways. The mysticism of Meister Eckhart, for instance, seems at times to be pure God-mysticism. It has been said of St John of the Cross that he is like a sponge full of Christianity; you can squeeze it all out and the full mystical theory remains. Yet it will be found that it is through Christ that they have been led into that 'wayless way in which all lovers lose themselves'. And it was Jesus Himself who said in the great discourse to His disciples at the Last Supper: 'When the Comforter is come whom I will send unto you from the Father, even the Spirit of truth, who proceedeth from the Father, He will testify of me. ... It is expedient for you that I go away; for if I go not away the Comforter will not come unto you; but if I depart, I will send Him unto you.'

This introductory note could easily become a full-length essay. We might discuss the debt St Paul might have owed to the Mystery religions with which he and certainly some of his converts would have come in contact. He freely uses many of the terms, such as pneuma (*spirit*), gnosis (*divine knowledge*), doxa (*glory*), sophia (*wisdom*), teleioi *(the initiated)*, etc., *which are found in the Mystery religions. The issue is, however, a highly controversial one and cannot be discussed here.**

The text used in the passages that follow is that of the Authorized Version, with occasional borrowings from the Revised Version. Except for the Prologue I have not included any passages from the Fourth Gospel. It is best that it should be read in its entirety.† From the Pauline Epistles the selected passages are arranged under headings.

The Prologue of the Fourth Gospel

THE LOGOS

In the beginning was the Word [the *Logos*], and the Word was with God, and the Word was God. The same was in the beginning with God. All things were made by Him; and without Him was not any thing made. That which was made was life in Him; and the life was the light of men. And the light shineth in darkness; and the darkness comprehended it not.‡

There was a man sent from God, whose name was John.

* Readers who might like to explore this issue further are referred to H. A. A. Kennedy: *St Paul and the Mystery Religions* (Hodder & Stoughton), where a mass of relevant evidence is set out.

† I would, however, draw particular attention to Jesus's conversation with Nicodemus in Chapter 3 and His last discourse to His disciples on the eve of His death, recorded in Chapters 14 to 17.

‡ In his beautiful anthology, *The Testament of Light* (Dent), Gerald Bullett gives this paraphrase:

> In the beginning was Imagination:
> in the beginning was the Seed.
>   And the Seed was in God:
>   And the Seed is God.
> All things are the flowering of That.
>   In the Seed was that Light
>   which lighteth every man
>   that cometh into the world.
>   The Light shineth in darkness,
>   And the darkness overpowers it not.

The same came for a witness, to bear witness of the Light, that all men through him might believe. He was not that Light, but was sent to bear witness of that Light. That was the true Light, which lighteth every man that cometh into the world. He was in the world, and the world was made by Him, and the world knew Him not. He came unto His own, and His own received Him not. But as many as received Him, to them gave He power to become the sons of God, even to them that believe on His name: which were born, not of blood, nor of the will of the flesh, nor of the will of man, but of God.

And the Word was made flesh, and dwelt among us (and we beheld His glory, the glory as of the only begotten of the Father), full of grace and truth.

John bore witness of Him, and cried, saying:

'This was He of whom I spake, He that cometh after me is preferred before me: for He was before me. And of His fulness have all we received, and grace for grace. For the law was given by Moses, but grace and truth came by Jesus Christ. No man hath seen God at any time; the only begotten Son, which is in the bosom of the Father, He hath declared Him.'

From the Pauline Epistles

THE MYSTIC VISION

I knew a man in Christ [St Paul refers to himself], above fourteen years ago (whether in the body, I cannot tell; or whether out of the body, I cannot tell: God knoweth); such an one caught up to the third heaven. And I knew such a man (whether in the body or out of the body, I cannot tell: God knoweth;) how that he was caught up into paradise, and heard unspeakable words, which it is not lawful for man to utter. Of such an one will I glory: yet of myself will I not glory, but in mine infirmities. For though I would desire to glory, I shall not be a fool; for I will say the truth: but now I forbear, lest any man should think of me above that which he seeth me to be, or that he heareth of me. And lest I should be exalted above measure through the abundance of the revelation, there was given me a thorn in the flesh, the messenger of Satan to buffet me, lest I should be exalted above measure. For this thing I besought the Lord thrice, that it might depart from me. And he said unto me: My grace is sufficient for thee; for My strength is made perfect in weakness.

II Corinthians 12

THE HIDDEN WISDOM

We speak wisdom among them that are perfect,*[1] yet not the wisdom of the world, nor of the princes of this world, that come to naught: but we speak the wisdom of God in a mystery, the hidden wisdom, which God ordained before the world unto our glory: which none of the princes of this world knew: for had they known it they would not have crucified the Lord of Glory. . . . But God hath revealed it unto us by His Spirit: for the Spirit searcheth all things, yea, the deep things of God.[2] For what man knoweth the things of a man save the spirit of man which is in him? Even so the things of God knoweth no man, but the Spirit of God. Now we have received, not the spirit of the world, but the Spirit which is of God; that we might know the things that are freely given to us of God. Which things also we speak, not in the words which man's wisdom teacheth, but which the Holy Ghost teacheth; comparing spiritual things with spiritual.[3] But the natural man receiveth not the things of the Spirit of God: for they are foolishness unto him: neither can he know them, because they are spiritually discerned.[4]

I Corinthians 2

---

* The meaning is clearer in the translation by J. B. Phillips, in *Letters to Young Churches* (Bles). I give his translation of the indicated sentences:
  1. We do, of course, speak 'wisdom' [i.e. secret doctrine not given to any but the initiated] among those who are spiritually mature.
  2. For nothing is hidden from the Spirit, not even the deep wisdom of God.
  3. . . . explaining spiritual things to those who are spiritual.
  4. But the unspiritual man simply cannot accept the matters which the Spirit deals with – they just don't make sense to him, for, after all, you must be spiritual to see spiritual things.

THE MYSTERY OF CHRIST

If any man be in Christ, he is a new creature: old things are passed away; behold, all things are become new. And all things are of God, Who hath reconciled us to Himself by Jesus Christ, and hath given to us the ministry of reconciliation; to wit, that God was in Christ, reconciling the world unto Himself.

II Corinthians 5

For this cause we also, since the day we heard it, do not cease to pray for you, and do desire that you be filled with the knowledge of His will in all wisdom and spiritual understanding; . . . giving thanks unto the Father, Who hath made us to be partakers of the inheritance of the saints in light: Who hath delivered us from the power of darkness, and hath translated us into the kingdom of His dear Son; in Whom we have redemption through his blood, even the forgiveness of sins. Who is the image of the invisible God, the First-born of every creature. For by Him were all things created, that are in heaven, and that are in earth, visible and invisible, whether they be thrones, or dominions, or principalities, or powers; all things were created by Him and for Him: and he is before all things, and by Him all things consist. And He is the Head of the Body, the Church; Who is the beginning, the First-born from the dead, that in all things He might have the pre-eminence. For it pleased the Father that in Him should all fulness dwell: and having made peace through the blood of His Cross, by Him to reconcile all things unto Himself; by Him, I say, whether they be things in earth, or things in heaven.

Colossians 1

Having made known unto us the mystery of His will, according to His good pleasure which He hath purposed in Himself that in the dispensation of the fulness of times He might gather in one all things in Christ.

Ephesians 1

Let this mind be in you which was also in Christ Jesus.

Who, being in the form of God, thought it no robbery to be equal with God: but made Himself of no reputation, and took upon Him the form of a servant, and was made in the likeness of men; and being found in fashion as a man, He humbled Himself, and became obedient unto death, even the death of the cross. Wherefore God hath highly exalted Him, and given Him a name which is above every name, that at the name of Jesus every knee should bow, of things in heaven, and things in earth, and things under the earth; and that every tongue should confess that Jesus Christ is Lord, to the glory of God the Father.

Philippians 2

THE SOUL'S UNION WITH CHRIST

I am crucified with Christ; nevertheless I live; yet not I, but Christ liveth in me.

Galatians 2

As many of you as have been baptized into Christ have put on Christ.

Galatians 3

If ye then be risen with Christ, seek those things which are above, where Christ sitteth on the right hand of God. Set your affection on things above, and not on things on the earth. For ye are dead, and your life is hid with Christ in God.

Colossians 3

Now if we be dead with Christ, we believe that we shall also live with Him: knowing that Christ being raised from the dead dieth no more; death hath no more dominion over Him. For in that He died, He died unto sin once: but in that He liveth He liveth unto God. Likewise reckon ye also yourselves to be dead indeed unto sin, but alive unto God through Jesus Christ our Lord.

Romans 6

The mystery which hath been hid from ages and from

generations, but now is made manifest to His saints: – which is Christ in you, the hope of glory.

Colossians 1

Our conversation is in heaven; from whence also we look for the Saviour, the Lord Jesus Christ: Who shall change our vile body, that it may be fashioned like unto His glorious body, according to the working whereby He is able to subdue all things unto Himself.

Philippians 3

I am persuaded that neither death, nor life, nor angels, nor principalities, nor powers, nor things present, nor things to come, nor height, nor depth, nor any other creature, shall be able to separate us from the love of God, which is in Christ Jesus our Lord.

Romans 8

THE MYSTERY OF RESURRECTION

Now is Christ risen from the dead, and become the first fruits of them that slept. For since by man came death, by man came also the resurrection of the dead. For as in Adam all die, even so in Christ shall all be made alive. But every man in his own order: Christ the firstfruits, afterwards they that are Christ's at his coming. Then cometh the end, when He shall have delivered up the kingdom to God, even the Father; when He shall have put down all rule and all authority and power. For He must reign, till He hath put all enemies under His feet. The last enemy that shall be destroyed is death. . . .

That which thou sowest is not quickened, except it die: and that which thou sowest, thou sowest not that body which shall be, but a bare grain, it may chance of wheat, or some other kind: but God giveth it a body as it pleaseth Him, and to every seed a body of its own. All flesh is not the same flesh: there is one flesh of men, another flesh of beasts, another of fishes, another of birds. There are also celestial bodies, and bodies terrestrial: the glory of the celestial is one, and the glory of the terrestrial is another. There is one glory of the sun, and another glory of the moon, and another glory of the stars: for one star differeth from another in glory. So also is the resurrection of the dead. It is sown in corruption; it is raised in incorruption. It is sown in dishonour; it is raised in glory. It is sown in weakness; it is raised in power. It is sown a natural body; it is raised a spiritual body. There is a natural body, and there is a spiritual body. And so it is written,

> The first Adam was made a living soul;
> The second Adam a quickening spirit.

Howbeit that was not first which is spiritual, but that which is natural: and afterwards that which is spiritual. The first man is of the earth, earthy: the second man is the Lord from heaven. As is the earthy, such are they also that are earthy: and as is the heavenly, such are they also that are heavenly. And as we have borne the image of the earthy, we shall also bear the image of the heavenly.

Now this I say, brethren, that flesh and blood cannot inherit the kingdom of God; neither does corruption inherit incorruption. Behold, I show you a mystery; We shall not all sleep, but we shall all be changed, in a moment, in the twinkling of an eye, at the last trump: for the trumpet shall sound, and the dead shall be raised incorruptible, and we shall be changed. For this corruptible must put on incorruption, and this mortal must put on immortality. So when this corruptible shall have put on incorruption, and this mortal shall have put on immortality, then shall be brought to pass the saying that is written, Death is swallowed up in victory. O death, where is thy sting? O grave, where is thy victory?

I Corinthians 15

THE REDEMPTION OF THE WHOLE CREATION

For I reckon that the sufferings of this present time are not worthy to be compared with the glory which shall be revealed in us. For the earnest expectation of the creature waiteth for the manifestation of the sons of God. For the creature was made subject to vanity, not willingly, but by reason of Him who hath subjected the same in hope. Because the creature itself also shall be delivered from the bondage of corruption into the glorious liberty of the sons of God.* For we know that the whole creation groaneth and travaileth in pain together until now. And not only they, but ourselves also, which have the firstfruits of the Spirit, even we ourselves groan within ourselves, waiting for the adoption, to wit, the redemption of our body.

Romans 8

THE ENDING OF THE HYMN TO LOVE

When I was a child, I spake as a child, I felt as a child, I thought as a child: Now that I have become a man, I have put away childish things. For now we see in a mirror, darkly; but then face to face:† now I know in part; but then shall I know even as also I am known. Now abideth faith, hope, love, these three; and the greatest of these is love.

I Corinthians 13

* Mgr Knox, in his translation of the New Testament (Burns & Oates), brings out the meaning of this passage very well. It runs as follows: 'Created nature has been condemned to frustration; not for some deliberate fault of its own, but for the sake of Him who so condemned it, with a hope to look forward to; namely, that nature in its turn will be set free from the tyranny of corruption, to share in the glorious freedom of God's sons.'

† Phillips, op. cit., translates as follows: 'At present all we see is the baffling reflection of reality; we are like men looking at a landscape in a small mirror [cf. Plato's image of the Cave; see Anthology, p. 155]. The time will come when we shall see reality whole and face to face.'

8. The Kingdom of Heaven is Within You

THE OXYRHYNCHUS SAYINGS
OF JESUS

At the end of the nineteenth and the beginning of the twentieth century two papyri were discovered in Egypt. The first, found in 1897, was in book, the second, found in 1903, in roll form. Both were in a mutilated condition and scholars have found difficulty in deciphering them, indeed, some of the readings are little more than conjecture. The two papyri, which were written in the third century A.D., contain a number of sayings of Jesus, some already known from the record of them in the Gospels, some unknown until the time of the discovery of the papyri. The most striking of these sayings of Jesus are printed below. Francis Thompson echoes one of them in his poem, The Kingdom of God:

> *The angels keep their ancient places; –*
> *Turn but a stone, and start a wing! –*
> *'Tis ye, 'tis your estranged faces,*
> *That miss the many-splendoured thing.*

Wherever there are two, they are not without God, and where there is one alone, I say I am with him. Raise the stone and there thou shalt find me; cleave the wood and there I am. Let not him who seeks cease until he finds, and when he finds he shall be astonished. Astonished he shall reach the Kingdom, and having reached the Kingdom, he shall rest.

*

Who then are they that draw us and when shall come the Kingdom that is in heaven?

The fowls of the air and of the beasts whatever is beneath the earth or upon the earth, and the fishes of the sea, these they are that draw you. And the Kingdom of heaven is within you and whosoever knoweth himself shall find it. And, having found it, ye shall know yourselves that ye are sons and heirs of the Father, the Almighty, and shall know yourselves that ye are in God and God in you. And ye are the City of God.

9. Departure and Return

THE HYMN OF THE ROBE
OF GLORY

THE Hymn of the Robe of Glory, or, *as it is sometimes called,*
The Hymn of the Soul, *is an early Christian poem or hymn of great
beauty, written in Old Syriac, possibly Gnostic in origin, and dated
about the second half of the second century* A.D. *It describes the
departure of the soul into the body (Egypt), where it forgets what it
is and where it belongs, its eventual remembrance of its divine origin
and its return to the heavenly kingdom, where it is received with joy
by the Father and restored to its original state.*

It is interesting to note the close resemblance between the Hymn
*and the parable of the Prodigal Son in St Luke's Gospel. In both
there are the two sons; in both the younger son goes down to Egypt
and there forgets his origin; in both there is the return and the welcome
by the father. The jealousy of the elder brother in the parable is,
however, absent from the Hymn. In the Hymn, too, is found the
symbol of the Pearl, carrying the same meaning, that of the divine
spark, the 'kingdom of heaven' within man, as in another parable
of Jesus, 'The kingdom of heaven is like unto a pearl of great price'
(Matthew 13).*

*I leave it to the reader to interpret the significance of this close
resemblance.*

*Parts of the Hymn are obscure and for the sake of clarity I have
omitted a number of the verses, reducing the one hundred and five of
the original to seventy.*

The translation is that contained in Echoes from the Gnosis *by
G. R. S. Mead (Theosophical Publishing Society).*

I

When, a quite little child, I was dwelling
In the House of my Father's Kingdom,

And in the wealth and the glories
Of my Up-bringers I was delighting,

From the East, our Home, my Parents
Forth-sent me with journey-provision.

Indeed from the wealth of our Treasure,
They bound up for me a load.

Large was it, yet was it so light
That all alone I could bear it. . . .

My Glorious Robe they took off me
Which in their love they had wrought me,

And my Purple Mantle (also)
Which was woven to match with my stature.

And with me They (then) made a compact;
In my heart wrote it, not to forget it;

'If thou goest down into Egypt,
And thence thou bring'st the one Pearl –

'(The Pearl) that lies in the Sea,
Hard by the loud-breathing Serpent, –

'(Then) shalt thou put on thy Robe
And thy Mantle that goeth upon it,

'And with thy Brother, Our Second,
Shalt thou be Heir in our Kingdom.'

2

I left the East and went down
With two Couriers (with me);

For the way was hard and dangerous,
For I was young to tread it. . . .

Down further I went into Egypt;
And from me parted my escorts.

Straightway I went to the Serpent;
Near to his lodging I settled,

To take away my Pearl
While he should sleep and should slumber.

Lone was I there, yea, all lonely;
To my fellow-lodgers a stranger.

However I saw there a noble,
From out of the Dawn-land my kinsman,

A young man fair and well favoured,
Son of Grandees; he came and he joined me.

I made him my chosen companion,
A comrade, for sharing my wares with.

He warned me against the Egyptians,
'Gainst mixing with the unclean ones.

For I had clothed me as they were,
That they might not guess I had come

From afar to take off the Pearl,
And so rouse the Serpent against me.

But from some occasion or other
They learned I was not of their country.

With their wiles they made my acquaintance;
Yea, they gave me their victuals to eat.

I forgot that I was a King's son,
And became a slave to their king.

I forgot all concerning the Pearl
For which my Parents had sent me;

And from the weight of their victuals
I sank down into a deep sleep.

3

All this that now was befalling,
My Parents perceived and were anxious.

It was then proclaimed in our Kingdom,
That all should speed to our Gate –

Kings and Chieftains of Parthia,
And of the East all the Princes.

And this is the counsel they came to;
I should not be left down in Egypt.

And for me they wrote out a Letter;
And to it each Noble his Name set:

'From Us – King of Kings, thy Father,
And thy Mother, Queen of the Dawn-land,

'And from Our Second, thy Brother –
To thee, Son, down in Egypt,
   Our Greeting!

'Up and arise from thy sleep,
Give ear to the words of Our Letter!

'Remember that thou art a King's son;
See whom thou hast served in thy slavedom.

'Bethink thyself of the Pearl
For which thou didst journey to Egypt.

'Remember thy Glorious Robe,
Thy Splendid Mantle remember,

'To put on and wear as adornment,
When thy Name may be read in
   the Book of the Heroes,

'And with Our Successor, thy Brother,
Thou mayest be Heir in our Kingdom.' . . .

It flew in the form of the Eagle,
Of all the winged tribes the king-bird;

It flew and alighted beside me,
And turned into speech altogether.

At its voice and the sound of its winging,
I waked and arose from my deep sleep.

Unto me I took it and kissed it;
I loosed its seal and I read it.

E'en as it stood in my heart writ,
The words of my Letter were written.

I remembered that I was a King's son,
And my rank did long for its nature.

I bethought me again of the Pearl,
For which I was sent down to Egypt.

And I began (then) to charm him,
The terrible loud-breathing Serpent.

I lulled him to sleep and to slumber,
Chanting o'er him the Name of my Father,

The Name of our Second (my Brother),
And (Name) of my Mother, the East-Queen.

And (thereon) I snatched up the Pearl,
And turned to the House of my Father.

Their filthy and unclean garments
I stripped off and left in their country.

To the way that I came I betook me
To the Light of our Home, to the Dawn-land. . . .

4

My Glorious Robe that I'd stripped off,
And my Mantle with which it was covered,

Down from the Heights of Hyrcānia,
Thither my Parents did send me. . . .

At once, as soon as I saw it,
The Glory looked like my own self.

I saw it all in all of me,
And saw me all in (all of) it —

That we were twain in distinction,
And yet again one in one likeness. . . .

And (now) with its kingly motions
Was it pouring itself out towards me,

And made haste in the hands of its Givers,
That I might (take and) receive it.

And me, too, my love urged forward
To run for to meet it, to take it.

And I stretched myself forth to receive it;
With its beauty of colour I decked me,

And my Mantle of sparkling colours
I wrapped entirely all o'er me.

I clothed me therewith, and ascended
To the Gate of Greeting and Homage.

I bowed my head and did homage
To the Glory of Him who had sent it,

Whose commands I (now) had accomplished,
And who had, too, done what He'd promised.

(And there) at the Gate of His House-sons
I mingled myself with His Princes;

For He had received me with gladness,
And I was with Him in His Kingdom. . . .

10. The One and the Many

PLOTINUS,

The *Enneads*

PLOTINUS, philosopher and mystic, was born in A.D. 205 and died in 270. He was thus a younger contemporary of Clement of Alexandria and Origen, two of the most mystically inclined of the early Fathers of the Christian Church. He was not, however, a Christian. He drew his chief inspiration from Plato, and is the clearest and most profound exponent of that Neoplatonism, which was to have so widespread an influence on the later development of speculative mysticism. There are close affinities between his spiritual teaching and that of Clement and Origen.

It is not easy to summarize the philosophy of Plotinus briefly and intelligibly. To understand it at all one must put aside all ideas of time and space, of before and after, of here and now, of this and that, as we are conscious of them in the phenomenal world.

Behind everything there is a transcendent First Principle, which Plotinus calls the One or the Good. The One is beyond the reach of human thought or language. Yet It is not a mere negation; rather it is a positive and dynamic Reality, the source of all defined and limited realities. The One is beyond being, and, therefore, cannot properly be said to 'exist'; yet It is the supreme Existent. No predicates can be applied to It nor, in reference to It, can any quasi-temporal or quasi-spatial concepts be used; nor can one attribute to It activity or planning or choice. All one can speak of is a spontaneous outgoing and self-giving of the Perfect. Though timeless Rest, It is dynamic through and through, unbounded Life, unbounded Power. Nor is It remote from us, but is present in the centre of our souls, or rather, Plotinus would prefer to say, we are in Him. In reference to the One he sometimes uses the impersonal It, sometimes the personal He.

From the One proceeds, by a timeless generation, though not in any spatial or temporal sense, the first of the derived realities, which Plotinus calls Nous. *It is the Divine Mind and also the World of Forms and Ideas in the Platonic sense. In this timeless generation there are two movements. In the first* Nous *is realized as potentiality; in the second it turns back to the One in contemplation and is filled with content, so that it becomes the totality of all real existence. Christian Neoplatonism equated the* Logos *of St John's Gospel, the Second Person of the Trinity, the divine Activity, the World Principle, the That which is the basis of the manifold, and which was incarnate in Jesus Christ, with the* Nous *of Plotinus. Both Clement and Origen call the* Logos *the Idea of Ideas.*

From Nous *proceeds Soul, the third of the three Hypostases of Plotinus. Soul is universal and is the intermediary between the 'intelligible' world of* Nous *and the phenomenal world of sense. Universal Soul has two levels, a higher and a lower, the former acting as a transcendent principle of form, order, and intelligent direction, the latter as an immanent principle of life and growth. Universal Soul, immaterial and immortal, is diffused everywhere; it is present in animals and plants as well as in man, imposing on all things the forms they bear and controlling their activity. The body is, according to Plotinus, in the soul rather than the soul in the body, the soul creating the body by imposing form on matter, which, in itself, is No-Thing. Space and time, bound up as they are with the material, are only forms of our thought.*

Individual souls are, as it were, 'parts' – it is impossible to find an exact word – of Universal Soul. The individual soul has three parts: the lowest, which is animal and sensual and closely bound up with the body; the next, the logical, reasoning soul, the distinctly human part which differentiates man from the rest of creation; and, thirdly, the highest, superhuman part, which is capable of being 'made one with Nous', *yet without losing its identity, 'so that they two are both one and two'. A man's eternal destiny depends on which level of the soul he allows to become dominant in him.*

It is possible, some consider probable, that Plotinus had some acquaintance with the thought of India. Certainly, his conception of the One has affinity with the Hindu doctrine of Spirit, 'the seed of all seeds', and his conception of Soul with the Hindu teaching on the Atman.

In the work of Plotinus is found the fine flowering of Neoplatonism which, in fertile association with the Christo-mysticism of St John and St Paul, was the foundation of speculative Christian mysticism. His canvas was indeed an immense and magnificent one, a picture of an 'intelligible' world, the real world, timeless, spaceless, and containing in itself the archetypes of the sensible world and having its existence in the mind of God; of the sensible world as an image of the Divine Mind, which is itself a reflection of the One; of the whole universe as a vast organism, an immense living being, held together by the Power and Logos of God, so that all existence, men, and things, is drawn by a sort of centripetal attraction towards God.

The mystical philosophy of Plotinus is not easy to understand. For one who wishes to explore it further, the best translation is that of A. H. Armstrong: Plotinus, published by Allen & Unwin. The parts of the Enneads which are translated are grouped under headings, the One or the Good, Nous, Soul, etc., thus making understanding easier. Further, the book contains a masterly introduction. The passages which follow are taken from this translation.

THE ONE OR THE GOOD

What is This which does not exist? We must go away silent, involved by our thought in utter perplexity, and seek no further: for what could anyone look for when there is nothing to which he can still go on? Every search moves to a first principle and stops when it has reached it.

Besides, we must consider that every inquiry is either about what a thing essentially is, or its quality, or its cause, or the fact of its existence. But the existence of That, in the sense in which we say that It exists, is known from the things which come after It; inquiry into Its cause is looking for another principle beyond It, and there is no principle of the Universal Principle. To seek Its quality is to seek what are Its incidental attributes, and It has none. To seek Its essential nature makes still more clear that we should make no inquiry about It, but only grasp It, if we can, in our intellect and learn that it is a profanation to apply any terms to It. . . .

We must not set Him in any place whatever, either as

eternally resting and established in it or as an incomer. We must think of Him only as existing (the necessity of discussion compels us to attribute existence to Him), and of place and everything else as later than Him – place latest and last of all. Conceiving this Placeless Existence as we do, we shall not set other things round Him in a sort of circle or be able to circumscribe Him and measure His dimensions; we shall not attribute quantity to Him at all, or quality either; for He has no form, not even intelligible form; nor is He related to anything else, for He exists in and by Himself before any other thing.

Since the nature of the One produces all things It is none of them. It is not a thing or quality or quantity or intellect or soul; It is not in motion or at rest, in place or in time, but exists in Itself, a unique Form; or rather It is formless, existing before all form, before motion, before rest; for these belong to being and make it multiple.

The essence* which is generated from the One is Form (one could not say that what is generated from that Source is anything else), not the form of some one thing but of everything, so that no other form is left outside it.

When you think of Him as Mind or God, He is still more: and when you unify Him in your thought, the degree of unity by which He transcends your thought is still greater than you imagine it to be. For He exists in and by Himself without any attributes. Substance needs Him in order to be one: but He does not need Himself; for He is Himself.

It has life in Itself and all things in Itself. Its thinking of Itself is Itself, and exists by a kind of immediate self-consciousness, in everlasting rest.

If the First is perfect, the most perfect of all, and the primal Power, It must be the most powerful of beings and the other powers must imitate It as far as they are able. Now when

* The Greek word *ousia*, the substantial form, the principle which gives a thing its particular, definite being, which makes it this thing and not anything else.

anything else comes to perfection we see that it produces, and does not endure to remain by itself, but makes something else. How then could the Most Perfect, the First Good, the Power of all things, remain in Itself as if It grudged Itself or was unable to produce? How would it then still be the Principle?

NOUS

How then does *Nous* see, and what does it see? How did it come into existence at all and arise from the One so as to be able to see? The soul now knows that these things must be, but longs to answer the question repeatedly discussed, even by the ancient philosophers, how from the One, if It is such as we say It is, a multiplicity or a duality or a number come into existence. Why did It not remain by Itself? How did so great a multitude flow from It as that which we see to exist in beings but think it right to refer back to the One? . . .

How did it come to be then? And what are we to think of as surrounding the One in Its repose? It must be a radiation from It while It remains unchanged, just like the bright light which surrounds the sun, which remains unchanged though the light springs from it continually. Everything that exists, as long as it remains in being, necessarily produces from its own substance, in dependence on its present power, a surrounding reality directed towards the external world, a kind of image of the archetype from which it was produced.

The One is always perfect and therefore produces everlastingly; and Its product is less than Itself. What then must we say about the Most Perfect? Nothing can come from It except that which is next greatest after It. *Nous* is next to It in greatness and second to It; for *Nous* sees It and needs It alone; but It has no need of *Nous*.

Since we say that this universe here is modelled on the world of *Nous*, every living thing must be There first; if the being of *Nous* is complete it must be everything. Heaven There must be a living thing. . . .

So he who inquires whence the living thing comes, is inquiring whence the heaven There comes; and this amounts to asking the origin of living reality There; and this is the same as asking whence comes life, and universal life and universal Soul and universal *Nous*, in that world There where there is no poverty or impotence, but everything is filled full of life, boiling with life. Things There flow in a way from a single source, not like one particular breath or warmth, but as if there were a single quality containing in itself and preserving all qualities, sweet taste and smell and the quality of wine with all other flavours, visions of colours and all that touch perceives, all too that hearing hears, all tunes and every rhythm.

SOUL

In the intelligible world is true being: *Nous* is the best of it. But there are souls There too; for it is from There that they come here. That world contains souls without bodies; this one, the souls which have come to be in bodies and are divided by their bodies. There all and every *Nous* is together, not separated or divided, and all souls are together in the one world, without spatial division. ...

We are not *Nous*; we are conformed to it by our primary reasoning power which receives it. ... The activities of *Nous* come from above, just as those proceeding from sense-perception come from below. *We* are the chief part of the soul, in the middle between two powers, a worse and a better, the worse being that of sense-perception and the better that of *Nous*. ... *Nous* is our king.

Nous is a self-contained activity, but soul has what we may call an inward part, which is that of it which is directed to *Nous*, and a part outside *Nous* which is directed to the outside world. By the one it is made like that from which it came, by the other, even though it has been made unlike, it becomes like, here below too, both in its action and its production. For even while it is active it contemplates, and when it produces it produces Forms (a kind of completed acts of intellect). So all things are traces of thought and *Nous*;

they proceed according to their original pattern; those which are near imitate *Nous* better, and the remotest keep an obscure image of it. This light of *Nous* shines in the soul and illumines it: that is, it makes it intelligent: that is, it makes it like itself, the light above.

It will be proper to investigate what it is that happens when a soul which is altogether pure and free from body takes upon itself a bodily nature. We should perhaps, or rather must, begin with the Soul of the All: and when talking about the Soul of the All we must consider that the terms 'entry' and 'ensoulment' are used in the discussion for the sake of clear explanation. For there never was a time when this universe did not have a soul, or when body existed in the absence of soul, or when matter was not set in order: but in discussing these things one can consider them apart from each other. When one is reasoning about any kind of composite thing it is always legitimate to analyse it in thought into its parts.

The truth is as follows. If body did not exist, soul would not go forth, since there is no place other than body where it is natural for it to be. But if it intends to go forth it will produce a place for itself, and so a body. . . .

But if the same soul is everywhere, how can there be a particular soul of each individual? And how is one good and another bad? The one soul is sufficient to provide for individuals as well as the whole, and contains all souls and all intellects. . . . Each one of them is not marked off from the others by boundaries; so in this way it is also one. It was not to have a single, but an unbounded life, and yet a single one too, single in this way, that all souls are together, not collected into a unity but springing from a unity and remaining in that from which they sprang; or rather they never did spring from it, but always were in this state, for nothing There comes into being, and so nothing is divided into parts; it is only the recipient who thinks that it is divided.

THE RETURN OF THE SOUL

But how shall we find the way? What method can we devise?
How can one see the inconceivable Beauty Which stays within
the holy sanctuary and does not come out where the profane
may see It? Let him who can, follow and come within, and
leave outside the sight of his eyes and not turn back to the
bodily splendours which he saw before. When he sees the
beauty in bodies he must not run after them; we must know
that they are images, traces, shadows, and hurry away to
That which they image. For if a man runs to the image and
wants to seize it as if it was the reality (like a beautiful reflection playing on the water, which some story somewhere, I
think, said riddlingly a man wanted to catch and sank down
into the stream and disappeared) then this man who clings to
beautiful bodies and will not let them go, will, like the man
in the story, but in soul, not in body, sink down into the dark
depths where *Nous* has no delight, and stay blind in Hades,
consorting with shadows there and here. This would be truer
advice, 'Let us fly to our dear country.' Where then is our
way of escape? How shall we put out to sea? Our country
from which we came is There, our Father is There. How shall
we travel to it, where is our way of escape? We cannot get
there on foot; for our feet only carry us everywhere in this
world, from one country to another. You must not get
ready a carriage, either, or a boat. Let all these things go,
and do not look. Shut your eyes and change to and wake
another way of seeing, which everyone has but few use.

11. The Divine Darkness

DIONYSIUS THE AREOPAGITE

The Mystical Theology

THE *identity of Dionysius the Areopagite, or, as he is often called, the Pseudo-Dionysius, is unknown. He was probably a Syrian monk, living at the end of the fifth and the beginning of the sixth century* A.D. *Since he ascribed his works to that Dionysius the Areopagite who was the friend of St Paul, and addressed them to St Paul's fellow-worker, Timothy, he was thought for centuries to have been a contemporary of the Apostle and his writings were given the same authority as those of the writers of the New Testament.*

His chief work was a priceless little treatise called The Mystical Theology, *the whole of which is printed below. Short as it is, it is one of the most important works in the whole history of speculative Christian mysticism. In it the Pseudo-Dionysius describes with extreme precision the working of the mystical consciousness at its most profound level. Quite apart from its religious significance, it is a psychological document of the highest worth. It is not surprising that later contemplatives found in it perpetual echoes of their own experiences and that the phrase 'Dionysius [or Denis or St Denis] saith' is of so frequent recurrence in their writings.*

The author of The Mystical Theology *gave to mystical literature some of its key ideas, notably the conception of the Supreme Godhead as the Divine Dark, the negation of all that the surface consciousness perceives. In his writings, too, are found, for the first time in Christian mysticism, the terms 'divine ignorance' and 'unknowing' as descriptions of the way the soul reaches the highest truth. We shall come across them again and again when we come to read the writings of the contemplatives, particularly those of the thirteenth and fourteenth centuries.*

In the writings of the Pseudo-Dionysius is found a fusion of

Oriental and Neoplatonist speculation. His thought has close affinities with that of Plotinus, though he does not attempt, as does Plotinus, to construct an elaborate philosophical system. There are some, Dean Inge for instance, who regard the Dionysian strain in Christian mysticism as an aberration, as an unfortunate departure from the pure Christo-mysticism of St John and St Paul, as not essentially Christian at all. Such judgement is limited. The mystic is compelled to follow his own gleam and, when he writes, is equally compelled to describe truthfully the way he has gone and what he has found on that way. Christian mysticism took into itself all that was best in Oriental and Neoplatonist religious philosophy and re-expressed it in the light of the revelation of Christ.

The translation is that published by the Shrine of Wisdom, Brook, Godalming. The section headings are those used in this edition. This edition contains some useful comments on the text.

WHAT IS THE DIVINE DARKNESS?

Supernal Triad, Deity above all essence, knowledge and goodness; Guide of Christians to Divine Wisdom; direct our path to the ultimate summit of Thy mystical Lore, most incomprehensible, most luminous, and most exalted, where the pure, absolute, and immutable mysteries of theology are veiled in the dazzling obscurity of the secret Silence, out-shining all brilliance with the intensity of their Darkness, and surcharging our blinded intellects with the utterly impalpable and invisible fairness of glories surpassing all beauty.

Let this be my prayer; but do thou, dear Timothy, in the diligent exercise of mystical contemplation, leave behind the senses and the operations of the intellect, and all things sensible and intellectual, and all things in the world of being and non-being, that thou mayest arise, by unknowing, towards the union, as far as is attainable, with Him Who transcends all being and all knowledge. For by the unceasing and absolute renunciation of thyself and of all things, thou mayest be borne on high, through pure and entire self-abnegation, into the superessential Radiance of the Divine Darkness.

But these things are not to be disclosed to the uninitiated, by whom I mean those attached to the objects of human thought, and who believe there is no superessential Reality beyond, and who imagine that by their own understanding they know Him Who has made Darkness His secret place. And if the principles of the divine Mysteries are beyond the understanding of these, what is to be said of others still more incapable thereof, who describe the transcendental First Cause of all by characteristics drawn from the lowest order of beings, while they deny that He is in any way above the images which they fashion after various designs; whereas, they should affirm that, while He possesses all the positive attributes of the universe (being the Universal Cause), yet, in a more strict sense, He does not possess them, since He transcends them all; wherefore there is no contradiction between the affirmations and the negations, inasmuch as He infinitely precedes all conceptions of deprivation, being beyond all positive and negative distinctions.

Thus, the blessed Bartholomew asserts that the divine science is both vast and minute, and that the Gospel is great and broad, yet concise and short; signifying by this, that the beneficent Cause of all is most eloquent, yet utters few words, or rather, is altogether silent, as having neither (human) speech nor (human) understanding, because He is superessentially exalted above created things, and reveals Himself in His naked Truth to those alone who pass beyond all that is pure or impure, and ascend above the topmost altitudes of holy things, and who, leaving behind them all divine light and sound and heavenly utterances, plunge into the Darkness where truly dwells, as the Oracles declare, that ONE Who is beyond all.

It was not without reason that the blessed Moses was commanded first to undergo purification himself and then to separate himself from those who had not undergone it; and after the entire purification heard many-voiced trumpets and saw many lights streaming forth with pure and manifold rays; and that he was thereafter separated from the multitude, with the elect priests, and pressed forward to the summit of the divine ascent. Nevertheless, he did not attain to the Presence of God Himself; he saw not Him (for He cannot be looked upon), but the Place where He dwells. And this I take to signify that the divinest and highest things seen by the eyes or contemplated by the mind are but the symbolical expressions of those that are immediately beneath Him Who is above all. Through these, His incomprehensible Presence is manifested upon those heights of His Holy Places; that then It breaks forth, even from that which is seen and that which sees, and plunges the mystic into the Darkness of Unknowing, whence all perfection of understanding is excluded, and he is enwrapped in that which is altogether intangible and noumenal, being wholly absorbed in Him Who is beyond all, and in none else (whether himself or another); and through the inactivity of all his reasoning powers is united by his highest faculty to Him who is wholly unknowable; thus by knowing nothing he knows that Which is beyond his knowledge.

THE NECESSITY OF BEING UNITED WITH AND OF RENDERING PRAISE TO HIM WHO IS THE CAUSE OF ALL AND ABOVE ALL

We pray that we may come unto this Darkness which is beyond light, and, without seeing and without knowing, to see and to know that which is above vision and knowledge through the realization that by not-seeing and by unknowing we attain to true vision and knowledge; and thus praise, super-essentially, Him Who is superessential, by the abstraction of the essence of all things; even as those who, carving a statue out of marble, abstract or remove all the surrounding material that hinders the vision which the marble conceals and, by that abstraction, bring to light the hidden beauty.

It is necessary to distinguish this negative method of abstraction from the positive method of affirmation, in which we deal with the Divine Attributes. For with these latter we begin with the universal and primary, and pass through the intermediate and secondary to the particular and ultimate attributes; but now we ascend from the particular to the universal conceptions, abstracting all attributes in order that without veil, we may know that Unknowing, which is enshrouded under all that is known and all that can be known, and that we may begin to contemplate the superessential Darkness which is hidden by all the light that is in existing things.

WHAT ARE THE AFFIRMATIONS AND NEGATIONS CONCERNING GOD?

In the *Theological Outlines* we have set forth the principal affirmative expressions concerning God, and have shown in what sense God's Holy Nature is One, and in what sense Three; what is within It which is called Paternity, and what Filiation, and what is signified by the name Spirit; how from the uncreated and indivisible Good, the blessed and perfect Rays of Its Goodness proceed, and yet abide immutably one both within Their Origin and within Themselves and each other, co-eternal with the act by which They spring from It; how the superessential Jesus enters an essential state in which the truths of human nature meet; and other matters made known by the Oracles are expounded in the same place.

Again, in the treatise on *Divine Names*, we have considered the meaning, as concerning God, of the titles of Good, of Being, of Life, of Wisdom, of Power, and of such other names as are applied to Him; further, in *Symbolical Theology*, we have considered what are the metaphorical titles drawn from the world of sense and applied to the nature of God; what is meant by the material and intellectual images we form of Him, or the functions and instruments of activity attributed to Him; what are the places where He dwells and the raiment in which He is adorned; what is meant by God's anger, grief, and indignation, or the divine inebriation; what is meant by God's oaths and threats, by His slumber and waking; and all sacred and symbolical representations. And it will be observed how far more copious and diffused are the last terms than the first, for the theological doctrine and the exposition of the *Divine Names* are necessarily more brief than the *Symbolical Theology*.

For the higher we soar in contemplation the more limited become our expressions of that which is purely intelligible; even as now, when plunging into the Darkness which is above the intellect, we pass not merely into brevity of speech, but even into absolute silence, of thoughts as well as of words. Thus, in the former discourse, our contemplations descended from the highest to the lowest, embracing an ever-widening number of conceptions, which increased at each stage of the descent; but in the present discourse we mount upwards from below to that which is the highest and, according to the degree of transcendence, so our speech is restrained, until, the entire ascent being accomplished, we become wholly voiceless, inasmuch as we are absorbed in Him Who is totally ineffable. 'But why,' you will ask, 'does the affirmative method begin from the highest attributions, and the negative method with the lowest abstractions?' The reason is because, when affirming the subsistence of That Which transcends all affirmation, we necessarily start from the attributes most closely related to It and upon which the remaining affirmations depend; but when pursuing the negative method to reach That Which is beyond all abstraction, we must begin by applying our negations to things which are most remote from It.

For is it not more true to affirm that God is Life and Goodness than that He is air or stone; and must we not deny to Him more emphatically the attributes of inebriation and wrath than the applications of human speech and thought?

THAT HE WHO IS THE PRE-EMINENT CAUSE OF ALL THINGS SENSIBLY PERCEIVED IS NOT HIMSELF ANY OF THOSE THINGS

We therefore maintain that the universal and transcendent Cause of all things is neither without being nor without life, nor without reason or intelligence; nor is He a body, nor has He form or shape, or quality, or quantity, or weight; nor has He any localized, visible, or tangible existence; He is not sensible or perceptible; nor is He subject to any disorder or inordination or influenced by any earthly passion; neither is He rendered impotent through the effects of material causes and events; He needs no light; He suffers no change, or corruption, or division, or privation, or flux; none of these things can either be identified with or attributed unto Him.

THAT HE WHO IS THE PRE-EMINENT CAUSE OF ALL THINGS INTELLIGENTLY PERCEIVED IS NOT HIMSELF ANY OF THOSE THINGS

Again, ascending yet higher, we maintain that He is neither soul nor intellect; nor has He imagination, opinion, reason, or understanding; nor can He be expressed or conceived, since He is neither number, nor order; nor greatness, nor smallness; nor equality, nor inequality; nor similarity, nor dissimilarity; neither is He standing, nor moving, nor at rest; neither has He power, nor is power, nor is light; neither does He live, nor is He life; neither is He essence, nor eternity, nor time; nor is He subject to intelligible contact; nor is He science, nor truth, nor kingship, nor wisdom; neither one, nor oneness; nor godhead, nor goodness; nor is He spirit according to our understanding, nor filiation, nor paternity; nor anything else known to us or to any other beings, of the things that are or the things that are not; neither does anything that is, know Him as He is; nor does He know existing things according to existing knowledge; neither can the reason attain to Him, nor name Him, nor know Him; neither is He darkness nor light, nor the false, nor the true; nor can any affirmation or negation be applied to Him, for although we may affirm or deny the things below Him, we can neither affirm nor deny Him, inasmuch as the all-perfect and unique Cause of all things transcends all affirmation, and the simple pre-eminence of His absolute nature is outside of every negation – free from every limitation and beyond them all.

12. Theosis: The Deification Of The Creature

THE MYSTICISM OF THE EASTERN ORTHODOX CHURCH

THE *theological thinking of the Eastern Orthodox Church is much more subtle and mystical than that of the Roman Catholic Church or of the Reformed Churches which separated themselves from it. Some of its most prominent theologians were themselves mystics and, in general, its contemplatives have been better understood and more highly regarded than in the West.*

If one looks for a reason for this it seems to lie in:

(i) differences in origin, environment, and ways of thinking;

(ii) an almost entire absence of the influence of Aristotelian thought, which played so great a part in the moulding of Catholic theology from the time of St Thomas Aquinas onwards;

(iii) the importance given to and the subtle interpretation of the doctrine of the Unity of the Holy Trinity, and of the doctrine of grace;

(iv) the greater coinherence of dogmatic theology and the insights and modes of expression of the mystics. Orthodox mystics had little difficulty in equating and describing their spiritual experience in terms of the formal theology of the Church.

In the formal theology of the Orthodox Church dogmatic and mystical concepts are closely interconnected. Indeed it may be aptly said that the symbols of Orthodox dogmatic theology are the result of an effort to give a dogmatic foundation to the mystical experience of union with God. In the Eastern Orthodox Church union with God is regarded as a spiritual state attainable by far more than the contemplative saint; it should be the objective of all Christians who would lead the Christian life in its fullness.

The theology of the Orthodox Church is essentially an apophatic (negative) theology. It has as its basis and it emphasizes the incomprehensibility of God (or, as Eckhart would say, the Godhead). The nature of God conceived as the Ultimate Reality is completely unapproachable and unknowable, beyond all that exists and all that can be thought.

THE EASTERN ORTHODOX CHURCH

But, if that is so how can He be known at all by man, by created being? Those familiar with the literature of mysticism will know that this antinomy has always been present in the mind of the mystic. Not seldom he has seen no need to resolve it at the level of intellect; he knows that he knows, and that is enough for him. At least one answer had been given by the Pseudo-Dionysius, when he wrote of a 'higher faculty' of the soul through which it is possible for men to be united 'to Him who is wholly unknowable; thus by knowing nothing he knows That which is beyond his knowledge'.

But how is it possible to resolve this antinomy, this contradiction, this paradox, in terms of dogmatic theology? It is only possible if dogmatic theology is willing to think in terms of, and to use a language of, polarity.

In Orthodox theology a distinction is made between the Divine Essence, Its uncreated Energies and the created being of man. God is made accessible and knowable to created being through the Trinity in Unity; not, however, through the essence of the Trinity which is one with the unknowable God, equally God, and therefore Itself inaccessible and unknowable, but through the uncreated Energies within It. The Trinity is more than Its Essence; within the Essence, and inseparable from It, there are the uncreated Energies, in and through which It goes forth from Itself and manifests, communicates and gives Itself to men. The uncreated Energies are the exterior *manifestations of God, outpourings of Itself, while still remaining Itself unchanged, into the realm of created being. The knowledge of the unknowable One by created being is said to fall within the sphere of divine* economy.*

I am aware that all this is not easy to understand. The theologians were well aware of this. St Gregory of Thessalonica wrote: 'The divine nature must be said to be at the same time both exclusive of and, in some sense, open to participation. We attain to participation in the divine nature, and yet at the same time it remains totally inaccessible. We need to affirm both at the same time and to preserve the antinomy as a criterion of right devotion.'

'Open to participation.' The holy, blessed and most glorious Trinity is a Mystery, like the Tao of Chinese mystical philosophy, the 'Mystery and Mysteries', inaccessible to thought and only to be

* The Greek word, *oikonomia* means literally the construction or administration of a house.

*known by participation in its divine life. Through this union or partici-
pation, men may attain to the state of* deification *and become co-heirs of
the divine nature, recreated after the pattern of the uncreated God,
possessing by grace (and only by grace) all that the Holy Trinity possesses
by nature.*

The doctrine of theosis, *of the possibility of the deification of
created being through grace, is at the very heart of Orthodox theology
and spirituality. This deification, or union, is in no way an annihilation
of 'personality', but rather its full flowering. The further a man
advances towards union with God, the greater his growth in consciousness.
Consciousness becomes an enlightened consciousness, no longer bound to
the senses, but one which the Divine Light is able to illuminate. The
doctrines not only of a Divine Darkness, of a Cloud of Unknowing
(see Section 22) into which the aspirant to enlightenment must be
prepared to enter in order that he may know the Unknowable, but also
of a Divine Light, shining in this Darkness, are not seldom found in the
writings of the theologians.*

*Spiritual directors in the West have tended to frown on any attempt
deliberately to seek mystical experience through spiritual exercises.
The objective of spiritual exercises they maintain is greater holiness. If
a man should be given the grace of mystical illumination well and good;
it must not, however, be deliberately sought.*

*The attitude of the Orthodox Church is different. That a man should
be able to attain to deification and union is the result of the grace of God,
it is true; but he is called upon to play his own part, to work for his
own transformation. A widely recognized way is through the Prayer of
Jesus, the Prayer of the Heart, the spiritual exercise called Hesychasm.*

*The words of the Jesus Prayer are simple, 'Lord Jesus Christ, Son
of God, have mercy on me, a sinner.' On the face of it, this looks like an
ordinary petitionary prayer. It has, however, a different objective, it is,
as one writer has put it, 'a scientific attempt to change the one who prays'.*

*Spiritual directors give precise directions on how the Jesus Prayer
should be used. First of all it is said aloud for a specific number of times
each day 'in silence and solitude'; then it is repeated silently an increased
number of times during the day and night. At length, as the aspirant
becomes more proficient, it is taken down from the 'head' centre of
consciousness into the 'heart' centre, where 'it lives itself in every heart
beat'. A prayer which begins by being 'thought', a prayer of the 'mind',*

is taken down into a deeper level of consciousness and becomes a prayer of the 'heart'.

One acquainted with the spiritual practices of the East will recognize that the Jesus Prayer is a mantra. *A mantra may be a single evocative word or a sacred sentence or some form of creative sound. It may be a microcosm of some eternal reality which one wishes to contemplate, a peg on which to hang one's most profound inner experience, a means of awakening dormant forces in the soul, and of polarizing the mind in the direction in which one wants it to go.**

In the writing of this introduction and in selecting the passages quoted below I have been immensely helped by Vladimar Lossky's The Mystical Theology of the Eastern Church (*James Clarke and Co.*) *and by* On the Prayer of Jesus *from the* Ascetic Essays *of Bishop Ignatius Brianchaninov,* trans. by Father Lazarus (*John M. Watkins*). *The passages quoted are translations of original documents quoted in Lossky, passages from* On the Prayer of Jesus, *and translations from the Greek* Patrologia, *specially made for me by my friend, Brother George Every of the Society of the Sacred Mission, to whom I am particularly grateful.*

ON THE NATURE AND REVELATION OF GOD

The Word was made man (hominized) that we might be made God (deified).

St Athanasius: De Incarnatione

God has from all eternity enjoyed the sublimity of His glory . . . His glory is the revelation, the manifestation, the reflection, the garment of his inner perfection. God reveals Himself to Himself from all eternity by the eternal generation of His consubstantial Son, and by the eternal procession of His consubstantial Spirit; and thus the unity within the Holy Trinity shines forth imperishable and unchangeable in its essential glory. . . . In this glory, uniquely proper to Himself, God dwells in perfect felicity above all glory, without having need of any witness, without admitting of any division. But as

* For a full discussion of the nature of mantras see my *The Journey Inwards* (Darton, Longman and Todd).

in His mercy and infinite love He desires to communicate His blessedness, to create for Himself beings capable of sharing in the joyfulness of His glory, He calls forth His infinite perfections and they disclose themselves in His creatures.

Philaret of Moscow

The divine nature must be said to be at the same time exclusive and, in some sense, open to participation. We attain to participation in the divine nature and at the same time it remains totally inaccessible. We need to affirm both at the same time and to preserve the antinomy as a criterion of right devotion.

St Gregory of Thessalonica

God is communicable in what He imparts to us; but He is not communicable in the uncommunicability of His essence.

St Maximus the Confessor

It is by his energies that we say we know our God: we do not say that we can come near to the essence itself, for his energies descend to us, but his essence remains unapproachable.

St Basil

The divine and deifying illumination and grace is not the essence but the energy of God.

St Gregory Palamas

We do not speak of things of which we are ignorant, but we bear witness to that which we know. For the light already shines in the darkness, in the night and in the day, in our hearts and minds. This light without change, without decline and never extinguished enlightens us; it speaks, it acts, it lives and gives life, and transforms into light those whom it illumes. God is Light and those whom He makes to see Him see Him as Light: those who receive Him, receive Him as Light.

St Symeon the New Theologian

God is called Light not with reference to His essence but to His energy.

St Gregory Palamas

He who participates in the divine energy, himself becomes to some extent, light; he is united to the light, and by that light he sees in full awareness all that remains hidden to those who have not this grace; thus he transcends not only the bodily senses, but also all that can be known by the intellect. . . . for the pure in heart see God . . . who being Light, dwells in them and reveals Himself to those who love Him, to His beloved.

St Gregory Palamas

When thought is with God, first of all the thinking mind seeks some understanding of His essence, burning with desire for this; it finds no comfort in any knowledge about Him, for this cannot be contrived or attained by any created nature. Rather it is comforted by the knowledge of what is around Him, I mean eternity, infinity, invisibility, goodness, wisdom, and the power that creates and judges everything. This alone about Him is universally intelligible, His infinitude, and to know this Nothing is to pass beyond the knowledge of the thinking mind, as the theologians have said, especially Gregory and Dionysius (i.e. of Nyssa and the Areopagite).

St Maximus the Confessor

Wonder is the total lifting of the powers of the soul towards what may be discerned of the entire majesty of glory. Or again wonder is a pure and entire outreaching of the mind towards the limitless power of light. But ecstasy is more than the taking up of the powers of the soul to the heavenly places, but it also involves their removal from all the actions of the senses; for love, the intoxicating drink of the spirit's desire, is twofold. There are two loves that rule masterfully in the spirit, the love of the heart and ecstatic love. The first is for them who are still being enlightened, the second to those perfected in love. Both work in the mind and draw it away from the senses, for the love of the spirit is a divine intoxicant that overpowers our natural wits, and through this our awareness of the forms of things is taken from us.

St Gregory of Sinai

He who desires to see the Lord within himself endeavours to

purify his heart by the unceasing remembrance of God. The spiritual land of a man pure in soul is within him. The sun which shines in it is the light of the Holy Trinity. The air which its inhabitant breathes is the All-Holy Spirit. The life, joy and gladness of that country is Christ, the Light of the Light – the Father. That is the Jerusalem or Kingdom of God hidden within us, according to the word of the Lord. Try to enter the cell within you, and you will see the heavenly cell. They are one and the same. By one entry you enter both. The ladder to the Heavenly Kingdom is within you. It is built mysteriously in your soul.

St Isaac the Syrian

There is a double point in food for the soul. It is fed on its progress with virtues and visions, but when it has passed through all there is, and comes to the measure of the stature of Christ's fullness, it stays there and ceases from all progress towards increase by intermediate means, but being fed directly, without intermediaries, in a way that passes our understanding and perhaps passes the possibility of growth, it receives an incorruptible food, given for its sustenance and completion in godlike being, and for showing to us the countless joys that this food brings. And so receiving power to be always like this and to live in this way, it becomes God by participation in the divine grace. When it has ceased from mental and sensible activity, and finished with the natural operations of the body, the process of becoming God is completed according to the participation which renders it like Him; and so God alone is manifested in soul and body, all their natural characteristics overwhelmed by the overflowing of His glory.

St Maximus the Confessor

ON THE PRAYER OF JESUS

The object of our search is the fire of grace which enters into the heart. . . . When the spark of God Himself – grace – appears in the heart, it is the prayer of Jesus which quickens it and fans it into flame. But it does not itself create the spark – it gives only the possibility that it may be received, by recollecting the thoughts and making ready the soul before the face of the Lord. The essential thing is to hold oneself ready before the Lord, calling out to Him from the depths of one's heart. . . . God is concerned with the heart.

Theophanes, known as 'the Recluse'

If then from the first you enter through the mind into the place of the heart, as I have shown you, give thanks to God and praise him with transports of joy for all this work in you, which will teach you what you could not otherwise know. It is needful to learn this while your mind is in this condition, and not to keep silent, and so be fruitless. For your unceasing occupation ought to be to keep on saying: 'Lord Jesus, Son of God, have mercy on me.' This practice of continual recollection gives no handle or opportunity to the suggestions of the enemy, but leads us on day by day to more love and longing for God.

Nicephorus the Solitary

Experience will soon show that in using this method (i.e. the Jesus Prayer), the words should be pronounced with extreme unhurriedness, so that the mind may be able to enter into the words as into forms. . . . One must train oneself as if one were reading by syllables – with the same unhurriedness.

Brianchaninov: On the Prayer of Jesus

In order that the true teaching on the elementary stages of this mental prayer should not be lost, they (i.e. the spiritual directors) expound in writing the actual beginning, ways and exercises – how beginners must train themselves to enter with the mind into the land of the heart, and there truly and without delusion perform prayer with the mind.

Brianchaninov

Try to restore, or more exactly, to enclose your thoughts in the words of the prayer. If on account of its infancy, it wearies and wanders, lead it in again.

St John of the Ladder, quoted by Brianchaninov

It is one thing frequently to look into the heart, and another to entrust the watch of the heart to the mind, that prince and bishop that offers spiritual sacrifices to Christ.

St John of the Ladder, quoted by Brianchaninov

Thus, he who prays by the method proposed by St John of the Ladder will pray with the lips and the mind and the heart. And when he becomes proficient in prayer he will acquire mental prayer and the prayer of the heart.

Brianchaninov

It is one thing to pray with attention with the participation of the heart. It is another thing to descend with the mind into the temple of the heart and from there to offer mystical prayer filled with the divine grace and power. The second is the result of the first. The attention of the mind during prayer draws the heart into sympathy. With the strengthening of the attention, sympathy of heart and mind is turned into unity of heart and mind. Finally when attention makes the prayer its own, the mind descends into the heart for the most profound and sacred service of prayer.

Brianchaninov

Once upon a time he was praying and saying secretly in his heart 'God, have mercy upon me, the sinner', when a single divine ray shone right down on him and the room was full of light, and the young man, the blessed young man, George I mean, stayed there in ecstasy, forgot his individual self, and found no walls around or roof over his head, because he saw light on every side, just as if he were out of doors; and he received no sense-impressions, not even of standing on the ground; he was rather walking on air. He had no bodily cares or concerns of this world on his mind, but forgot the world and was wholly dissolved to become one with the divine light, so that it seemed to him that he was the light. He was filled with tears and joy unspeakable. After this his mind went up to the heavenly places and there he saw a fuller and a brighter light, and looking into this it seemed to him that the elder was standing who gave him the little book by St Mark (the hermit) and his own rule of life. . . . And so it was in truth that love and the desire he had for God took him out of the world in the spirit, and he forgot the world and the flesh and all the vain business of this life and was translated wholly into God. . . . Yet he lived in a city and had business in government offices, and was steward in the house of a great ruler, with many slaves and servants, discharging important duties there.

St Simeon the New Theologian, telling the
story of a young man called George

13. The Mysticism of the Intellect

ST AUGUSTINE,

The Confessions

ST AUGUSTINE is one of the supremely dominant figures of Western Christianity and through his Confessions, *the story of the spiritual struggles which resulted in his return to Catholicism, is one of the best known.*

He was born in North Africa in A.D. *354. For ten years he was a Manichaean. Manichaeism was a syncretism of Persian and Christian ideas, dualistic in character, which pictured the world-process as an eternal battle between the powers of light and darkness. His acute mind was not, however, satisfied and, as he began to read the writings of the Neoplatonists, particularly of Plotinus, he was gradually led towards the Catholic Faith. In 387 he was baptized by St Ambrose of Milan; in 391 ordained priest and, in 396, consecrated Bishop of Hippo in North Africa, where he remained until his death in 430.*

St Augustine lived in troublous times. The Western Roman Empire was collapsing under the pressure of the Teutonic barbarians. In 410 the Eternal City of Rome was sacked by Alaric and his Visigoths; in 429, a year before St Augustine's death, the province of North Africa was overrun by the Vandals. His ponderings on the historical situation in which he found himself led to his writing one of his greatest books, The City of God.

While Dean Inge considers that it is hardly justifiable to claim St Augustine as a mystic at all, Dom Cuthbert Butler o.s.b., *the author of* Western Mysticism, *calls him the 'Prince of Mystics', since in him is found in a unique form a combination of penetrating intellectual vision of spiritual things and passionate love of God.*

While I should not be inclined to give St Augustine the title of Prince of Mystics, I share Dom Butler's view of his importance in the history of Christian mysticism. While he never reached the heights of mystical vision of a Ruysbroeck or a St John of the Cross, nor wrote any treatise of the highest order on the Contemplative Life, the experiences he describes in the Confessions *are undeniably mystical in character. His importance lies in his balance, his breadth, his universality, his vast charity. He was able to combine in himself the practical administrator, the brilliant philosophical and theological thinker, and the mystic. There is in him no conflict between the personal, the institutional, and the intellectual sides of religion, between the life of contemplation and the life of action. Though animated by a passionate love, his mysticism is primarily one of the intellect, a mysticism of knowledge and understanding. In addition, he showed forth in his dedicated life in a particularly vivid way what I have called the mysticism of action.*

The translation used in the passages printed is that by Dr E. B. Pusey, of which there have been numerous editions.

And being thence admonished to return to thyself, I entered even into my inward self, Thou being my Guide; and able I was, for Thou wert become my Helper. And I entered and beheld with the eye of my soul (such as it was), above the same eye of my soul, above my mind, the Light Unchangeable. Not this ordinary light, which all flesh may look upon, nor, as it were, a greater of the same kind, as though the brightness of this should be manifold brighter, and with its greatness take up all space. Not such was this light, but other, yea, far other from all these. Nor was it above my soul, as oil is above water, nor yet as heaven above earth; but above my soul, because It made me; and I below It, because I was made by It. He that knows the Truth, knows what that Light is; and he that knows It, knows eternity. Love knoweth it. O Truth Who art Eternity! and Love Who art Truth! and Eternity Who art Love! Thou art my God, to Thee do I sigh night and day. Thee when I first knew, Thou liftedst me up, that I might see there was what I might see, and that I was not yet such as to see. And Thou didst beat back the weakness of my sight, streaming forth Thy beams of light upon me most strongly, and I trembled with love and awe: and I perceived myself to be far off from Thee, in the region of unlikeness, as if I heard this Thy voice from on high: 'I am the food of grown men; grow, and thou shalt feed upon Me; nor shalt thou convert Me, like the food of thy flesh, into thee, but thou shalt be converted into Me. . . .'

And I wondered that now I loved Thee, and no phantasm for Thee. And yet did I not press on to enjoy my God; but was borne up to Thee by Thy beauty, and soon borne down from Thee by mine own weight, sinking with sorrow into these inferior things. This weight was carnal custom. Yet dwelt there with me a remembrance of Thee; nor did I any way doubt, that there was One to whom I might cleave, but that I was not yet such as to cleave to Thee: for that the body which is corrupted, presseth down the soul, and the earthly tabernacle weigheth down the mind that museth upon many things. And most certain I was, that Thy invisible works from the creation of the world are clearly seen, being understood by the things that are made, even Thy eternal power and God-head. For examining, whence it was that I admired the beauty of bodies celestial or terrestrial; and what aided me in judging soundly on things mutable, and pronouncing, 'This ought to be thus, this not'; examining, I say, whence it was that I so judged, seeing I did so judge, I had found the unchangeable and true Eternity of Truth, above my changeable mind. And thus by degrees, I passed from bodies to the soul, which through the bodily senses perceives; and thence to its inward faculty, to which the bodily senses represent things external, whitherto reaches the faculties of beasts; and thence again to the reasoning faculty, to which what is received from the senses of the body, is referred to be judged. Which, finding itself also to be in me a thing variable, raised itself up to its own understanding, and drew away my thoughts from the power of habit, withdrawing itself from those troops of contradictory phantasms; that so it might find what that light was, whereby it was bedewed, when, without all doubting, it cried out, 'That the unchangeable was to be preferred to the changeable'; whence also it knew That Unchangeable, which, unless it had in some way known, it had had no sure ground to prefer it to the changeable. And thus with the flash of one trembling glance it arrived at THAT WHICH IS. And then I saw Thy invisible things understood by the things which are made. But I could not fix my gaze thereon; and my infirmity being struck back, I was thrown again on my wonted habits, carrying along with me only a loving memory thereof, and a longing for what I had, as it were, perceived the odour of, but was not yet able to feed on.

Book VII

And when our discourse was brought to that point,* that the very highest delight of the earthly senses, in the very purest material light, was, in respect of the sweetness of that life, not only not worthy of comparison, but not even of mention; we, raising up ourselves with a more glowing affection towards the 'self-same', did by degrees pass through all things bodily, even the very heaven, whence sun and moon, and stars shine upon the earth; yea, we were soaring higher yet, by inward musing, and discourse, and admiring of Thy works; and we came to our own minds, and went beyond them, that we might arrive at that region of never-failing plenty, where Thou feedest Israel for ever with the food of truth, and where life is the Wisdom by whom all these things are made, and what have been, and what shall be; and she† is not made, but is, as she hath been, and so shall she be ever; yea rather, to 'have been' and 'hereafter to be' are not in her, but only 'to be', seeing she is eternal. For to 'have been' and to 'be hereafter', are not eternal. And while we were discoursing and panting after her, we slightly touched on her with the whole effort of our heart; and we sighed, and there we left bound the first fruits of the Spirit; and returned to vocal expressions of our mouth, where the word spoken has beginning and end.

Book IX

Not without doubting, but with assured consciousness, do

---

* St Augustine is writing of a talk with his mother, Monica, just before her death.

† i.e. Wisdom.

I love Thee, Lord. Thou hast stricken my heart with Thy word, and I loved Thee. Yea also heaven and earth, and all that therein is, behold on every side, they bid me love Thee; nor cease to say so unto all, that they may be without excuse. ... But what do I love, when I love Thee? not beauty of bodies, nor the fair harmony of time, nor the brightness of the light, so gladsome to our eyes, nor sweet melodies of varied songs, nor the fragrant smell of flowers, and ointments, and spices, not manna and honey, not limbs acceptable to embracements of flesh. None of these I love, when I love my God; and yet I love a kind of light, and melody, and fragrance, and meat, and embracement, when I love my God, the light, melody, fragrance, meat, embracement of my inner man; where there shineth unto my soul, what space cannot contain, and there soundeth, what time beareth not away, and there smelleth, what breathing disperseth not, and there tasteth, what eating diminisheth not, and there clingeth, what satiety divorceth not. This is it which I love, when I love my God.

And what is this? I asked the earth, and it answered me, 'I am not He'; and whatsoever are in it confessed the same. I asked the sea and the deeps, and the living creeping things, and they answered, 'We are not thy God, seek above us.' I asked the moving air; and the whole air with his inhabitants answered, 'Anaximenes was deceived, I am not God.' I asked the heavens, sun, moon, stars, 'Nor (say they) are we the God whom thou seekest.' And I replied unto all the things which encompass the door of my flesh: 'Ye have told me of my God, that ye are not He; tell me something of Him.' And they cried out with a loud voice, 'He made us.' My questioning them, was my thoughts on them; and their form of beauty gave the answer. And I turned myself unto myself, and said to myself, 'Who art thou?' And I answered, 'A man.' And behold, in me there present themselves to me, soul and body, one without, the other within. By which of these ought I to seek my God? I had sought Him in the body from earth to heaven, so far as I could send messengers, the beams of mine eyes. But the better is the inner, for to it as presiding and judging, all the bodily messengers reported the answers of heaven and earth, and all things therein, who said, 'We are not God, but He made us.' These things did my inner man know by the ministry of the outer: I the inner, knew them; I, the mind, through the senses of my body. I asked the whole frame of the world about my God; and it answered me, 'I am not He, but He made me.' . . .

What then do I love, when I love my God? who is He above the head of my soul? By my very soul will I ascend to Him. I will pass beyond that power whereby I am united to my body, and fill its whole frame with life. Nor can I by that power find my God; for so horse and mule that have no understanding, might find Him; seeing it is the same power, whereby even their bodies live. But another power there is, not that only whereby I animate, but that too whereby I imbue with sense my flesh, which the Lord hath framed for me: commanding the eye not to hear, and the ear not to see; but the eye, that through it I should see, and the ear, that through it I should hear; and to the other senses severally, what is to each their own peculiar seats and offices; which, being divers, I the one mind, do through them enact. I will pass beyond this power of mine also; for this also have the horse and mule, for they also perceive through the body.

I will pass then beyond this power of my nature also, rising by degrees unto Him, who made me. And I come to the fields and spacious palaces of my memory, where are the treasures of innumerable images, brought into it from things of all sorts perceived by the senses. . . .

Great is the power of memory, a fearful thing, O my God, a deep and boundless manifoldness; and this thing is the mind, and this am I myself. . . . I will pass even beyond this power of mine which is called memory: yea, I will pass beyond it, that I may approach unto Thee, O sweet Light. . . .

Where then did I find Thee, that I might learn Thee? For in my memory Thou wert not, before I learned Thee. Where then did I find Thee, that I might learn Thee, but in Thee above me? Place there is none; we go backward and forward, and there is no place. Everywhere, O Truth, dost Thou give audience to all who ask counsel of Thee, and at once answerest all, though on manifold matters they ask Thy counsel. Clearly dost Thou answer, though all do not clearly hear. All consult Thee on what they will, though they hear not always what they will. He is thy best servant, who looks not so much to hear that from Thee, which himself willeth; as rather to will that, which from Thee he heareth.

Too late loved I Thee, O Thou Beauty of ancient days, yet ever new! too late I loved Thee! And behold, Thou wert within, and I abroad, and there I searched for Thee; deformed I, plunging amid those fair forms, which Thou hadst made. Thou wert with me, but I was not with Thee. Things held me far from Thee, which, unless they were in Thee, were not at all. Thou calledst, and shoutedst, and burstest my deafness. Thou flashedst, shonest, and scatteredst my blindness. Thou breathedst odours and I drew in breath and pant for Thee. I tasted, and hunger and thirst. Thou touchedst me, and I burned for Thy peace.

Book X

14. The Mysticism of Love

ST BERNARD OF CLAIRVAUX

In 1112 the young Bernard, with four of his brothers and twenty-five companions, entered the Cistercian Abbey of Cîteaux. A great century in European history had just opened. It was a century of vigorous, flowering life, the century of the Crusades, of the rise of towns, of the beginnings of Gothic architecture, of the emergence of vernacular literature, of the revival of Latin studies, and the founding of the first European universities, and, through contacts with the Moslem world, of the rediscovery of Greek science. Of this twelfth-century Renaissance the revival of spiritual and mystical life among the Carthusian, Benedictine, Cistercian, and Augustinian Orders is an important and essential part. The chief figures in this mystical revival are the Cistercians, William of Saint-Thierry and St Bernard, and the Augustinians, Hugh and Richard of St Victor.

The men of the twelfth century were deeply concerned with the problem of love, carnal as well as spiritual. The century saw the emergence of that ideal of romantic love, so vividly mirrored in its literature, and its mysticism is fundamentally the mysticism of love. The foundation stone of St Bernard's mysticism is the love of God. One finds in him little if anything of the Divine Dark of the Pseudo-Dionysian tradition, which is so evident in the later German and Flemish mystics. For St Bernard God is love and the Mystic Way is, for him therefore, chiefly, indeed one might say solely, a continuous apprenticeship in love. The condition of knowledge of and union with God is, for him, the possession of pure and ardent love.

Before the soul can be united to God, two things must, according to St Bernard, take place. First of all, there must be a rectification of the reason by the Word, the Wisdom of God; out of this is born humility. Secondly, there must be a rectification of the will by the Holy Spirit; out of this association of the Spirit of God and the human will is born charity.

Of these two faculties of the soul, that is to say reason and will [he wrote], the one is taught by the Word of Truth, the other inspired by the Spirit of Truth; the one is sprinkled with the hyssop of humility, the other is set on fire by charity. And now become a perfect soul from which humility has removed all stains, and in which charity has left no wrinkle, in which the will no longer resists reason, nor does reason trifle with truth, then does the Father unite it closely with Himself as His glorious Bride, in such wise that reason is no longer allowed to think of itself, nor may the will think of the neighbour, but the entire delight of that blessed soul will be to say: 'Introduxit me Rex in cubiculum suum [the King has led me into his bed].'*

The fact of earthly love is St Bernard's starting-point. There is first the love of oneself and one's own interests; then love in a higher form, the love of one's neighbour; and then love at its highest, the love of God; and in this there is a reciprocal action which has its fount in God. We can love God because He first loved us. St Bernard would have been in full agreement with the Moslem mystic, Abu Yazid, when he said: 'I sought for God for thirty years; I thought it was I who desired Him, but, no, it was He who desired me.'

The passages printed below, from St Bernard's Sermons on the Song of Songs, *have been specially translated for me by my friend Dr A. L. Peck, Fellow of Christ's College, Cambridge.*

THE NATURE OF MYSTICAL EXPERIENCE

But now bear awhile with my foolishness. I would tell you, as indeed I promised, how it is with me in these matters. I confess, then, that the Word has come even to me (I speak as a fool), and has come many times. Yet although He has often come in unto me, I have never perceived the moment of His coming; I have perceived Him present, I remember He has been present; sometimes I have actually been able to have a premonition of His entry, but never to be aware of it when it happens, nor of His going out from me. For whence He came into my soul, and whither He went when He left it again, by what way He came in or went out, even now I confess I do not know, as the Gospel says, 'Thou canst not

* Quoted in Gilson, *The Mystical Theology of St Bernard* (Sheed & Ward), from the *Sermons on the Song of Songs*.

tell whence He cometh or whither He goeth.' Nor is this to be wondered at, for He is that very one to whom these words were spoken, 'And thy footsteps are not known.' Certainly it was not by the eyes that He entered, for He has no colour; nor by the ears, for He made no sound; nor by the nostrils, for He blends not with the air but with the soul; nor did He make the air fragrant – He *made it*. Nor again did He enter through the mouth, for He is not to be eaten or drunk; nor could He be discerned by touch, for He is impalpable. By what way then did He enter? Can it be that He did not enter at all, because He did not come from outside? for He is not one of the things that are without. Yet again, He did not come from within me, for He is good, and I know that *no good thing dwelleth in me*. I have gone up to the highest that I have, and behold, the Word was towering yet higher. My curiosity took me to my lowest depth to look for Him, nevertheless He was found still deeper. If I looked outside me, I found He was beyond my farthest; if I looked within, He was more inward still. And so I have understood the truth of that I had read, 'In Him we live and move and have our being.' But blessed is the man in whom He is, who lives unto Him, who moves by Him.

74 : 5

You ask, then, since His ways are thus beyond all searching out, how did I know the Word was present? Because He is living, and powerful to act and to do; and as soon as He came within He roused my sleeping soul, He stirred and softened and wounded my heart, for it was hard and stony and poor in health. He began, too, to pluck out and to destroy, to build up and to plant, to water the dry places, to lighten the dark corners, to throw open the closed doors, to enkindle the chilled regions, *to make the crooked straight and the rough places plain*, so that *my soul blessed the Lord, and all that was within me praised His holy Name*. So then, the Word, the Bridegroom, though several times He has come in unto me, has never made known His entry by any signs or tokens, neither by voice, nor by sight, nor by gait. In fine, it was by no movements of His that He became known to me, nor could I tell by any senses of mine that He had passed into my inmost parts; only by the movement of my heart, as I said at the outset, did I recognize His presence; and by the flight of all vices from me, and by the suppression of all carnal desires, I was aware of the power of His might; and from the discovery and conviction of my secret faults I came to wonder at the depth of His wisdom; and from the amendment (small though it were) of my life and conversation I learnt of His goodness and loving kindness; and through the renewing and refashioning of the spirit of my mind, that is, of my inner man, I perceived in some measure His excellent beauty; and from gazing upon all these things together I was filled with awe at His abundant greatness.

74 : 6

THE MARRIAGE OF LOVE

It is this conformity which brings about the marriage of the soul with the Word, when the soul, being already like unto Him in nature, shows itself like unto Him also in will, loving as itself is loved. So, if it love thus perfectly, it is wedded to Him. Is there anything more joyful than this conformity? Is there anything more to be desired than charity, charity which makes thee, O soul, no longer content with human tutelage, go forward of thine own accord with full confidence to approach the Word, to cleave steadfastly to the Word, to address thy questions to Him as to a friend, to ask his counsel upon every matter, as receptive in thine intelligence as thou art fearless in thy desire? This is the marriage-contract of a truly spiritual and holy union: no, contract is too weak a description; it is an embrace. . . . Nor need we fear that the inequality of the two partners will make the concurrence of their wills halting or lame, for love is no respecter of persons, and it is from loving, not from paying honour, that love takes its name. Indeed, one who is horror-stricken, one who is filled with amazement, or with fear, or with wonder, may well pay honour; but to a lover all these have lost their meaning. Love provides its own sufficiency: where love has come to be, it subdues all other affections and makes them part of itself; and that is why the soul that loves, loves and knows naught else at all. He who is a worthy object of honour, of amazement, of admiration, he loves rather in order to be loved. They are Bridegroom and Bride.

83 : 3

This Bridegroom is not only loving, he is love. ... God demands to be feared, as Lord; to be honoured, as Father; as Bridegroom, to be loved. Which of these is the highest, which the noblest? Love, we cannot doubt. Without love, fear hath torment and honour hath no grace. Fear is servile, so long as love set it not free; and honour which flows not out from love is not honour but flattery. Truly honour and glory are due to God alone; but God will not accept of either, unless they be seasoned with the honey of love. Love is sufficient of itself; it is pleasant of itself and for its own sake. Love itself is a merit, and itself its own reward. Beyond itself love seeks neither cause nor outcome: the outcome of it is one with the practice of it. I love, because I love; I love, that I may love. A great reality is love, if only it return to its source, if it be restored again to its first beginning, if it be poured back into its fount and ever draw therefrom whence it perpetually flows. Of all the movements of the soul, of all its feelings and affections, it is love alone by which the creature responds to its creator, though in less than equal measure, and pays back to him somewhat of that it has received. ... When God loves, he wants nothing else than to be loved; for he loves for no other purpose than that he may be loved, knowing that those who love him are blessed by that very love.

83 : 4

Love then is a great reality; but there are degrees of love, and highest of all stands the bride. Children love their fathers, but they are thinking about the inheritance they expect to get, and so long as they are afraid that somehow they may lose it, their respect for their father is the greater and their love for him the less. I am suspicious of that love which I see to be animated by the hope of getting something. It is weak, for if that hope is taken away, then it goes out altogether, or its flame burns low. It is impure, for it desires something else. Pure love is not mercenary. Pure love does not draw its strength from hope, nor is it injured by distrust. This is the love that the bride has; for all and everything she is, is this. All her being, all her hope, is love and love alone. The bride overflows with love, and therewith the bridegroom is content. He seeks nought else from her; she has nought else to give. It is this which makes him the bridegroom, her the bride. This is the love which belongs only to those who are joined in marriage, the love which none other, not even a son, can attain unto.

83 : 5

Rightly, then, does the bride renounce all other affections and give herself up wholly to love and to love alone, for she is able to make some return to love by loving him back again. For when she has poured her whole self forth into love, how little this is when compared with that fountain which flows in a never-failing stream! Truly they flow not in equal volume, the Lover and love himself, the soul and the Word, the bride and the Bridegroom, the Creator and the creature: it is as though we were to compare a thirsty man with the spring he drinks from. Well then: shall the prayer of the bride that is to be, the deep longing of her aspirations, her loving fervour, her confident anticipation, come to nought and be wholly cast away, on this account, that she cannot keep pace with this Giant who runs ahead, that she cannot vie in sweetness with the honey, in gentleness with the lamb, in whiteness with the lily, in clarity with the sun, in charity with Him who is Himself Charity? No; for though the creature may love less than He, for that she is less, yet if she love with her whole self, nought is wanting there where the whole is given. Wherefore, as I have said, thus to love is to be joined together in wedlock, for it is impossible that a soul should love thus and not be beloved; and it is the unity of their two wills that makes the complete and perfect marriage, to which nothing is lacking.

83 : 6

15. The Four Degrees of Passionate Love

RICHARD OF ST VICTOR

RICHARD OF ST VICTOR, *a contemporary of St Bernard, who died in 1173 as prior of the Abbey of St Victor in Paris, is not numbered among the best-known of the mystics. Yet in the history of Christian mysticism he occupies an important place. He was the first mystical writer to put his hand to the systematizing of mystical theology and he anticipates the Scholastic faith in reason.*

His approach is primarily psychological; he was intensely interested in the way the rational and non-rational faculties combine, not only in mystical states, but also in all acts of perception and thought. He held that contemplation was capable of a wider meaning than the restricted one that is sometimes given to it. He dealt with it as a mode of knowing, a way of considering every kind of knowledge, from sense objects to the Being of God.

Even in contemplation in the strictly mystical sense, ordinary rational modes of knowledge have, according to Richard, a part to play; and the intellect or intelligence, in the sense medieval philosophers used the term, is, according to him, the instrument in the contemplative act, at least in its earlier stages.

Particularly in the Benjamin Major, *the second of his two major works – the other, the* Benjamin Minor, *deals as its sub-title indicates, with the preparation of the soul for contemplation – Richard gives much attention to the psychological study of the non-rational and the psycho-physical phenomena of union, which was to receive so much attention later. He speaks of a state of revelation or shewing, and of a double unveiling, at the same time that of the eye of man, so that he may see God, and of the mystery which he is then enabled to see. He speaks, too, of that state of unknowing, which we came across in* The Mystical Theology, *when the highest consciousness of the intelligence ceases to function. He calls it* excessus mentis *or* alienatio, *an abstraction or alienation of the faculties; or sometimes* extasis.

*Just before his death Richard wrote a little treatise on the mystical
life called* The Four Degrees of Passionate Charity. *Compared
with the* Benjamin Major *and the* Benjamin Minor *it is very
short. It is, however, though not well known, one of the most beautiful
pieces of writing in the whole range of mystical literature. Nowhere
else, so far as I remember, is it more emphasized that the highest stage
of the mystical life is not one of selfish withdrawal from all concern
with the world and its sorrows, but is one in which a man, who has
attained the state of union, humbles himself and becomes the servant
of his fellow-men, following the pattern of the divine–human life, as
it was seen in Christ.*

*The passage printed below is an abridgement of the second half of
this exquisite exposition of the stages of the mystical life in the
translation of Clare Kirchberger, included in her* Richard of St
Victor: Select Writings on Contemplation (*Faber and Faber*).
This book, which also includes the two Benjamins, *has an excellent
sixty-page introduction.*

*A word ought to be said on Richard's style of writing. Like so
many medieval writers, he incorporates freely the words of Scripture
into the body of his sentences, so that sometimes they read like a
collection of texts. He also constantly employs the allegorical method
of interpreting Scripture, whereby characters and incidents of the
Old Testament are treated as 'types', which is common in these
writers.*

Let us go deeper and speak more openly. In the first degree
the soul thirsts for God, in the second she thirsts to go to
God, in the third she thirsts to be in God, in the fourth she
thirsts in God's way. She thirsts for God when she desires to
experience what that inward sweetness is that inebriates the
mind of man, when he begins to taste and see how sweet the
Lord is. She thirsts for God when she desires to be raised
above herself by the grace of contemplation and to see the
Lord in all His beauty, that she may truly say: 'For I
have seen the Lord face to face, and my life is preserved.' She
thirsts in God, when in ecstasy she desires to pass over into
God altogether, so that having wholly forgotten herself she
may truly say: 'Whether in the body or out of the body I

cannot tell.' She thirsts in God's way when, by her own will, I do not mean in temporal matters only but also in spiritual things, the soul reserves nothing for her own will but commits all things to God, never thinking about herself but about the things of Jesus Christ, so that she may say: 'I came not to do my own will but the will of the Father which is in heaven.'

In the first degree, God enters into the soul and she turns inward into herself. In the second, she ascends above herself and is lifted up to God. In the third the soul, lifted up to God, passes over altogether into Him. In the fourth the soul goes forth on God's behalf and descends below herself. In the first she enters into herself, in the second she goes forth from herself. In the first she reaches her own life, in the third she reaches God. In the first she goes forth on her own behalf, in the fourth she goes forth because of her neighbour. In the first she enters in by meditation, in the second she ascends by contemplation, in the third she is led into jubilation, in the fourth she goes out by compassion.

In the first degree spiritual feeling sweeter than honey enters into her soul and inebriates her with its sweetness, so that she has honey and milk on her tongue and her lips distil the honeycomb. Those who have felt this will give forth a memorial of abundant sweetness, for the mouth speaketh out of the abundance of the heart. This is the first consolation which they who renounce the world receive at first and it generally confirms them in their good intention. This is the heavenly food which is wont to refresh those who go forth from Egypt and to feed them in the wilderness; this is the hidden manna which no man knoweth who hath not received it. . . .

But first we must leave Egypt* behind, first we must cross the Red Sea. First the Egyptians must perish in the waves, first we must suffer famine in the land of Egypt before we can

* Egypt was commonly used as the symbol of the material world (cf. *The Hymn of the Robe of Glory*, pages 176–81). As the Israelites had to leave Egypt and endure the rigours of the desert of Sinai before reaching the Promised Land, so the soul must shake off the shackles of the material in order that it may find the Heavenly City.

receive this spiritual nourishment and heavenly food. He who desires that food of heavenly solitude let him abandon Egypt both in body and heart, and altogether set aside the love of the world. Let him cross the Red Sea, let him try to drive all sadness and bitterness out of his heart, if he desires to be filled with inward sweetness. First the Egyptians must be swallowed up. Let perverse ways perish lest the angelic citizens disdain an ignoble companion. First the foods of Egypt must fail, and carnal pleasures be held in abomination before we may experience the nature of those inner and eternal pleasures.

In this state the Lord often visits the hungry and thirsty soul, often He fills her with inward delight and makes her drink with the sweetness of His spirit. Nevertheless He reveals His presence but without showing His face. He infuses His sweetness but does not show His fair beauty. His loveliness is felt but His form is not discerned. Even now the clouds and darkness are round about Him and His throne is in the pillar of the cloud. Gentle and soothing is that which is felt, but altogether dark, what is seen. For He does not yet appear in the light, and though He be seen in the fire, the fire is a burning rather than an illumination. For He kindles the affection but does not yet illuminate the intellect. He inflames the desire but does not yet enlighten the intelligence. In this state the soul can feel her beloved but she cannot see Him. And if she does see Him it is as one sees by night. She sees as it were in a cloud, she sees Him at last in a mirror and darkly, not yet face to face.

At times [the mind] begins to be more bold and to ask for higher things. Nevertheless it does not receive immediately what it asks, nor according to its desire, though it may ask with deep desire. But knowing that he who asketh receiveth, who seeketh findeth, and that the door is opened to him that knocketh, again and again he is given confidence and his strength is renewed and he says: 'My face hath sought Thee. Thy face, O Lord, will I seek.' When the mind therefore goes forward to the grace of contemplation with great effort and ardent desire, it moves as it were into the second degree of

love, where it deserves to look, by divine shewing, upon that
which the eye cannot see nor the ear hear nor shall it enter the
heart of man, so that it may truly say: 'But to us, God hath
revealed them by His spirit.'

The shewing of the divine light in this state and the wonder
of the revelation arising from it, together with the perennial
memory thereof bind the soul indissolubly so that she is not
able to forget the happiness of her experience. And as in the
earlier degree, the delight which she has tasted satisfied the
soul and transfixes the affections, so in this degree, the brightness she has looked upon binds the thoughts that she may
neither forget it nor think about anything else.

The third degree of love is when the mind of man is ravished
into the abyss of divine light so that the soul, having forgotten
all outward things, is altogether unaware of itself and passes
out completely into its God. In this state it is wholly subdued,
the host of carnal desires are deeply asleep and there is silence
in heaven as it were for half an hour. And any suffering that
is left is absorbed in glory. In this state, while the soul is
abstracted from itself, ravished into that secret place of divine
refuge, when it is surrounded on every side by the divine fire
of love, pierced to the core, set alight all about, then it sheds
its very self altogether and puts on that divine life, and being
wholly conformed to the beauty it has seen passes wholly
into that glory. . . .

As soon as she is admitted to that inner secret of the divine
mystery, through the greatness of her wonder and the
abundance of joy, she is wholly dissolved in herself, or rather
into Him who speaks, when she begins to hear words that it is
not lawful for man to utter and to understand the strange and
hidden things of God. In this state she who cleaves to the
Lord is one spirit with him. In this state, as we have said, the
soul is altogether melted into him whom she loves and is
herself fainting away. . . .

Similarly those who have reached the third degree of love,
do nothing according to their own will, they leave nothing
at their own desire, but commit all things to the providence
of God. Every wish or desire of theirs hangs upon God's

sign and awaits the divine good pleasure. And as the first degree wounds the affection and the second binds the thoughts, so the third hinders action, so that a man cannot be occupied about anything unless the power of the divine will draws or drives him. When in this way the soul has been reduced in the divine fire, softened to the very core and wholly melted, nothing is wanting except that she should be shown what is God's good will, all pleasing and perfect, even the form of perfect virtue, to which she must be conformed. For just as the metal workers, when the metals are melted and the moulds set out, shape any form according to their will and produce any vessel according to the manner and mould that has been planned, so the soul applies herself in this degree, to be readily at the beck and call of the divine will, indeed she adapts herself with spontaneous desire to every demand of God and adjusts her own will, as the divine good pleasure requires. And as liquefied metal runs down easily wherever a passage is opened, so the soul humbles herself spontaneously to be obedient in this way, and freely bows herself in all acts of humility according to the order of divine providence.

In this state the image of the will of Christ is set before the soul so that these words come to her: 'Let this mind be in you, which was also in Christ Jesus: who being in the form of God, thought it not robbery to be equal with God, but emptied himself, and took upon him the form of a servant, and was made in the likeness of men, and was found in the habit of man; he humbled himself and became obedient unto death, even the death of the cross.' This is the form of the humility of Christ to which every man must conform himself, who desires to attain to the highest degree of perfect charity. For greater love has no man than this, that a man lay down his life for his friends. Those who are able to lay down their lives for their friends have reached the highest peak of charity and are already placed in the fourth degree of charity. They can fulfil the Apostle's bidding: 'Be ye therefore followers of God, as dear children: and walk in love, as Christ also hath loved us, and hath given himself for an offering and a sacrifice to God for a sweetsmelling savour.'

Therefore in the third degree the soul is glorified, in the fourth she is humbled for God's sake. In the third she is conformed to the divine light, in the fourth she is humbled for God's sake. In the third she is conformed to the divine light, in the fourth she is conformed to the humility of Christ. And though in the third she is in a way almost in the likeness of God, nevertheless in the fourth she begins to empty herself, taking the form of a servant, and begins to be found in fashion as a man. In the third degree she is as it were put to death in God, in the fourth she is raised in Christ. He that is in the fourth degree may say truly: 'I live yet not I, Christ liveth in me.' Such a man begins to live in newness of life, and for the rest, 'to him to live is Christ and to die gain'. He is truly in a strait between two desires, to be dissolved and be with Christ which is far better, but to remain in the flesh is necessary for our sakes. The charity of Christ compels him. Such a man becomes a new creature, for old things are passed away and lo! all things are made new. For in the third degree he is put to death, in the fourth, as it were, he rises from the dead, now he dieth no more, death hath no more dominion over him, for in that he liveth he liveth unto God.

Therefore, in this fourth degree, the soul is made in some way immortal and impassible. How can it be mortal if it cannot die? and how can it die if it cannot be separated from Him who is life? We know who said this: 'I am the way, the truth, and the life.' How then can a man die who cannot be separated from Him? 'For I am sure,' he saith, 'that neither death nor life, nor angels nor principalities, nor powers, nor things present, nor things to come, nor might, nor height, nor depth, nor any other creature, shall be able to separate us from the love of God which is in Christ Jesus.' Besides, does a man not seem, in some degree, impassible, who does not feel the misfortunes that he bears, who rejoices in injuries, and whatever pain he suffers he counts it to be glory? according to the saying of the Apostle: 'Gladly therefore I will glory in my infirmities that the power of Christ may dwell in me.' He who takes pleasure in sufferings and contumely for Christ, also seems to be impassible. 'Therefore, I take pleasure in infirmities, in reproaches, in necessities, in persecutions, in distresses for Christ's sake.' He who is in this degree can say confidently: 'I can do all things in him who strengtheneth me,' in that he knows how to be filled and how to be hungry, to abound and to suffer poverty. In this degree of charity he 'beareth all things, believeth all things, hopeth all things, endureth all things'. In this degree charity is long-suffering and is kind, is not ambitious, seeketh not her own, does not render evil for evil nor curse for a curse. But rather blesseth. He who ascends to this degree of charity is truly in the state of love that can say: 'I am made all things to all men that I might save all.' And such a man then desires to be made anathema from Christ for his brethren's sake. What shall we say then? In this degree of love the soul of man might seem to be mad, in that it will not suffer his zeal to be kept within bounds or measure. Is it not complete madness to reject true life, to accuse the highest wisdom, to resist omnipotence? And if a man desires to be separated from Christ for his brethren's sake, is that not a rejection of true life? . . . Consider to what boldness of presumption the perfection of charity can raise up the mind of man: behold how it induces him to presume beyond the power of a man! That which he hopes of God, what he does for God and in God and effects with God, is more than merely human. How utterly wondrous and amazing! The more he hopes from God the more he abases himself for God. The more he rises up in boldness, the more he descends in humility. Just as the goal to which he ascends by confidence is above man, so is the point to which he descends by patience, beyond man.

Therefore as we have said, in the first degree, the soul returns to itself; in the second it ascends to God; in the third it passes out into God; in the fourth it descends below itself. In the first and second it is raised; in the third and fourth it is transfigured. In the first it ascends to itself; in the second it transcends itself; in the third it is conformed to the glory of Christ; in the fourth it is conformed to the humility of Christ. Again, in the first it is led back; in the second it is transferred; in the third it is transformed; in the fourth it is resurrected.

16. The Sufi Path of Love

THE emergence of a rich mystical tradition in the heart of Islam, the most transcendental of all the higher religions, may seem at first sight surprising. That it should emerge suggests that mystical experience is the fundamental stuff of religion, that it is bound to burst out and be given expression, however alien to it the theological tenets in which a particular religious belief is expressed may seem to be.

While the mystical experiences described by the Sufi mystics follow the same general pattern as those described by the mystics of other religions, there are elements in Sufism which make it of great interest to the student of mysticism. A particular combination of historical, environmental, and psychological circumstance gave it a quality all its own.

To the Sufi mystic self-renunciation is the essential thing if any real progress in the higher stages of the spiritual life is to be made. It is not, however, as in some mystics, a renunciation of the world, in the sense of turning one's back on the world. Rather, the Sufi aspirant to union with God is bidden to plunge into the world, to merge himself in it, so that he may be able to understand what it truly is.

This process of self-mergence in the world is, however, different from that of the typical nature-mystic. For the Sufi aspirant was taught that, in order to be able to see the world as it really is, the senses must be purified; the would-be mystic must free himself from egocentric judgement, his organs of perception must become clear and unclouded, his I-hood must be surrendered, his affections and will must be subjugated. Then, and only then, can his heart become the measure of Divinity; then, and only then, can the rhythm of his inner life be in tune with the Universal Life, with Spirit, with Self, with the 'Love which moves the sun and the other stars'. Because the mystic has become 'merged' in God, he is able to see the world as it is, that is, as God sees it. It then assumes a new complexion. Beauty and *serenity are seen beneath all its apparent deformity and inhumanity. He hears in it a new music, sees a new colour, smells a new fragrance. God-mysticism and nature-mysticism coalesce.*

Self-mergence alike in God and in the world naturally expressed itself in poetry. Sufism produced a galaxy of poets, whose vision was one of God as Absolute Beauty and Absolute Love, and for whom earthly beauty and earthly love imaged and revealed the Divine Beauty and the Divine Love.

Whatever the path trod, the quest for complete and absolute self-mergence in Divinity is beset with danger. When the contemplative, to whatever religion he belongs, attains the state of the Unitive Life and undergoes the experiences which mark that state, he feels as though his individual self has ceased to exist, that it has been entirely lost in God. One need not go to the Sufi mystics to find this. It is there in Ruysbroeck, in Eckhart, in St John of the Cross's 'each seems to be God', in St Paul's 'I live; yet not I, but Christ liveth in me'. It is at the heart of the Hindu Tat twam asi *(Thou art That) formulation. It can, however, easily result in an egocentric deification, which is not a loss of selfhood, but a glorification of the individual ego, and be expressed in exaggerated outbursts, such as:* I am the One Real! Glory be to me! How great is my glory!

Some of the Sufis were guilty of using such exaggerated forms of expression to describe experiences which are known to many of the great contemplative saints. There were, however, men such as Al-Ghazali, who were not only mystics, but were also of high intellectual calibre and mental balance, who were able to interpret and express the Sufi experience of Union in terms which did not conflict with orthodox Moslem theology.

The descriptions of the quest for and union with God by these Sufi mystics are not only psychologically and intellectually illuminating, but are also often given exquisite expression; for, as we have said, Sufism produced men who were not only true mystics, but also poets. Persia, that home of poetry, produced more poet-mystics, inspired by the most profound spiritual experience, than any other country has done. Christianity has only one poet-mystic, St John of the Cross, who is comparable with Rumi, 'Attar, and some other Persian poet-mystics.

Enough has been written to introduce a school of mystics, unfamiliar

to many to whom the great contemplatives of Christendom are not
unknown. Let them speak for themselves.

1. THE VISION OF GOD IN EVERYTHING

In the market, in the cloister – only God I saw.
In the valley and on the mountain – only God I saw.
Him I have seen beside me oft in tribulation;
In favour and in fortune – only God I saw.
In prayer and fasting, in praise and contemplation,
In the religion of the Prophet – only God I saw.
Neither soul nor body, accident nor substance,
Qualities nor causes – only God I saw.
I oped mine eyes and by the light of His face around me
In all the eye discovered – only God I saw.
Like a candle I was melting in His fire:
Amidst the flames outflanking – only God I saw.
Myself with mine own eyes I saw most clearly,
But when I looked with God's eyes – only God I saw.
I passed away into nothingness, I vanished,
And lo, I was the All-living – only God I saw.

Baba Kuhi of Shiraz,* trans. by R. A. Nicholson

2. THE DIVINE BEAUTY AND LOVE

The Absolute Beauty is the Divine Majesty endued with
the attributes of power and bounty. Every beauty and perfection manifested in the various grades of beings is a ray of
His perfect beauty reflected therein. It is from these rays that
exalted souls have received their impress of beauty and their
quality of perfection. Whosoever is wise derives his wisdom
from the Divine wisdom. Wherever intelligence is found it
is the fruit of the Divine intelligence. In a word, all are attributes of Deity which have descended from the zenith of
the Universal and Absolute to the nadir of the particular and
relative. [They have descended] to the end that they may

---

* Baba Kuhi was the earliest Sufi poet of Persia; he died in 1050.

direct thy course from the part towards the Whole, and from
the relative deduce the Absolute, and not imagine the part
to be distinct from the Whole, nor to be so engrossed with
what is merely relative as to cut thyself off from the Absolute.

> The Loved One's rose-parterre I went to see,
> That beauty's Torch espied me, and, quoth He,
> 'I am the tree; these flowers My offshoots are.
> Let not these offshoots hide from thee the tree.'

> What profit rosy cheeks, forms full of grace,
> And ringlets clustering round a lovely face?
> When Beauty Absolute beams all around,
> Why linger finite beauties to embrace?

Jami,* trans. by E. H. Whinfield

From all eternity the Beloved unveiled His beauty in the
  solitude of the Unseen;
He held up the mirror to His own face, He displayed His
  loveliness to Himself.
He was both the spectator and the spectacle: no eye but His
  had surveyed the universe.
All was One, there was no duality, no pretence of 'mine' or
  'thine'.
The vast orb of Heaven, with its myriad incomings and out-
  goings, was concealed in a single point.
The Creation lay cradled in the sleep of non-existence, like a
  child ere it has breathed.
The eye of the Beloved, seeing what was not, regarded non-
  existence as existent.
Though He beheld His attributes and qualities as a perfect
  whole in His own essence,
Yet he desired that they should be displayed to Him in another
  mirror,
And that each of His eternal attributes should become manifest
  accordingly in a diverse form.

---

* Jami, saint and mystic, is commonly called the last great classical poet
of Persia. He wrote numerous lyrics and idylls, as well as many prose
works. He died in 1492.

Therefore He created the verdant fields of Time and Space
    and the life-giving garden of the world,
That every bough and fruit might show forth His various
    perfections.
The cypress gave a hint of His comely stature, the rose gave
    tidings of His beauteous countenance.
Wherever Beauty peeped out, Love appeared beside it;
    wherever Beauty shone in a rosy cheek, Love lit his torch
    from that flame.
Wherever Beauty dwelt in dark tresses, Love came and found a
    heart entangled in their coils.
Beauty and Love are as body and soul; Beauty is the mine
    and Love the precious stone.
They have always been together from the first: never have
    they travelled but in each other's company.

                                 Jami, trans. by R. A. Nicholson

    Beauty, wherever it is seen, whether in humanity or in
the vegetable or mineral world, is God's revelation of Himself; He is the all-beautiful, those objects in which we perceive
beauty being, as it were, so many mirrors in each of which
some fraction of His essential self is revealed. By virtue of its
Divine origin, the beauty thus perceived exercises a subtle
influence over the beholder, waking in him the sense of love,
whereby he is at last enabled to enter into communion with
God Himself. Thus God is the ultimate object of every
lover's passion; but while this is as yet unrealized by the
lover, while he still imagines that the earthly fair one is the
true inspirer and final goal of his affection, his love is still
in the 'typal' stage, and he himself still on the allegoric
'Bridge'.
    So Love is the guide to the World Above, the stair leading
up to the portal of Heaven; through the fire of Love iron is
transmuted into gold, and the dark clay into a shining gem.
Love it is that makes the heedless wise, and changes the
ignorant into an adept of the Divine mysteries; Love is the
unveiler of the Truth, the hidden way into the Sanctuary of
God. And as for the true Lover, he is pure of heart and holy

of life, worldly things are of no account with him, dust and
gold being equal in his eyes; generosity and gentleness
distinguish him; carnal desire stirs him not.

Fazil,* trans. by E. J. W. Gibb

3. THE SOUL AND GOD

Played by Thy Hand, the soul makes melody,
How art Thou in, and yet without the soul?
With Thee, my flame, I burn, without Thee, die;
   How farest Thou without me, O my Whole?

Whom seekest thou? What fever fills thy mind?
'Tis He is patent, thou the veil behind;
   Search after Him, and but thyself thou'lt see,
Search after Self, and naught but Him thou'lt find.

Thou only art in the Creator's 'Be'!
Thou only art the Sign that none may see;
   Then tread more fearlessly the road of life,
The world's broad plain containeth only thee.

The origins of Selfhood no man knows,
To dawn and eve no fellowship it owes,
   I heard this wisdom from the Heavenly Guide:
'Not older than its waves the Ocean flows.'

Heart, in the rosebud view life's mystery:
   Truth in Contingent there unveiled is shewn;
Although it springeth from the shadowed earth,
   Its gaze is fixed upon the radiant sun.

Garden and mead are in His radiance dight,
His wine the rose adorns in lustre bright,

---

* Fazil was a well-known Turkish poet; he died in 1811.

None in this world benighted He hath left,
His brand hath kindled in each heart a light.

> *Muhammad Iqbal,* trans. by A. J. Arberry*

When at thy love a lamp we light
Our barn of being is ablaze,
And of that inward glow so bright
A wisp of smoke to heaven we raise.

Turn thou on us thy beauty's sun:
Our day is dark without thy face,
But we are blind to every one
When we have seen thy matchless grace.

Lo, we have cast, and made our stake;
Our life and heart hang on a spin;
What better throw could gambler make
If, giving all, thy love he win?

Like children in thy school of love
The alphabet of love we learn;
Along thy path to death I move,
And I am glad; I will not turn.

> *'Iraqi,† trans. by A. J. Arberry*

4. THE EXPERIENCE OF THE MYSTIC

The heavenly rider passed;
The dust rose in the air;
He sped; but the dust cast
Yet hangeth there.

Straight forward thy vision be,
And gaze not left or right;

---

* Iqbal of Lahore (1876–1938), an eminent lawyer, philosopher, and statesman as well as a mystic and a poet. He was one of the founders of Pakistan.

† 'Iraqi, Persian poet and mystic, died in 1289.

His dust is here, and he
In the infinite.

*

As salt resolved in the ocean
I was swallowed in God's sea,
Past faith, past unbelieving,
Past doubt, past certainty.

Suddenly in my bosom
A star shone clear and bright;
All the suns of heaven
Vanished in that star's light.

*

Flowers every night
Blossom in the sky;
Peace in the Infinite;
At peace am I.

Sighs a hundredfold
From my heart arise;
My heart, dark and cold,
Flames with my sighs.

*

He that is my soul's repose
Round my heart encircling goes
Round my heart and soul of bliss
He encircling is.

Laughing, from my earthly bed
Like a tree I lift my head,
For the Fount of living mirth
Washes round my earth.

*

Happy was I
In the pearl's heart to lie;
Till, lashed by life's hurricane,
Like a tossed wave I ran.

The secret of the sea
I uttered thunderously;
Like a spent cloud on the shore
I slept, and stirred no more.

*

He set the world aflame,
And laid me on the same;
A hundred tongues of fire
Lapped round my pyre.

And when the blazing tide
Engulfed me, and I sighed,
Upon my mouth in haste
His hand he placed.

*

Through every way I try
His whim to satisfy,
His every answering word
Is a pointed sword.

See how the blood drips
From his finger-tips;
Why does He find it good
To wash in my blood?

*

Remembering Thy lip
The ruby red I kiss;
Having not that to sip,
My lips press this.

Not to Thy far sky
Reaches my stretched hand,
Wherefore, kneeling, I
Embrace the land.

*

I sought a soul in the sea
And found a coral there;
Beneath the foam for me
An ocean was all laid bare.

Into my heart's night
Along a narrow way
I groped; and lo! the light,
An infinite land of day.

Rumi,* trans. by A. J. Arberry

5. THE LOSS OF SELFHOOD

Whoever leaves this world behind him passes away from
mortality, and when he has passed away from mortality, he
attains to immortality. If thou dost desire to reach this abode
of immortality, and to attain this exalted station, divest thyself
first of self, and then summon unto thyself a winged steed
out of nothingness, to bear thee aloft. Clothe thyself with the
garment of nothingness and drink the cup of annihilation.
Cover thy breast with a nothingness, and draw over thy head
the robe of non-existence. Set thy foot in the stirrup of
complete renunciation and, looking straight before thee,
ride the steed of non-being to the place where nothing is.
Thou wilt be lost again and again, yet go on thy way in
tranquillity, until at last thou shalt reach the world where
thou art lost altogether to Self.

'Attar,† trans. by Margaret Smith

* Jalalud-din Rumi (1207–73), saint and mystic, and one of the most
profound of the Sufi poets.

† Farid al-din 'Attar (1119–1230?), saint and mystic, and one of the
most voluminous of Persian writers. He is possibly best known through
the elaborate allegory of the soul's quest for God, *The Conference of the
Birds*, the ending of which is printed below.

Wherefore it behoves thee to strive and hide thy *self* from thy sight, and occupy thyself with Very Being, and concern thyself with the 'Truth'. For the various grades of created things are theatres of His revealed beauty, and all things that exist are mirrors of His perfections.

And in this course thou must persevere until He mingles Himself with thy soul, and thine own individual existence passes out of thy sight. Then, if thou regardest thyself, it is He whom thou art regarding: if thou speakest of thyself, it is He of whom thou art speaking. The relative has become the Absolute, and 'I am the Truth' is equivalent to 'He is the Truth'.

Jami, trans. by E. H. Whinfield

6. THE ATTAINMENT OF UNION

The one who has passed beyond states and stages is distant from knowing aught save God Most High to such a degree that he is distant from knowledge of his own self and its states and intercourse and is like one stupefied, a diver in the very sea of Witnessing. . . . Of such as are in this condition the Sufis use the expression *faniya*, 'he has passed away from himself and come to an end', and whenever anyone passes away from himself he must pass away from all beside himself; then it is as though he passed away from everything except the One – the witnessed one. . . . Such a condition as this sometimes suddenly appears with regard to created things, and sometimes, also, with regard to the Creator. For the most part it is like swift lightning which stands not and lasts not: if it should last, human strength could not endure it. . . . This is the rank of him who wades the deep sea of verities and has passed the shoreland of states and works, and has occupied himself with the purity of the Unity and is confirmed in absolute sincerity.

Al-Ghazali,* trans. by R. B. Macdonald

* Abu Hamid Muhammad b. Muhammad al-Ghazali, the 'Proof of Islam' (1059–1111), was one of the leading scholars and theologians of his day. Converted to Sufism, he spent the latter days of his life as a simple mystic and tried more than anyone else to reconcile Sufi experience and teaching with the orthodox doctrine of Islam.

Those gnostics, on their return from their Ascent into the heaven of Reality, confess with one voice that they saw nought existent there save the One Real. Some of these arrived at this scientifically, and others experimentally and subjectively. From these last the plurality of things fell away in its entirety. They were drowned in the absolute Unitude, and their intelligences were lost in Its abyss. . . . Therein became they as dumbfoundered things. No capacity remained within them save to recall ALLAH; yea, not so much as the capacity to recall their own selves. So there remained nothing with them save ALLAH. They became drunken with a drunkenness wherein the sway of their own intelligence disappeared; so that one exclaimed, 'I am the ONE REAL!' and another, 'Glory be to ME! How great is MY glory!', and another, 'Within this robe is nought but Allah!' . . . But the words of Lovers Passionate in their intoxication and ecstasy must be hidden away and not spoken of. . . .

Now, when this state prevails, it is called in relation to him who experiences it, Extinction, nay, Extinction of Extinction, for the soul has become extinct to itself, extinct to its own extinction; for it becomes unconscious of itself and unconscious of its own unconsciousness, since were it conscious of its own unconsciousness, it would be conscious of itself. In relation to the man, immersed in this state, the state is called, in the language of metaphor, 'Identity'; in the language of reality, 'Unification'.

Al-Ghazali, trans. by W. H. T. Gairdner

Till of the mighty host that fledged the dome
Of heaven and floor of earth on leaving home,
A handful reached and scrambled up the knees
Of Kaf whose feet dip in the Seven Seas;
And of the few that up his forest-sides
Of Light and Darkness where the Presence hides,
But thirty – thirty desperate draggled things,
Half-dead, with scarce a feather on their wings,
Stunned, blinded, deafened with the crash and craze
Of rock and sea collapsing in the blaze

That struck the sun to cinder – fell upon
The Threshold of the Everlasting One,
With but enough of life in each to cry,
On THAT which all absorbed.

       And suddenly
Forth flashed a winged Harbinger of Flame
And Tongue of Fire, and 'Who?' and 'Whence they came?'
And 'Why?' demanded. And the Tajidar
For all the Thirty answered him: 'We are
Those fractions from the sum of Being, far
Dis-spent and foul disfigured, that once more
Strike for admission at the Treasury Door.'

To whom the Angel answered: 'Know ye not
That he you seek recks little who or what
Of Quantity and Kind – himself the Fount
Of Being Universal needs no count
Of all the drops that overflow his urn,
In what degree they issue or return?'
Then cried the Spokesman: 'Be it even so:
Let us but see the Fount from which we flow,
And, seeing, lose ourselves therein!' And lo!
Before the word was uttered, or the Tongue
Of Fire replied, or portal open flung,
They were *within* – they were before the Throne,
Before the Majesty that sat thereon,
But wrapt in so insufferable a blaze
Of glory as beat down their baffled gaze,
Which, downward dropping, fell upon a scroll
That, lightning-like, flashed back on each the whole
Past half-forgotten story of his soul;
Like that which Yusuf in his glory gave
His brethren as some writing he would have
Interpreted; and at a glance, behold
Their own indenture for their brother sold!
And so with these poor Thirty; who, abasht
In memory all laid bare and conscience lasht,
In full confession and self-loathing flung

The rags of carnal self that round them clung;
And, their old selves self-knowledged and self-loathed,
And in the soul's integrity reclothed,
Once more they ventured from the dust to raise
Their eyes – up to the Throne – into the blaze,
And in the centre of the Glory there
Beheld the Figure of *themselves* as 'twere
Transfigured – looking to *themselves*, beheld
The Figure on the Throne en-miracled,
Until their eyes themselves and *That* between
Did hesitate which Seer was, which Seen;
They That, That they: Another, yet the same;
Dividual, yet One: from whom there came
A Voice of awful answer, scarce discerned,
From *which* to Aspiration *whose* returned
They scarcely knew; as when some man apart
Answers aloud the question in his heart:
'The Sun of my Perfection is the glass
Wherein from *Seeing* into *Being* pass
All who, reflecting as reflected see
Themselves in Me and Me in them: not *Me*,
But all of Me that a contracted eye
Is comprehensive of Infinity;
Nor yet themselves: no selves, but of the All
Fractions, from which they split and whither fall.
As water lifted from the deep again
Falls back in individual drops of rain,
Then melts into the universal main.
All you have been, and seen, and done, and thought,
Not *you* but *I*, have seen, and been, and wrought:
I was the Sin which from Myself rebelled;
I the Remorse that toward Myself compelled;
I was the Tajidar who led the track:
I was the little Briar that pulled you back:
Sin and Contrition – Retribution owed,
And cancelled – Pilgrim, Pilgrimage, and Road,
Was but Myself toward Myself; and your
Arrival but *Myself* at my own door;

Who in your fraction of Myself behold
Myself within the mirror Myself hold
To see Myself in, and each part of Me
That sees himself, though drowned, shall ever see.
Come, you lost atoms, to your Centre draw,
And *be* the Eternal Mirror that you saw;
Rays that have wandered into darkness wide,
Return, and back into your Sun subside.'

'Attar, The ending of The Conference of the Birds,
trans. Edward Fitzgerald

17. Intellectual Vision

DANTE

THE poet's vision of God is, most commonly, one of God as immanent in the natural world. His experience is of the 'pan-en-henic' type, an experience of the All in the One, of the One in the All. His mysticism is, most frequently, some sort of Nature-mysticism. A combination of high poetic genius with the most profound kind of mystical experience is comparatively rare. It is found in a pre-eminent degree in some of the Sufi poet-mystics of Islam and in St John of the Cross. One of the outstanding examples of it is in the last hundred lines of Dante's Paradiso. Here we have a description of an 'intellectual' vision of the most profound order, a description in great poetry of what one cannot but believe was an experience actually undergone in some form or other by the poet of The Divine Comedy.

This passage in the Paradiso is an extremely difficult one to translate effectively. The translation used here is that of Barbara Reynolds in her completion of the Penguin Classics translation of The Divine Comedy, which Dorothy Sayers left unfinished at her death. In some places I feel that the blank verse translation of Henry Francis Cary may bring out the sense more clearly, as, for instance, in his version of the lines beginning, in Barbara Reynolds's translation, 'In that abyss I saw how love held bound . . .', which he translates as follows:

> 'and, in that depth,
> Saw in one volume, clasped of love, whate'er
> The universe unfolds; all properties
> Of substance and of accident, beheld
> Compounded, yet one individual light
> The whole. And of such bond methinks I saw
> The universal form.'

Some of the most puzzling lines are those beginning, 'The sphering

*thus begot. . . .' In the heart of the blazing circles of the Blessed Trinity
Dante sees the image of a Man. What is he trying to convey? It has
been suggested that the reference is to the mystery of the Incarnation.
That is probably true, but I would suggest that it may be something
more, that what Dante glimpsed was something similar to what was
seen by the birds in 'Attar's allegory, when, at the end of their long
pilgrimage, they at last enter the Presence,*

> And in the centre of the Glory there
> Beheld the Figure of themselves as 'twere
> Transfigured – looking to themselves beheld
> The Figure on the Throne en-miracled.

*In short, that what he saw was the supreme mystery of the inter-
relationship of the essence of God and the essence of man.*

*Dante Alighieri is too well known for it to be necessary to write
more than a few words about him here. He was born at Florence in
1265. He therefore overlaps Richard of St Victor and is a contemporary of Meister Eckhart. His life was an active one, spent amid the
turbulent political conditions of thirteenth- and fourteenth-century
Italy. His romantic, spiritual love for Beatrice has become a legend
and his greatest literary work,* The Divine Comedy, *which tells
of his pilgrimage through Hell, Purgatory, and Paradise, has placed
him among the small group of supremely great European poets. He
died, still exiled from his native Florence, in 1321.*

For now my sight, clear and yet clearer grown,
Pierced through the ray of that exalted light,
Wherein, as in itself, the truth is known.

Henceforth my vision mounted to a height
Where speech is vanquished and must lag behind,
And memory surrenders in such plight.

As from a dream one may awake to find
Its passion yet imprinted on the heart,
Although all else is cancelled from the mind,

So of my vision now but little part
Remains, yet in my inmost soul I know
The sweet instilling which it did impart.

So the sun melts the imprint on the snow,
Even so the Sybil's wisdom that was penned
On light leaves vanished on the winds that blow.

O Light supreme, by mortal thought unscanned,
Grant that Thy former aspect may return,
Once more a little of Thyself relend.

Make strong my tongue that in its words may burn
One single spark of all Thy glory's light
For future generations to discern.

For if my memory but glimpse the sight
Whereof these lines would now a little say,
Men may the better estimate Thy might.

The piercing brightness of the living ray
Which I endured, my vision had undone,
I think, if I had turned my eyes away.

And I recall this further led me on,
Wherefore my gaze more boldness yet assumed
Till to the Infinite Good it last had won.

O grace abounding, whereby I presumed
So deep the eternal light to search and sound
That my whole vision was therein consumed!

In that abyss I saw how love held bound
Into one volume all the leaves whose flight
Is scattered through the universe around;

How substance, accident, and mode unite
Fused, so to speak, together, in such wise
That this I tell of is one simple light.

Yea, of this complex I believe mine eyes
Beheld the universal form – in me,
Even as I speak, I feel such joy arise.

One moment brings me deeper lethargy
Than twenty-five centuries brought the quest that dazed
Neptune when Argo's shadow crossed the sea.

And so my mind, bedazzled and amazed,
Stood fixed in wonder, motionless, intent,
And still my wonder kindled as I gazed.

That light doth so transform a man's whole bent
That never to another sight or thought
Would he surrender, with his own consent;

For everything the will has ever sought
Is gathered there, and there is every quest
Made perfect, which apart from it falls short.

Now, even what I recall will be exprest
More feebly than if I could wield no more
Than a babe's tongue, yet milky from the breast;

Not that the living light I looked on wore
More semblances than one, which cannot be,
For it is always what it was before;

But as my sight by seeing learned to see,
The transformation which in me took place
Transformed the single changeless form for me.

That light supreme, within its fathomless
Clear substance, showed to me three spheres, which bare
Three hues distinct, and occupied one space;

The first mirrored the next, as though it were
Rainbow from rainbow, and the third seemed flame
Breathed equally from each of the first pair.

How weak are words, and how unfit to frame
My concept – which lags after what was shown
So far, 'twould flatter it to call it lame!

Eternal light, that in Thyself alone
Dwelling, alone dost know Thyself, and smile
On Thy self-love, so knowing and so known!

The sphering thus begot, perceptible
In Thee like mirrored light, now to my view –
When I had looked on it a little while –

Seemed in itself, and in its own self-hue,
Limned with our image; for which cause mine eyes
Were altogether drawn and held thereto.

As the geometer his mind applies
To square the circle, nor for all his wit
Finds the right formula, howe'er he tries,

So strove I with that wonder – how to fit
The image to the sphere; so sought to see
How it maintained the point of rest in it.

Thither my own wings could not carry me,
But that a flash my understanding clove,
Whence its desire came to it suddenly.

High phantasy lost power and here broke off;
Yet, as a wheel moves smoothly, free from jars,
My will and my desire were turned by love,

The love that moves the sun and the other stars.

From Canto xxxiii

18. Godhead, God, and the Soul

MEISTER ECKHART

MEISTER ECKHART, Dominican friar, brilliant and original preacher, and ardent Christian evangelist, born at Hochheim in Thuringia in 1260, is one of the most important and arresting figures in the history of mysticism. His place in Christian mysticism is unique.

A great part of Rudolf Otto's book, Mysticism, East and West, *is given over to a comparative study of the doctrines of Eckhart and the ninth-century Indian philosopher–mystic, Sankara. In his book Otto brings out clearly the basic similarity in the doctrines of the two men. He quotes this passage from Eckhart:*

When I came out from God, that is, into multiplicity, then all proclaimed, 'There is a God' [i.e. the personal God, Creator of all things]. Now this cannot make me blessed, for hereby I realize myself as creature. But in the breaking through [i.e. through all limitations], I am more than all creatures, I am neither God nor creature; I am that which I was and shall remain for evermore. There I receive a thrust which carries me above all angels. By this sudden touch I am become so rich that God [i.e. God as opposed to Godhead] is not sufficient for me, so far as he is only God and in all his divine works. For in this breaking through I perceive what God and I are in common. There I am what I was. There I neither increase nor decrease. For there I am the immovable which moves all things. Here man has won again what he is eternally [i.e. in his essential being] and ever shall be. Here God [i.e. the Godhead] is received into the soul.

This is Eckhart's teaching in a nutshell. Sankara would have used different terms, but it is his teaching too.

So here we have a sincere, believing Catholic Christian, whose language is the language of the Catholic Faith, whose mysticism is deeply Christo-centric, the 'adorable, lovable Master', 'who always taught the truth', 'from whom God hid nothing' (I quote from his contemporaries), the inspiration of Tauler, Suso, and Ruysbroeck, speaking a language which would not have been alien to the mystic of the East.

This surely is significant. But if mystical insight and experience is what we have presumed it to be, knowing no boundaries of race or creed, it is perhaps not surprising.

Though there are striking similarities, there are, as Otto points out, fundamental differences in conception between Eckhart and Sankara; Sankara's God (Brahman) is Being and Spirit through and through, utterly opposed to all matter. He is the resting, immobile Sat. Though there is in the God of Eckhart an eternal repose of the Godhead, God is for him the beginning and ending of a vast movement, a mighty eternal process of perpetually flowing life, in which He pours Himself out into the world of matter, multiplicity and time and draws it back into his unity and eternity; He is a living God. Sankara's idea of God is static, Eckhart's, because it is Christian, dynamic.

It is necessary, in order to understand Eckhart's thought – and this is also true of Ruysbroeck – to grasp the distinction he makes between Godhead and God. The Godhead is the abiding potentiality, containing in Itself all distinctions as yet undeveloped. The Godhead cannot therefore be the object of worship or knowledge. It is Darkness and Formlessness. God, the Blessed Trinity, is 'evolved from', or 'flows out from' – it is difficult to find a precise phrase – the Godhead. The three Persons, Father, Son, and Holy Spirit, of the Trinity are, however, not merely modes or accidents of the Divine Subsistence, emanations or appearances of the Absolute; they are inherent in the Godhead Itself.

The same dynamism which is found in Eckhart's conception of God is also found in his conception of Christ. He is the eternal Word, the only-begotten of the Father before all worlds; He is also the Word made flesh, entering the time process in a stable at Bethlehem. He is also the Word perpetually being born in the human soul.

With his God-mysticism Eckhart, like Sankara, combines soul-mysticism, a doctrine of the nobility of the soul in its essential nature. To find and know one's soul, to realize its glory, to penetrate to the abyss of the self and there discover the divine nature of the soul, on this theme Eckhart waxes lyrical (see below). In Eckhart's teaching, beneath sense perception, beneath the sensuous will, beneath the higher

powers of memory, reason, and reasonable will, lies the soul, the
apex, the spark, the heaven within. It is here that man may find God.

It is not easy to make selections from Eckhart's writings. They
are very voluminous. Moreover, his language is that of the Scholastic
philosophy of his time, with the result that his superb gems of spiritual
insight are not seldom buried in what to the modern reader seems to be
masses of unintelligible verbiage. Further, in his zeal to make his
point he sometimes indulges in wild exaggeration and paradox. This
got him into trouble with the ecclesiastical authorities; he had to
stand his trial for suspected heresy. I have selected a number of
passages from his Sermons *and* Tractates, *which bring out the main*
essentials of his teaching. They are taken from the Pfeiffer edition
of his works, translated, with some omissions and additions, by C. de
B. Evans, two volumes (Watkins).

ON THE NATURE OF THE DIVINE BEING
AND THE NOBILITY OF THE SOUL

God is his own form and matter; his form emerges from his
matter and according to this form does he form all things that
become. But his simple nature is in form formless, in mode
modeless, cause uncaused, being without becoming which
transcends all things becoming and all that becomes comes to
an end therein.

God is eternal and all things have been in him eternally.
They were not in themselves. Ere God created creatures he
was nothing whatever to creatures, in their understanding,
though in himself he was to them eternally the same as he is
now and always shall be. . . .

God in the Godhead is spiritual substance, so elemental
that we can say nothing about it excepting that it is naught.
To say it is aught were more lying than true. God in the Trinity
is the living light in its radiant splendour, a complex of one
nature with distinct Persons. . . . God in human nature is a
lamp of living light and this light shines in the darkness and
the darkness comprehends not this light. Darkness ever flees
from light as night does from the day. Thence comes her
knowledge of God's will. . . .

The Trinity is the heart of divine and human nature and human nature flows into the Trinity in a steady stream of love. Supposing the soul crosses over, then she sinks down and down in the abysm of the Godhead nor ever finds a footing unless it be that she has taken with her some temporal thing: resting on temporal things brings her back into the Trinity. ... Suppose one dropped a millstone from the sun to earth, the earth being pierced straight through the centre, the millstone would stop falling at the centre of the earth. Here is the heart of the earth, the stopping-place of everything on earth. So is the Trinity the stopping-place of creatures as a whole, all the Godhead has being gotten impartible and eternal from itself. The Father is the manifestation of the Godhead, the Son is the image and countenance of the Father and the Holy Ghost is the light of his countenance and the love of them both; all they have have they gotten eternally from their own selves. But the three Persons stooped in compassion towards human nature and the Son was made man and in this world was more despised than any man on earth, suffering want and pain from creatures himself had made in conjunction with his Father, by whose will he became man. Christ lived in time down to his death and then, arising from the dead, this most despised of men is seen united with the Godhead in the Person of the Christ who came on earth. Human nature wedded with the divine nature; her eternal portion, fellowship with divine nature in the same Person.

From Tractate XI

God has wrought one act eternally in which act he made the soul in his own (likeness), and out of which act and by means of which act the soul issued forth into her created existence, becoming unlike God and estranged from her own prototype, and in her creation she made God, who was not before the soul was made. ... I am the cause that God is God. God is gotten of the soul, his Godhead of himself; before creatures were, God was not God albeit he was Godhead which he gets not from the soul. Now when God finds a naughted soul whose self and whose activity have been brought to naught by means of grace, God works his eternal work in her above grace, raising her out of her created nature. Here God naughts himself in the soul and then neither God nor soul is left. Be sure that this is God indeed. When the soul is capable of conceiving God's work she is in the state of no longer having any God at all; the soul is then the eternal image as which God has always seen her, his eternal Word.

From Tractate XIX

While I subsisted in the ground, in the bottom, in the river and fount of Godhead, no one asked me where I was going or what I was doing: there was no one to ask me. When I was flowing all creatures spake God. If I am asked, Brother Eckhart, when went ye out of your house? Then I must have been in. Even so do all creatures speak God. And why do they not speak the Godhead? Everything in the Godhead is one, and of that there is nothing to be said. God works, the Godhead does no work, there is nothing to do; in it is no activity. It never envisaged any work. God and Godhead are as different as active and inactive. ... When I go back into the ground, into the depths, into the wellspring of the Godhead, no one will ask me whence I came or whither I went. No one missed me: God passes away.

From Sermon LVI

Thou shalt know him without image, without semblance and without means. – 'But for me to know God thus, with nothing between, I must be all but he, he all but me.' – I say, God must be very I, I very God, so consummately one that this he and this I are one *is*, in this is-ness working one work eternally; but so long as this he and this I, to wit, God and the soul, are not one single here, one single now, the I cannot work with nor be one with that he. ... 'How then shall I love him?' – Thou shalt love God non-spiritually, thy soul must be de-spiritualized: stripped of spirituality. For while thy soul is specifically spirit, she has form; the while she has form she has neither unity nor union; the while she lacks union she has never really loved God, for actual love lies in union. Wherefore let thy soul be de-spirited of all spirit; let it be spiritless; if thou lovest God as God, as spirit, as Person or as image, that must all go. – 'Then how shall I love him?' – Love him as he is: a not-God, a not-spirit, a not-Person, a not-image; as sheer, pure, limpid unity, alien from all duality. And in this one let us sink down eternally from nothingness to nothingness.

From Sermon XCIX

O wonder of wonders! when I think of the union of the soul with God! He makes the soul to flow out of herself in joyful ecstasy, for no named things content her. And since she is herself a nature named, therefore she fails to content herself. The divine love-spring surges over the soul, sweeping her out of herself into the unnamed being in her original source, for that is all God is. Creatures have given him names, but in himself he is nameless essence. Thus the soul arrives at the height of her perfection.

Further as concerns the noble nature of the soul. St Augustine says, 'As with God so with the soul.' Had God not made the soul in the likeness of himself, to be God by grace, she could never be God above grace. Her likeness to the pattern of the blessed Trinity we see by comparing her with God.

God is threefold in Person and onefold in his nature. God is in all places and in each place whole. In other words, all places are the place of God. And the same with her. God has prevision of all things and everything is pictured in his providence. This is natural to God. And also to the soul. She too is threefold in her powers and simple in her nature. She too exists in all her members and in each member whole. So that all her members are the place of the soul. She too has foresight and imagines such things as she is able. To anything that we can predicate of God, soul has a certain likeness. Or, in the words of St Augustine, 'Like God like the soul.' God had endowed the soul with his own likeness, which did she not possess she could not be God by grace nor above grace either; whereas in this likeness she is able to attain to being

God by grace and also above grace. And she must equal him in divine love and divine activity. So much for the soul as being God by grace. . . .

Let us see how the soul becomes God above grace. What God has given her is changeless, for she has reached a height where she has no further need of grace. In this exalted state she has lost her proper self and is flowing full-flood into the unity of the divine nature. But what, you may ask, is the fate of this lost soul: does she find herself or not? My answer is, it seems to me that she does find herself and that at the point where every intelligence sees itself with itself. For though she sink all sinking in the oneness of divinity she never touches bottom. Wherefore God has left her one little point from which to get back to herself and find herself and know herself as creature. For it is of the very essence of the soul that she is powerless to plumb the depths of her creator. Henceforth I shall not speak about the soul, for she has lost her name yonder in the oneness of divine essence. There she is no more called soul: she is called infinite being.

From Tractate II

God is not light nor life nor love nor nature nor spirit nor semblance nor anything we can put into words. God flows into God and God flows out of God and God knows himself God in himself and knows himself God in his creatures in general and he knows himself God in the noble soul in particular. The Father is almighty in the soul, the Son all-wise, the Holy Ghost all loving, loving all creatures with the same love. But he manifests as *different* and the soul is destined to know things as they are and conceive things as they are when, seized thereof, she plunges into the bottomless well of the divine nature and becomes so one with God that she herself would say that she is God.

From Tractate II

I have spoken about one power in the soul; in her first issue she lays hold of God not as being good nor yet as truth: delving deeper still she grasps him in his loneliness, in his solitude; she finds him in his desert, in his actual ground. But being still unsatisfied, on she goes in quest of what it is that is in his Godhead, of the special property of his peculiar nature. They say no property (or union) is closer than that of the three Persons being one God. And next they put the union of the soul with God. When the soul, being kissed by God, is in absolute perfection and in bliss, then at last she knows the embrace of unity, then at the touch of God she is made uncreaturely, then, with God's motion, the soul is as noble as God is himself. God moves the soul after his own fashion. God contemplating creature gives it life; creature finds life in contemplating God. The soul has intelligent, noetic being, and therefore where God is, there is the soul and where the soul is, there is God.

From Sermon LXXXIII

ON THE DIVINE BIRTH IN THE SOUL

Here in time we make holiday because the eternal birth which God the Father bore and bears unceasingly in eternity is now born in time, in human nature. St Augustine says this birth is always happening. But if it happen not in me what does it profit me? What matters is that it shall happen in me.

We intend therefore to speak of this birth as taking place in us: as being consummated in the virtuous soul; for it is in the perfect soul that God speaks his Word. What I shall say is true only of the perfected man, of him who has walked and is still walking in the way of God; not of the natural undisciplined man who is entirely remote from and unconscious of this birth.

There is a saying of the wise man: 'When all things lay in the midst of silence then leapt there down into me from on high, from the royal throne, a secret word.' This sermon is about this word. . . .

First we will take the words: 'In the midst of the silence there was spoken in me a secret word.'

– But, Sir, where is the silence and where the place in which the word is spoken?

As I said just now, it is in the purest part of the soul, in the noblest, in her ground, aye in the very essence of the soul. That is mid-silence, for thereinto no creature did ever get, nor any image, nor has the soul there either activity or understanding, therefore she is not aware of any image either of herself or any creature. Whatever the soul effects she effects with her powers. When she understands she understands with her intellect. When she remembers she does so with her memory. When she loves she does so with her will. She works then with her powers and not with her essence. Now every exterior act is linked with some means. The power of seeing is brought into play only through the eyes; elsewhere she can neither do nor bestow such a thing as seeing. And so with all the other senses: their operations are always effected through some means or other. But there is no activity in the essence of the soul; the faculties she works with emanate from the ground of the essence, but in her actual ground there is mid-stillness; here alone is rest and a habitation for this birth, this act, wherein God the Father speaks his Word, for it is intrinsically receptive of naught save the divine essence, without means. Here God enters the soul with his all, not merely with a part. God enters the ground of the soul. None can touch the ground of the soul but God only. No creature is admitted into her ground, it must stop outside in her powers. . . .

What does it behove a man to do in order to deserve and procure this birth to come to pass and be consummated in him: is it better for him to do his part towards it, to imagine and think about God, or should he keep still in peace and quiet so that God can speak and act in him while he merely waits on God's operation? At the same time I repeat that this speaking, this act, is only for the good and perfect, those who have so absorbed and assimilated the essence of virtue that it emanates from them naturally, without their seeking; and above all there must live in them the worthy life and lofty teaching of our Lord Jesus Christ. Such are permitted to know that the very best and utmost of attainment in this life is to remain still and let God act and speak in thee. When the powers have all been withdrawn from their bodily forms and functions, then this Word is spoken. Thus he says: 'in the midst of the silence the secret word was spoken to me.' The more completely thou art able to in-draw thy faculties and forget those things and their images which thou hast taken in, the more, that is to say, thou forgettest the creature, the nearer thou art to this and the more susceptible thou art to it. . . .

Mark now the fruit and use of this mysterious Word and of this darkness. In this gloom which is his own the heavenly Father's Son is not born alone: thou too art born there a child of the same heavenly Father and no other, and to thee also he gives power. Observe how great the use. No truth learned by any master by his own intellect and understanding, or ever to be learned this side the day of judgement, has ever been interpreted at all according to this knowledge, in this ground. Call it, if thou wilt, an ignorance, an unknowing, yet there is in it more than in all knowing and understanding without it, for this outward ignorance lures and attracts thee from all understood things and from thyself.

From Sermon I, a sermon preached at Christmastide

ON MULTIPLICITY AND TIME

Time is fulfilled when time is no more. He who in time has his heart established in eternity and in whom all temporal things are dead, in him is the fullness of time. Three things prevent a man from knowing God at all. The first is time, the second corporality, and the third is multiplicity or number. As long as these three things are in me God is not in me nor is he working in me really. St Augustine says, 'Because the soul is greedy, because she wants to have and hold so much, therefore she reaches into time and, snatching at the things of time and number, loses what she already has.' While there is more and less in thee God cannot dwell nor work in thee. These things must go out for God to come in; except thou have them in a higher, better way; if multiplicity has become one in thee, then the more of multiplicity the more there is of unity, for the one is changed into the other. . . .

These three things stand for three kinds of knowledge. The first is sensible. The eye sees from afar what is outside it. The second is rational and is a great deal higher. The third corresponds to an exalted power of the soul, a power so high and noble it is able to see God face to face in his own self. This power has nothing common with anything else, it knows no yesterday or day before, no morrow or day after (for in eternity there is no yesterday or morrow); there is only a present now; the happenings of a thousand years ago, a thousand years to come, are there in the present and the antipodes the same as here.

From Sermon XC*

The now wherein God made the world is as near this time as the now I am speaking in this moment, and the last day is as near this now as was yesterday.

From Sermon LXXXIV

The soul's day and God's day are different. In her natural day the soul knows all things above time and place; nothing is far or near. And that is why I say, this day all things are of equal rank. To talk about the world as being made by God to-morrow, yesterday, would be talking nonsense. God makes the world and all things in this present now. Time gone a thousand years ago is now as present and as near to God as this very instant. The soul who is in the here and now, in her the Father bears his one-begotten Son and in that same birth the soul is born back into God. It is one birth; as fast as she is reborn into God, the Father is begetting his only Son in her.

From Sermon LXXXIII

* For the sake of greater clarity a few words and phrases have been altered.

19. The Active, Inward, and Superessential Lives

THE BLESSED JOHN RUYSBROECK

IT *may be that the Blessed John Ruysbroeck cannot be numbered among the great original exponents of mystical theology. He has not the high intellectual quality of St Augustine, nor the supreme metaphysical audacity of Eckhart, nor the austere precision of St John of the Cross. He came at the end of a great sequence. He gathers into his thought and feeling the hoarded riches of that greatest epoch of Catholic mysticism, the thirteenth and fourteenth centuries. Yet he has a splendour and quality all his own which places him very high among the exponents of the spiritual life. Nowhere else can one find so sure and illuminating a guide to the journey from the life of dedicated activity to superessential life in which God in his fullness is met. Highly speculative and theological though his approach is, it is essentially robust and practical; he describes the stages of the Mystic Way from his own intimate experience of it. From few other writers can one gain so vivid an idea of what at its best Christian mysticism is.*

Moreover, there is a definite modern feel about him. His vision is framed in the terms of traditional Catholic dogmatic and mystical theology; but it is essentially dynamic. Two words, Rest and Activity, constantly occur in his writings. He describes the Nature of God as an eternal flowing from the Unchanging One through the activity of the Persons of the Blessed Trinity back to the One again. Had he lived in the twentieth century one feels that such concepts as energy, structure, organism (in the sense of living pattern) and complementarity would not have been alien to his thought.

The Adornment of the Spiritual Marriage, *from which the passages which follow are taken, is divided into three books. The first deals with the dedicated active life and is, for the most part, concerned with the cultivation of the moral virtues, such as charity, humility, generosity, temperance, etc., without which any further advance in the spiritual life is impossible; before his retirement with two friends to the old hermitage of Groenendaal, in the forest of Soignies, at the age of fifty, Ruysbroeck was for twenty-six years a secular parish priest in Brussels.*

In some of those who lead the dedicated active life there arises an ardent desire to penetrate more deeply into the world of spirit. In the second book Ruysbroeck describes the stages of the Interior Life which such men and women should strive to lead, a way of life which can lead to the 'highest degree of the most interior life', which seems to differ little, if at all, from that which some call the Unitive Life. The book ends with a vigorous attack on false mysticism.

Ruysbroeck envisages a stage even higher than that which he calls 'the highest degree of the most interior life'. In the short third book he deals with what he calls the Superessential or God-seeing Life, a stage of active meeting with and loving embrace of God, 'the wayless being which all interior spirits have chosen above all others', 'the dark silence in which all lovers lose themselves'.

There are several words which Ruysbroeck constantly uses which must be understood in order that his meaning may be clear. The first is fruition. *By this is meant a total attainment, a complete and permanent possession. Ruysbroeck speaks of fruitive love or fruitive possession as opposed to striving, dynamic love and partial and conditional possession.* Simple *and* simplicity, *words frequently found in the literature of mysticism, convey the meaning of wholeness, completeness, synthesis. They are used to describe a total, undifferentiated act of perception in which there is no analysis into partial aspects. Ruysbroeck uses two opposites to describe two modes or degrees of perception, e.g.* in some wise *and* in no wise. *Within our ordinary experience, and also in the lower stages of the spiritual life, we dwell in a conceptual world; reality is mediated to us through symbols and images which the intellect can grasp, i.e.* in some wise. *In the advanced stage of the mystical life knowledge transcends the categories of thought; there is direct, unmediated, spiritual intuition; it is modeless, unconditioned, i.e.* in no wise: *'In the Darkness he is enwrapped and falls into somewhat that is in no wise, even as one who has lost his way.'*

Finally, Ruysbroeck employs the words superessential *and*

superessence *to describe a state which is more than being (essence).*
Beyond the Persons of the Blessed Trinity is the Superessential Unity
of the Godhead. In man there is a 'fathomless ground' which has a
potential relationship with this superessential reality, so that it is
possible for man to enter into a superessential life.

The translation used is that of C. A. Wynschenk Dom, published
by Dent. The book also contains, in addition to The Adornment
of the Spiritual Marriage, The Sparkling Stone, *and* The Book
of Supreme Truth.

THE CULMINATION OF THE ACTIVE LIFE

A man who lives this life, i.e. *the active life*, in its perfection,
as it has here been shown, and who is offering up his whole
life, and all his works, to the worship and praise of God, and
who wills and loves God above all things, is often stirred by
a desire to see, to know, and to prove what, in Himself, this
Bridegroom Christ is: Who for man's sake became man and
laboured in love unto death, and delivered us from sin, and
the devil, and has given us Himself and His grace, and left
us His sacraments, and has promised us His kingdom and
Himself as an eternal wage; Who also gives us all that is
needful for the body, and inward consolation and sweetness,
and innumerable gifts of all kinds, according to the needs
of each.

When a man beholds all this, he feels an unmeasured impulse
to see Christ his Bridegroom, and to know Him as He is in
Himself. Though he knows Him in His works, this does not
seem to him enough. Then he must do as the publican Zac-
cheus did, who longed to see Jesus, who He was. He must
run before the crowd, that is the multiplicity of creatures;
for these make us so little and so low that we cannot see God.
And he must climb up into the tree of faith, which grows
from above downwards, for its roots are in the Godhead.
This tree has twelve branches, which are the twelve articles
of faith. The lower speak of the Divine Humanity, and of
those things which belong to our salvation of soul and of
body. The upper part of the tree tells of the Godhead, of the

Trinity of Persons, and of the Unity of the Nature of God. And the man must cling to that unity, in the highest part of the tree; for there it is that Jesus must pass with all His gifts.

Here comes Jesus, and sees the man, and shows to him, in the light of faith, that He is according to His Godhead immeasurable and incomprehensible and inaccessible and abysmal, transcending every created light and every finite conception. And this is the highest knowledge of God which any man may have in the active life: that he should confess in the light of faith that God is incomprehensible and unknowable. And in this light Christ says to man's desire: *Make haste and come down, for today I must abide at thy house.* This hasty descent, to which he is summoned by God, is nothing else than a descent through desire and through love into the abyss of the Godhead, which no intelligence can reach in the created light. But where intelligence remains without, desire and love go in. When the soul is thus stretched towards God, by intention and by love, above everything that it can understand, then it rests and dwells in God, and God in it. When the soul climbs with desire above the multiplicity of creatures, and above the works of the senses, and above the light of nature, then it meets Christ in the light of faith, and becomes enlightened, and confesses that God is unknowable and incomprehensible. When it stretches itself with longing towards this incomprehensible God, then it meets Christ, and is filled with His gifts. And when it loves and rests above all gifts, and above itself, and above all creatures, then it dwells in God, and God dwells in it.

This is the way in which we shall meet Christ on the summit of the active life. When you have laid the foundation of righteousness, charity, and humility; and have established on it a dwelling-place, that is, those virtues which have been named heretofore; and have met Christ through faith, by intention and by love; then you dwell in God and God dwells in you, and you possess the true active life.

I : 26

THE UNITY OF MAN AND GOD

A threefold unity is found in all men by nature, and also in all good men according to a supernatural manner.

The first and highest unity of man is in God; for all creatures depend upon this unity for their being, their life, and their preservation; and if they be separated in this wise from God, they fall into the nothingness and become nought. This unity is in us essentially, by nature, whether we be good or evil. And without our own working it makes us neither holy nor blessed. This unity we possess within us and yet above us, as the ground and the preserver of our being and of our life.

The second unity or union is also in us by nature. It is the unity of our higher powers; forasmuch as these spring naturally as active powers from the unity of the mind or of the spirit. This is that same unity which depends upon God; but with this difference, that here it is active and there essential. Nevertheless, the spirit is wholly and perfectly understood according to the fulness of its substance, in each unity. This unity we possess within us, above our senses; and from it there proceed memory, understanding, and will, and all the powers of ghostly action. In this unity, the soul is called 'spirit'.

The third unity which is in us by nature is the source of all the bodily powers, in the unity of the heart; origin and beginning of the bodily life. This unity the soul possesses in the body and in the quickening centre of the heart, and therefrom flow forth all bodily activities, and the five senses. And therein the soul is called 'soul'; for it is the forming principle of the body, and quickens this carcase; that is, gives it life and keeps it therein.

These three unities abide in man by nature as one life and one kingdom. In the lowest we are sensible and animal; in the middle we are rational and spiritual; and in the highest we are kept according to our essence. And thus are all men by nature.

Now these three unities, as one kingdom and one eternal dwelling-place, are adorned and inhabited in a supernatural way by the moral virtues through charity and the active life. And they are still more gloriously adorned and more excellently perfected by inward exercises united with a spiritual life. But they are most gloriously and blessedly adorned by a supernatural and contemplative life.

II : 2

Now the grace of God, pouring forth from God, is an inward thrust and urge of the Holy Ghost, driving forth our spirit from within and exciting it towards all virtues. This grace flows from within, and not from without; for God is more inward to us than we are to ourselves, and His inward thrust or working within us, be it natural or supernatural, is nearer to us and more intimate to us, than our own working is. And therefore God works in us from within outwards; but all creatures work from without inwards. And thus it is that grace, and all the gifts of God, and the Voice of God, come from within, in the unity of our spirit; and not from without, into the imagination, by means of sensible images.

II : 3

The unity of our spirit has two conditions; it is essential, and it is active. You must know that the spirit, according to its essence, receives the coming of Christ in the nakedness of its nature without means and without interruption. For the being and the life which we are in God, in our Eternal Image, and which we have within ourselves according to our essence, this is without means and indivisible. And this is why the spirit, in its inmost and highest part, that is in its naked nature, receives without interruption the impress of its Eternal Archetype, and the Divine Brightness; and is an eternal dwelling-place of God in which God dwells as an eternal Presence, and which He visits perpetually, with new comings and with new instreamings of the ever-renewed brightness of His eternal birth. For where He comes, there He is; and where He is, there He comes. And where He has never been, thereto He shall never come; for neither chance nor change are in Him. And everything in which He is, is in Him; for He never goes out of Himself. And this is why the spirit in its essence possesses God in the nakedness of its nature, as God does the spirit; for it lives in God and God in it. And it is able, in its highest part, to receive, without intermediary, the Brightness of God, and all that God can fulfil. And by means of the brightness of its Eternal Archetype, which shines in it essentially and personally, the spirit plunges itself and loses itself, as regards the highest part of its life, in the Divine Being, and there abidingly possesses its eternal blessedness; and it flows forth again, through the eternal birth of the Son, together with all the other creatures, and is set in its created being by the free will of the Holy Trinity. And here it is like unto the image of the most high Trinity in Unity, in which it has been made. And, in its created being, it incessantly receives the impress of its Eternal Archetype, like a flawless mirror, in which the image remains steadfast, and in which the reflection is renewed without interruption by its ever-new reception in new light. This essential union of our spirit with God does not exist in itself, but it dwells in God, and it flows forth from God, and it depends upon God, and it returns to God as to its Eternal Origin. And in this wise it has never been, nor ever shall be, separated from God; for this union is within us by our naked nature, and, were this nature to be separated from God, it would fall into pure nothingness. And this union is above time and space, and is always and incessantly active according to the way of God. But our nature, forasmuch as it is indeed like unto God but in itself is creature, receives the impress of its Eternal Image passively. This is that nobleness which we possess by nature in the essential unity of our spirit, where it is united with God according to nature. This neither makes us holy nor blessed, for all men, whether good or evil, possess it within themselves; but it is certainly the first cause of all holiness and all blessedness. This is the meeting and the union between God and our spirit in the nakedness of our nature.

II : 57

THE HIGHEST DEGREE OF THE INTERIOR LIFE

That measureless Splendour of God, which together with the incomprehensible brightness, is the cause of all gifts and of all virtues – that same Uncomprehended Light transfigures the fruitive tendency of our spirit and penetrates it in a way that is wayless; that is, through the Uncomprehended Light. And in this light the spirit immerses itself in fruitive rest; for this rest is wayless and fathomless, and one can know of it in no other way than through itself – that is, through rest. For, could we know and comprehend it, it would fall into mode and measure; then it could not satisfy us, but rest would become an eternal restlessness. And for this reason, the simple, loving, and immersed tendency of our spirit works within us a fruitive love; and this fruitive love is abysmal. And the abyss of God calls to the abyss; that is, of all those who are united with the Spirit of God in fruitive love. This inward call is an inundation of the essential brightness, and this essential brightness, enfolding us in an abysmal love, causes us to be lost to ourselves, and to flow forth from ourselves into the wild darkness of the Godhead. And, thus united without means, and made one with the Spirit of God, we can meet God through God, and everlastingly possess with Him and in Him our eternal bliss.

At times, the inward man performs his introspection simply, according to the fruitive tendency, above all activity and above all virtues, through a simple inward gazing in the fruition of love. And here he meets God without intermediary. And from out the Divine Unity, there shines into him a simple light; and this light shows him Darkness and Nakedness and Nothingness. In the Darkness, he is enwrapped and falls into somewhat which is in no wise, even as one who has lost his way. In the Nakedness, he loses the perception and discernment of all things, and is transfigured and penetrated by a simple light. In the Nothingness, all his activity fails him; for he is vanquished by the working of God's abysmal love, and in the fruitive inclination of his spirit he vanquishes God, and becomes one spirit with Him. And in this oneness with the Spirit of God, he enters into a fruitive tasting and possesses the Being of God. . . . And in the deeps of his ground he knows and feels nothing, in soul or in body, but a singular radiance with a sensible well-being and an all-pervading savour. This is the first way, and it is the way of emptiness; for it makes a man empty of all things, and lifts him up above activity and above all the virtues. And it unites the man with God, and brings about a firm perseverance in the most interior practices which he can cultivate.

At times such an inward man turns towards God with ardent desire and activity; that he may glorify and honour Him, and offer up and annihilate in the love of God, his selfhood and all that he is able to do. . . . And here the hunger and thirst of love become so great that he perpetually surrenders himself, and gives up his own works, and empties himself, and is noughted in love, for he is hungry and thirsty for the taste of God; and, at each irradiation of God, he is seized by God, and more than ever before is newly touched by love. Living he dies, and dying he lives again. And in this way the desirous hunger and thirst of love are renewed in him every hour.

This is the second way, which is the way of longing, in which love dwells in the Divine likeness, and longs and craves to unite itself with God. This way is more profitable and honourable to us than the first, for it is the source of the first; for none can enter into the rest which is above all works save the man who has loved love with desire and with activity. . . .

From these two ways the third way arises; and this is an inward life according to justice. Now understand this: God comes to us without ceasing, both with means and without means, and demands of us both action and fruition, in such a way that the one never impedes, but always strengthens, the other. And therefore the most inward man lives his life in these two ways; namely, in work and in rest. And in each he is whole and undivided; for he is wholly in God because he rests in fruition, and he is wholly in himself because he loves in activity: and he is perpetually called and urged by

God to renew both the rest and the work. And the justice
of the spirit desires to pay every hour that which is demanded
of it by God. And therefore, at each irradiation of God, the
spirit turns inward, in action and in fruition; and thus it is
renewed in every virtue, and is more deeply immersed in
fruitive rest. For God gives, in one gift, Himself and His
gifts; and the spirit gives, at each introversion, itself and all
its works. . . . Thus the man is just; and he goes *towards* God
with fervent love in eternal activity; and he goes *in* God with
fruitive inclination in eternal rest. And he dwells in God,
and yet goes forth towards all creatures in universal love, in
virtue, and in justice. And this is the supreme summit of the
inward life. All those men who do not possess both rest and
work in one and the same exercise, have not yet attained this
justice. This just man cannot be hindered in his introversion,
for he turns inward both in fruition and in work; but he is
like to a double mirror, which receives images on both sides.
For in his higher part, the man receives God with all His
gifts; and, in his lower part, he receives bodily images through
the senses.

II : 64, 65

THE SUPERESSENTIAL OR GOD-SEEING LIFE

The inward lover of God, who possesses God in fruitive love,
and himself in adhering and active love, and his whole life in
virtues according to righteousness; through these three
things, and by the mysterious revelation of God, such an
inward man enters into the God-seeing life. Yea, the lover
who is inward and righteous, him will it please God in His
freedom to choose and to lift up into a superessential contemplation, in the Divine Light and according to the Divine
Way. This contemplation sets us in purity and clearness above
all our understanding, for it is a singular adornment and a
heavenly crown, and besides the eternal reward of all virtues
and of our whole life. And to it none can attain through
knowledge and subtlety, neither through any exercise whatsoever. Only he with whom it pleases God to be united in His

Spirit, and whom it pleases Him to enlighten by Himself, can see God, and no one else.

Few men can attain to this Divine seeing, because of their own incapacity and the mysteriousness of the light in which one sees. And therefore no one will thoroughly understand the meaning of it by any learning or subtle consideration of his own; for all words, and all that may be learnt and understood in a creaturely way, are foreign to, and far below, the truth which I mean. But he who is united with God, and is enlightened in this truth, he is able to understand the truth by itself. For to comprehend and to understand God above all similitudes, such as He is in Himself, is to be God with God, without intermediary, and without any otherness that can become a hindrance or an intermediary. And therefore I beg every one who cannot understand this, or feel it in the fruitive unity of his spirit, that he be not offended at it, and leave it for that which it is: for that which I am going to say is true, and Christ, the Eternal Truth, has said it Himself in His teaching in many places, if we could but show and explain it rightly. And therefore, whosoever wishes to understand this must have died to himself, and must live in God, and must turn his gaze to the eternal light in the ground of his spirit, where the Hidden Truth reveals Itself without means.

Now if the spirit would see God with God in this Divine light without means, there needs must be on the part of man three things.

The first is that he must be perfectly ordered from without in all the virtues, and within must be unencumbered, and as empty of every outward work as if he did not work at all: for if his emptiness is troubled within by some work of virtue, he has an image; and as long as this endures within him, he cannot contemplate.

Secondly, he must inwardly cleave to God, with adhering intention and love, even as a burning and glowing fire which can never more be quenched. As long as he feels himself to be in this state, he is able to contemplate.

Thirdly, he must have lost himself in a Waylessness and

in a Darkness, in which all contemplative men wander in
fruition and wherein they never again can find themselves
in a creaturely way. In the abyss of this darkness, in which
the loving spirit has died to itself, there begin the manifestation of God and eternal life. For in this darkness there shines
and is born an incomprehensible Light, which is the Son of
God, in Whom we behold eternal life. And in this Light one
becomes seeing; and this Divine Light is given to the simple
sight of the spirit, where the spirit receives the brightness
which is God Himself, above all gifts and every creaturely
activity, in the idle emptiness in which the spirit has lost itself
through fruitive love, and where it receives without means
the brightness of God, and is changed without interruption
into that brightness which it receives. Behold, this mysterious
brightness, in which one sees everything that one can desire
according to the emptiness of the spirit: this brightness is
so great that the loving contemplative, in his ground wherein
he rests, sees and feels nothing but an incomprehensible
Light; and through that Simple Nudity which enfolds all
things, he finds himself, and feels himself, to be that same
Light by which he sees, and nothing else. And this is the first
condition by which one becomes seeing in the Divine Light.
Blessed are the eyes which are thus seeing, for they possess
eternal life. . . .

Now the Spirit of God says in the secret outpouring of our
spirit: *Go ye out*, in an eternal contemplation and fruition,
according to the way of God. All the riches which are in
God by nature we possess by way of love in God, and God
in us, through the unmeasured love which is the Holy Ghost;
for in this love one tastes of all that one can desire. And therefore through this love we are dead to ourselves, and have
gone forth in loving immersion into Waylessness and Darkness. There the spirit is embraced by the Holy Trinity, and
dwells for ever within the superessential Unity, in rest and
fruition. And in that same Unity, according to Its fruitfulness,
the Father dwells in the Son, and the Son in the Father, and
all creatures dwell in Both. And this is above the distinction of the Persons; for here by means of the reason we

understand Fatherhood and Sonhood as the life-giving fruit-fulness of the Divine Nature.

Here there arise and begin an eternal going out and an eternal work which is without beginning; for here there is a beginning with beginning. For, after the Almighty Father had perfectly comprehended Himself in the ground of His fruitfulness, so the Son, the Eternal Word of the Father, came forth as the Second Person in the Godhead. And, through the Eternal Birth, all creatures have come forth in eternity, before they were created in time. So God has seen and known them in Himself, according to distinction, in living ideas, and in an otherness from Himself; but not as something other in all ways, for all that is in God is God. This eternal going out and this eternal life, which we have and are in God eternally, without ourselves, is the cause of our created being in time. And our created being abides in the Eternal Essence, and is one with it in its essential existence. And this eternal life and being, which we have and are in the eternal Wisdom of God, is like unto God. For it has an eternal immanence in the Divine Essence, without distinction; and through the birth of the Son, it has an eternal outflowing in a distinction and otherness, according to the Eternal Idea. And through these two points it is so like unto God that He knows and reflects Himself in this likeness without cessation, according to the Essence and according to the Persons. For, though even here there are distinction and otherness according to intellectual perception, yet this likeness is one with that same Image of the Holy Trinity, which is the wisdom of God and in which God beholds Himself and all things in an eternal NOW, without before and after. In a single seeing He beholds Himself and all things. And this is the Image and the Likeness of God, and our Image and our Likeness; for in it God reflects Himself and all things. In this Divine Image all creatures have an eternal life, outside themselves, as in their eternal Archetype; and after this eternal Image, and in this Likeness, we have been made by the Holy Trinity. And there-fore God wills that we shall go forth from ourselves in this Divine Light, and shall reunite ourselves in a supernatural way with this Image, which is our proper life, and shall possess it with Him, in action and in fruition, in eternal bliss. . . .

When the inward and God-seeing man has thus attained to his Eternal Image, and in this clearness, through the Son, has entered into the bosom of the Father: then he is enlightened by Divine truth, and he receives anew, every moment, the Eternal Birth, and he goes forth according to the way of the light, in a Divine contemplation. And here there begins the fourth and last point; namely, a loving meeting, in which, above all else, our highest blessedness consists. . . .

Now this active meeting and this loving embrace are in their ground fruitive and wayless; for the abysmal Waylessness of God is so dark and so unconditioned that it swallows up in itself every Divine way and activity, and all the attributes of the Persons, within the rich compass of the essential Unity; and it brings about a Divine fruition in the abyss of the Ineffable. And here there is a death in fruition, and a melting and dying into the Essential Nudity, where all the Divine names, and all conditions and all the living images which are reflected in the mirror of Divine Truth, lapse in the Onefold and Ineffable, in waylessness and without reason. For in this unfathomable abyss of the Simplicity, all things are wrapped in fruitive bliss; and the abyss itself may not be comprehended, unless by the Essential Unity. To this the Persons, and all that lives in God, must give place; for here there is nought else but an eternal rest in the fruitive embrace of an outpouring Love. And this is that wayless being which all interior spirits have chosen above all other things. This is the dark silence in which all lovers lose themselves.

                                                        III : 1, 3, 4

20. Nothing Burns in Hell but Self-will

THE THEOLOGIA GERMANICA

THIS little manual of the spiritual life, which has on its title page these words: 'Here begins the Frankfurter and speaks very lofty and lovely things concerning a perfect life', is a delightful example of the German School of mysticism. Though in the same tradition, there is in it little of the inspired sweep of theological and psychological speculation which is found in Eckhart, Tauler, and Ruysbroeck. It is written in a lower key. It is a comparatively simple guide, vigorously expressed, to union with God through Christ, by the complete conquest of self-love and self-will, of the 'I, Mine, Me, and the like'. There are other elements in the book, but this is its main theme, and it is on its exposition of this theme that I have concentrated in the choice of the passages which follow.

Who the Frankfurter was no one knows. All that is known is that he was a Teutonic Knight, a priest and a warden in the House of the Teutonic Knights at Frankfurt. His book was written sometime in the second half of the fourteenth century. The earliest manuscript is dated 1497.

The book has had a chequered history. In his earlier period Luther was strongly influenced by it, and, in 1516, published it, without name or title, but with this heading: 'A spiritual, noble little book. Of right discrimination and reason. What the old man is and what the new. What is Adam's child and what is God's, and how Adam shall die in us and Christ arise.' It had considerable popularity in the early days of the Reformation, but as Protestantism became more rigid and less spiritual, it came to be less regarded. Calvin condemned it as 'a bag of tricks produced by Satan's cunning to confound the whole simplicity of the Gospel'. After the beginning of the seventeenth century interest in the book seems to have faded altogether, not to be revived until the nineteenth century.

The translation used is that of Susanna Winkworth, the first, I believe, to be made into the English language.

Sin is nought else, but that the creature turneth away from the unchangeable Good and betaketh itself to the changeable; that is to say, that it turneth away from the Perfect, to 'that which is in part' and imperfect, and most often to itself. Now mark: when the creature claimeth for its own anything good, such as Substance, Life, Knowledge, Power, and in short whatever we should call good, as if it were that, or possessed that, or that were itself, or that proceeded from it – as often as this cometh to pass, the creature goeth astray.

What did the devil do else, or what was his going astray and his fall else, but that he claimed for himself to be also somewhat, and would have it that somewhat was his, and somewhat was due to him? This setting up of a claim and his I and Me and Mine, these were his going astray, and his fall. And thus it is to this day.

Chapter II

What else did Adam do but this same thing? It is said, it was because Adam ate the apple that he was lost, or fell. I say, it was because of his claiming something for his own, and because of his I, Mine, Me, and the like. Had he eaten seven apples, and yet never claimed anything for his own, he would not have fallen: but as soon as he called something his own, he fell and would have fallen if he had never touched an apple. Behold! I have fallen a hundred times more often and deeply, and gone a hundred times farther astray than Adam; and not all mankind could amend his fall, or bring him back from going astray. But how shall my fall be amended? It must be healed as Adam's fall was healed, and on the self-same wise. By whom, and on what wise was that healing brought to pass? Mark this: man could not without God, and God should not without man. Wherefore God took human nature or manhood upon himself and was made man, and man was made divine. Thus the healing was brought to pass. So also must my fall be healed. I cannot do the work without God, and God may not or will not without me; for if it shall be accomplished in me, too, God must be made man; in such sort that God must take to himself all that is in me, within and without, so that there may be nothing in me which striveth against God or hindereth his work. Now if God took to himself all men that are in the world, or ever were, and were made man in them, and they were made divine in him, and this work were not fulfilled in me, my fall and my wandering would never be amended except it were fulfilled in me also. And in this bringing back and healing, I can, or may, or shall do nothing of myself, but just simply yield to God, so that He alone may do all things in me and work, and I may suffer him and all his work and his divine will. And because I will not do so, but I count myself to be my own, and say 'I', 'Mine', 'Me', and the like, God is hindered, so that he cannot do his work in me alone and without hindrance; for this cause my fall and my going astray remain unhealed. Behold! this all cometh of my claiming somewhat for my own.

Chapter III

All that in Adam fell and died, was raised again and made alive in Christ, and all that rose up and was made alive in Adam, fell and died in Christ. But what was that? I answer, true obedience and dis-obedience. But what is true obedience? I answer, that a man should so stand free, being quit of himself, that is, of his I, and Me, and Self, and Mine, and the like, that in all things, he should no more seek or regard himself, than if he did not exist, and should take as little account of himself as if he were not, and another had done all his works. Likewise, he should count all the creatures for nothing. What is there then, which is, and which we may count for somewhat? I answer, nothing but that which we may call God. Behold! This is very obedience in the truth, and thus it will be in a blessed Eternity. There nothing is sought nor thought of, nor loved, but the one thing only.

Hereby we may mark what disobedience is: to wit, that a man maketh some account of himself, and thinketh that he is, and knoweth, and can do somewhat, and seeketh himself and his own ends in the things around him, and hath regard to and loveth himself, and the like. Man is created for true obedience, and is bound of right to render it to God. And this

obedience fell and died in Adam, and rose again and liveth
in Christ. Yea, Christ's human nature was so utterly bereft
of Self, and apart from all creatures, as no man's ever was,
and was nothing else but 'a house and habitation of God'.
Neither of that in him which belonged to God, nor of that
which was a living human nature and a habitation of God,
did he, as man, claim any thing for his own. His human
nature did not even take unto himself the Godhead, whose
dwelling it was, nor any thing that this same Godhead willed,
or did or left undone in him, nor yet any thing of all that his
human nature did or suffered; but in Christ's human nature
there was no claiming of any thing, nor seeking nor desire,
saving that what was due might be rendered to the Godhead.
and he did not call this very desire his own.

Chapter XV

Nothing burneth in hell but self-will. Therefore it hath been
said 'Put off thine own will, and there will be no hell'. Now
God is very willing to help a man and bring him to that which
is best in itself, and is of all things the best for man. But to
this end, all self-will must depart, as we have said. And God
would fain give man his help and counsel thereunto, for so
long as a man is seeking his own good, he doth not seek what
is best for him, and will never find it. For a man's highest
good would be and truly is, that he should not seek himself
nor his own things, nor be his own end in any respect, either
in things spiritual or things natural, but should seek only
the praise and glory of God and His holy will. This doth
God teach and admonish us.

Chapter XXXIV

What is Paradise? All things that are; for all are goodly and
pleasant, and therefore may fitly be called a Paradise. It is said
also that Paradise is an outer court of Heaven. Even so this
world is verily an outer court of the Eternal, or of Eternity,
and specially whatever in time, or any temporal things or
creatures, manifesteth or remindeth us of God or Eternity;
for the creatures are a guide and a path unto God and Eternity.

Thus this world is an outer court of Eternity, and therefore it may well be called a Paradise, for it is such in truth. And in this Paradise, all things are lawful, save one tree and the fruits thereof. That is to say: of all things that are, nothing is forbidden and nothing is contrary to God but one thing only: that is, Self-will, or to will otherwise than as the Eternal Will would have it. Remember this. For God saith to Adam, that is, to every man, 'Whatever thou art, or doest, or leavest undone, or whatever cometh to pass, is all lawful and not forbidden if it be not done from or according to thy will, but for the sake of and according to My will. But all that is done from thine own will is contrary to the Eternal Will.'

Chapter L

21. The Royal Road of the Holy Cross

THOMAS À KEMPIS

The Imitation of Christ

IT *would not be surprising if some, having read through the foregoing pages, sat back and said to themselves: 'This high speculative spirituality is doubtless of profound interest and importance; but how remote it is from the sort of spirituality and experience possible to ordinary men.' He will be quite right; the rare air of the summit is not for the normal climber of the Mount of God.*

In the second half of the fourteenth century there sprang up in the Low Countries what was called the devotio moderna, *the new devotion. Its chief promoter was Gerald Groote, the founder of the Brethren of the Common Life. While it drew its inspiration from Ruysbroeck, it was a much more practical type of spirituality, less speculative and less mystical in the limited sense, and, while demanding complete surrender of selfhood, much more attuned to the needs and capacities of ordinary men and women.*

Out of it came a book which, next to the Bible, has had a more profound and widespread influence throughout Christendom than any other, the Imitation of Christ. *Men so diverse in temperament and point of view as Sir Thomas More, General Gordon, St Ignatius Loyola, John Wesley, and Dr Samuel Johnson, all acknowledged their debt to it.*

There has been some controversy as to the authorship of the Imitation. *The evidence is, however, strongly in favour of Thomas à Kempis, to whom it has been commonly attributed.*

The life of Thomas à Kempis, which lasted for over ninety years, from 1380 to 1471, was an uneventful one; the greater part was spent at the monastery of Mount St Agnes near Zwolle – close to the Zuider Zee – and need not detain us here. Our concern is with the Imitation. *There is in it little of the sort of speculative mysticism*

found in the writings of Eckhart and Ruysbroeck, nothing of the
Wayless Way, the Dark Silence, or the abyss of the Godhead.
Strongly Christo-centric, it concerns itself rather with the path to
union with God than with the union itself. Its theme is the following
of Christ along the Royal Road of the Holy Cross, which leads
ultimately to union with Christ and God.

The translation used is that of Leo Sherley-Price, for the Penguin
Classics edition of the Imitation.

ON THE INNER LIFE IN CHRIST

'The Kingdom of God is within you,' says Our Lord. Turn to
the Lord with all your heart, forsake this sorry world, and
your soul shall find rest. Learn to turn from worldly things,
and give yourself to spiritual things, and you will see the
Kingdom of God come within you. For the Kingdom is
peace and joy in the Holy Spirit; these are not granted to the
wicked. Christ will come to you, and impart his consolations
to you, if you prepare a worthy dwelling for Him in your
heart. All true glory and beauty is within, and there He
delights to dwell. He often visits the spiritual man, and holds
sweet discourse with him, granting him refreshing grace,
great peace, and friendship exceeding all expectation.

Come then, faithful soul; prepare your heart for your
Divine Spouse, that He may deign to come to you and dwell
with you. For He says, 'If any man love Me, he will keep My
word; and We will come and make Our abode with him'.
Therefore welcome Christ, and deny entrance to all others.
When you possess Christ, you are amply rich, and He will
satisfy you. He will dispose and provide for you faithfully in
everything, so that you need not rely on man. For men soon
change and fail you; but Christ abides for ever, and stands
firmly by you to the end.

Never place your whole trust and reliance in weak and
mortal man, however helpful and dear to you he may be;
nor should you grieve overmuch if sometimes he opposes and
contradicts you. Those who take your part today may tomorrow oppose you; for men are as changeable as the weather.

Put your whole trust in God; direct your worship and love to Him alone. He will defend you, and will dispose all things for the best. Here you have no abiding city, and wherever you may be, you are a stranger and pilgrim; you will never enjoy peace until you become inwardly united to Christ.

What do you seek here, since this world is not your resting place? Your true home is in Heaven; therefore remember that all the things of this world are transitory. All things are passing, and yourself with them. See that you do not cling to them, lest you become entangled and perish with them. Let all your thoughts be with the Most High, and direct your humble prayers unceasingly to Christ. If you cannot contemplate high and heavenly things, take refuge in the Passion of Christ, and love to dwell within His Sacred Wounds. For if you devoutly seek the Wounds of Jesus and the precious marks of His Passion, you will find great strength in all troubles. And if men despise you, you will care little, having small regard for the words of your detractors.

Christ Himself was despised by men, and in His direst need was abandoned by his friends and acquaintances to the insults of His enemies. Christ was willing to suffer and to be despised; and do you presume to complain? Christ had enemies and slanderers; and do you expect all men to be your friends and benefactors? How will your patience be crowned, if you are not willing to endure hardship? Suffer with Christ, and for Christ, if you wish to reign with Christ.

Had you but once entered perfectly into the Heart of Jesus, and tasted something of His burning love, you would care nothing for your own gain or loss; for the love of Jesus causes a man to regard himself very humbly. The true, inward lover of Jesus and the Truth, who is free from inordinate desires, can turn freely to God, rise above self, and joyfully rest in God.

He who knows all things at their true worth, and not as they are said or reputed to be, is truly wise, for his knowledge comes from God, and not from man. He who walks by an inner light, and is not unduly influenced by outward things, needs no special time or place for his prayers. For the man of

inner life easily recollects himself, since he is never wholly
immersed in outward affairs. Therefore his outward occupa-
tions and needful tasks do not distract him, and he adjusts
himself to things as they come. The man whose inner life is
well-ordered and disposed is not troubled by the strange and
perverse ways of others; for a man is hindered and distracted
by such things only so far as he allows himself to be concerned
by them.

If your inner life were rightly ordered and your heart pure,
all things would turn to your good and advantage. As it is,
you are often displeased and disturbed, because you are not
yet completely dead to self, nor detached from all worldly
things. Nothing defiles and ensnares the heart of man more
than a selfish love of creatures. If you renounce all outward
consolation, you will be able to contemplate heavenly things,
and often experience great joy of heart.

II : 1

ON THE ROYAL ROAD OF THE HOLY CROSS

Jesus has many who love His Kingdom in Heaven, but few
who bear His Cross. He has many who desire comfort, but
few who desire suffering. He finds many to share His feast,
but few His fasting. All desire to rejoice with Him, but few
are willing to suffer for His sake. Many follow Jesus to the
Breaking of Bread, but few to the drinking of the Cup of
His Passion. Many admire His miracles, but few follow Him
in the humiliation of His Cross. Many love Jesus as long as no
hardship touches them. Many praise and bless Him, as long
as they are receiving any comfort from Him. But if Jesus
withdraw Himself, they fall to complaining and utter dejection.

They who love Jesus for His own sake, and not for the sake
of comfort to themselves, bless Him in every trial and anguish
of heart, no less than in the greatest joy. And were He never
willing to bestow comfort on them, they would still always
praise Him and give Him thanks.

Oh, how powerful is the pure love of Jesus, free from all
self-interest and self-love! Are they not all mercenary, who

are always seeking comfort? Do they not betray themselves
as lovers of self rather than of Christ, when they are always
thinking of their own advantage and gain? Where will you
find one who is willing to serve God without reward?

Seldom is anyone so spiritual as to strip himself entirely of
self-love. Who can point out anyone who is truly poor in
spirit and entirely detached from creatures? His rare worth
exceeds all on earth. If a man gave away all that he possessed,
yet it is nothing. And if he did hard penance, still it is little.
And if he attained all knowledge, he is still far from his goal.
And if he had great virtue and most ardent devotion, he still
lacks much, and especially the 'one thing needful to him'.
And what is this? That he forsake himself and all else, and
completely deny himself, retaining no trace of self-love. And
when he has done all that he ought to do, let him feel that he
has done nothing.

Let him not regard as great what others might esteem great,
but let him truthfully confess himself an unprofitable servant.
For these are the words of the Truth Himself: 'When you
shall have done all those things that are commanded you,
say, "We are unprofitable servants."' Then he may indeed
be called poor and naked in spirit, and say with the Prophet,
'I am alone and poor.' Yet there is no man richer, more
powerful, or more free than he who can forsake himself and
all else, and set himself in the lowest place.

'Deny yourself, take up your cross, and follow Me.' To
many this saying of Jesus seems hard. But how much harder
will it be to hear that word of doom, 'Depart from Me, you
cursed, into everlasting fire.' For those who now cheerfully
hear and obey the word of the Cross will not tremble to hear
the sentence of eternal damnation. The sign of the Cross will
appear in the heavens, when Our Lord comes as Judge. Then
will all the servants of the Cross, who in their lives conformed
themselves to the Crucified, stand with confidence before
Christ their Judge.

Why, then, do you fear to take up the Cross, which is the
road to the Kingdom? In the Cross is salvation; in the Cross
is life; in the Cross is protection against our enemies; in the

Cross is infusion of heavenly sweetness; in the Cross is
strength of mind; in the Cross is joy of spirit; in the Cross
is excellence of virtue; in the Cross is perfection of holiness.
There is no salvation of soul, no hope of eternal life, save
in the Cross. Take up the Cross, therefore, and follow Jesus,
and go forward into eternal life. Christ has gone before you,
bearing His Cross; He died for you on the Cross, that you also
may bear your cross, and desire to die on the cross with Him.
For if you die with Him, you will also live with Him. And if
you share His sufferings, you will also share His glory.

See how in the Cross all things consist, and in dying on it all
things depend. There is no other way to life and to true inner
peace, than the way of the Cross, and of daily self-denial. Go
where you will, seek what you will; you will find no higher
way above nor safer way below than the road of the Holy
Cross. Arrange and order all things to your own ideas and
wishes, yet you will still find suffering to endure, whether you
will or not; so you will always find the Cross. For you will
either endure bodily pain, or suffer anguish of mind and spirit.

At times God will withdraw from you; at times you will be
troubled by your neighbour, and, what is more, you will
often be a burden to yourself. Neither can any remedy or
comfort bring you relief, but you must bear it as long as God
wills. For God desires that you learn to bear trials without
comfort, that you may yield yourself wholly to Him, and
grow more humble through tribulation. No man feels so
deeply in his heart the Passion of Christ as he who has to
suffer in like manner. The Cross always stands ready, and
everywhere awaits you. You cannot escape it, wherever you
flee; for wherever you go, you bear yourself, and always find
yourself. Look up or down, without you or within, and
everywhere you will find the Cross. And everywhere you
must have patience, if you wish to attain inner peace, and
win an eternal crown. . . .

Resolve, then, as a good and faithful servant of Christ,
manfully to bear the cross of your Lord, who was crucified
for love of you. Prepare yourself to endure many trials and
obstacles in this vale of tears; for such will be your lot

wherever you are, and you will encounter them wherever
you conceal yourself. It must needs be so; nor is there any
remedy or means of escape from ills and griefs; you must
endure them. Drink lovingly the cup of your Lord, if you
wish to be His friend, and to share all with Him. Leave
consolations to God, to dispose as He wills. But set yourself
to endure trials, regarding them as the greatest of all comforts,
'for the sufferings of this present time are not worthy to be
compared with the glory to come', even though you alone
were to endure them all.

When you have arrived at that state when trouble seems
sweet and acceptable to you for Christ's sake, then all is well
with you, for you have found paradise upon earth. . . .

Be assured of this, that you must live a dying life. And the
more completely a man dies to self, the more he begins to
live to God. No man is fit to understand heavenly things,
unless he is resigned to bear hardships for Christ's sake. Nothing is more acceptable to God, and nothing more salutary
for yourself, than to suffer gladly for Christ's sake. And if
it lies in your choice, you should choose rather to suffer hardships for Christ's sake, than to be refreshed by many consolations; for thus you will more closely resemble Christ and
all His Saints. For our merit and spiritual progress does not
consist in enjoying much sweetness and consolation, but
rather in the bearing of great burdens and troubles.

Had there been a better way, more profitable to the salvation
of mankind than suffering, then Christ would have revealed
it in His word and life. But He clearly urges both His own
disciples and all who wish to follow Him to carry the cross,
saying, 'If any will come after Me, let him deny himself, and
take up his cross and follow me.'

II : 11, 12

22. God May Well be Loved but not Thought

THE CLOUD OF UNKNOWING

In the sphere of speculative mysticism this country has produced no great figures, such as St Augustine and Eckhart. The flowering of mysticism in England came late and, as a vigorous movement, lasted only a hundred years. The sequence opens with Richard Rolle of Hampole (1300–49), continues later in the century with Walter Hilton and the author of The Cloud of Unknowing, *and ends with Julian of Norwich, who died shortly after 1413. The advent of Protestantism was its deathblow. That is not to say that there were no English mystics after 1500; the Catholic tradition of Hilton and the* Cloud *was, for instance, continued in the work of the seventeenth-century Venerable Augustine Baker. The expression of the mystical consciousness in England after the Reformation, however, took a different form.*

Yet, though not among the giants, these fourteenth-century English mystics have an attractive quality which is all their own. There are some mystics who have felt compelled in their quest for God to put aside all material concepts and images and to seek Him 'without means' in the wayless way and the dark desert 'where no one is at home'. There are others who have joyfully used the wayside sacraments of earthly things. Both have been right, for God is in all things and can be seen by more than one mode of spiritual perception. The questing soul can, however, never rest permanently in these wayside sacraments. 'Our soul,' said Julian of Norwich, 'can never have rest in things that are beneath itself.' It has to go farther. They are, nevertheless, one way which leads to illumination and to union with God.

The Mystical Theology *of Dionysius the Areopagite, which had so profound an influence on the shape and development of Catholic mysticism, was translated into English in the mid fourteenth century under the title of* Dionise Hid Divinite. *Appearing as it did at a time of great spiritual vitality, it had a large circulation. Except for the author of the* Cloud, *who is thought to have been its translator, however, its influence on the four mystics mentioned above does not seem to have been very great. This fourteenth-century English mysticism is essentially practical, essentially 'homely', to use a word constantly found in Julian of Norwich. It is not intent on rising to great metaphysical and speculative heights. While its head is in heaven, its feet are kept firmly fixed on the ground.*

Further, it has the quality of what Richard of St Victor called jubilatio. *There is in these English mystics a sense of joy. Their mysticism is the mysticism of the 'heat, sweetness, and song' of Richard Rolle. Though, except for Julian of Norwich, they have a good deal to say about the need of asceticism and the 'Mending of Life' (the title of one of the works of Richard Rolle), one finds in them little of that strain and pain so evident in, for instance, St John of the Cross. And time and time again one comes across homely similes, half-humorous asides and little human touches. Even the author of the* Cloud *can compare those terribly cheerful, hearty religious people, whom we all know, to 'giggling girls and japing jugglers', and constantly criticizes those who 'can neither sit still, stand still, nor be still, unless they be either wagging with their feet or else somewhat doing with their hands'.*

The author of The Cloud of Unknowing *is unknown. The book itself is a manual of instruction for those who would enter on the contemplative life. It is closer to the main European mystical tradition, as it is seen in Richard of St Victor, Eckhart, and Ruysbroeck, than the writings of the other English mystics. Yet it has a quality all its own. It has also the literary charm which is characteristic of these fourteenth-century English mystics.*

The 'cloud of unknowing' is of course, the 'divine dark' of Dionysius and his followers – indeed, at times Dionysius uses the same word – that night of the intellect when a plane of spiritual experience is reached with which the intellect cannot deal. The view of the contemplative life found in the Cloud *is, however, thoroughly healthy and manly; it is no short cut to hidden knowledge or supersensual experience, but demands a keen employment of the will, coupled with self-knowledge, humility, and charity. There is in it no trace of quietism or spiritual limpness, but an insistence on controlled activity and wholeness of experience. 'A man,' it says, 'may not be fully active, but he be in part contemplative; nor yet fully contemplative, as it may be here, but he be in part active.'*

The text used is that edited by Evelyn Underhill from the British Museum MS. Harl. 674, which has the title, A Book of Contemplation the which is called the Cloud of Unknowing, in the which a soul is oned with God, *published by John M. Watkins. Chapters 6 to 8, inclusive, are printed in full.*

But now thou askest me and sayest, 'How shall I think on Himself, and what is He?' and to this I cannot answer thee but thus: 'I wot not.'

For thou hast brought me with thy question into that same darkness, and into that same cloud of unknowing, that I would thou wert in thyself. For of all other creatures and their works, yea, and of the works of God's self, may a man through grace have fullhead of knowing, and well he can think of them: but of God Himself can no man think. And therefore I would leave all that thing that I can think, and choose to my love that thing that I cannot think. For why; He may well be loved, but not thought. By love may He be gotten and holden; but by thought never. And therefore, although it be good sometime to think of the kindness and the worthiness of God in special, and although it be a light and a part of contemplation: nevertheless yet in this work it shall be cast down and covered with a cloud of forgetting. And thou shalt step above it stalwartly, but listily, with a devout and a pleasing stirring of love, and try for to pierce that darkness above thee. And smite upon that thick cloud of unknowing with a sharp dart of longing love; and go not thence for thing that befalleth.

Chapter 6

And if any thought rise and will press continually above thee betwixt thee and that darkness, and ask thee saying, 'What seekest thou, and what wouldest thou have?' say thou, that it is God that thou wouldest have. 'Him I covet, Him I seek, and nought but Him.'

And if he ask thee, 'What is that God?' say thou, that it is God that made thee and bought thee, and that graciously hath called thee to thy degree. 'And in Him,' say, 'thou hast no skill.' And therefore say, 'Go thou down again,' and tread him fast down with a stirring of love, although he seem to thee right holy, and seem to thee as he would help thee to seek Him. For peradventure he will bring to thy mind diverse full fair and wonderful points of His kindness, and say that He is full sweet, and full loving, full gracious, and full merciful. And if thou wilt hear him, he coveteth no better; for at the last he will thus jangle ever more and more till he bring thee lower, to the mind of His Passion.

And there will he let thee see the wonderful kindness of God, and if thou hear him, he careth for nought better. For soon after he will let thee see thine old wretched living, and peradventure in seeing and thinking thereof he will bring to thy mind some place that thou hast dwelt in before this time. So that at the last, or ever thou wit, thou shalt be scattered thou wottest not where. The cause of this scattering is, that thou heardest him first wilfully, then answeredst him, receivedst him, and lettest him alone.

And yet, nevertheless, the thing that he said was both good and holy. Yea, and so holy, that what man or woman that weeneth to come to contemplation without many such sweet meditations of their own wretchedness, the passion, the kindness, and the great goodness, and the worthiness of God coming before, surely he shall err and fail of his purpose. And yet, nevertheless, it behoveth a man or a woman that hath long time been used in these meditations, nevertheless to leave them, and put them and hold them far down under the cloud of forgetting, if ever he shall pierce the cloud of unknowing betwixt him and his God. Therefore what time that thou purposest thee to this work, and feelest by grace that thou art called of God, lift then up thine heart unto God with a meek stirring of love; and mean God that made thee, and bought thee, and that graciously hath called thee to thy degree, and receive none other thought of God. And yet not all these, but if thou list; for it sufficeth enough, a naked intent direct unto God without any other cause than Himself.

And if thee list have this intent lapped and folden in one word, for thou shouldest have better hold thereupon, take thee but a little word of one syllable: for so it is better than of two, for ever the shorter it is the better it accordeth with the work of the Spirit. And such a word is this word GOD or this word LOVE. Choose thee whether thou wilt or another; as thee list, which that thee liketh best of one syllable. And fasten this word to thine heart, so that it never go thence for thing that befalleth.

This word shall be thy shield and thy spear, whether thou ridest on peace or on war. With this word, thou shalt beat on this cloud and this darkness above thee. With this word, thou shalt smite down all manner of thought under the cloud of forgetting. Insomuch, that if any thought press upon thee to ask thee what thou wouldest have, answer him with no more words but with this one word. And if he proffer thee of his great clergy to expound thee that word and to tell thee the conditions of that word, say him: That thou wilt have it all whole, and not broken nor undone. And if thou wilt hold thee fast on this purpose, be thou sure, he will no while abide. And why? For that thou wilt not let him feed him on such sweet meditations of God touched before.

Chapter 7

But now thou askest me, 'What is he, this that thus presseth upon me in this work; and whether it is a good thing or an evil? And if it be an evil thing, then have I marvel,' thou sayest, 'why that he will increase a man's devotion so much. For sometimes me think that it is a passing comfort to listen after his tales. For he will sometime, me think, make me weep full heartily for pity of the Passion of Christ, sometime for my wretchedness, and for many other reasons, that me thinketh be full holy, and that done me much good. And therefore me thinketh that he should on nowise be evil; and if he be good, and with his sweet tales doth me so much good withal, then I have great marvel why that thou biddest me put him down and away so far under the cloud of forgetting?'

Now surely me thinketh that this is a well moved question, and therefore I think to answer thereto so feebly as I can. First when thou askest me what is he, this that presseth so fast upon thee in this work, proffering to help thee in this work; I say that it is a sharp and a clear beholding of thy natural wit, printed in thy reason within in thy soul. And where thou askest me thereof whether it be good or evil, I say that it behoveth always be good in its nature. For why, it is a beam of the likeness of God. But the use thereof may be both good and evil. Good, when it is opened by grace for to see thy wretchedness, the passion, the kindness, and the wonderful works of God in His creatures bodily and ghostly. And then it is no wonder though it increase thy devotion full much, as thou sayest. But then is the use evil, when it is swollen with pride and with curiosity of much clergy and letterly cunning as in clerks; and maketh them press for to be holden not meek scholars and masters of divinity or of devotion, but proud scholars of the devil, and masters of vanity and of falsehood. And in other men or women what so they be, religious or seculars, the use and the working of this natural wit is then evil, when it is swollen with proud and curious skills of worldly things, and fleshly conceits in coveting of worldly worships and having of riches and vain pleasaunce and flatterings of others.

And where that thou askest me, why that thou shall put it down under the cloud of forgetting, since it is so, that it is good in its nature, and thereto when it is well used it doth thee so much good and increaseth thy devotion so much. To this I answer and say – That thou shall well understand that there be two manner of lives in Holy Church. The one is active life, and the other is contemplative life. Active is the lower, and contemplative is the higher. Active life hath two degrees, a higher and a lower: and also contemplative life hath two degrees, a lower and a higher. Also, these two lives be so coupled together that although they be divers in some part, yet neither of them may be had fully without some part of the other. For why? That part that is the higher part of active life, that same part is the lower part of contemplative life. So that a man may not be fully active, but if he be in part contemplative; nor yet fully contemplative, as it may be here, but if he be in part active. The condition of active life is such, that it is both begun and ended in this life; but not so of contemplative life. For it is begun in this life, and shall last without end. For why? That part that Mary chose shall never be taken away. Active life is troubled and travailed about many things; but contemplative sitteth in peace with one thing.

The lower part of active life standeth in good and honest bodily works of mercy and of charity. The higher part of active life and the lower part of contemplative life lieth in goodly ghostly meditations, and busy beholding unto a man's own wretchedness with sorrow and contrition, unto the Passion of Christ and of His servants with pity and compassion, and unto the wonderful gifts, kindness, and works of God in all His creatures bodily and ghostly with thanking and praising. But the higher part of contemplation, as it may be had here, hangeth all wholly in this darkness and in this cloud of unknowing; with a loving stirring and a blind beholding unto the naked being of God Himself only.

In the lower part of active life a man is without himself and beneath himself. In the higher part of active life and the lower part of contemplative life, a man is within himself and even with himself. But in the higher part of contemplative life, a man is above himself and under his God. Above himself he is: for why, he purposeth him to win thither by grace, whither he may not come by nature. That is to say, to be knit to God in spirit, and in onehead of love and accordance of will. And right as it is impossible, to man's understanding, for a man to come to the higher part of active life, but if he cease for a time of the lower part; so it is that a man shall not come to the higher part of the contemplative life, but if he cease for a time of the lower part. And as unlawful a thing as it is, and as much as it would let* a man that sat in his meditations, to have regard then to his outward bodily works, the which he had done, or else should do, although they were

* Hinder.

never so holy works in themselves: surely as unlikely a thing it is, and as much would it let a man that should work in this darkness and in this cloud of unknowing with an affectuous stirring of love to God for Himself, for to let any thought or any mediation of God's wonderful gifts, kindness, and works in any of His creatures bodily or ghostly, rise upon him to press betwixt him and his God; although they be never so holy thoughts, nor so profound, nor so comfortable.

And for this reason it is that I bid thee put down such a sharp subtle thought, and cover him with a thick cloud of forgetting, be he never so holy nor promise he thee never so well for to help thee in thy purpose. For why, love may reach to God in this life, but not knowing. And all the whiles that the soul dwelleth in this deadly body, evermore is the sharpness of our understanding in beholding of all ghostly things, but most specially of God, mingled with some manner of fantasy; for the which our work should be unclean. And unless more wonder were, it should lead us into much error.

Chapter 8

23. Practical Directions for the Following of the Spiritual Life

WALTER HILTON

The Ladder of Perfection

OF *Walter Hilton little is known. He was probably of Midland stock and became a Canon Regular of St Augustine at the Priory of Saint Peter at Thurgarton, near Southwell. He died at the Priory in 1395. Before entering the Augustinian Order he is said to have lived as a hermit.*

Walter Hilton is pre-eminently the spiritual director, the practical teacher of those who desire to enter into the interior life. Though he never intended what he wrote for those whose destiny it is to lead the active life of the world – he makes that clear at the beginning of his book – much of his teaching is applicable to those in the world who aim at leading in some degree a recollected life. Hilton's exposition is very simple and straightforward, and it is not surprising that his treatise, The Ladder (or Scale) of Perfection, *quickly became a classic of the spiritual life. While he was influenced by the Pseudo-Dionysius and Richard of St Victor, he shows little knowledge or appreciation of that state of dim contemplation which finds so full a place in the writings of Ruysbroeck and St John of the Cross. True, he uses the concepts of darkness and nothingness; but he seems to use them in a sense different from that in which they are used by these two. He is the practical guide of souls rather than the exponent of a speculative mysticism in the Neoplatonist tradition. And it is therein that his value lies. The reader of the passages from* The Ladder of Perfection *which follow cannot but be impressed by the expert precision of Hilton's spiritual direction.*

The text used is that of Leo Sherley-Price in the Penguin Classics. It is based on the edition of Evelyn Underhill, published by Watkins, but is translated into present-day English. Though something of the flavour of the Middle English is lost, it is thus made easier for the general reader to understand.

THROUGH DARKNESS TO LIGHT

Whoever loves God dwells in light. But anyone who realizes that the love of this world is false and transitory, and therefore wishes to abandon it and seek the love of God, cannot at once experience His love, but must remain awhile in the night. He cannot pass suddenly from one light to the other, that is, from the love of this world to the perfect love of God. This night is nothing other than a complete withdrawal of the soul from earthly things by an intense desire to love, see, and know Jesus and the things of the spirit. This is a real night, for just as night is dark, hiding all created things and bringing all bodily activity to a halt, similarly one who sets himself to think of Jesus and to desire His love alone must try to withdraw his thoughts and affections from created things. In so doing his mind will be set free and his affections liberated from enslavement to anything of a nature inferior to his own. If he can do this, then it is night for him, for he is in darkness.

But this is a night pregnant with good, a glowing darkness, for it shuts out the false love of this world and ushers in the dawn of the true day. Indeed, the darker this night, the nearer the true day of the love of Jesus, for the farther the soul in its longing for Jesus retires from the clamour of worldly desires and impure thoughts, the nearer it approaches to experiencing the light of His love. Indeed, it is very close. . . .

However, this light is sometimes full of pain, and sometimes pleasant and consoling. When one who is deeply contaminated by sin wishes to enter this darkness it is at first painful to him, for grace has not as yet accustomed him to it; so he tries to fix his mind and will on God as best he can, and to think of Him alone. And because he finds this difficult, he is troubled. Sinful habits, with the memory of former worldly affections, interests, and doings crowd in upon him with such force that his soul is dragged back to them, and he is unable to escape their influence as quickly as he would wish. So this darkness is full of pain for him, and especially at times when he has little grace to help him. Nevertheless, if this is so in your case do not be too discouraged, and do not overstrain yourself as though you could force these thoughts out of your mind, for you cannot do it. Therefore wait for God's grace, persevere, and do not overtax yourself. If you can do so gently and without forcing them, guide the desires and powers of your soul towards Jesus. Understand that when you desire Jesus and wish to think of nothing but Him, but cannot do so properly because of worldly thoughts crowding into your mind, you have in fact left the false daylight and are entering this darkness. But you will not find this darkness peaceful because it is strange to you, who are not yet enlightened and cleansed. Therefore enter it often, and by the grace of God it will gradually become easier and more peaceful. Your soul will become so free, strong, and recollected that it will have no desire to think of anything worldly, while no worldly thing will prevent it from thinking of nothing. This darkness will then bring blessing to the soul. . . .

What, then, is the nature of this darkness? It arises solely from a grace-inspired desire to have the love of Jesus. This desire and longing for the love of God, to see Him and to possess Him, drives out of the heart all worldly considerations and affections. It moves the soul to recollection, and to ponder how it may come to this love; in this way it brings it into this precious nothing. But the soul is not in complete darkness and nothingness during this time, for although it conceals it from the false light it does not entirely conceal it from the true light. For Jesus, who is both love and light, is in this darkness, whether it brings pain or peace. He is at work in the soul, moving it to anguish with desire and longing for the light, but not as yet allowing it to rest in love, nor showing it His light. This state is called night and darkness, because the soul is hidden from the false light of the world, and has not yet fully enjoyed the true light, but is awaiting the blessed love of God which it desires. . . .

This darkness and night, then, springs solely from the soul's desire and longing for the love of Jesus, combined with a blind groping of the mind towards Him. And since it brings so much blessing and peace to the soul, albeit of short duration, how much better and more blessed must it be to experience His love, to be bathed in His glorious and invisible light, and to see all truth. It is this light which a soul receives as night passes and day dawns.

II : 24, 25

WARNING AGAINST SPIRITUAL PRIDE

Some people seem to forsake the love of the world and wish to attain the love of God and the light of understanding, but they are not willing to pass through this darkness that I have mentioned. They will not look at themselves honestly and humbly, and examine their former life and present sinful state, nor recognize their own nothingness before God. They make no effort to enter upon an interior life, and put aside all wordly things. They will not stamp out the sinful impulses of pride, envy, anger, and such like that arise in their hearts, by constantly reaching out to Jesus in prayer and meditation, silence, and tears, and in other spiritual and corporal exercises as devout and holy people have done in the past. But directly they have outwardly forsaken the world – or soon after – they imagine that they are holy, and able to understand the inner meaning of the Gospels and holy scripture. And provided that they can fulfil the commandments of God literally and avoid bodily sin, they think that they love God perfectly. So at once they want to preach and instruct everyone else, under the misapprehension that they have received the grace of understanding and perfect charity by a special gift of the Holy Spirit. They are even more strongly impelled to do this when they feel themselves suddenly endowed with great knowledge after little previous effort on their part, or with what seems to be fervent love which drives them to preach truth and righteousness to their fellow-men. They regard this as a grace from God, a blessed light granted to themselves before all others. But if they examine these things carefully, they will realize that this light of knowledge and fervour does not come from the true Sun, that is our Lord Jesus, but from the noonday devil who makes his spurious light resemble the sun. ... Those whose knowledge comes from these sources are full of spiritual pride. They are so blinded by this spurious light that they regard their own conceit and disobedience to the laws of Holy Church as perfect compliance with the Gospel and laws of God. They imagine that the following of their own inclination is freedom of spirit. ...

The true Sun of Righteousness, that is our Lord Jesus, will shine upon you who fear Him; that is, on humble souls who, acknowledging their own weakness, esteem themselves less than their neighbours, and cast themselves down before God. They know that they themselves are nothing, and they attain perfect humility through reverent fear and constant contemplation of God. Upon these souls the true Sun will rise and illumine their minds to know truth, and will kindle their affections with burning love, so that they burn and shine. Under the influence of this heavenly Sun they will burn with perfect love and shine with the knowledge of God.

II : 26

FIRST KNOW THYSELF

A soul that desires to attain knowledge of spiritual things must first know itself, for it cannot acquire knowledge of a higher kind until it first knows itself. The soul does this when it is so recollected and detached from all earthly preoccupations and from the influence of the senses that it understands itself as it is in its own nature, taking no account of the body. So if you desire to know and see your soul as it is, do not look for it within your body as though it were hidden in your heart in the same way that the heart is hidden within the body. If you look for it in this way you will never find it. The more you search for it as a material object, the farther you are from it, for your soul is not tangible, but a living and invisible spirit. It is not hidden and enclosed in your body in the way that a lesser object is hidden and enclosed within a greater; on the contrary, it is the soul that sustains and gives life to the body, and is possessed of much greater strength and virtue. . . . The soul is a living spirit, immortal and invisible, with power in itself to see and know supreme Truth and to love supreme Good, which is God. Once you have grasped this, you have some understanding of yourself.

Your soul is a spiritual mirror in which you may see the likeness of God. First, then, find your mirror, and keep it bright and clean from the corruption of the flesh and worldly vanity. Hold it well up above the earth so that you can see it, and our Lord reflected in it. In this life all chosen souls direct their effort and intention to this end although they may not be fully conscious of it. It is for this reason, as I said earlier, that at the beginning and early stages of their spiritual life many souls enjoy great fervour and sweetness of devotion, and seem all afire with love; but this is not the perfect love or spiritual knowledge of God. You can be certain that however intense the fervour felt by a soul – even if it is so intense that the body appears unable to bear it or melts into tears – so long as its conception and experience of God is largely or wholly dependent on imagination rather than on knowledge, it has not yet attained perfect love or contemplation.

Understand, then, that the love of God has three degrees, all of which are good, but each succeeding degree is better then the other. The first degree is reached by faith alone, when no knowledge of God is conveyed by grace through the imagination or understanding. This love is common to every soul that is reformed in faith, however small a degree of charity it has attained; and it is good, for it is sufficient for salvation. The second degree of love is attained when the soul knows God by faith and Jesus in His manhood through the imagination. This love, where imagination is stimulated by grace, is better than the first, because the spiritual perceptions are awakened to contemplate our Lord's human nature. In the third degree the soul, as far as it may in this life, contemplates the Godhead united to manhood in Christ. This is the best, highest, and most perfect degree of love, and it is not attained by the soul until it is reformed in feeling. Those at the beginning and early stages of the spiritual life do not possess this degree of love, for they cannot think of Jesus or love Him as God, but always think of Him as a man living under earthly conditions. All their thoughts and affections are shaped by this limitation. They honour Him as a man, and they worship and love Him principally in His human aspect, and go no farther. For instance, if they have done wrong and offended against God, they think that God is angry with them as a man would be had they offended him. So they fall down as it were at the feet of our Lord with heartfelt sorrow and ask for mercy, trusting that our Lord will mercifully pardon their offence. And although this practice is commendable, it is not as spiritual as it might be. Similarly, when they wish to worship God they imagine our Lord in a bodily form aglow with wondrous light; then they proceed to honour, worship, and revere Him, throwing themselves on His mercy and begging Him to do with them what He wills. In the same way, when they wish to love God, they think of Him, worship Him, and reverence Him as a man, recalling the Passion of Christ or some other event in His earthly life. Nevertheless, when they do this they are deeply stirred to the love of God.

Such devotion is good and inspired by grace, but it is much inferior to the exercise of the understanding, when grace moves the soul to contemplate God in Man. For there are two natures in our Lord, that of God, and that of Man. And as the divine nature is higher and nobler than the human, so the soul's contemplation of the Godhead in the manhood of Jesus is more exalted, more spiritual, and more valuable than the contemplation of His manhood alone, whether the soul is thinking of His manhood as passible or glorified. For the same reason the love felt by a soul when grace enables it to contemplate God in man is more exalted, more spiritual, and more valuable than the fervour of devotion aroused by the contemplation of Jesus's manhood alone, however strong the outward signs of this love. For this latter love is a natural love, and the former a spiritual love; and our Lord does not reveal Himself to the imagination as He is, for the frailty of man's nature is such that the soul could not endure His glory.

Nevertheless, in order that the devotion of those souls
that are incapable of such elevated contemplation of the Godhead should not be misdirected, but be comforted and
strengthened by some form of interior contemplation of
Jesus to forsake sin and the love of the world, God tempers
the ineffable light of His divinity and cloaks it in the bodily
form of Jesus's humanity. He reveals it in this way to the
inward vision of the soul, and sustains it spiritually through
the love of His precious manhood.

II : 30

24. The Homeliness of God

JULIAN OF NORWICH

Revelations of Divine Love

DAME JULIAN, *or Juliana, was an anchoress of Norwich at the end of the fourteenth and the beginning of the fifteenth century, to whom was given a series of 'revelations' or 'shewings', which she describes in her book,* Revelations of Divine Love. *Her visions were mostly of the Passion of Christ. Such visions were not uncommon among recluses and might have been dismissed as of no special significance, except for herself, had they been all. With them were associated, however, 'shewings' which she received in her 'understanding', and which continued for many years after the visions of the Passion had ceased. As she herself puts it: 'All this was shewed by three parts — that is to say, by bodily sight, by words formed in my understanding, and by ghostly sight [i.e. spiritual intuition].'*

These shewings are marked by a spiritual insight of a high order. Though she appears to have been almost entirely lacking in book-learning, Julian is led spontaneously to those doctrines on the nature of the soul and its relation with God which are found in different forms throughout the whole range of speculative mysticism.

Julian's great appeal lies, however, in a serene joyousness and sunny hopefulness which shines out from every page she wrote. This is coupled with a homeliness of thought and expression and a delightful humour. To her everything is good because God is good. Why then, she asks, are there such things as pain and sin? This is one of the main themes of her book, and her answer is founded on her own intimate vision of God as that Love which she celebrates so exquisitely in her final chapter: 'Wouldst thou learn the meaning of this thing [i.e. of her shewings]? Learn it well. Love was His meaning. Who shewed it thee? Love. What shewed He thee? Love. Wherefore shewed it He? For Love.'

The text used is the version of the Sloane manuscript in the British Museum, edited by Grace Warrack (Methuen).

A LITTLE THING, THE QUANTITY OF AN HAZEL-NUT

In this same time our Lord shewed me a spiritual* sight of His homely loving.

I saw that He is to us everything that is good and comfortable for us: He is our clothing that for love wrappeth us, claspeth us, and all encloseth us for tender love, that He may never leave us; being to us all-thing that is good, as to mine understanding.

Also in this He shewed me a little thing, the quantity of an hazel-nut, in the palm of my hand; and it was as round as a ball. I looked thereupon with eye of my understanding, and thought: What may this be? And it was answered generally thus: It is all that is made. I marvelled how it might last, for methought it might suddenly have fallen to naught for little(ness). And I was answered in my understanding: It lasteth, and ever shall (last) for that God loveth it. And so All-thing hath the Being by the love of God.

In this Little Thing I saw three properties. The first is that God made it, the second that God loveth it, the third that God keepeth it. But what is to me verily the Maker, the Keeper, and the Lover – I cannot tell; for till I am Substantially oned to Him, I may never have full rest nor very bliss: that is to say, till I be so fastened to Him, that there is right nought that is made betwixt my God and me.

It needeth us to have knowing of the littleness of creatures and to hold as nought all-thing that is made, for to love and have God that is unmade. For this is the cause why we be not all in ease of heart and soul: that we seek here rest in those things that are so little, wherein is no rest, and know not our God that is All-mighty, All-wise, All-good. For He is the Very Rest. God willeth to be known, and it pleaseth Him that we rest in Him; for all that is beneath Him sufficeth not us.

* MS: ghostly.

And this is the cause why that no soul is rested till it is made nought as to all things that are made. When it is willingly made nought, for love, to have Him that is all, then is it able to receive spiritual rest.

V

THE MARVELLOUS COURTESY AND HOMELINESS OF GOD

Verily it is the most joy that may be, as to my sight, that He that is highest and mightiest, noblest and worthiest, is lowest and meekest, homeliest and most courteous: and truly and verily this marvellous joy shall be shewn us all when we see Him.

And this willeth our Lord that we seek for and trust to, joy and delight in, comforting us and solacing us, as we may with His grace and with His help, unto the time that we see it verily. For the most fulness of joy that we shall have, as to my sight, is the marvellous courtesy and homeliness of our Father, that is our Maker, in our Lord Jesus Christ that is our Brother and our Saviour.

VII

I SAW NO WRATH BUT ON MAN'S PART

Our good Lord the Holy Ghost, which is endless life dwelling in our soul, full securely keepeth us; and worketh therein a peace and bringeth it to ease by grace, and accordeth it to God and maketh it pliant. And this is the mercy and the way that our Lord continually leadeth us in as long as we be here in this life which is changeable.

For I saw no wrath but on man's part; and that forgiveth He in us. For wrath is not else but a frowardness and a contrariness to peace and love; and either it cometh of failing of might, or of failing of wisdom, or of failing of goodness: which failing is not in God, but is on our part. For we by sin and wretchedness have in us a wretched and continuant contrariness to peace and to love. And that shewed He full often in His lovely Regard of Ruth and Pity. For the ground of mercy is love, and the working of mercy is our keeping in love. And this was shewed in such manner that I could not have perceived of the part of mercy but as it were alone in love; that is to say, as to my sight.

Mercy is a sweet gracious working in love, mingled with plenteous pity: for mercy worketh in keeping us, and mercy worketh turning to us all things to good.

XLVIII

VERILY GOD IS OUR MOTHER

All this bliss we have by Mercy and Grace: which manner of bliss we might never have had nor known but if that property of Goodness which is God had been contraried: whereby we have this bliss. For wickedness hath been suffered to rise contrary to the Goodness, and the Goodness of Mercy and Grace contraried against the wickedness and turned all to goodness and to worship, to all these that shall be saved. For it is the property in God which doeth good against evil. Thus Jesus Christ that doeth good against evil is our Very Mother: we have our Being of Him – where the Ground of Motherhood beginneth – with all the sweet Keeping of Love that endlessly followeth. As verily as God is our Father, so verily God is our Mother; and that shewed He in all, and especially in these sweet words where He saith: I it am. That is to say, I it am, the Might and the Goodness of the Fatherhood; I it am, the Wisdom of the Motherhood; I it am, the Light and the Grace that is all blessed Love: I it am, the Trinity; I it am, the Unity; I am the sovereign Goodness of all manner of things. I am that maketh thee to love: I am that maketh thee to long: I it am, the endless fulfilling of all true desires.

For there the soul is highest, noblest, and worthiest, where it is lowest, meekest, and mildest: and (out) of this Substantial Ground we have all our virtues in our Sense-part by gift of Nature, by helping and speeding of Mercy and Grace: without the which we may not profit.

Our high Father, God Almighty, which is Being, He knew and loved us from afore any time: of which knowing, in His marvellous deep charity and the foreseeing counsel of all the blessed Trinity, He willed that the Second Person should

become our Mother. Our Father (willeth), our Mother
worketh, our good Lord the Holy Ghost confirmeth: and
therefore it belongeth to us to love our God in whom we have
our being: Him reverently thanking and praising for our
making, mightily praying to our Mother for mercy and pity,
and to our Lord the Holy Ghost for help and grace.

For in these three is all our life: Nature, Mercy, Grace:
whereof we have meekness and mildness; patience and pity;
and hating of sin and of wickedness – for it belongeth
properly to virtue to hate sin and wickedness. And thus is
Jesus our Very Mother in Nature (by virtue) of our first
making; and He is our Very Mother in Grace, by taking our
nature made. All the fair working, and all the sweet natural
office of dearworthy Motherhood is impropriated to the
Second Person: for in Him we have this Godly Will whole
and safe without end, both in Nature and in Grace, of His
own proper Goodness. I understand three manners of beholding of Motherhood in God: the first is grounded in our
Nature's making; the second is taking of our nature – and
there beginneth the Motherhood of Grace; the third is
Motherhood of working – and therein is a forth-spreading
by the same Grace, of length and breadth and height and of
deepness without end. And all is one Love.

LIX

OUR SUBSTANCE IS IN GOD

I saw full assuredly that our Substance is in God, and also I
saw that in our sense-soul* God is: for in the self-(same) point
that our Soul is made sensual, in the self-(same) point is the
City of God ordained to Him from without beginning; into
which seat He cometh, and never shall remove (from) it. For
God is never out of the soul: in which He dwelleth blissfully
without end. . . .

And all the gifts that God may give to creatures, He hath
given to His Son Jesus for us: which gifts He, dwelling in
us, hath enclosed in Him unto the time that we be waxen

* MS.: sensualite.

and grown – our soul with our body and our body with our soul, either of them taking help of other – till we be brought up unto stature, as nature worketh. And then, in the ground of nature, with working of mercy, the Holy Ghost graciously inspireth into us gifts leading to endless life.

And thus was my understanding led of God to see in Him and to understand, to perceive and to know, that our soul is made-trinity, like to the unmade blissful Trinity, known and loved from without beginning, and in the making oned to the Maker.

LV

Thus I saw full surely that it is readier to us to come to the knowing of God than to know our own Soul. For our Soul is so deep-grounded in God, and so endlessly treasured, that we may not come to the knowing thereof till we have first knowing of God, which is the Maker, to whom it is oned. . . .

God is nearer to us than our own Soul: for He is (the) Ground in whom our Soul standeth, and He is (the) Mean that keepeth the Substance and the Sense-nature together so that they shall never dispart. For our soul sitteth in God in very rest, and our soul standeth in God in very strength, and our Soul is kindly rooted in God in endless love: and therefore if we will have knowledge of our Soul, and communing and dalliance therewith, it behoveth to seek unto our Lord God in whom it is enclosed.

And as anent our Substance and our Sense-part, both together may rightly be called our Soul: and that is because of the oneing that they have in God. The worshipful City that our Lord Jesus sitteth in is our Sense-soul, in which He is enclosed: and our Kindly Substance is enclosed in Jesus with the blessed Soul of Christ sitting in rest in the Godhead.

LVI

And thus I understood in verity that our Soul may never have rest in things that are beneath itself. And when it cometh above all creatures into the Self, yet may it not abide in the beholding of its Self, but all the beholding is blissfully set in God that is the Maker dwelling therein. For in Man's Soul is His very dwelling; and the highest light and the brightest shining of the City is the glorious love of our Lord, as to my sight.

LXVII

SIN IS BEHOVABLE*

And after this I saw God in a Point, that is to say, in mine understanding – by which sight I saw that He is in all things.

I beheld and considered, seeing and knowing in sight, with a soft dread, and thought: What is sin?

For I saw truly that God doeth all-thing, be it never so little. And I saw truly that nothing is done by hap nor by adventure, but all things by the foreseeing wisdom of God: if it be hap or adventure in the sight of man, our blindness and our unforesight is the cause. For the things that are in the foreseeing wisdom of God from without beginning, which rightfully and worshipfully and continually He leadeth to the best end, as they come about fall to us suddenly, ourselves unwitting; and thus by our blindness and our unforesight we say: these be haps and adventures. But to our Lord God they be not so.

Wherefore me behoveth needs to grant that all-thing that is done, it is well-done: for our Lord God doeth all. For in this time the working of creatures was not shewed, but (the working) of our Lord God in the creature: for He is in the Mid-point of all thing, and all He doeth. And I was certain He doeth no sin.

And here I saw verily that sin is no deed: for in all this was not sin shewed.

XI

After this the Lord brought to my mind the longing that I had to Him afore. And I saw that nothing letted me but sin. And so I looked, generally, upon us all, and methought: If sin had not been, we should all have been clean and like to our Lord, as He made us. . . .

But Jesus, who is this Vision, informed me of all that is

* i.e. necessary, plays a needful part.

needful to me, answered by this word and said: *It behoved that there should be sin;** *but all shall be well, and all shall be well, and all manner of thing shall be well.*

In this naked word sin, our Lord brought to my mind, generally, all that is not good, and the shameful despite and the utter noughting that He bare for us in this life, and His dying; and all the pains and passions of all His creatures, ghostly and bodily; for we be all partly noughted, and we shall be noughted following our Master, Jesus, till we be full purged, that is to say, till we be fully noughted of our deadly flesh and of all our inward affections which are not very good; and the beholding of this, with all pains that ever were or ever shall be – and with all these I understand the Passion of Christ for most pain, and over-passing. All this was shewed in a touch and quickly passed over into comfort: for our good Lord would not that the soul were affeared of this terrible sight.

But I saw not sin: for I believe it hath no manner of substance nor no part of being, nor could it be known but by the pain it is cause of.

And thus pain, it is something, as to my sight, for a time; for it purgeth, and maketh us to know ourselves and to ask mercy. For the Passion of Our Lord is comfort to us against all this, and so is His blessed will. And for the tender love that our good Lord hath to all that shall be saved, He comforteth readily and sweetly, signifying thus: It is sooth that sin is cause of all this pain; but all shall be well, and all shall be well, and all manner (of) thing shall be well. . . .

And in these words I saw a marvellous high mystery† hid in God, which mystery He shall openly make known to us in Heaven: in which knowing we shall verily see the cause why He suffered sin to come. In which sight we shall endlessly joy in our Lord God.

XXVII

---

* MS.: Synne is behovabil.
† MS.: privity.

ALL THING SHALL BE WELL

One time our good Lord said: *All thing shall be well*; and another time he said: *Thou shalt see thyself that all* MANNER (*of*) *thing shall be well*; and in these two (sayings) the soul took sundry understandings.

One was that He willeth we know* that not only He taketh heed to noble things and to great, but also to little and to small, to low and to simple, to one and to other. And so meaneth He in that He saith: ALL MANNER OF THINGS shall be well. For He willeth we know that the least thing shall not be forgotten.

Another understanding is this, that there be deeds evil done in our sight, and so great harms taken, that it seemeth to us that it were impossible that ever it should come to good end. And upon this we look, sorrowing and mourning therefore, so that we cannot resign us unto the blissful beholding of God as we should do. And the cause of this is that the use of our reason is now so blind, so low, and so simple, that we cannot know that high marvellous Wisdom, the Might and the Goodness of the blissful Trinity. And thus signifieth He when He saith: THOU SHALT SEE THYSELF if [i.e. that] all manner of things shall be well. . . .

For like as the blissful Trinity made all things of nought, right so the same blessed Trinity shall make well all that is not well.

And in this sight I marvelled greatly and beheld our Faith, marvelling thus: Our Faith is grounded in God's word, and it belongeth to our Faith that we believe that God's word shall be saved in all things; and one point of our Faith is that many creatures shall be condemned: as angels that fell out of Heaven for pride, which be now fiends; and man in earth that dieth out of the Faith of Holy Church: that is to say, they that be heathen men; and also man that hath received christendom and liveth unchristian life and so dieth out of charity: all these shall be condemned to hell without end, as

* MS.: wit.

Holy Church teacheth me to believe. And all this (so) standing, methought it was impossible that all manner of things should be well, as our Lord shewed in the same time.

And as to this I had no other answer in Shewing of our Lord God but this: That which is impossible to thee is not impossible to me: I shall save my word in all things and I shall make all things well. Thus I was taught, by the grace of God, that I should steadfastly hold me in the Faith as I had afore-hand understood, (and) therewith that I should firmly believe that all things shall be well, as our Lord shewed in the same time.

For this is the Great Deed that our Lord shall do, in which Deed He shall save His word and He shall make all well that is not well. How it shall be done there is no creature beneath Christ that knoweth it, nor shall know it till it is done; according to the understanding that I took of our Lord's meaning in this time.

XXXII

LOVE WAS OUR LORD'S MEANING

This book is begun by God's gift and His grace, but it is not yet performed, as to my sight.

For Charity pray we all; (together) with God's working, thanking, trusting, enjoying. For thus will our good Lord be prayed to, as by the understanding that I took of all His own meaning and of the sweet words where He saith full merrily: I am the Ground of thy beseeching. For truly I saw and understood in our Lord's meaning that He shewed it for that He willeth to have it known more than it is: in which knowing He will give us grace to love Him and cleave to Him. For He beholdeth His heavenly treasure with so great love on earth that He willeth to give us more light and solace in heavenly joy, in drawing to Him of our hearts, for sorrow and darkness which we are in.

And from that time that it was shewed I desired oftentimes to learn what was our Lord's meaning. And fifteen years after, and more, I was answered in ghostly understanding, saying

thus: Wouldst thou learn thy Lord's meaning in this thing?
Learn it well: Love was His meaning. Who shewed it thee?
Love. What shewed He thee? Love. Wherefore shewed it
He? For Love. Hold thee therein and thou shalt learn and
know more in the same. But thou shalt never know nor learn
therein other thing without end. Thus was I learned that Love
was our Lord's meaning.

And I saw full surely that ere God made us He loved us;
which love was never slacked, nor ever shall be. And in this
love He hath done all His works; and in this love He hath
made all things profitable to us; and in this love our life is
everlasting. In our making we had beginning; but the love
wherein He made us was in Him from without beginning:
in which love we have our beginning. And all this shall we
see in God, without end.

LXXXVI

25. The Coincidence of Opposites

NICHOLAS OF CUSA

THE *fifteenth century was a period of crisis in the history of Europe. The medieval system of universal Church and universal Empire was beginning to break up. The unity of the Church had been undermined by the Babylonian Captivity and the Great Schism and was soon to be torn asunder by the Reformation. The ideal of a universal Christian state, embodied in the Holy Roman Empire, had ceased to have any reality; nationalism was in the air. In the Renaissance of the fifteenth century one sees the flowering of that humanistic idealism which was to dominate the thought and action of the Modern Age.*

In the midst of this period of crisis stood the remarkable figure of Nicholas of Cusa, born in 1401, the son of a well-to-do boat-owner, at Cues on the Moselle; Papal Legate, Bishop and Cardinal; philosopher, mathematican, and mystic; practical man of affairs playing an important role in the Councils of the Church which were called to try to end the scandal of the Great Schism, and, at the same time, a leader of the thought of his age.

Until recently Nicholas of Cusa was known in this country only as a political theorist – Dunning, in Political Theories, Ancient and Medieval, *gives a whole section to his political thinking – other and for us more important aspects of his thought were neglected or unknown. It is perhaps not surprising. Not only were the Latin texts of his writings difficult to obtain, but also none of his religious works were translated into English until 1928, when a translation of the* Visio Dei (The Vision of God) *by Emma Gurney Salter appeared. The first English translation of his best-known work,* De Docta Ignorantia (Of Learned Ignorance), *by Fr Germain Heron was not published until 1954 (Routledge & Kegan Paul). I believe there is only one critical biography in English, that of Henry Bett in Methuen's 'Great Medieval Churchman' series.*

What is the significance of this subtle philosopher and precise mathematician in the history of speculative Christian mysticism?

In the Dedicatory Letter to the Lord Cardinal Julian of the De docta ignorantia Nicholas tells of the mystical experience which happened to him on a sea voyage from Greece, through which he was 'led in that learning which is ignorance to grasp the incomprehensible'; and this, he says, he was able to achieve 'not by way of comprehension but by transcending those perennial truths that can be reached by reason'.

This mystical experience did not set Nicholas on the road of Contemplation; but it influenced the whole of his thinking henceforth. In him we see the interplay in a manner almost unique — there is something of the same interplay in St Augustine — of rational speculation and intuition founded on mystical vision.

The philosophy of Nicholas of Cusa may be summed up briefly as follows: He had the mathematician's passion for unity. He was impatient of the opposites which conditioned his perception, the opposition of infinite and finite, of thought and being, of good and evil, of time and eternity; i.e. the old, old problem of the One and the Many. He burned to break through these opposites and to find the unity which he felt existed beyond and above them. His resolution of the dilemma is expressed in his doctrine of the coincidence of opposites (or contradictories) in God. His thinking here has some affinity with ancient Chinese metaphysics, in which the phenomenal universe is envisaged as coming into existence by the breaking asunder of Tao, the Primal Meaning, into the polar opposites evident in the material world.

He envisaged reality as having two aspects: an invisible and ultimate reality, which is God, and a visible and derived reality, which is the world. God is the originative and communicative, the world the originated and communicated reality. As uncreated all is God; as created all is the world. All begins from God and ends in God, as motion begins from rest and ends in rest.

God is thus the superessential unity which is opposed to all otherness, and in Him all contraries coincide. (Here there are similarities to the teaching of Hinduism.) Not only that, since all things in God are God, and since the essence of them is in the thought of God, everything is one with God.

This is the merest summary of a system of thought which is both

rich and subtle. One finds also in Nicholas of Cusa a teaching on
the apprehension of God by man and the way he can be spoken of
which has affinities with that found in the writings of the Pseudo-
Dionysius, i.e. that the negations are true and the affirmations are true;
but the negations are more true than the affirmations.†*

The first three passages quoted below are from The Vision of
God (Dent). *This is one of Nicholas's smaller and less elaborate
works. It contains, however, the essence of his teaching and has,
moreover, what I can only call a quality of excitement. Time and time
again one feels that Nicholas is writing in a sort of ecstasy of intellectual joy in his vision. Of* Learned Ignorance *is much more
elaborately mathematical in its argument and moves more sedately.
Further, the argument is too continuous to make selective quotation
easy. I have, however, selected the fourth passage from the Third
Book, in Fr Heron's translation, in which Nicholas uses his philosophical system to interpret the central mystery of the Christian faith.*

ON THE COINCIDENCE OF OPPOSITES

Apart from Thee, Lord, naught can exist. If, then, Thine
essence pervade all things, so also doth Thy sight,‡ which
is Thine essence. For even as no created thing can escape
from its own proper essence, so neither can it from Thine
essence, which giveth essential being to all beings. . . .
Accordingly, Thou, Lord, seest all things and each thing at
one and the same time, and movest with all that move, and
standest with them that stand. And because there be some that
move while others stand, Thou, Lord, dost stand and move

* A good account of the philosophy of Nicholas of Cusa will be found
in Bett: *Nicholas of Cusa*.

† See *Of Learned Ignorance*, Book I, Chapter XXVI.

‡ Or, perhaps better, *gaze*. The little treatise on the mystical life, the
Visio Dei, was sent by Nicholas of Cusa to the Abbot and Brethren of
Tegernsee, accompanied by a picture of an omnivoyant, i.e. a picture of
a face which, from whatever angle it is looked at, seems to be looking
straight at the beholder. Nicholas calls it in the Preface to the book 'the
icon of God', and uses it extensively in the first part of the treatise to
bring out what he is saying. The word, *visio*, may be translated 'gaze'
when it refers to God's regard of man, 'vision' when it refers to man's
regard of God.

at the same time, at the same time Thou dost proceed and rest. For if both motion and rest can be individuated at the same time in divers beings, and if naught can exist apart from Thee, and no motion be apart from Thee, nor any rest; then Thou, Lord, art wholly present to all these things, and to each, at one and the same time. And yet Thou dost not move nor rest, since Thou art exalted above all, and freed from all that can be conceived or named. Wherefore, Thou standest and proceedest, and yet at the same time dost not stand or proceed. . . .

Hence I observed how needful it is for me to enter into the darkness, and to admit the coincidence of opposites, beyond all the grasp of reason, and there to seek the truth where impossibility meeteth me. And beyond that, beyond even the highest ascent of intellect, when I shall have attained unto that which is unknown to every intellect, and which every intellect judgeth to be most far removed from truth, there, my God art Thou, who art Absolute Necessity. And the more that dark impossibility is recognized as dark and impossible, the more truly doth His Necessity shine forth, and is more unveiledly present, and draweth nigh.

Wherefore I give Thee thanks, my God, because Thou makest plain to me that there is none other way of approaching Thee than that which to all men, even the most learned philosophers, seemeth utterly inaccessible and impossible. For Thou hast shown me that Thou canst not be seen elsewhere than where impossibility meeteth and faceth me. Thou hast inspired me, Lord, who art the Food of the strong, to do violence to myself, because impossibility coincideth with necessity, and I have learnt that the place wherein Thou art found unveiled is girt round with the coincidence of contradictories, and this is the wall of Paradise wherein Thou dost abide. The door whereof is guarded by the most proud spirit of Reason, and, unless he be vanquished, the way in will not lie open. Thus 'tis beyond the coincidence of contradictories that Thou mayest be seen, and nowhere this side thereof.

Chapter IX

Whence I begin, Lord, to behold Thee in the door of the coincidence of opposites, which the angel guardeth that is set over the entrance into Paradise. For Thou art there where speech, sight, hearing, taste, touch, reason, knowledge, and understanding are the same, and where seeing is one with being seen, and hearing with being heard, and tasting with being tasted, and touching with being touched, and speaking with hearing, and creating with speaking. . . .

Thou conceivest the heaven, and it existeth as Thou conceivest it; Thou conceivest the earth, and it existeth as Thou conceivest it; while Thou conceivest, Thou dost see and speak and work, and do all else that can be named. Marvellous art Thou, my God, Thou conceivest once, Thou speakest once! How, then, do not all things come into being simultaneously, but many of them successively? How do such diverse things spring from one only concept? Thou dost enlighten me while I am on the threshold of the door, showing me that Thy concept is pure and simple eternity itself. 'Tis impossible that aught should be made after eternity pure and simple. For infinite duration, which is eternity's self, includeth all succession, and all which seemeth to us to be in succession existeth not posterior to Thy concept, which is eternity. For Thy one and only concept, which is also Thy Word, enfoldeth all and each, while Thine eternal Word cannot be manifold, nor diverse, nor changeable, nor mutable, because it is simple eternity.

Thus, Lord, I perceive that naught existeth posterior to Thy concept, but that all things exist because Thou dost conceive them. Thou conceivest in eternity, but in eternity succession is without succession, 'tis eternity's self, 'tis Thy very Word, O Lord God. Thou hast no sooner conceived aught that appeareth to us in time than it is. For in eternity in which Thou conceivest, all succession in time coincideth in the same NOW of eternity. There is no past nor future where future and past are one with present. The reason why things in this world exist as earlier and later is that Thou didst not earlier conceive such things to exist: hadst Thou earlier conceived them they would have existed earlier. But he in whose thought earlier and later can occur, in such a way that he conceives one thing first and then another, is not almighty. Thus, because Thou art God Almighty, Thou dwellest within the wall of Paradise, and this wall is that coincidence where later is one with earlier, where the end is one with the beginning, where Alpha and Omega are the same. . . .

That which seemeth impossible is necessity itself, for NOW and THEN are posterior to Thy Word. This is why for him that approacheth Thee, they meet in the wall surrounding the place where Thou abidest in coincidence. For NOW and THEN coincide in the circle of the wall of Paradise. But, O my God, the Absolute and Eternal, it is beyond the Present and the Past that Thou dost exist and utter speech!

Chapter X

GOD AS CREATOR YET NOT CREATOR

If with Thee to see is to create, and Thou seest naught other than Thyself, but art Thyself the object of Thyself (for Thou seest, and art to be seen, and art Sight) – how then dost Thou create things other than Thyself – for Thou wouldst seem to create Thyself even as Thou seest Thyself? But Thou dost strengthen me, Life of my spirit! For, although the wall of absurdity, which is the coincidence of creating with being created, should seem as if it were impossible, in that creating and being created are one (for to admit this would seem to be to affirm that a thing existeth before it existeth, since when He createth it it existeth, and yet it existeth not because it is created) – yet this is no real difficulty, since with Thee creation and existence are the same. And creating and being created alike are naught else than the sharing of Thy Being among all, that Thou mayest be All in all, and yet mayest abide freed from all. For to call into being things which are not is to make Nothing a sharer in Being: thus to call is to create, while to share is to be created. And beyond this coincidence of creating and being created art Thou, Absolute and Infinite God, neither creating nor creatable, albeit all things are what they are because Thou art.

O height of riches, how beyond understanding art Thou! While I imagine a Creator creating, I am still on this side of the wall of Paradise! While I imagine a Creator as creatable, I have not yet entered, but I am in the wall. But when I behold Thee as Absolute Infinity, to whom is befitting neither the name of creating Creator nor of creatable Creator – then indeed I begin to behold Thee unveiled, and to enter in to the garden of delights! For Thou art naught such as can be spoken or imagined, but art infinitely and absolutely exalted high above all such things. Wherefore, albeit without Thee naught is made or can be made, Thou art not a Creator, but infinitely more than a Creator; unto Thee be praise and glory through endless ages.

Chapter XII

OF LEARNED IGNORANCE

Thus, while I am borne to loftiest heights, I behold Thee as infinity. By reason of this, Thou mayest not be attained, or comprehended, or named, or multiplied, or beheld. He that approacheth Thee must needs ascend above every limit and end and finite thing. But how shall he attain unto Thee who art the End toward whom he striveth, if he must ascend above the end? He who ascendeth above the end, doth he not enter into what is undefined and confused, and thus, in regard to the intellect, into ignorance and obscurity, which pertain to intellectual confusion? It behoveth, then, the intellect to become ignorant and to abide in darkness if it would fain see Thee. But what, O my God, is this intellectual ignorance? Is it not an instructed ignorance? Thou, God, who art infinity, canst only be approached by him whose intellect is in ignorance, to wit, by him who knows himself to be ignorant of Thee.

How can the intellect grasp Thee, who art infinity? The intellect knoweth that it is ignorant, and that Thou canst not be grasped because Thou art infinity. For to understand infinity is to comprehend the incomprehensible. The intellect knoweth that it is ignorant of Thee, because it knoweth Thou canst not be known, unless the unknowable could be known, and the invisible beheld, and the inaccessible attained. . . .

Thou art the great God, of whose greatness there is no end, and thus I perceive Thee to be the immeasurable measure of all things, even as the infinite end of all. Wherefore, Lord, being infinite, Thou art without beginning and end; Thou art beginning without beginning and end without end; Thou art beginning without end and end without beginning; Thou art equally beginning as end and end as beginning, yet neither beginning nor end, but above beginning and end, absolute infinity itself, blessed for ever!

Chapter XIII

ON THE MYSTERIES OF FAITH

Our ancient writers are at one in asserting that faith lies at the root of all understanding. In every science certain things must be accepted as first principles if the subject matter is to be understood; and these first postulates rest only upon faith. He who wishes to rise to knowledge must first believe those things without which knowledge is impossible. Says Isaias: 'Unless you believe you shall not understand.' Faith, therefore, embraces every intelligible thing. Understanding is the unfolding of what was wrapped up in faith. The intelligence is therefore directed by faith; and faith is extended by understanding. Without sound faith then there is no true understanding. There is no mistaking the kinds of conclusions that are reached from faulty principles and from a weak foundation: and on the other hand, there is no faith more perfect than that which is founded upon the truth itself, which is Jesus. . . .

Now this most wholesome faith in Christ, constantly strengthened in simplicity, can, in our accepted doctrine of ignorance, be extended and unfolded. The greatest and profoundest mysteries of God, though hidden from the wise, may be revealed to little ones and humble folk living in the world by their faith in Jesus: for in Jesus are hidden all the treasures of wisdom and knowledge, so that without Him no man can do anything. For He is the Word, and the power by whom God made the world, He the most high having alone power over everything in heaven and on earth. He cannot be apprehended within the context of this world. Here we are led by reason, opinion, or doctrine from the better known to the less known by symbols; whereas he is grasped only when movement ceases and faith takes its place. By this faith we are caught up into simplicity above all reason and intelligence to the third heaven of most pure simple* intellectuality;† that in the body we may contemplate him incorporeally, because in spirit, and on the earth in an entirely unearthly fashion and rather in a heavenly and incomprehensible manner, whereby we perceive that He cannot be comprehended because of the immensity of His excellence. And this is none other than that very learned ignorance – by which the blessed Paul himself, raised higher and into a closer knowledge, perceived that the Christ with whom he was at one time acquainted, he never really knew.

We, then, believers in Christ, are led in learned ignorance to the mountain that is Christ, which our animal nature is forbidden to touch; and when we endeavour to gaze upon Him with the eye of the mind we fall into darkness, knowing that in that very darkness is the mount in which He is pleased to dwell for the sake of all those who live a life of the spirit. But if, in the constancy of a firmer faith we approach Him, we are snatched away from the eyes of them that live by sensuality, to perceive with interior hearing the voices and the thunder and the dread signs of His majesty. We are given to realize that he alone is the Lord whom all things obey. And step by step we come close even to certain incorruptible footprints of Him (as to most divine characters) in which, hearing the voice not of mortal creatures but of God Himself in His holy organs and in the words of His prophets and saints, we come, as in a cloud of most transparent quality, to perceive Him more clearly.

Book III, Chapter XI

* In the sense used by the mystics, conveying the meaning of wholeness, completeness, synthesis.

† With the meaning of *intellectus*, a higher faculty than *ratio*.

26. The Degrees of Prayer

ST TERESA OF ÁVILA

On *28 March 1515 there was born, in the Spanish town of Ávila, a girl, Teresa de Cepeda y Ahumada, destined to become one of the best-known and best-loved contemplative saints of the Christian Church. Two years later, Luther nailed his ninety-five theses against indulgences to the church door of Wittenberg, and, in so doing, heralded in that Protestant Reformation which was to split Western Christendom in twain.*

At first the Roman Catholic Church did not take the German revolt very seriously. After all, there had been other revolts, which had come to nothing. Twenty years later it had become clear that a more dangerous attack against the unity of the Church than ever before had been launched. The response of the Roman Church to the Protestant Reformation is known as the Counter-Reformation. It is not necessary to describe here the form it took. It is sufficient to say that it had its roots in the reforms of the Spanish Church which had been carried out by Isabella of Castile a little less than a century earlier, and it was in Spain that, associated with it, there was a flowering of mystical life equal to that which had flourished in earlier centuries in Germany and the Low Countries. Its outstanding figures were St Teresa of Ávila (or, as she is sometimes named, Teresa of Jesus) and St John of the Cross.

These two were intimately associated in the work of the reform of the Carmelite Order. Yet how different they are. St John of the Cross, the 'mystic's mystic', was withdrawn, austere, of brilliant and keen intellect, a poet who is numbered among the great poets of Spain. Teresa was a typical woman, practical and vigorous, humorous and attractive, a born leader and organizer, and, at the same time, a contemplative saint whose writings on the spiritual life stand high in the literature of mysticism.

There is no room here to tell her story. It is exquisitely told by

*the late Professor Allison Peers, chief English authority on St
Teresa and St John of the Cross, in* Mother of Carmel *(S.C.M.
Press). Until her death in 1582 her life was one of intense activity,
of struggles with the ecclesiastical authorities to allow her to carry
out the work of the reform of the Carmelite Order, to which she felt
herself called by God, of weary journeyings over wild and difficult
country, of the founding of convent after convent, of intense literary
activity – her books and letters fill five volumes in Allison Peers's
edition – the whole sustained by the mystical prayer, at which she
was adept.*

Her greatest work is The Interior Castle, *in which she describes
the Seven Mansions through which the soul passes on its way from
purgation to union. I have decided, however, to let her speak through
the chapters of the* Life, *one of the most charmingly intimate and self-
revealing spiritual autobiographies ever written, in which she describes
from her own experience the degrees of prayer. To get the full flavour
these chapters ought to be read* in extenso. *Nevertheless the passages
quoted give some idea of St Teresa's style. All the time she is strug-
gling to put down as exactly as possible the character of the experiences she is trying to describe. This results in a certain diffuseness and
repetition, very different from the extreme precision of St John of the
Cross, as the reader will realize when he compares these passages with
those from the writing of St John of the Cross which follow. Yet it is
this naïveté, the refusal to be clever or learned, the extremely humble
effort to be as truthful as possible, which give the writings of St
Teresa not only their charm but also their particular value and
effectiveness, especially for one who desires to enter on at least the
earlier stages of mystical prayer.*

*The translation used is that by J. M. Cohen, published in the
Penguin Classics. The passages quoted are taken from Chapter 11
and from Chapters 14 to 18 of the* Life, *and are arranged to form a
continuous narrative.*

THE FOUR DEGREES (OR STAGES) OF PRAYER

I shall have to make use of a comparison, though being a
woman and writing only what I have been commanded to
write, I should like to avoid it. But this spiritual language is

so difficult to use for those like myself who have no learning, that I must find some other means of expression. It may be that my comparisons will not very often be effective, in which case your Reverence will be amused at my stupidity. It strikes me that I have read or heard this one before. But as I have a bad memory I do not know where it occurred or what it illustrated. But for the present it will serve my purpose.

A beginner must look on himself as one setting out to make a garden for his Lord's pleasure, on most unfruitful soil which abounds in weeds. His Majesty roots up the weeds and will put in good plants instead. Let us reckon that this is already done when a soul decides to practise prayer and has begun to do so. We have then, as good gardeners, with God's help to make these plants grow, and to water them carefully so that they do not die, but produce flowers which give out a good smell, to delight this Lord of ours. Then He will often come to take His pleasure in this garden and enjoy these virtues.

Now let us see how this garden is to be watered, so that we may understand what we have to do, and what labour it will cost us, also whether the gain will outweigh the effort, or how long it will take. It seems to me that the garden may be watered in four different ways. Either the water must be drawn from a well, which is very laborious; or by a water-wheel and buckets, worked by a windlass – I have sometimes drawn it in this way, which is less laborious than the other, and brings up more water – or from a stream or spring, which waters the ground much better, for the soil then retains more moisture and needs watering less often, which entails far less work for the gardener; or by heavy rain, when the Lord waters it Himself without any labour of ours; and this is an incomparably better method than all the rest.

Now to apply these four methods of watering, by which this garden is to be maintained and without which it will fail. This is my purpose, and will, I think, enable me to explain something about the four stages of prayer, to which the Lord has, in His kindness, sometimes raised my soul.

Chapter 11

ON THE FIRST DEGREE OF PRAYER

We may say that beginners in prayer are those who draw the water up out of the well; which is a great labour, as I have said. For they find it very tiring to keep the senses recollected, when they are used to a life of distraction. Beginners have to accustom themselves to pay no attention to what they see or hear, and to put this exercise into practice during their hours of prayer, when they must remain in solitude, thinking whilst they are alone of their past life. Although all must do this many times, the advanced as well as the beginners, all need not do so equally, as I shall explain later. At first they are distressed because they are not sure that they regret their sins. Yet clearly they do, since they have now sincerely resolved to serve God. They should endeavour to meditate on the life of Christ, and thus the intellect will grow tired. Up to this point we can advance ourselves, though with God's help of course, for without it, as everyone knows, we cannot think one good thought. . . .

But what shall a man do here who finds that for many days on end he feels nothing but dryness, dislike, distaste, and so little desire to go and draw water that he would give it up altogether if he did not remember that he is pleasing and serving the Lord of the garden; if he did not want all his service to be in vain, and if he did not also hope to gain something for all the labour of lowering the bucket so often into the well and bringing it up empty? It will often happen that he cannot so much as raise his arms to the task, or think a single good thought. For by this drawing of water I mean, of course, working with the understanding.

Well, what, I repeat, shall the gardener do now? He shall be glad and take comfort, and consider it the greatest favour that he is working in the garden of so mighty an Emperor. He knows that He is pleasing his Master in this, and his purpose must be to please Him and not himself. Let him praise him greatly, for having placed such trust in him, and for seeing that though he receives no payment he is carefully carrying out the task assigned to him. . . .

These labours bring their reward. I endured them for many years, and when I drew one drop of water from this blessed well I thought of it as a mercy from God. I know that they are very great labours, and that more courage is needed for them than for most worldly trials. But I have clearly seen that God does not fail to reward them highly, even in this life. A single one of those hours in which He has allowed me to taste of His sweetness has seemed to me afterwards a certain recompense for all the afflictions I bore during my long perseverance in prayer.

Chapter 11

ON THE SECOND DEGREE OF PRAYER

Having spoken of the effort and physical labour entailed in watering the garden, and what efforts it costs to raise the water from the well, let us now turn to the second method of drawing it which the Owner of the plot has ordained. By means of a device with a windlass, the gardener draws more water with less labour, and so is able to take some rest instead of being continuously at work. I apply this description to the prayer of quiet, which I am now going to describe.

Now the soul begins to be recollected, and here it comes into touch with the supernatural, to which it could not possibly attain by its own efforts. True, sometimes it seems to have grown weary through turning the wheel, and toiling with its mind, and filling the buckets. But in this state the level of the water is higher, and so much less labour is required than for drawing it from a well. I mean that the water is closer because grace reveals itself more clearly to the soul. This entails a gathering of the faculties within oneself so as to derive a greater savour from that pleasure. But they are not lost or asleep. The will alone is occupied in such a way that it is unconsciously taken captive. It simply consents to be God's prisoner, since it well knows how to surrender to One whom it loves. O Jesus, my Lord, how precious Your love is to us then! It binds our own love so closely to it as to leave us no liberty to love anything but you!

The other two faculties – the memory and the imagination – help the will to make itself more and more capable of enjoying this great blessing, though, on the other hand, it sometimes happens that they are a great hindrance to it, even when the will is in union. But then it should never pay attention to them but stay in its joy and quiet. For if it tried to make them recollected, both it and they might lose the way. . . .

Everything that happens now brings very great consolation, and costs so little labour that, even if prayer is continued for some time, it brings no weariness. The intellect now works very gently and draws up a great deal more water than it drew from the well. . . .

On arriving at this state, the soul begins to lose the desire for earthly things – and no wonder! It clearly sees that not even one moment of this joy is to be obtained here on earth, and that there are no riches, estates, honours, or delights that can give it such satisfaction even for the twinkling of an eye. For this is the true joy, the content that can be seen to satisfy. Those of us who are on earth, it seems to me, rarely understand where this satisfaction lies. It is always up and down. First we have it, then it leaves us, and we find that it has all gone and that we cannot get it back, since we have no idea how to do so. . . .

This satisfaction lodges in the innermost part of the soul, which does not know whence nor how it came. Often it does not even know what to do or wish or ask for. It seems to find everything at once, and yet not to know what it has found. I do not know how to explain this. . . .

I very much wish the Lord would help me to describe the effects of these things on the soul, now that they begin to be supernatural, so that men may know by the results whether they are from the spirit of God. I mean that I would have them know in so far as anything can be known here below, for it is always well to proceed with fear and caution. Even if they are from God, the devil can at times transform himself into an angel of light, and if the soul is not very experienced, it will not realize this. To realize this, indeed, it must have so much experience that it must have attained to the very summit of prayer. . . .

This quiet and recollection of the soul manifests itself largely in the peace and satisfaction, the very joy and repose of the faculties, and the most sweet delights that it brings with it. As the soul has never gone beyond this stage, it thinks that there is nothing left to desire, and would, like St Peter, gladly make its home here. It dares not move or stir, for fear that this blessing may slip through its fingers; sometimes it is afraid even to breathe. The poor creature is not aware that, just as it could do nothing to acquire this blessing, so it is still less able to hold it any longer than the Lord wishes. I have already said that in this first recollection and stillness the powers of the soul are not suspended. But the soul is so replete with God that, although two of its faculties may be distracted, yet so long as recollection lasts, peace and quiet are not lost, since the will is in union with God. On the contrary the will gradually calls the intellect and the memory back again. Although it is not yet completely absorbed, it is so occupied, without knowing with what, that whatever efforts the distracted faculties may make they cannot rob it of its joy and contentment. In fact it effortlessly helps to keep this little spark of love for God from going out. . . .

This prayer, then, is a little spark of true love for Him which the Lord begins to kindle in the soul. He wishes the soul to come to understand the nature of this love with its attendant joy. This quiet and recollection, and this little spark – so long as it proceeds from the spirit of God and is not a sweetness given by the devil or induced by ourselves – is not a thing that can be acquired, as anyone who has experience of it must immediately realize. But this nature of ours is so greedy for moments of sweetness that it seeks for them in every way. But soon it becomes very cold. For however much we try to kindle the fire in order to catch this sweetness, we seem merely to be pouring water on it and putting it out. Now this God-given spark, however tiny it may be, causes a great noise; and if we do not quench it through our own fault it begins to light the great fire which – as I shall tell in due course – throws out flames of that mighty love of God, with which His Majesty endows the souls of the perfect.

ST TERESA OF ÁVILA 349

This little spark is a sign or pledge that God gives to this soul to show that He is already choosing it for great things, if it will prepare itself to receive them. It is a great gift, far greater indeed than I can say.

All that the soul has to do at these times of quiet is merely to be calm and make no noise. By noise I mean working with the intellect to find great numbers of words and reflections with which to thank God for this blessing, and piling up its sins and faults to prove to itself that it does not deserve it. Then the commotion starts, the intellect works and the memory seethes. Indeed these faculties sometimes tire me out, for though I have very little memory I cannot keep it under control. The will must quietly and wisely understand that we cannot deal violently with God; and that our efforts are like great logs of wood indiscriminately piled on, which will only put out the spark. It must admit this and humbly ask: 'Lord, what can I do now?'

Chapters 14 and 15

ON THE THIRD DEGREE OF PRAYER

Let us now go on to speak of the third water that feeds this garden, which is flowing water from a stream or spring. This irrigates it with far less trouble, though some effort is required to direct it into the right channel. But now the Lord is pleased to help the gardener in such a way as to be, as it were, the gardener Himself. For it is He who does everything. The faculties of the soul are asleep, not entirely lost nor yet entirely conscious of how they are working. The pleasure, sweetness, and delight are incomparably more than in the previous state, for the water of grace has risen to the soul's neck, and it is powerless, knowing neither how to advance nor to retreat; what it wants is to enjoy its very great glory. It is like a man with the funeral candle in his hand, on the point of dying the death he desires. It takes unutterable delight in the enjoyment of its agony, which seems to me like nothing else but an almost complete death to all the things of this world, and a fulfilment in God. I know of no other words with which to describe or explain it. The soul does not know what to do; it cannot tell whether to speak or be silent, whether to laugh or weep. It is a glorious bewilderment, a heavenly madness, in which true wisdom is acquired, and to the soul a fulfilment most full of delight.

It is, I believe, five or six years since the Lord first granted me frequent and abundant experience of this sort of prayer; and I have never understood it or been able to explain it. . . . I knew very well that it was not a complete union of all the faculties, and yet it was clearly higher than the previous state of prayer. But I confess that I could not decide or understand where the difference lay. . . . Very often I was, so to speak, bewildered and intoxicated with love, and yet could never understand how it was. I knew very well that this was God's work, but I could never understand the way in which He worked here. In effect the faculties are in almost complete union, yet not so absorbed that they do not act. I am greatly delighted that I have understood it at last. Blessed be the Lord, who has given me this gift!

The faculties retain only the power of occupying themselves wholly with God. None of them seems to dare even to stir, nor can we make any one of them move without great and deliberate efforts to fix the attention on some external thing, though I do not think that at such times we can entirely succeed in doing this. Many words are then spoken in praise of the Lord. But they are disorderly, unless the Lord himself imposes order on them. The intellect, at any rate, is of no value here. The soul longs to pour out words of praise. But it is in a sweet unrest, and cannot contain itself. Already the flowers are opening, and beginning to give off scent. . . .

This state of prayer seems to me a most definite union of the whole soul with God, complete but for the fact that His Majesty appears to allow the faculties to be conscious of and to enjoy the great work that He is doing. Sometimes – indeed very often – the will being in union, the soul is aware of it and sees that it is rejoicing in its captivity. There is the will, alone and abiding in great peace, while the understanding and the memory, on the other hand, are so free that they can attend to business or do works of charity. I tell you this, my Father, so that you may see that it can happen, and may recognize the experience when it comes to you: I myself was driven quite frantic by it, and that is why I speak of it here.

Although it may appear to be the same, this differs from the prayer of quiet, of which I have spoken. In that first state the soul does not wish to move or stir but delights in the blessed repose of a Mary, whereas in this second state it can be like Martha also. Thus it is, as it were, leading the active and the contemplative life at once, and can apply itself to works of charity, to its professional business and to reading as well. Yet in this state we are not wholly masters of ourselves, but are well aware that the better part of the soul is elsewhere. It is as if we were speaking to one person, while someone else were speaking to us, so that we cannot attend properly to either.

In all these states of prayer that I have described whilst speaking of this last water, which comes from a spring, the soul's bliss and repose is so great that even the body shares in its joy and delight to a clearly perceptible extent, and the virtues are highly developed also, as I have said. It seems that the Lord has been pleased thus to reveal these states in which the soul may find itself, and to do so as clearly, I believe, as is possible here upon this earth.

Chapters 16 and 17

ON THE FOURTH DEGREE OF PRAYER

May the Lord teach me words with which to convey some idea of the fourth water. I shall indeed need His help more now than ever before. In this state, the soul still feels that it is not altogether dead, as we may say, though it is entirely dead to the world. But, as I have said, it retains the sense to know that it is still here and to feel its solitude; and it makes use of outward manifestations to show its feelings, at least by signs. Throughout, in every stage of the prayer that I have described, the gardener performs some labour, though in these later stages the labour is accompanied by so much bliss and comfort to the soul that the soul would never willingly abandon it. So the labour is not felt as such, but as bliss.

Here there is no sense of anything but enjoyment, without any knowledge of what is being enjoyed. The soul realizes that it is enjoying some good thing that contains all good things together, but it cannot comprehend this good thing. All the senses are taken up with this joy so that none of them is free to act in any way, either outwardly or inwardly. Previously, as I have said, the senses were permitted to give some indication of the great joy they feel. But now the soul enjoys incomparably more, and yet has still less power to show it. For there is no power left in the body – and the soul possesses none – by which this joy can be communicated. At such a time anything of the sort would be a great embarrassment, a torment and a disturbance of its repose. If there is really a union of all the faculties, I say, then the soul cannot make it known, even if it wants to – while actually in union I mean. If it can, then it is not in union.

How what is called union takes place and what it is, I cannot tell. It is explained in *mystical theology*, but I cannot use the proper terms; I cannot understand what *mind* is, or how it differs from *soul* or *spirit*. They all seem one to me, though the soul sometimes leaps out of itself like a burning fire that has become one whole flame and increases with great force. The flame leaps very high above the fire. Nevertheless it is not a different thing, but the same flame which is in the fire. . . .

What I want to explain is the soul's feelings when it is in this divine union. It is plain enough what union is; in union two separate things become one. O my Lord, how good You are! May You be blessed for ever, O my God, and may all things praise You for so loving us that we can truly speak of Your communication with souls, even here in our exile! . . .

I am now speaking of that rain that comes down abundantly from heaven to soak and saturate the whole garden. . . .

The heavenly rain very often comes down when the gardener least expects it. Yet it is true that at the beginning it almost always comes after long mental prayer. Then, as one stage succeeds another, the Lord takes up this small bird and puts it into the nest where it may be quiet. He has watched it fluttering for a long time, trying with its understanding and its will and all its strength to find God and please Him; and now He is pleased to give it its reward in this life. And what a reward! One moment of it is enough to repay all the trials it can ever have endured.

While seeking God in this way, the soul is conscious that it is fainting almost completely away in a kind of swoon, with a very great calm and joy. Its breath and all its bodily powers progressively fail it, so that it can hardly stir its hands without great effort. Its eyes close involuntarily, and if they remain open, they see almost nothing. If a person reads in this state he can scarcely make out a single letter; it is as much as he can do to recognize one. He sees that there are letters, but as the understanding offers no help, he cannot read them, even if he wants to. He hears but does not understand what he hears. In the same way, his senses serve no purpose except to prevent the soul from taking its pleasure; and so they tend to do him harm. It is the same with the tongue, for he cannot form a word, nor would he have the strength to pronounce one. The whole physical strength vanishes and the strength of the soul increases for the better enjoyment of its bliss. The outward joy that is now felt is great and most perceptible.

However long this prayer lasts, it does no harm. At least it has never done me any; however ill I might have been when the Lord granted me this grace, I never remember an occasion when I experienced any bad effects from it. On the contrary I was left feeling much better. But what harm can so great a blessing possibly do? The outward results are so evident that there can be no doubt some great thing has taken place. Nothing else could have robbed us of our bodily strength, yet have given us so much joy that it is returned to us increased. . . .

Let us now come to the soul's inward sensations in this condition. These should be spoken of by those who know them; for as they are beyond understanding, so are they beyond description. I was wondering when I decided to write this – after taking Communion and experiencing that state of prayer of which I am writing – how the soul is occupied at that time. Then the Lord said to me: 'It dissolves utterly, my daughter, to rest more and more in Me. It is no longer itself that lives; it is I.' As it cannot comprehend what it understands, it understands by not understanding.

Anyone who has experienced this will to some extent understand. It cannot be expressed more clearly, since all that happens is so obscure. I can only say that the soul conceives itself to be near God, and that it is left with such a conviction that it cannot possibly help believing. All the faculties are in abeyance, and so suspended, as I have said, that their operations cannot be followed. If the soul has previously been meditating on any subject, it vanishes from the memory at once, as completely as if it had never been thought of. If it has been reading, it is unable to remember it or dwell on the words; and it is the same with vocal prayer. So the restless little moth of the memory has its wings burned, and can flutter no more. The will must be fully occupied in loving, but does not understand how it loves. If it understands, it does not understand how it understands, or at least, cannot comprehend anything of what it understands. I do not think that it understands at all, because, as I have said, it does not understand itself. Nor can I myself understand this.

Chapter 18

27. The Way of Absolute Detachment

ST JOHN OF THE CROSS

To some this gentle little Carmelite saint, as he has been called, the devoted companion of St Teresa, is utterly repellent. Of him one writer uses these words: 'terrible, sanglant et les yeux secs'; another labels him 'l'ascète terrible'. Yet others find him the most attractive of the contemplative saints. Why are there these apparently conflicting responses? The answer is not far to seek. St John of the Cross has two faces; he is both the apostle of absolute detachment and also the apostle of absolute love. He teaches a detachment so absolute that it appears, taken alone, to be a complete abandonment of everything earthly, a philosophy of world-negation of a most extreme type. But he can also write such sentences as: 'All the ability of my soul and body is moved through love, all that I do I do through love, and all that I suffer I suffer for love's sake,' and, in one of his letters: 'Where there is no love, put love in and you will draw love out.' And these two elements are intimately intertwined; the detachment is absolute because the love is absolute.

Speaking of the first impression produced by a reading of St John of the Cross, Professor Allison Peers writes:

Few persons, however spiritually minded, will fail to find it repellent. It strikes a deadly chill, not only into the unhealthy heat of sense-affection, but into the glowing warmth of what one had hoped and believed to be pure love of God. It calls on one to go out from God-given light into a black and unknown darkness.

To understand the doctrine of St John of the Cross and to appreciate his breadth, one must read more than the famous chapter on detachment in The Ascent of Mount Carmel, *and the descriptions of the two 'nights' in this book and in* The Dark Night of the Soul; *one must read also* The Spiritual Canticle *and* The Living Flame of Love *and the lovely lyrics of the spiritual quest, which take rank among the greatest mystical poems of all ages. If one does so, one will realize how well he deserves the description given of him by the twentieth-century Spanish poet, Antonio Machado:*

John of the Cross, spirit of ardent flame.

This is what he is, a spirit of flame, on fire with the love of God, the supreme spiritual mountaineer, comparable, on a higher plane, with those climbers who pit their endurance, courage, and skill against the summit of Everest or the deadly North Face of the Eiger.

He has been aptly called the 'mystic's mystic'. His way is not one to be followed by everyone. He writes not for the spiritually immature but for those who would tread the way of dim contemplation. Yet even for those of us who totter along in the lower reaches of the spiritual life he has immense value. His astringent quality acts as an ice-cold douche, awakening us from our lethargy and complacency. He speaks with the voice of Jesus when he was asked by the rich young ruler how he might attain perfection: 'Go, sell all that thou hast, and follow me.'

As an analyst and describer of mystical states St John of the Cross stands in the highest rank, so much so that there has been a tendency among Catholic writers on mysticism to regard him too much as a norm for the testing of what religious experience should be labelled mystical; an unfortunate tendency, since mystical experience is too varied to be made to fit into any one precise scheme. I myself prefer the dazzling and penetrating beauty of Ruysbroeck's descriptions. I acknowledge, however, that there is a certain vagueness about them. St John of the Cross writes with a scientific precision, founded on intimate personal knowledge of the psychological states he describes, which Ruysbroeck lacks. Since, however, he is a poet, his prose often has a poetic quality and at times he is certainly not lacking in warmth. Nevertheless one does not find in him, except in the lyrics, those personal touches which make, for instance, Julian of Norwich and St Augustine so attractive. His presentation is almost invariably objective.

Because of the vastness of his range, it is not easy to make selections from his writings, which in fact make up a complete mystical library, capable of giving anything like a complete picture of his doctrine. The passages printed below are all taken from the authoritative three-volume edition of his works by Professor Allison Peers, published by

Burns and Oates. Allison Peers has also written an excellent short biography, Spirit of Flame, *published by S.C.M. Press.*

It would, however, be unfair if the greatest of Christian poet-mystics were represented only by his prose, particularly so since so many of the Sufi poet-mystics have been given a place in this Anthology. The prose passages are, therefore, preceded by Roy Campbell's translation of 'En una noche oscura', printed in his The Poems of St John of the Cross *(Harvill Press and Penguin Classics). Its full title is 'Songs of the soul in rapture at having arrived at the height of perfection, which is union with God by the road of spiritual negation'.*

Upon a gloomy night,
With all my cares to loving ardours flushed,
(O venture of delight!)
With nobody in sight
I went abroad when all my house was hushed.

In safety, in disguise,
In darkness up the secret stair I crept,
(O happy enterprise!)
Concealed from other eyes,
When all my house at length in silence slept.

Upon a lucky night
In secrecy, inscrutable to sight,
I went without discerning
And with no other light
Except for that which in my heart was burning.

It lit and led me through
More certain than the light of noonday clear
To where One waited near
Whose presence well I knew,
There where no other presence might appear.

Oh night that was my guide!
Oh darkness dearer than the morning's pride,
Oh night that joined the lover
To the beloved bride
Transfiguring them each into the other.

Within my flowering breast
Which only for himself entire I save
He sank into his rest
And all my gifts I gave
Lulled by the airs with which the cedars wave.

Over the ramparts fanned
While the fresh wind was fluttering his tresses,
With his serenest hand
My neck he wounded, and
Suspended every sense with its caresses.

Lost to myself I stayed
My face upon my lover having laid
From all endeavour ceasing:
And all my cares releasing
Threw them among the lilies there to fade.

ON THE TWO NIGHTS

For a soul to attain to the state of perfection, it has ordinarily first to pass through two principal kinds of night, which spiritual persons call purgations or purifications of the soul; and here we call them nights, for in both of them the soul journeys, as it were, by night, in darkness.

The first night or purgation is of the sensual part of the soul; and the second is of the spiritual part.

And this first night pertains to beginners, occurring at the time when God begins to bring them into the state of contemplation; in this night the spirit likewise has a part. ... And the second night, or purification, pertains to those who are already proficient, occurring at the time when God desires to bring them to the state of union with God.

We may say that there are three reasons for which this journey made by the soul to union with God is called night. The first has to do with the point from which the soul goes forth, for it has gradually to deprive itself of desire for all the worldly things which it possessed, by denying them to itself;

the which denial and deprivation are, as it were, night to all the senses of man. The second reason has to do with the mean, or the road along which the soul must travel to this union – that is, faith, which is likewise as dark as night to the understanding. The third has to do with the point to which it travels – namely, God, Who, equally, is dark night to the soul in this life. These three nights must pass through the soul – or, rather, the soul must pass through them – in order that it may come to Divine union with God.

The Ascent of Mount Carmel, I : 1 and 2

ON DETACHMENT

It now remains for me to give certain counsels whereby the soul may know how to enter this night of sense and may be able so to do. To this end it must be known that the soul habitually enters this night of sense in two ways: the one is active; the other passive. The active way consists in that which the soul can do, and does of itself, in order to enter therein, whereof we shall now treat in the counsels which follow. The passive way is that wherein the soul does nothing, and God works in it, and it remains, as it were, patient. . . .

These counsels for the conquering of the desires, which now follow, albeit brief and few, I believe to be as profitable and efficacious as they are concise; so that one who sincerely desires to practise them will need no others, but will find them all included in these.

First, let him have an habitual desire to imitate Christ in everything that he does, conforming himself to His life; upon which life he must meditate so that he may know how to imitate it, and to behave in all things as Christ would behave.

Secondly, in order that he may be able to do this well, every pleasure that presents itself to the senses, if it be not purely for the honour and glory of God, must be renounced and completely rejected for the love of Jesus Christ, Who in this life had no other pleasure, neither desired any, than to do the will of His Father, which He called His meat and food.

I take this example. If there present itself to a man the pleasure of listening to things that tend not to the service and honour of God, let him not desire that pleasure, nor desire to listen to them; and if there present itself the pleasure of looking at things that help him not Godward, let him not desire the pleasure or look at these things; and if in conversation or in aught else soever such pleasure present itself, let him act likewise. And similarly with respect to all the senses, in so far as he can fairly avoid the pleasure in question; if he cannot, it suffices that, although these things may be present to his senses, he desire not to have this pleasure. And in this wise he will be able to mortify and void his senses of such pleasure, as though they were in darkness. If he takes care to do this, he will soon reap great profit.

For the mortifying and calming of the four natural passions, which are joy, hope, fear, and grief, from the concord and pacification whereof come these and other blessings, the counsels here following are of the greatest help, and of great merit, and the source of great virtues.

Strive always to prefer, not that which is easiest, but that which is most difficult;

Not that which is most delectable, but that which is most unpleasing;

Not that which gives most pleasure, but rather that which gives least;

Not that which is restful, but that which is wearisome;

Not that which is consolation, but rather that which is disconsolateness;

Not that which is greatest, but that which is least;

Not that which is loftiest and most precious, but that which is lowest and most despised;

Not that which is a desire for anything, but that which is a desire for nothing;

Strive to go about seeking not the best of temporal things, but the worst.

Strive thus to desire to enter into complete detachment and emptiness and poverty, with respect to everything that is in the world, for Christ's sake.

And it is meet that the soul embrace these acts with all its heart and strive to subdue its will thereto. For, if it perform them with its heart, it will very quickly come to find in them great delight and consolation, and to act with order and discretion.

These things that have been said, if they be faithfully put into practice, are quite sufficient for entrance into the night of sense; but, for greater completeness, we shall describe another kind of exercise which teaches us to mortify the concupiscence of the flesh and the concupiscence of the eyes, and the pride of life, which, says St John, are the things that reign in the world, from which all the other desires proceed.

First, let the soul strive to work in its own despite, and desire all to do so. Secondly, let it strive to speak in its own despite and desire all to do so. Third, let it strive to think humbly of itself, in its own despite, and desire all to do so. . . .

In order to arrive at having pleasure in everything,
    Desire to have pleasure in nothing.
In order to arrive at possessing everything,
    Desire to possess nothing.
In order to arrive at being everything,
    Desire to be nothing.
In order to arrive at knowing everything,
    Desire to know nothing.
In order to arrive at that wherein thou hast no pleasure,
    Thou must go by a way wherein thou hast no pleasure.
In order to arrive at that which thou knowest not,
    Thou must go by a way that thou knowest not.
In order to arrive at that which thou possessest not,
    Thou must go by a way that thou possessest not.
In order to arrive at that which thou art not,
    Thou must go through that which thou art not. . . .

When thy mind dwells upon anything,
    Thou art ceasing to cast thyself upon the All.
For, in order to pass from the all to the All,
    Thou hast to deny thyself wholly in all.
And, when thou comest to possess it wholly,

Thou must possess it without desiring anything.
For, if thou wilt have anything in having all,
Thou hast not thy treasure purely in God.

In this detachment the spiritual soul finds its quiet and
repose; for, since it covets nothing, nothing wearies it when
it is lifted up, and nothing oppresses it when it is cast down,
because it is in the centre of its humility; but, when it covets
anything, at that very moment it becomes wearied.

The Ascent of Mount Carmel, I : 13

ON THE CENTRE OF THE SOUL

The centre of the soul is God; and, when the soul has attained
to Him according to the whole capacity of its being, and according to the force of its operation, it will have reached the
last and the deep centre of the soul, which will be when with
all its powers it loves and understands and enjoys God; and
so long as it attains not as far as this, although it be in God,
Who is its centre by grace and by His own communication,
still, if it has the power of movement to go farther and
strength to do more, and is not satisfied, then, although it is
in the centre, it is not in the deepest centre, since it is capable
of going still farther. Love unites the soul with God, and the
more degrees of love the soul has, the more profoundly does
it enter into God and the more is it centred in Him; and thus
we can say that, as are the degrees of love of God, so are the
centres, each one deeper than another, which the soul has in
God; these are the many mansions which, He said, were in
His Father's house. And thus the soul which has one degree
of love is already in its centre in God, since one degree of
love suffices for a soul to abide in Him through grace. If it
have two degrees of love, it will have entered into another
and a more interior centre with God; and, if it attain to
three, it will have entered into the third. If it attain to the
last degree, the love of God will succeed in wounding the
soul even in its deepest centre – that is, in transforming and
enlightening it as regards all the being and power and virtue

of the soul, such as it is capable of receiving, until it be brought into such a state that it appears to be God. In this state the soul is like the crystal that is clear and pure; the more degrees of light it receives, the greater concentration of light there is in it, and this enlightenment continues to such a degree that at last it attains a point at which the light is centred in it with such copiousness that it comes to appear to be wholly light, and cannot be distinguished from the light, for it is enlightened to the greatest possible extent and thus appears to be light itself.

The Living Flame of Love, *Stanza I*

ON THE SPIRITUAL BETROTHAL

By this spiritual flight which we have just described is denoted a lofty estate and union of love wherein after much spiritual exercise God is wont to place the soul, which is called spiritual betrothal with the Word, the Son of God. And at the beginning, when this is done for the first time, God communicates to the soul great things concerning Himself, beautifying it with greatness and majesty, decking it with gifts and virtues, and clothing it with knowledge and honour of God, just as if it were a bride on the day of her betrothal. And upon this happy day, not only is there an end of the soul's former vehement yearnings and plaints of love, but, being adorned with the good things which I am describing, she enters into an estate of peace and delight and sweetness of love wherein she does naught else but relate and sing the wonders of her Beloved, which she knows and enjoys in Him, by means of the aforementioned union of the betrothal. . . .

This spiritual sleep which the soul has in the bosom of its Beloved comprises enjoyment of all the calm and rest and quiet of the peaceful night, and it receives in God together with this a profound and dark Divine intelligence; and for this reason the Bride says that her Beloved is to her 'the tranquil night'.

But this tranquil night, she says, is not as the dark night, but as the night which is already near the rising of the morning; that is, it appears together with the rising because this calm and quiet in God is not complete darkness to the soul, as is the dark night, but is tranquillity and quiet in the Divine light, in a new knowledge of God, wherein the spirit is most gently tranquil, being raised to the Divine light. And here she very fitly calls this Divine light the rising of the dawn, which means the morning; for, even as the rising of the morning dispels the darkness of the night and reveals the light of the day, even so this spirit that is tranquil and quiet in God is raised from the darkness of natural knowledge to the morning light of the supernatural knowledge of God – not brightly, but, as we say, darkly, like the night at the time of the rising of the dawn; for even as the night at the time of such rising is neither wholly night nor wholly day, but, as men say, 'between two lights', so this Divine tranquillity and solitude is neither informed with the Divine light in all its clearness nor does it fail in some measure to participate thereof.

In this tranquillity the understanding sees itself raised up in a new and strange way, above all natural understanding, to the Divine light, much as one who, after a long sleep, opens his eyes to the light which he was not expecting.

In that aforesaid tranquillity and silence of the night, and in that knowledge of the Divine light, the soul is able to see a marvellous fitness and disposition of the wisdom of God in the diversities of all His creatures and works, all and each of which are endowed with a certain response to God, whereby each after its manner testifies to that which God is in it, so that it seems to hear a harmony of sublimest music surpassing all concerts and melodies of the world. . . .

Although that music is silent to the senses and the natural faculties, it is a most sounding solitude to the spiritual faculties; for when these are alone and empty of all natural forms and apprehensions they can readily and most sonorously receive in the spirit the spiritual sound of the excellence of God, in Himself and in His creatures. . . .

The soul is able to see, in that tranquil wisdom, how of all the creatures – not the higher creatures alone, but also the lower, according to that which each of them has received in itself from God – each one raises its voice in testimony to that which God is. She sees that each one after its manner exalts God, since it has God in itself according to its capacity; and thus all these voices make one voice of music, extolling the greatness of God and His marvellous knowledge and wisdom.

Although we have said that the soul in this estate of betrothal enjoys all tranquillity, and that all the other things that are possible in this life are communicated to her, it is not for that reason to be understood that the tranquillity is only according to the higher part, because the sensual part never, until the estate of the Spiritual Marriage, completely loses its imperfections, neither is its strength completely subdued. . . . That which is here communicated to it is the most that is possible in the estate of the Betrothal; for in the Spiritual Marriage its profit is much greater. In the Betrothal, although in the visits of the Spouse the Bride-Soul enjoys these great blessings which we have described, she nevertheless suffers from His absences, and from perturbations and disturbances coming from her lower part, and from the devil, all of which things cease in the estate of the Marriage.

The Spiritual Canticle, *Stanzas XIV and XV*

ON THE SPIRITUAL MARRIAGE

. . . As each living creature lives by its operation, as the philosophers say, having its operations in God, through the union that they have with God, the soul lives the life of God and its death has been changed into life. For the understanding, which before this union understood in a natural way with the strength and vigour of its natural light, is now moved and informed by another principle, that of the supernatural light of God, and has been changed into the Divine, for its understanding and that of God are now both one. And the will, which aforetime loved after the manner of death, that is to say, meanly and with its natural affection, has now been changed into the life of Divine love; for it loves after a lofty manner with Divine affection and is moved by the Holy

Spirit in Whom it now lives, since its will and His will are
now only one. And the memory, which of itself perceived
only the forms and figures of created things, has become
changed, so that it has in its mind the eternal years. And the
desire, which enjoyed only creature food that wrought death,
is now changed so that it tastes and enjoys Divine food, being
now moved by another and a more living principle, which is
the delight of God; so that it is now the desire of God. And
finally, all the movements and operations which the soul had
aforetime, and which belonged to the principle of its natural
life, are now in this union changed into movements of God.
For the soul, like the true daughter of God that it now is,
is moved wholly by the Spirit of God, even as Saint Paul
says: 'That they that are moved by the Spirit of God are
sons of God.' So the understanding of the soul is now the
understanding of God; and its will is the will of God; and
its memory is the memory of God; and its delight is the delight
of God; and the substance of the soul, although it is not the
Substance of God, for into this it cannot be changed, is
nevertheless united in Him and absorbed in Him, and is thus
God by participation in God, which comes to pass in this
perfect state of the spiritual life, although not so perfectly as
in the next life. And in this way by 'slaying, thou hast changed
death into life'. And for this reason the soul may here say
very truly with Saint Paul: 'I live, now not I, but Christ
liveth in me.' And thus the death of this soul is changed into
the life of God, and the soul becomes absorbed in life, since
within it there is likewise fulfilled the saying of the Apostle:
'Death is absorbed in victory.'

The Living Flame of Love, *Stanza II*

28. Nature-Mysticism and Christo-Mysticism

THOMAS TRAHERNE

THOUGH *Thomas Traherne cannot be numbered among the great mystics, he demands a place in any anthology of mysticism. Nowhere else does one find a similar fusion of nature-mysticism and Christo-mysticism as exquisitely balanced, so that both are essential parts of his consciousness, neither being complete without the other.*

His mysticism is a mysticism of joy. For him the object of life is happiness, which he calls felicity; not happiness as the world conceives it, but something more profound. One might call it 'theo-centric' happiness. Men should be happy because God is good, desires happiness for His children, and has for them created a world so wonderful that if only one's eyes are opened to its beauty, one is compelled to rejoice in it and in its Creator.

There is in Traherne nothing of the 'wayless way' and the 'dark silence' of a Ruysbroeck; nothing of the austerities of a Suso; detachment, yes, but a detachment very different from that of St John of the Cross. His life was a living of that saying of Jesus, 'Unless ye become as little children ye shall in no wise enter the kingdom of heaven.' He has the utter trust, the unspoilt simplicity, and the as not yet disillusioned confidence of a child. Read the opening sections of the Third Century of the Meditations, which are printed below, in which he describes the world as he saw it as a child, a vision which he was able to recover as a man, passages which compare not unfavourably with the opening stanzas of Wordsworth's Intimations of Immortality. And, in order to understand him fully, set these sections and many more side by side with the lyrical passages on the Cross of Christ in the First Century. Then the two strains of Traherne's mystical vision will become clear.

Of this man, mystic, saint, and poet, little is known and little need be said. Born about 1634, the son of a shoemaker of Hereford, he was of the same century as George Herbert and Henry Vaughan,

*with both of whom, as a poet, he has kinship. He entered Brasenose
College, Oxford, became a Master of Arts, was ordained a priest
of the Anglican Church, and was for a time Rector of Credenhill.
He then became private chaplain to Sir Orlando Bridgman who, in
1667, became Lord Keeper of the Seals. In his own time such fame
as he achieved rested on two books,* Roman Forgeries *and* Christian
Ethics, *published after his death in 1674. These books are long
forgotten. His enduring fame is through the poems and the* Centuries
of Meditations, *both of which, for hundreds of years after his death,
remained in manuscript and, had it not been for Bertram Dobell,
who gave them to the world shortly after 1900, might still be unknown.*

The Centuries of Meditations, *from which the passages printed
below are taken, is made up of four books and a small part of a fifth,
each consisting of a hundred 'meditations', usually falling into series.
The edition used is that published by the Faith Press, by permission
of the Clarendon Press. The passages are arranged in an order
different from that of the original, but the books and sections from
which they are taken is indicated. Traherne's use of capital letters
has been retained.*

THE EARTHLY SPLENDOUR

Will you see the infancy of this sublime and celestial greatness?
Those pure and virgin apprehensions I had from the womb,
and that divine light wherewith I was born are the best unto
this day, wherein I can see the Universe. By the Gift of God
they attended me into the world, and by His special favour
I remember them till now. Verily they seem the greatest gifts
His wisdom could bestow, for without them all other gifts
had been dead and vain. They are unattainable by book, and
therefore I will teach them by experience. Pray for them
earnestly: for they will make you angelical, and wholly
celestial. Certainly Adam in Paradise had not more sweet
and curious apprehensions of the world, than I when I was
a child.

All appeared new, and strange at first, inexpressibly rare
and delightful and beautiful. I was a little stranger, which at
my entrance into the world was saluted and surrounded with

innumerable joys. My knowledge was Divine. I knew by intuition those things which, since my Apostasy, I collected again by the highest reason. My every ignorance was advantageous. I seemed as one brought into the Estate of Innocence. All things were spotless and pure and glorious: yea, and infinitely mine, and joyful and precious. I knew not that there were any sins, or complaints or laws. I dreamed not of poverties, contentions or vices. All tears and quarrels were hidden from mine eyes. Everything was at rest, free and immortal. I knew nothing of sickness or death or rents or exaction, either for tribute or bread. In the absence of these I was entertained like an Angel with the works of God in their splendour and glory, I saw all in the peace of Eden; Heaven and Earth did sing my Creator's praises, and could not make more melody to Adam than to me. All Time was Eternity, and a perpetual Sabbath. Is it not strange, that an infant should be heir of the whole World, and see those mysteries which the books of the learned never unfold?

The corn was orient and immortal wheat, which never should be reaped, nor was ever sown. I thought it had stood from everlasting to everlasting. The dust and stones of the street were as precious as gold: the gates were at first the end of the world. The green trees when I saw them first through one of the gates transported and ravished me, their sweetness and unusual beauty made my heart to leap, and almost mad with ecstasy, they were such strange and wonderful things. The men! O what venerable and reverend creatures did the aged seem! Immortal Cherubims! And young men glittering and sparkling Angels, and maids strange seraphic pieces of life and beauty! Boys and girls tumbling in the street, and playing, were moving jewels. I knew not that they were born or should die; But all things abided eternally as they were in their proper places. Eternity was manifest in the Light of the Day, and something infinite behind everything appeared: which talked with my expectation and moved my desire. The city seemed to stand in Eden, or to be built in Heaven. The streets were mine, the temple was mine, the people were mine, their clothes and gold and silver were mine, as much as their sparkling eyes, fair skins, and ruddy faces. The skies were mine, and so were the sun and moon and stars, and all the World was mine; and I the only spectator and enjoyer of it. I knew no churlish proprieties, nor bounds, nor divisions: but all proprieties and divisions were mine: all treasures and the possessors of them. So that with much ado I was corrupted, and made to learn the dirty devices of this world. Which now I unlearn, and become, as it were, a little child again that I may enter into the Kingdom of God.

III : 1, 2, 3

ON HAPPINESS

Felicity is a glorious though an unknown thing. And certainly it was the infinite wisdom of God that did implant by instinct so strong a desire of Felicity in the Soul, that we might be excited to labour after it, though we know it not, the very force wherewith we covet it supplying the place of understanding. That there is a Felicity, we all know by the desires after, that there is a most glorious Felicity we know by the strength and vehemence of those desires. And that nothing but Felicity is worthy of our labour, because all other things are the means only which conduce unto it. I was very much animated by the desires of philosophers which I saw in heathen books aspiring after it. But the misery is *It was unknown*. An altar was erected to it like that in Athens with this inscription: TO THE UNKNOWN GOD.

III : 56

The image of God implanted in us, guided me to the manner wherein we were to enjoy. For since we were made in the similitude of God, we were made to enjoy after His similitude. Now to enjoy the treasures of God in the similitude of God, is the most perfect blessedness God could devise. For the treasures of God are the most perfect treasures, and the manner of God is the most perfect manner. To enjoy therefore the treasures of God after the similitude of God is to enjoy the most perfect treasures in the most perfect manner. Upon which I was infinitely satisfied in God, and knew there was a Deity because I was satisfied. For in exerting Himself wholly in achieving thus an infinite Felicity He was infinitely delightful, great and glorious, and my desires so august and insatiable that nothing less than a Deity could satisfy them.

This spectacle once seen, will never be forgotten. It is a great part of the beatific vision. A sight of Happiness is Happiness. It transforms the Soul and makes it Heavenly, it powerfully calls us to communion with God, and weans us from the customs of this world. It puts a lustre upon God and all His creatures and makes us to see them in a Divine and Eternal Light. I no sooner discerned this but I was (as Plato saith, *In summa Rationis arce quies habitat*) seated in a throne of repose and perfect rest. All things were well in their proper places, I alone was out of frame and had need to be mended. For all things were God's treasures in their proper places, and I was to be restored to God's Image. Whereupon you will not believe, how I was withdrawn from all endeavours of altering and mending outward things. They lay so well, methought, they could not be mended: but I must be mended to enjoy them.

III : 59, 60

YOU NEVER ENJOY THE WORLD ARIGHT, TILL . . .

You never enjoy the world aright, till you see how a sand exhibiteth the power and wisdom of God: and prize in everything the service which they do you, by manifesting His glory and goodness to your Soul, far more than the visible beauty on their surface, or the material services they can do your body. . . . Your enjoyment of the world is never right, till every morning you awake in Heaven; see yourself in your Father's Palace; and look upon the skies, the earth, and the air as Celestial Joys: having such a reverend esteem of all, as if you were among the Angels. . . . You never enjoy the world aright, till the Sea itself floweth in your veins, till you are clothed with the heavens, and crowned with the stars: and perceive yourself to be the sole heir of the whole world, and more than so, because men are in it who are every one sole heirs as well as you. Till you can sing and rejoice and delight in God, as misers do in gold, and Kings in sceptres, you never enjoy the world.

Till your spirit filleth the whole world, and the stars are your jewels; till you are as familiar with the ways of God in all Ages as with your walk and table: till you are intimately acquainted with that shady nothing out of which the world was made: till you love men so as to desire their happiness, with a thirst equal to the zeal of your own; till you delight in God for being good to all: you never enjoy the world. Till you more feel it than your private estate, and are more present in the hemisphere, considering the glories and the beauties there, than in your own house: Till you remember how lately you were made, and how wonderful it was when you came into it: and more rejoice in the palace of your glory, than if it had been made but today morning.

Yet further, you never enjoy the world aright, till you so love the beauty of enjoying it, that you are covetous and earnest to persuade others to enjoy it. And so perfectly hate the abominable corruption of men in despising it, that you had rather suffer the flames of Hell than willingly be guilty of their error. There is so much blindness and ingratitude and damned folly in it. The world is a mirror of infinite beauty, yet no man sees it. It is a Temple of Majesty, yet no man regards it. It is a region of Light and Peace, did not men disquiet it. It is the Paradise of God. It is more to man since he is fallen than it was before. It is the place of Angels and the Gate of Heaven.

I : 27–31

THE CROSS

The Cross is the abyss of wonders, the centre of desires, the school of virtues, the house of wisdom, the throne of love, the theatre of joys, and the place of sorrows; It is the root of happiness, and the gate of Heaven. Of all the things in Heaven and Earth it is the most peculiar. It is the most exalted of all objects. It is an Ensign lifted up for all nations. . . . If Love be the weight of the Soul, and its object the centre, all eyes and hearts may convert and turn unto this Object: cleave unto this centre, and by it enter into rest. There we might see all nations assembled with their eyes and hearts upon it. There we may see God's goodness, wisdom, and power: yea His mercy and anger displayed. There we may see man's sin and infinite value. His hope and fear, his misery and happiness. There we might see the Rock of Ages, and the Joys of Heaven. There we may see a Man loving all the world, and God dying for mankind. There we may see all types and ceremonies, figures and prophecies. And all kingdoms adoring a male-factor: An innocent malefactor, yet the greatest in the world. There we may see the most distant things in Eternity united: all mysteries at once couched together and explained. . . . It is the Root of Comforts and the Fountain of Joys. It is the only supreme and sovereign spectacle in all Worlds. It is a Well of Life beneath in which we may see the face of Heaven above: and the only mirror, wherein all things appear in their proper colours: that is, sprinkled in the blood of our Lord and Saviour.

That Cross is a tree set on fire with invisible flame, that illuminateth all the world. The flame is Love: the Love in His bosom who died on it. In the light of which we see how to possess all the things in Heaven and Earth after His similitude. For He that suffered on it was the Son of God as you are: tho' He seemed only a mortal man. He had acquaintance and relations as you have, but He was a lover of Men and Angels. Was he not the Son of God; and Heir of the whole World? To this poor, bleeding, naked Man did all the corn and wine, and oil, and gold and silver in the world minister in an invisible manner, even as He was exposed lying and dying upon the Cross. . . .

O Jesus, Thou King of Saints, whom all adore: and the Holy imitate, I admire the perfection of Thy love in every soul! Thou lovest every one wholly as if him alone. Whose soul is so great an Image of Thine Eternal Father, that Thou camest down from Heaven to die for him, and to purchase

mankind that they might be His treasures. I admire to see
Thy cross in every understanding, Thy passion in every
memory, Thy crown of thorns in every eye, and Thy bleeding,
naked, wounded body in every soul. Thy death liveth in every
memory, Thy crucified person is embalmed in every affection,
Thy pierced feet are bathed in every one's tears, Thy blood
all droppeth on every soul: Thou wholly communicatest
Thyself to every soul in all kingdoms, and art wholly seen
in every saint, and wholly fed upon by every Christian. It is
my privilege that I can enter with Thee into every soul, and
in every living temple of Thy manhood and Thy Godhead,
behold again, and enjoy Thy glory.

I : 58-60, 86

LOVE

Love is so divine and perfect a thing, that it is worthy to be the
very end and being of the Deity. It is His goodness, and it is
His glory. We therefore so vastly delight in Love, because all
these excellencies and all other whatsoever lie within it. By
Loving a Soul does propagate and beget itself. By Loving it
does dilate and magnify itself. By Loving it does enlarge
and delight itself. By Loving also it delighteth others, as by
Loving it doth honour and enrich itself. But above all by
Loving it does attain itself. Love also being the end of Souls,
which are never perfect till they are in act what they are in
power. They were made to love, and are dark and vain and
comfortless till they do it. . . . Love is so noble that it enjoyeth
others' enjoyments, delighteth in giving all unto its object,
and in seeing all given to its object. So that whosoever loveth
all mankind, he enjoyeth all the goodness of God to the whole
world. . . . God is present by Love alone. By Love alone He
is great and glorious. By Love alone He liveth and feeleth
in other persons. By Love alone He enjoyeth all the creatures,
by Love alone He is pleasing to Himself, by Love alone He is
rich and blessed. O why dost not thou by Love alone seek
to achieve all these, by Love alone attain another self, by
Love alone live in others, by Love attain thy glory? The Soul

is shrivelled up and buried in a grave that does not Love.
But that which does love wisely and truly is the joy and end
of all the world, the King of Heaven, and the Friend of God,
the shining Light and Temple of Eternity: the Brother of
Christ Jesus, and one Spirit with the Holy Ghost.

II : 48–50

PRAYER TO THE HOLY TRINITY

O Adorable Trinity! What hast Thou done for me? Thou hast
made me the end of all things, and all the end of me. I in all,
and all in me. In every soul whom Thou hast created, Thou
hast given me the Similitude of Thyself to enjoy! Could my
desires have aspired unto such treasures? Could my wisdom
have devised such sublime enjoyments? Oh! Thou hast done
more for us than we could ask or think. I praise and admire,
and rejoice in Thee: who are infinitely infinite in all Thy doings.

I: 69

29. The Divine Indwelling

WILLIAM LAW

THERE *are some who may feel that an anthology of the writings of the mystics is deficient if it includes nothing of Jacob Boehme, the 'inspired shoemaker' of Görlitz, possibly the best known of Protestant mystics. It was never my plan, however, to attempt the tremendous task of compiling an anthology which would cover the whole of mystical literature, and Boehme is so obscure that much of what he wrote is incomprehensible to one unfamiliar with his particular terminology and symbolism. William Law, whom many regard as the greatest of English post-Reformation mystics, was strongly influenced by the teaching of Boehme. He is, however, as lucid as Boehme is obscure.*

Law was born in 1686, became a Fellow of Emmanuel College, Cambridge, but lost his fellowship as a result of his refusing to take the oath of allegiance to George I. He then lived as tutor and spiritual director with the Gibbon family until 1740, when he returned to his birthplace, Kings Cliffe, near Stamford, and became the centre of a small spiritual community there until his death in 1762.

Law is best known as the author of a work which is in no way mystical, the Serious Call to a Devout and Holy Life, *which so strongly influenced John Wesley. It was not until later life that he wrote his lesser-known mystical treatises, which include* The Spirit of Prayer, *passages from which are printed below.*

Boehme's central doctrine has, though he gives it an original turn, similarities with that of Nicholas of Cusa on the coincidence of opposites. In his teaching all manifestation and existence involves the clash of opposites and their ultimate resolution in a new unity. None of this, however, appears in The Spirit of Prayer. *The stress there is on another central doctrine of Boehme, that of the divine indwelling in the soul of man. Often as it has appeared in mystical literature, there is no expression of it more lucid and beautiful than in Law's spiritual manual, redolent with a lovely charity. Though it is doubtful whether Law had even heard of Meister Eckhart, one finds in* The Spirit of Prayer *a similar teaching on the divine birth in the soul, and his image of the Pearl is akin to that in* The Hymn of the Robe of Glory. *Law may not be numbered among the great contemplatives. He is, however, in the great mystical tradition.*

There have been several editions of The Spirit of Prayer. *It is included in* Selected Mystical Writings of William Law, *edited by Stephen Hobhouse (C. W. Daniel Company) and, in an abbreviated form, in* The Pocket William Law, *edited by A. W. Hopkinson (Latimer House).*

Heaven is as near to our souls as this world is to our bodies; and we are created, we are redeemed, to have our conversation in it. God, the only good of all intelligent natures, is not an absent or distant god, but is more present in and to our souls than our own bodies; and we are strangers to Heaven and without God in the world for this only reason, because we are void of that spirit of prayer which alone can and never fails to unite us with the One only Good, and to open Heaven and the kingdom of God within us. . . .

We are all of us by birth the offspring of God – more nearly related to Him than we are to one another, for in Him we live, and move, and have our being. The first man that was brought forth from God had the breath and Spirit of Father, Son, and Holy Ghost breathed into him, and so he became a living soul. Thus was our first father born of God, descended from Him, and stood in Paradise in the image and likeness of God. He was the image and likeness of God, not with any regard to his outward shape or form, for no shape has any likeness to God; but he was in the image and likeness of God because the Holy Trinity had breathed their own nature and Spirit into him. And as the Deity, Father, Son, and Holy Spirit are always in Heaven and make Heaven to be everywhere, so this Spirit, breathed by them into man, brought Heaven into man along with it; and so man was in Heaven as well as on earth; that is, in Paradise, which signifies an heavenly state or birth of life.

*

It is manifest that no one can fail of the benefit of Christ's salvation but through an unwillingness to have it, and from the same spirit and tempers which made the Jews unwilling to receive it. But if thou wouldst still further know how this great work, the birth of Christ, is to be effected in thee, then let this joyful truth be told thee, that this great work is already begun in every one of us. For this holy Jesus that is to be formed in thee, that is to be the Saviour and new life of thy soul, that is to raise thee out of the darkness of death into the light of life and give thee power to become a son of God, is already within thee, living, stirring, calling, knocking at the door of thy heart and wanting nothing but thy own faith and good will to have as real a birth and form in thee as He had in the Virgin Mary. For the eternal Word or Son of God did not then first begin to be the Saviour of the world when he was born in Bethlehem of Judea; but that Word which became man in the Virgin Mary did from the beginning of the world enter as a word of life, a seed of salvation, into the first father of mankind, was inspoken into him as an ingrafted word under the name and character of a Bruiser of the Serpent's head. Hence it is that Christ said to His disciples, 'The Kingdom of God is within you'; that is, the the divine nature is within you, given unto your first father, into the light of his life, and from him rising up in the life of every son of Adam. Hence also the holy Jesus is said to be the 'Light which lighteth every man that cometh into the world'. Not as He was born at Bethlehem, not as He had a human form upon earth; in these respects He could not be said to have been the light of every man that cometh into the world; but as He was that eternal Word by which all things were created, which was the life and light of all things, and which had as a second Creator entered again into fallen man as a Bruiser of the Serpent; in this respect it was truly said of our Lord when on earth that He was that Light which lighteth every man that cometh into the world. For He was really and truly all this, as He was the Immanuel, the God with us, given unto Adam and in him to all his offspring. See here the beginning and glorious extent of the Catholic Church of

Christ; it takes in all the world. It is God's unlimited, universal mercy to all mankind; and every human creature, as sure as he is born of Adam, has a birth of the Bruiser of the Serpent within him, and so is infallibly in covenant with God through Jesus Christ. Hence also it is that the holy Jesus is appointed to be Judge of all the world; it is because all mankind, all nations and languages have in Him and through Him been put into covenant with God and made capable of resisting the evil of their fallen nature.

*

Poor sinner! consider the treasure thou hast within thee; the Saviour of the world, the eternal Word of God lies hid in thee, as a spark of the divine nature which is to overcome sin and death and hell within thee, and generate the life of Heaven again in thy soul. Turn to thy heart, and thy heart will find its Saviour, its God within itself. Thou seest, hearest, and feelest nothing of God, because thou seekest for Him abroad with thy outward eyes, thou seekest for Him in books, in controversies, in the church and outward exercises, but there thou wilt not find Him till thou hast first found Him in thy heart. Seek for Him in thy heart, and thou wilt never seek in vain, for there He dwells, there is the seat of His Light and holy Spirit.

For this turning to the light and Spirit of God within thee is thy only true turning unto God; there is no other way of finding Him but in that place where He dwelleth in thee. For though God be everywhere present, yet He is only present to thee in the deepest and most central part of thy soul. Thy natural senses cannot possess God or unite thee to Him; nay, thy inward faculties of understanding, will, and memory can only reach after God, but cannot be the place of His habitation in thee. But there is a root or depth in thee from whence all these faculties come forth, as lines from a centre or as branches from the body of the tree. This depth is called the centre, the *fund* or bottom of the soul. This depth is the unity, the eternity, I had almost said the infinity of thy soul; for it is so infinite that nothing can satisfy it or give it any rest but the infinity of God. In this depth of the soul the Holy Trinity brought forth its own living image in the first created man, bearing in himself a living representation of Father, Son, and Holy Ghost, and this was his dwelling in God and God in him. This was the kingdom of God within him and made Paradise without him. But the day that Adam did eat of the forbidden earthly tree, in that day he absolutely died to this kingdom of God within him. This depth or centre of his soul having lost its God, was shut up in death and darkness and became a prisoner in an earthly animal that only excelled its brethren, the beasts, in an upright form and serpentine subtlety. Thus ended the fall of man. But from that moment that the God of mercy inspoke into Adam the Bruiser of the Serpent, from that moment all the riches and treasures of the divine nature came again into man, as a seed of salvation sown into the centre of the soul, and only lies hidden there in every man till he desires to rise from his fallen state and to be born again from above.

Awake, then, thou that sleepest, and Christ, who from all eternity has been espoused to thy soul, shall give thee light. Begin to search and dig in thine own field for this pearl of eternity that lies hidden in it; it cannot cost thee too much, nor canst thou buy it too dear, for it is *all*; and when thou has found it thou wilt know that all which thou hast sold or given away for it is as mere a nothing as a bubble upon the water.

*

See here in short the state of man as redeemed. He has a spark of the light and Spirit of God as a supernatural gift of God given into the birth of his soul, to bring forth by degrees a new birth of that life which was lost in Paradise. This holy spark of the divine nature within him has a natural, strong, and almost infinite tendency or reaching after that eternal light and Spirit of God from whence it came forth. It came forth from God, it came out of God, it partaketh of the divine nature, and therefore it is always in a state of tendency and return to God. And all this is called the breathing, the moving, the quickening of the Holy Spirit within us, which are so many operations of this spark of life tending towards God. On the other hand, the Deity as considered in itself and without the soul of man has an infinite, unchangeable tendency of love and desire towards the soul of man, to unite and communicate its own riches and glories to it, just as the spirit of air without man unites and communicates its riches and virtues to the spirit of the air that is within man. This love or desire of God towards the soul of man is so great that He gave His only begotten Son, the brightness of His glory, to take the human nature upon Him in its fallen state, that by this mysterious union of God and man all the enemies of the soul of man might be overcome and every human creature might have a power of being born again according to that image of God in which he was first created. The Gospel is the history of this love of God to man. Inwardly he has a seed of the divine life given into the birth of his soul, a seed that has all the riches of eternity in it and is always wanting to come to the birth in him and be alive in God. Outwardly he has Jesus Christ, who as a sun of righteousness is always casting forth His enlivening beams on this inward seed, to kindle and call it forth to the birth, doing that to this seed of Heaven in man which the sun in the firmament is always doing to the vegetable seeds in the earth. ... But here let it be well observed that this desire on both sides cannot have its effect till the husk and gross part of the grain falls into a state of corruption and death; till this begins, the mystery of life hidden in it cannot come forth.

*

This pearl of eternity is the Church or Temple of God within thee, the consecrated place of divine worship, where alone thou canst worship God in spirit and in truth. In spirit, because thy spirit is that alone in thee, which can unite and cleave unto God and receive the workings of His divine Spirit upon thee. In truth, because this adoration in spirit is that truth and reality, of which all outward forms and rites, though instituted by God, are only the figure for a time; but this worship is eternal. Accustom thyself to the holy service of this inward temple. In the midst of it is the fountain of living water, of which thou mayest drink and live for ever. There the mysteries of thy redemption are celebrated, or rather opened in life and power. There the Supper of the Lamb is kept; the bread that came down from Heaven, that giveth life to the world, is thy true nourishment: all is done and known in real experience, in a living sensibility of the work of God on the soul. There the birth, the life, the sufferings, the death, the resurrection and ascension of Christ are not merely remembered, but inwardly found and enjoyed as the real states of thy soul, which has followed Christ in the regeneration. When once thou art well grounded in this inward worship, thou wilt have learnt to live unto God above time and place. For every day wilt be Sunday to thee, and wherever thou goest thou wilt have a priest, a church, and an altar along with thee. For when God has all that He should have of thy heart, when renouncing the will, judgement, tempers and inclinations of thy old man, thou art wholly given up to the obedience of the light and Spirit of God within thee, to will only in His will, to love only in His love, to be wise only in His wisdom, then it is that everything thou doest is as a song of praise and the common business of thy life is a conforming to God's will on earth as angels do in Heaven.

*

Now there is but one possible way for man to attain this salvation or life of God in the soul. There is not one for the Jew, another for a Christian, and a third for the heathen. No; God is one, human nature is one, salvation is one, and the way to it is one; and that is, the desire of the soul turned to God. When this desire is alive and breaks forth in any creature under Heaven, then the lost sheep is found and the shepherd has it upon his shoulders. Through this desire the poor Prodigal Son leaves his husks and swine and hastens to his father; it is because of this desire that the father sees the son while yet afar off, that he runs out to meet him, falls on his neck and kisses him. See here how plainly we are taught that no sooner is this desire arisen and in motion towards God, but the operation of God's Spirit answers to it, cherishes and welcomes its first beginnings – signified by the father's seeing and having compassion on his son whilst yet afar off, that is, in the first beginnings of his desire. Thus does this desire do all, it brings the soul to God and God into the soul, it unites with God, it cooperates with God, and is one life with God. Suppose this desire not to be alive, not in motion, either in a Jew or a Christian, and then all the sacrifices, the service, the worship either of the Law or the Gospel are but dead works that bring no life into the soul nor beget any union between God and it. Suppose this desire to be awakened and fixed upon God, though in souls that never heard either of the Law or Gospel, and then the divine life or operation of God enters into them, and the new birth in Christ is formed in those who never heard of His name. And these are they 'that shall come from the East, and from the West, and sit down with Abraham and Isaac in the Kingdom of God'. . . .

When, therefore, the first spark of a desire after God arises in thy soul, cherish it with all thy care, give all thy heart into it, it is nothing less than a touch of the divine loadstone that is to draw thee out of the vanity of time into the riches of eternity. Get up, therefore, and follow it as gladly as the Wise Men of the East followed the star from Heaven that appeared to them. It will do for thee as the star did for them: it will lead thee to the birth of Jesus, not in a stable at Bethlehem in Judea, but to the birth of Jesus in the dark centre of thy own fallen soul.

30. Nature-Mysticism and Soul-Mysticism

RICHARD JEFFERIES

I DO *not think that there could be anyone more appropriate with whom to end this anthology than Richard Jefferies (1848–87). He was the son of a Wiltshire farmer and during his lifetime won a wide reputation as a writer who combined a remarkable power of observing nature with a deep poetical and philosophical insight. His books, such as* Wild Life in a Southern County *and* Bevis, *are still remembered.*

Shortly before his death he wrote a spiritual autobiography, The Story of my Heart, *which, owing to its particular quality and burning sincerity, gives him a significant place in the literature of mysticism.*

In what does this significance consist? Why should Richard Jefferies be given a place in an anthology of mysticism in which so many greater mystics, such as the two Catherines, St Catherine of Siena and St Catherine of Genoa, Jacob Boehme, and St François de Sales are not included? He cannot be described as a contemplative, in the sense that we have used that word. He never attained to a state of mystical prayer as Catholic writers would define it. He was regarded in his own time as an atheist. He had no certainty that he was not merely 'a product of combustion', with no past or future beyond the span of his natural life.

What one finds in Richard Jefferies, however, is a man in whom mystical consciousness was very highly developed, but who could not find within the religious thought-patterns with which he was familiar satisfactory answers to the questions which his mystical consciousness posed for him. Such answers as he was able to find he found solely through the contemplation of nature and of his own soul. There is in him a combination of nature-mysticism and soul-mysticism of a unique kind, springing out of a purely personal vision, which, since the material was not available to him, he had no means of interpreting and expressing except in concepts which he had to invent for himself.

His quest was for what he called the Fourth Idea. 'It is,' he wrote, 'beyond, or beside, the three discovered by the Cavemen; it is additional to the existence of the soul; it is additional to immortality; and beyond the idea of deity.' Since the experience and writings of the mystics were unknown to him, he did not know that the Fourth Idea had already been explored by them. They knew and had expressed what he strove to know and express. They knew that which is beyond soul, beyond immortality, beyond deity.

Yet how far Jefferies managed to penetrate simply out of his own experience and his meditation on it! He found that 'eternal now' of which the mystics had spoken. He reached a doctrine of the 'nobility of the soul', which is akin to that of Eckhart and Sankara. Though the only idea of God with which he was acquainted was that of the religion of his own environment, in his conception of a 'deity' beyond 'deity' he tried to express in fumbling words what Eckhart and Ruysbroeck had expressed so much more adequately in the distinction they drew between the Godhead and God.

Had Jefferies been acquainted with the wide stream of mystical tradition, he would doubtless have written very differently. But he was not; and, for ourselves, we may be glad. For he would not have written The Story of my Heart, *that glowing and lovely history of the journeyings of a great soul.*

The story of my heart commences seventeen years ago. In the glow of youth there were times every now and then when I felt the necessity of a strong inspiration of soul-thought. My heart was dusty, parched for want of the rain of deep feeling; my mind arid and dry, for there is a dust which settles on the heart as well as that which falls on a ledge. It is injurious to the mind as well as to the body to be always in one place and always surrounded by the same circumstances. A species of thick clothing slowly grows about the mind, the pores are choked, little habits become a part of existence, and by degrees the mind is inclosed in a husk. When this began to form I felt eager to escape from it, to throw it off like heavy clothing, to drink deeply once more at the fresh fountains of life. An inspiration – a long deep breath of the pure air of thought – could alone give health to the heart.

There was a hill to which I used to resort at such periods. The labour of walking three miles to it, all the while gradually ascending, seemed to clear my blood of the heaviness accumulated at home. On a warm summer day the slow continued rise required continual effort, which carried away the sense of oppression. The familiar everyday scene was soon out of sight; I came to other trees, meadows, and fields; I began to breathe a new air and to have a fresher aspiration. I restrained my soul till I reached the sward of the hill; psyche, the soul that longed to be loose. . . .

Moving up the sweet short turf, at every step my heart seemed to obtain a wider horizon of feeling; with every inhalation of rich pure air, a deeper desire. The very light of the sun was whiter and more brilliant here. By the time I had reached the summit I had entirely forgotten the petty circumstances and the annoyances of existence. I felt myself, myself. There was an intrenchment on the summit, and going down into the fosse I walked round it slowly to recover breath. On the south-western side there was a spot where the outer bank had partially slipped, leaving a gap. There the view was over a broad plain, beautiful with wheat, and inclosed by a perfect amphitheatre of green hills. Through these hills there was one narrow groove, or pass, southwards, where the white clouds seemed to close in the horizon. Woods hid the scattered hamlets and farmhouses, so that I was quite alone.

I was utterly alone with the sun and the earth. Lying down on the grass, I spoke in my soul to the earth, the sun, the air, and the distant sea far beyond sight. I thought of the earth's firmness – I felt it bear me up; through the grassy couch there came an influence as if I could feel the great earth speaking to me. I thought of the wandering air – its pureness, which is its beauty; the air touched me and gave me something of itself. I spoke to the sea: though so far, in my mind I saw it, green at the rim of the earth and blue in deeper ocean; I desired to have its strength, its mystery and glory. Then I addressed the sun, desiring the soul equivalent of his light and brilliance, his endurance and unwearied race. I turned to the blue heaven over, gazing into its depth, inhaling its exquisite colour and sweetness. The rich blue of the unattainable flower of the sky drew my soul towards it, and there it rested, for pure colour is rest of heart. By all these I prayed; I felt an emotion of the soul beyond all definition; prayer is a puny thing to it, and the word is a rude sign to the feeling, but I know no other.

By the blue heaven, by the rolling sun bursting through untrodden space, a new ocean of ether every day unveiled. By the fresh and wandering air encompassing the world; by the sea sounding on the shore – the green sea white-flecked at the margin and the deep ocean; by the strong earth under me. Then, returning, I prayed by the sweet thyme, whose little flowers I touched with my hand; by the slender grass; by the crumble of dry chalky earth I took up and let fall through my fingers. Touching the crumble of earth, the blade of grass, the thyme flower, breathing the earth-encircling air, thinking of the sea and the sky, holding out my hand for the sunbeams to touch it, prone on the sward in token of deep reverence, thus I prayed that I might touch to the unutterable existence infinitely higher than deity.

With all the intensity of feeling which exalted me, all the intense communion I held with the earth, the sun and sky, the stars hidden by the light, with the ocean – in no manner can the thrilling depth of these feelings be written – with these I prayed, as if they were the keys of an instrument, of an organ, with which I swelled forth the notes of my soul, redoubling my own voice by their power. The great sun burning with light; the strong earth, dear earth; the warm sky; the pure air; the thought of ocean; the inexpressible beauty of all filled me with a rapture, an ecstasy, an inflatus. With this inflatus, too, I prayed. Next to myself I came and recalled myself, my bodily existence. I held out my hand, the sunlight gleamed on the skin and the iridescent nails; I recalled the mystery and beauty of the flesh. I thought of the mind with which I could see the ocean sixty miles distant, and gather to myself its glory. I thought of my inner existence, that consciousness which is called the soul. These, that is, myself – I threw into the balance to weigh the prayer the heavier. My strength of body, mind, and soul, I flung into it; I put forth my strength; I wrestled and laboured, and toiled in might of prayer. The prayer, this soul-emotion was in itself – not for an object – it was a passion. I hid my face in the grass, I was wholly prostrated, I lost myself in the wrestle, I was rapt and carried away.

Becoming calmer, I returned to myself and thought, reclining in rapt thought, full of aspiration, steeped to the lips of my soul in desire. I did not then define, or analyse, or understand this. I see now that what I laboured for was soul-life, more soul-nature, to be exalted, to be full of soul-learning. Finally I rose, walked half a mile or so along the summit of the hill eastwards, to soothe myself and come to the common ways of life again. Had any shepherd accidentally seen me lying on the turf, he would only have thought that I was resting a few minutes; I made no outward show. Who could have imagined the whirlwind of passion that was going on within me as I reclined there! I was greatly exhausted when I reached home. Occasionally I went upon the hill deliberately, deeming it good to do so; then, again, this craving carried me away up there of itself. Though the principal feeling was the same, there were variations in the mode in which it affected me.

Through every grass blade in the thousand, thousand grasses; through the million leaves, veined and edge-cut, on bush and tree; through the song-notes and the marked feathers of the birds; through the insects' hum and the colour of the butterflies; through the soft warm air, the flecks of clouds dissolving – I used them all for prayer. With all the energy the sunbeams had poured unwearied on the earth since Sesostris was conscious of them on the ancient sands; with all the life that had been lived by vigorous man and beauteous woman since first in dearest Greece the dream of the gods was woven; with all the soul-life that had flowed a long stream down to me, I prayed that I might have a soul more than equal to, far beyond my conception of, these things of the past, the present, and the fulness of all life. Not only equal to these, but beyond, higher, and more powerful than I could imagine. That I might take from all their energy, grandeur, and beauty, and gather it into me. That my soul might be more than the cosmos of life.

I prayed with the glowing clouds of sunset and the soft light of the first star coming through the violet sky. At night with the stars, according to the season; now with the Pleiades, now with the Swan or burning Sirius, and broad Orion's constellation, red Aldebaran, Arcturus, and the Northern Crown; with the morning star, the light-bringer, once now and then when I saw it, a white-gold ball in the violet-purple sky, or framed about with pale summer vapour floating away as red streaks shot horizontally in the east. A diffused saffron ascended into the luminous upper azure. The disk of the sun arose over the hill, fluctuating with throbs of light; his chest heaved in fervour of brilliance. All the glory of the sunrise filled me with broader and furnace-like vehemence of prayer. That I might have the deepest of soul-life, the deepest of all, deeper far than all this greatness of the visible universe and even of the invisible; that I might have a fulness of soul till now unknown, and utterly beyond my own conception.

Chapter I

Sweetly the summer air came up to the tumulus, the grass sighed softly, the butterflies went by, sometimes alighting on the green dome. Two thousand years! Summer after summer the blue butterflies had visited the mound, the thyme had flowered, the wind sighed in the grass. The azure morning had spread its arms over the low tomb; and full glowing noon burned on it; the purple of sunset rosied the sward. Stars, ruddy in the vapour of the southern horizon, beamed at midnight through the mystic summer night, which is dusky and yet full of light. White mists swept up and hid it; dews rested on the turf; tender harebells drooped; the wings of the finches fanned the air – finches whose colours faded from the wings how many centuries ago! Brown autumn dwelt in the woods beneath; the rime of winter whitened the beech clump on the ridge; again the buds came on the wind-blown hawthorn bushes, and in the evening the broad constellation of Orion covered the east. Two thousand times! Two thousand times the woods grew green, and ringdoves built their nests. Day and night for two thousand years – light and shadow sweeping over the mound – two thousand years of labour by day and slumber by night. Mystery gleaming in the stars, pouring down in the sunshine, speaking in the night, the wonder of the sun and of far space, for twenty centuries round about this low and green-grown dome. Yet all that mystery and wonder is as nothing to the Thought that lies therein, to the spirit that I feel so close.

Realizing that spirit, recognizing my own inner consciousness, the psyche, so clearly, I cannot understand time. It is eternity now. I am in the midst of it. It is about me in the sunshine; I am in it, as the butterfly floats in the light-laden air. Nothing has to come; it is now. Now is eternity; now is the immortal life. Here this moment, by this tumulus, on earth, now; I exist in it. The years, the centuries, the cycles are absolutely nothing; it is only a moment since this tumulus was raised; in a thousand years more it will still be only a moment. To the soul there is no past and no future; all is and will be ever, in now. For artificial purposes time is mutually agreed on, but there is really no such thing. The shadow goes on upon the dial, the index moves round upon the clock, and what is the difference? There may be time for the clock, the clock may make time for itself; there is none for me.

Chapter III

Three things only have been discovered of that which concerns the inner consciousness since before written history began. Three things only in twelve thousand written, or sculptured, years, and in the dumb, dim time before then. Three ideas the Cavemen primeval wrested from the unknown, the night which is round us still in daylight – the existence of the soul, immortality, the deity. These things found, prayer followed as a sequential result. Since then nothing further has been found in all the twelve thousand years, as if men had been satisfied and had found these to suffice. They do not suffice me. I desire to advance farther, and to wrest a fourth, and even still more than a fourth, from the darkness of thought.

I want more ideas of soul-life. I am certain that there are more yet to be found. A great life – an entire civilization – lies just outside the pale of common thought. Cities and countries, inhabitants, intelligences, culture – an entire civilization. Except by illustrations drawn from familiar things, there is no way of indicating a new idea. I do not mean actual cities, actual civilization. Such life is different from any yet imagined. A nexus of ideas exists of which nothing is known – a vast system of ideas – a cosmos of thought. There is an Entity, a Soul-Entity, as yet unrecognized. These, rudely expressed, constitute my Fourth Idea. It is beyond, or beside, the three discovered by the Cavemen; it is in addition to the existence of the soul; in addition to immortality; and beyond the idea of the deity. I think there is something more than existence.

There is an immense ocean over which the mind can sail, upon which the vessel of thought has not yet been launched. I hope to launch it. The mind of so many thousand years has worked round and round inside the circle of these three ideas as a boat on an inland lake. Let us haul it over the belt of land, launch on the ocean, and sail outwards.

There is so much beyond all that has ever yet been imagined. As I write these words, in the very moment, I feel that the whole air, the sunshine out yonder lighting up the ploughed earth, the distant sky, the circumambient ether, and that far space, is full of soul-secrets, soul-life, things outside the experience of all the ages. The fact of my own existence as I write, as I exist at this second, is so marvellous, so miracle-like, strange, and supernatural to me, that I unhesitatingly conclude I am always on the margin of life illimitable, and that there are higher conditions than existence. Everything around is supernatural; everything so full of unexplained meaning. . . .

The ashes of the man interred in the tumulus are indistinguishable; they have sunk away like rain into the earth; so his body has disappeared. I am under no delusion; I am fully aware that no demonstration can be given of the three stepping-stones of the Cavemen. The soul is inscrutable; it is not in evidence to show that it exists; immortality is not tangible.

Full well I know that reason and knowledge and experience tend to disprove all three; that experience denies answer to prayer. I am under no delusion whatever; I grasp death firmly in conception as I can grasp this bleached bone; utter extinction, annihilation. That the soul is a product at best of organic composition; that it goes out like a flame. This may be the end; my soul may sink like rain into the earth and disappear. Wind and earth, sea, and night and day, what then? Let my soul be but a product, what then? I say it is nothing to me; this only I know, that while I have lived – now, this moment, while I live – I think immortality, I lift my mind to a Fourth Idea. If I pass into utter oblivion, yet I have had that.

The original three ideas of the Cavemen became encumbered with superstition; ritual grew up, and ceremony, and long ranks of souls were painted on papyri waiting to be weighed in the scales, and to be punished or rewarded. These cobwebs grotesque have sullied the original discoveries and cast them into discredit. Erase them altogether, and consider only the underlying principles. The principles do not go far enough, but I shall not discard all of them for that. Even supposing the pure principles to be illusions, and annihilation the end, even then it is better – it is something gained to have thought them. Thought is life; to have thought them is to have lived them. Accepting two of them as true in principle, then I say that these are but the threshold. For twelve thousand years no effort has been made to get beyond that threshold. These are but the primer of soul-life; the merest hieroglyphics chipped out, a little shape given to the unknown.

Not tomorrow but today. Not the tomorrow of the tumulus, the hour of the sunshine now. This moment give me to live soul-life, not only after death. Now is eternity, now I am in the midst of immortality; now the supernatural crowds around me. Open my mind, give my soul to see, let me live it now on earth, while I hear the burring of the larger bees, the sweet air in the grass, and watch the yellow wheat wave beneath me. Sun and earth and sea, night and day – these are the least of things. Give me soul-life. . . .

There is an existence, a something higher than soul – higher, better, and more perfect than deity. Earnestly I pray to find this something better than a god. There is something superior, higher, more good. For this I search, labour, think, and pray. If after all there be nothing, and my soul has to go out like a flame, yet even then I have thought this while it lives. With the whole force of my existence, with the whole force of my thought, mind, and soul, I pray to find this Highest Soul, this greater than deity, this better than god. Give me to live the deepest soul-life now and always with this Soul. For want of words I write soul, but I think that it is something beyond soul.

Chapters III and IV

31. Epilogue:
The Mysticism of the Divine Milieu

PIERRE TEILHARD DE CHARDIN

MYSTICAL intuition can, as we have seen, express itself in different forms. In Pierre Teilhard de Chardin (d. 1955), priest of the Society of Jesus and eminent palaeontologist and scientist, it takes on a unique quality. His mysticism is of a type which could not have come into being until our own day. For in him the deep insights of the Christian Faith and the new knowledge of the universe, laid bare by the discoveries of modern science, are fused in a remarkable manner, each illuminating and enriching the other.

Out of this fusion of religious and scientific insights there came to Father Teilhard a vision of the universe as a divine milieu, *permeated through and through by the omnipresence of God. Evolution he saw as a divinely controlled and organized process, ever moving, in accordance with its own nature, through stress and suffering, towards an ultimate Christification in the mysterious Pleroma, 'in which the substantial* one *and the created* many *fuse without confusion in a whole', and all things are gathered together, unified, and redeemed in the total Christ. This Pleroma he calls, in his penetrating analysis of the evolutionary process in* The Phenomenon of Man, Omega. *'The Kingdom of God,' he wrote, 'is a prodigious biological operation. To create, to fulfil and to purify the world is to God to unify it by uniting it organically with Himself.'*

His mystic way is thus one very different from the via negativa *of Dionysius and St John of the Cross. For him union with God was not through withdrawal from the activity of the world but through a dedicated, integrated, and subliminated absorption in it. At the end of his life he said: 'Throughout my life, by means of my life, the world has little by little caught fire in my sight until, aflame all around me, it has become almost luminous from within. . . . Such has been my experience in contact with the earth – the diaphany of the Divine at the heart of a universe on fire. . . . Christ; the heart; a fire; capable of penetrating everywhere and, gradually, spreading everywhere.'*

For Father Teilhard human activity in all its forms was capable of divination. His mysticism is thus a mysticism of action, action springing from the inspiration of a universe seen as moved and com-penetrated by God in the totality of its evolution. And, in its vision of Christ as the All-in-everything, it is also a Christo-mysticism, expanding and reinterpreting the Christo-mysticism of St Paul.

This is essentially a new type of mysticism, the result of a profound, life-long, reconciling meditation on religious and scientific truth; and it is thus of immense relevance and significance for a scientific age such as ours.

The passages printed below are taken from Le Milieu Divin, Letters from a Traveller, *and* The Phenomenon of Man, *all published by Collins and Harper & Row Inc., and from three essays,* 'Christ in Matter', 'The Meaning and Constructive Value of Suffering', *and* 'Memories and Letters' *(by Lucile Swan), included in* The Wind and the Rain, *an anthology edited by Neville Braybrooke, published by Secker and Warburg.*

THE DIVINE MILIEU

By means of all created things, without exception, the divine assails us, penetrates us and moulds us. We imagined it as distant and inaccessible, whereas we live steeped in its burning layers. . . .

God reveals Himself everywhere, beneath our groping efforts, *as a universal milieu*, only because He is *the ultimate point* on which all realities converge. Each element of the world, whatever it may be, only subsists, *hic et nunc*, in the manner of a cone whose generatrices meet in God who draws them together (meeting at the term of their individual perfection and at the term of the general perfection of the world which contains them). It follows that all created things, every one of them, cannot be looked at, in their nature and action, without the same reality being found in their innermost being – like sunlight in the fragments of a broken mirror – one beneath its multiplicity, unattainable beneath its proximity, and spiritual beneath its materiality. No object can influence us by its essence without being touched by the radiance of the focus of the universe. Our minds are incapable of grasping a reality, our hearts and hands of seizing the essentially desirable in it, without our being compelled *by the very structure of things* to go back to the first source of its perfections. This focus, this source, is thus everywhere. It is *precisely because* He is so deep and yet so akin to an extensionless point that God is infinitely near, and dispersed everywhere. It is *precisely because* He is the centre that He fills the whole sphere. The omnipresence of the divine is simply the effect of its extreme spirituality and is the exact contrary of the fallacious ubiquity which matter seems to derive from its extreme dissociation and dispersal. In the light of this discovery, we may resume our march through the inexhaustible wonders which the divine *milieu* has in store for us.

However vast the divine *milieu* may be, it is in reality a *centre*. It therefore has the properties of a centre, and above all the absolute and final power to unite (and consequently to complete) all beings within its breast. In the divine *milieu* all elements of the universe *touch each other* by that which is most inward and ultimate in them. There they concentrate, little by little, all that is purest and most attractive in them without loss and without danger of subsequent corruption.

from Le Milieu Divin

I live in the heart of a single element, the centre and detail of All, personal love and cosmic power.

In attaining it and merging myself in it, I have the whole universe in front of me, with its noble endeavours, its entrancing search for knowledge, with its myriads of souls to be perfected and healed. I can and must plunge breathlessly into the midst of human labour. The greater share I take, the more weight I will bring to bear on the whole surface of the real, the nearer I will attain to Christ and the faster I shall grapple myself to him.

We could say that God, eternal being in Himself, *for us* is in process of formation all around us.

And God, too, is *the Heart of Everything*. This is so true that the vast setting of the universe might founder and perish or be snatched away from me by death without diminishing my fundamental joy. When that dust is scattered that was made animate by a halo of glory and power, there still remains untouched the reality of substance in which all perfection is subsumed and incorruptible. The rays are refracted in their source, and there, all converged, I would still hold them.

from Christ in Matter

Over the centuries an all-embracing plan seems in truth to be unfolding around us. . . . Something is afoot in the universe . . . the birth of a spiritual reality formed by the souls of men and by the matter which they bear along with them. Laboriously, through that medium and by virtue of human activity, the new earth is gathering its forces, emerging and purifying itself.

from The Meaning and Constuctive Value of Suffering

. . . . the coming of His Kingdom as I see it in my dreams. I mean the 'implosive' encounter in human consciousness of the 'ultra-human' and the 'Christic' impulses – or, as I often express it, of the Forward (i.e. the progress of mankind by 'convergence') and the Upward (the spiritual ascent of mankind towards Christ, in whom it will find its completion and consummation, when, in St Paul's words, God will be 'all in all'). I am more and more convinced – judging from my own infinitesimal experience – that this process is indeed possible, and is actually in operation, and that it will psychologically transfigure the world of tomorrow.

from Letters from a Traveller

We cannot be fundamentally happy but in a personal unification with something Personal (with the Personality of the Whole) in the whole. This is the ultimate call of what is termed 'love'.

Hence the substantial joy of life is found in the consciousness of feeling, that by *everything* we enjoy, create, overcome, discover or suffer in ourselves and in others in every line of life or death (organic, social, artistic, scientific, etc.), we are gradually increasing (and we are gradually incorporated into) the growing Soul or Spirit of the World. . . .

The Centre of this spiritualized Matter (spiritual Whole) has to be supremely *conscious* and *personal*. The Ocean collecting all the spiritual streams of the universe is, not only something, but *somebody*. It has, Itself, a face and a heart.

from Memories and Letters by Lucile Swan

THE UNIVERSAL CHRIST

We can say as a first approximation that the *milieu* whose rich and mobile homogeneity has revealed itself all around us as a condition and a consequence of the most Christian attitudes (such as right intention and resignation) is formed by the divine omnipresence. The immensity of God is the essential attribute which allows us to seize Him everywhere, within us and around us. . . .

Under what form, proper to our creation and adapted to our universe, does the divine immensity manifest itself to, and become relevant to, mankind? . . . What is, when all is said and done, the concrete link which binds all these universal entities together and confers on them a final power of gaining hold of us?

The essence of Christianity consists in asking oneself that question, and in answering: 'The Word Incarnate, Our Lord Jesus Christ.'

Let us examine step by step how we can validate to ourselves this prodigious identification of the Son of Man and the divine *milieu*.

A first step, unquestionably, is to see the divine omnipresence in which we find ourselves plunged as *an omnipresence of action*. God enfolds us and penetrates us by creating and preserving us.

Now let us go a little further. Under what form, and with what end in view, has the Creator given us, and still preserves in us, the gift of participated being? Under the form of an essential aspiration towards Him – and with a view to the unhoped-for cleaving which is to make us one and the same complex thing with Him. The action by which God maintains us in the field of His presence is *a unitive transformation*.

Let us go further still. What is the supreme and complex reality for which the divine operation moulds us? It is revealed to us by St Paul and St John. It is the quantitative repletion and the qualitative consummation of all things; it is the mysterious Pleroma, in which the substantial *one* and the created *many* fuse without confusion in a *whole* which, without adding anything essential to God, will nevertheless be a sort of triumph and generalization of being.

At last we are nearing our goal. What is the active centre, the living link, the organizing soul of the Pleroma? St Paul, again, proclaims it with all his resounding voice: it is He in whom all things are consummated – through whom the whole created edifice receives its consistency – Christ dead and risen *qui replet omnia, in quo omnia constant* (who fills all things and in whom all things consist).

And now let us link the first and last terms of this long series of identities. We shall see with a wave of joy that *the divine omnipresence* translates itself within our universe by the network of the organizing forces of the total Christ. God exerts pressure, in and upon us – through the intermediary of all the powers of heaven, earth, and hell – only in the act of forming and consummating Christ who saves and sur-animates the world. And since, in the course of this operation, Christ Himself does not act as a dead or passive point of convergence, but as a centre of radiation for the energies which lead the universe back to God through His humanity, the layers of divine action finally come to us impregnated with His organic energies.

The divine *milieu* henceforward assumes for us the savour and the specific features which we desire. In it we recognize an omnipresence which acts upon us by assimilating us in it, *in unitate corporis Christi* (in the unity of the body of Christ). As a consequence of the Incarnation the divine immensity has transformed itself for us into *the omnipresence of Christification*. All the good that I can do *opus et operatio* (both in the act and in the carrying out of it) is physically gathered in, by something of itself, into the reality of the consummated Christ. Everything I endure, with faith and love, by way of diminishment or death, makes me a little more closely an integral part of His mystical body. Quite specifically it is *Christ whom we make or whom we undergo in all things*. Not only *diligentibus omnia convertuntur in bonum* (everything is converted into good for those who love) but, more clearly still, *convertuntur in Deum* (converted into God) and, quite explicitly, *convertuntur in Christum* (converted into Christ).

from Le Milieu Divin

THE NATURE OF OMEGA

Omega – in its flower and its integrity – the hoard of consciousness liberated little by little on earth by noogenesis* adds itself together and accumulates. . . .

The very centre of our consciousness, deeper than all its radii; that is the essence which Omega, if it is to be truly Omega, must reclaim. And that essence is obviously not something of which we can dispossess ourselves for the benefit of others as we might give away a coat or pass on a torch. For we are the very flame of that torch. To consummate itself, my ego must subsist through abandoning itself or the gift will fade away. The conclusion is inevitable that the concentration of a conscious universe would be unthinkable if it did not reassemble in itself *all consciousnesses* as well as all *the conscious*; each particular consciousness remaining conscious of itself at the end of the operation, and even (this must be absolutely understood) each particular consciousness becoming still more itself and more distinct from others the closer it gets to them in Omega. . . .

* See pp. 33–4

In any domain – whether it be the cells of the body, the members of a society, or the elements of a spiritual synthesis – *union differentiates*. In every organized whole, the parts perfect themselves and fulfil themselves. . . . Following the confluent orbits of their centres, the grains of consciousness do not tend to lose their outline and blend, but, on the contrary, to accentuate the depth and incommunicability of their *egos*. The more 'other' they become in conjunction, the more they find themselves as 'self'. How could it be otherwise since they are steeped in Omega? Could a centre dissolve? Or rather, would not its particular way of dissolving be to supercentralize itself? . . .

Thus it would be mistaken to represent Omega to ourselves simply as a centre born of the fusion of elements which it collects, or annihilating them in itself. By its structure Omega, in its ultimate principle, can only be a *distinct Centre radiating at the core of a system of centres*; a grouping in which personalization of the All and personalizations of the elements reach their maximum, simultaneously and without merging, under the influence of a supremely autonomous focus of union. . . .

In the light of our experience it is abundantly clear that emergence *in the course of evolution* can only happen successively and with mechanical dependence on what precedes it. First the grouping of the elements; then the manifestation of 'soul' whose operation only betrays, from the point of view of energy, a more and more complex and subliminated involution of the powers transmitted by the chains of the elements. The radial function of the tangential: a pyramid whose apex is supported by its base: that is what we see during the course of the process. And it is in the same way that Omega is discovered to us at the end of the whole processus, inasmuch as in it the movement of synthesis culminates. Yet we must be careful to note that under this evolutive facet Omega still only reveals *half of itself*. While being the last term of its series, it is also *outside all series*. Not only does it crown, but it also closes. Otherwise the sum would fall short of itself, in organic contradiction with the whole operation. When, going beyond the elements, we come to speak of the conscious Pole of the world, it is not enough to say that it *emerges* from the rise of consciousness: we must add that from this genesis it has already *undergone emergence*; without which it could neither subjugate into love nor fix in incorruptibility. If by its very nature it did not escape from the time and space which it gathers together, it would not be Omega.

from The Phenomenon of Man

Index

Index

MORE ABOUT PENGUINS
AND PELICANS

Penguinews, which appears every month, contains details of all the new books issued by Penguins as they are published. From time to time it is supplemented by *Penguins in Print*, which is a complete list of all books published by Penguins which are in print. (There are well over four thousand of these.)

A specimen copy of *Penguinews* will be sent to you free on request. For a year's issues (including the complete lists) please send 30p if you live in the United Kingdom, or 60p if you live elsewhere. Just write to Dept EP, Penguin Books Ltd, Harmondsworth, Middlesex, enclosing a cheque or postal order, and your name will be added to the mailing list.

Some other books published by Penguins are described on the following pages.

Note: *Penguinews* and *Penguins in Print*
are not available in the U.S.A. or Canada

MAHARISHI MAHESH YOGI
ON THE BHAGAVAD-GITA

A New Translation and Commentary

The first six chapters of the *Bhagavad-Gita* with the original Sanskrit text, an introduction, and a commentary designed to restore the fundamental truths of the teachings delivered by the Lord Krishna to Arjuna on the battlefield.

THE PELICAN GUIDE TO MODERN THEOLOGY

Theology today can mean anything from reverence for the living God to the proposition that God is dead. How has the 'science of thinking about God' reached this dilemma?

The Pelican Guide to Modern Theology, which is under the general editorship of Professor R. P. C. Hanson, discusses the outlook of modern Christian thinkers and their attitude to the work of past theologians. Its three volumes, which examine the very foundations of Christianity in such questions as 'What and how is God?', cover the philosophy of religion, historical theology, and the study of the Bible: they help to explain why, even in these secular days, some people find theology the most attractive, exacting, and satisfying intellectual pursuit of all.

The first two volumes are published together: the third will follow.

VOLUME I

SYSTEMATIC AND PHILOSOPHICAL THEOLOGY

William Nicholls

In modern times theology has run into that same crisis which has been induced in the whole of civilized culture by the advance of science. This first volume outlines the directions of thought adopted by such modern theologians as Barth, Bultmann, Bonhoeffer and Tillich in the face of the scientific challenge. Though concerned in the main with what must be recognized as a German Protestant tradition, Professor Nicholls's study does much to clarify the latest developments in Catholic theology as well. It reveals a liveliness and openness in modern religious thought which suggests that, whatever it may become in the future, theology is not dying.

POEMS FROM THE SANSKRIT

Translated by John Brough

For many readers in the West, Indian literature means the
Bhagavad-Gita or the *Kamasutra*; this anthology of secular poems
from the classical Sanskrit redresses the balance. These poems
were written between the fourth and tenth centuries A.D. and
illustrate the great diversity of subject-matter, style and imagination in a highly artistic aspect of Indian culture. A purely
literary language by the fourth century, Sanskrit contains a
wealth of synonyms and lends itself to a strict metrical form
with complex and subtle sound patterns. In his introduction
John Brough confesses his affection for Sanskrit poems – an
affection which is reflected in his verse translations.

THE UPANISHADS

Translated by Juan Mascaró

The Upanishads represent for the Hindu approximately what the New Testament represents for the Christian. The earliest of these spiritual treatises, which vary greatly in length, were put down in Sanskrit between 800 and 400 B.C.

This selection from twelve Upanishads, with its illuminating introduction by Juan Mascaró, reveals the paradoxical variety and unity, the great questions and simple answers, the spiritual wisdom and romantic imagination of these 'Himalayas of the Soul'.

'Your translation. . . . has caught from those great words the inner voice that goes beyond the boundaries of words' – Rabindranath Tagore in a letter to the translator.

Also by F. C. Happold

PRAYER AND MEDITATION

Prayer and Meditation is the third of the three volumes which Dr Happold has written for Pelicans. This work on the nature and practice of prayer, meditation and contemplation is divided into two parts. The first is a study of the nature of prayer and its expression at all levels of spirituality in all the main religions; the second is a collection of prayers, devotions and meditations for 'all sorts and conditions of men', and containing much original material in prose and verse never before printed.

Dr Happold's clear style makes difficult ideas fully comprehensible and he also explains the relevance of the life of prayer to the life of action.